AF373904

STAR SKY Book Four

A Constellation in Ashes

T. M. BENNETT

ISBN 979-8-3304-2503-7

For my family. The path through this world is not always easy to follow, but help comes from those walking alongside us.

Table of Contents

Chapter 1

Teluthia, Airitha's home world, faded into the distant recesses of my mind. Pain and weariness paralyzed me, not in my body only but also in my mind. I could not shake the pure terror coursing through my veins. They knew. They had power over Tranto and me.

They were in control.

Whimpering and crying, like that of a very young and scared child, sounded softly to my left. I tried to open my eyes, but in my mind a hand balled into a fist and shattered my weak attempt to control my own body. I recoiled and called for Tranto. His comforting presence fled in and out of reach. When my consciousness brushed his, raw fear leeched from him into me, furthering my paralysis.

I wasn't fighting. I couldn't fight. My friends would disappear. We were defeated.

As I lay flat on my back for countless rays, I saw myself going numb as though I were observing someone else's body.

A click later, laughter tickled my ears. I jerked my head and found I could control it once again.

"Kammiel? Kammiel?" Airitha cried.

My leg was shaken.

"Kammiel," she nearly shouted with a voice hoarse from fright and the strain of tears, "we'll be alright, but right now you have to get up."

I shook my head. The laughter continued. It's undulations reverberated menacingly.

"Kammiel," my leg shook again as Airitha tried to rouse the youngest of our group.

Vertigo wrestled against me as I propped myself up and glimpsed the situation. Darvian, the boy who had healed Ahdah's broken leg, sat on his knees in a fetal position with his fists pressed hard against his ears. His sister, Meisha, whom we had only just rescued rays before, cowered beside him, shielding the side of her face where fresh bruises and scabs darkened her purple and green skin. Kammiel lay haphazardly on my left shin with her mul'li splayed across both of my legs. Airitha, bent over her little body. She glanced at me with a frantic plea as she desperately tried to wake the little girl. Lastly, Kelita, the girl from my home world, lay face down behind Airitha.

"Jax," Airitha rushed to me and hugged my neck. Before I could reply she tugged me to sit upright, "Help me.

Kammiel's not waking up. She seemed alright, then she started trembling and muttering, then she collapsed."

My words slurred too much for even me to understand myself when I replied. I had meant to say, "What's wrong with her?"

"Jax?" Airitha looked lost as she jerked her frazzled attention between Kammiel's limp body and me. "I need help," she cried to no one in particular.

My arm slammed into the floor, scraping my knuckles and bending my elbow the wrong way. Complete control had not yet fully returned.

The foreboding laughter turned to speech. It was a slow, crackly voice holding tightly to a thick accent which placed a dark twist on all of the syllables. "You've no need to fret over the little one. Little Kammiel is quite alright. She is simply tired. Little does she know what she's accomplished," soft laughter accentuated the owner's statements. "You, Jax of Geoteous," the voice all but spat the name of my planet, "on the other hand, may not be quite alright."

I lost control of my body and fell back onto the floor. I struggled feebly against the invisible force suppressing me. I needed to see the owner of the voice and the laughter.

"You see, my young friend, you have something that I have wanted returned for a very long time," the last three words were drawn out into an extraordinarily long hiss.

Since I could not see the unknown being, I studied Airitha who stared open-mouthed in the direction of the voice. She knelt beside me where she'd been. I knew her well enough to know that, even though her body sat motionless, inside she was seething with anger that would soon master her fear.

"What did you do to her?" Airitha demanded, anger clearly boiling over.

"Do you prefer Miss Airitha, or may I call you Airitha?" the voice asked mockingly.

"What did you do to her?" Airitha's fists balled at her sides.

The voice made no reply, but a click later Airitha grabbed her head and doubled over and whimpered pitifully.

My head shook from exerting my fatigued muscles. The last thing I saw before blacking out was Darvian's green eyes boring into me. In that look, his green gems of eyes told in stark detail of the erans of slavery and torment he'd survived and the fear and hatred that came hand in hand with oppression. I tried to shake my head as the voice spoke again, but darkness took me.

***

"The starship is still here," Darvian was saying as I came to.

"Darvian," Meisha sighed, "we cannot fly that thing out of here. We don't know where we are."

"It's right over there," the boy muttered in a harsh whisper.

"Darvi," Airitha joined the discussion, "your sister's right. We don't know what's going on. Kammiel, Kelita and Jax are all out cold. We wouldn't be able to load them up even if we could get out of these bonds."

I rolled my head and felt my arm slap my chest.

"I'm here, Jax," Airitha instantly held my arm and lifted my torso as I raised myself to sit.

She searched my face as I blinked repeatedly to force my eyes to focus.

"Is he still," I swallowed the urge to puke and started over. "Is he still here? The laughing voice?"

"Naw," Darvian jumped in. "He's gone."

"Jax," Airitha sat beside me and pulled me to her so that I leaned against her. "Something weird is going on. That guy that was laughing and walking toward us seems to have some awful power over our minds. He forced Kammiel to sing him our languages. He looked dreadful. Half of his face all sunken and scarred and all the twisted, orange markings on his body."

She shuddered as Darvian and Meisha looked at each other. "He was like Shahn'Nahsh," Meisha offered. "Only he seemed more sinister."

That caught my attention. The oppressor of their own people on the world of Grael had looked mean enough to take on a dragon with only a knife and come out the winner. Kelita had shot him, though, and he fell just as quickly as anyone else. The events of the fight in Shahn'Nahsh's starship flashed through my mind.

"What about Tranto?" words still came sluggishly from my lips.

"Oh, Jax," Airitha looked ready to cry. "They took him. They came with these spears or sticks or things that buzzed and sang every time they moved them—kind of like the stunsticks my Ahdah's soldiers sometimes use if they don't want to hurt anyone. He didn't even put up a fight. He just left with them."

Something pecked at the back of my mind. It wasn't Tranto, but it was something I knew I needed to remember.

I chose to address the issue of Tranto's apparent betrayal later. "So, where are we?"

Airitha answered, "They took us out of the starship." She glanced over her shoulder to where the starship sat on its gleaming hull. The ramp reached down from the hatch and rested on polished, black stone not more than twenty feet away. "And sat us down here. I don't see any cage or bars or cuffs of any kind, but we can't leave this circle." She drew an imaginary circle about ten feet in diameter around us. "It's like they're using a forcefield. We've tried to make them on Teluthia, but we could never get them to reach more than a quarter inch or so. These are completely invisible and *strong*."

The black floor flowed in all directions toward intricate beams and tresses that looked carved from whole trees complete with branches. Designs that flowed with no perceivable beginning or end ran the entire height of the tree beams. From their lofty branches, small lanterns twinkled. As I continued to study the area, I realized the trees formed two rows marching toward a raised platform upon which sat a chair constructed of curled wood entwining a giant crystal of pure black tipped with white. The chair or throne sat empty. Indeed, the entire area we were in was devoid of life apart from our own.

"If he comes back laughing at us, I'm gonna make him stop," Darvian growled, leaping to his feet and pacing. He bumped into the forcefield a couple times, and Airitha and Meisha pulled him down to sit between them. He rubbed his head as if he had bumped it hard.

Meisha looked completely spent with no fight or will to continue on lighting her dull, green eyes. "We've been freed from one prison only to be shoved into another," she murmured as silent tears ran from her eyes. She ducked her head, sniffed and smeared at them with limp hands.

I knew what Omoah would do, and I didn't think that was the right thing to do for this girl who was a few erans older than me. I could imagine Darvian's sister thinking I was some cute little kid trying to comfort her and doing such a poor job all I was doing was causing her shame.

Airitha scooched around Darvian and wrapped Meisha in her slender arms. The older girl cried against Airitha's temple and murmured, "It's so much like what Shahn'Nahsh did. He beat us, me and the others, whenever he didn't like something. It didn't matter whether we were boys or girls or how old we were. I watched so many of them bleed on the floor after he struck them. If we cried out, he'd hit them again and then we'd be next, but it could be a few clicks or half a cycle later before he lashed out at us. We never knew when it would be."

Airitha listened and kept hugging the older girl. Apparently, some things were always guaranteed to be the right thing to do for someone hurting.

I turned back to glancing around the room. I had to make sense of it so we could escape. It was quiet—too quiet. We were in the open, yet we were trapped.

Further, I could not feel Tranto anywhere. Why had they taken him? He didn't belong to them. He didn't actually belong to anyone, right? I hoped he was still alive and would return, bounding around some corner I hadn't noticed yet. I held onto such hope despite the complete absence of his presence.

Chapter 2

We sat on the floor, making only small comments now and then. Nothing could remove the oppressive silence and aloneness suffocating us. Airitha tended Kammiel and Kelita as well as she could, and I slipped in and out of fitful sleep.

One time when I dozed nearly awake, Darvian was arguing with Airitha that he had tried to help Kammiel, but he couldn't find anything to heal.

The next time I awoke fully, Darvian was grunting and muttering as he prodded Kelita's leg. Meisha held the younger girl's head in her lap and restrained her arms by pinning them under her legs. Kelita moaned and shook her head as she strained against Meisha's grip.

I just made sense of the scene when Darvian rocked back on his heels, saying, "I don't know. I can't do nothing. I can't do nothing."

Nausea kept me from standing or sitting, so I slowly scooched myself beside Kelita and took her hand.

She looked at me with glazed eyes. "It broke again," she whispered. "It hurts so much I can't take it."

"Darvian will figure it out," I tried to encourage her. "He healed Ahdah's leg."

She shook her head and moaned. "No, all he's doing is making it hurt more."

I studied her leg. It had swollen to nearly twice the size of her good leg. Darvian brushed his fingers along the biggest lump. Kelita bit her lip and winced.

"Give her a break," I scolded the younger boy.

"I'm sorry," Darvian hung his head. "I'm sorry. Can't do nothing."

Airitha knee-walked to him and hugged him, "Don't be so hard on yourself, Darvi. You didn't even know you had an ability until a cycle ago."

Her comfort had no noticeable impact on him. He pulled away and sat cross-legged at the edge of our unseen cage. Faint murmuring reached my ears until it was drowned out by echoing footsteps.

The footsteps sounded from all around us. However, the acoustics in the room proved so contorted that only one source came into view once the group rounded one of the carved trees beside the starship. They possessed the two head tails, or mul'li, of Ti'Kahn, but bore markings of iridescent orange with eyes flashing with orange irises of the same hue as the lava flows in the jagged, red mountains of Teluthia. Each of the three appeared to be a man clothed in what seemed to be a single sheet of orange fabric wrapped around their waists with a brown belt before being draped over the left shoulder.

The man in the lead stooped with age but bore only a few wrinkles on the healthy side of his face. The other side was a maze of whorled, orange scars and twisted purple skin. He held a staff that buzzed like hundreds of tiny shells cascading onto a drum each time he swung it forward. His feet were bare, slapping the polished floor like the bare feet of his escorts.

He stopped ten feet from Darvian who quickly edged back and stood with his face declined in a watchful glare.

"I am sorry for the length of time I have been away," the man with the scarred face said in the same voice with the thick accent and halting words. "Pardon me for my inhospitality." He flashed an ugly grin where only the healthy side of his face responded.

"I thank you, Jax, for returning that which was not given to you," he addressed me with an appraising glance.

"The rest of you have done well to accompany your friend and see that he has returned my Oogluk," the man smiled again.

I forced myself to my knees, ignoring the vertigo spinning in my head, and pressed what I hoped was a rebellious glare onto my face.

"Once again," the man stared directly at me, "please forgive my thoughtlessness. As your host, I should have introduced myself."

His lips ceased moving, but inside my mind, in much the same way Tranto and I talked, his voice rang darkly, "I am Gen'tahn'Gen." He paused before continuing, "I know each of you and your names. Your little servant was quite informative as she cooperated in allowing us to communicate freely."

Darvian screamed and rushed at the man with fists already pulled back to punch. He stopped suddenly and fell to the floor, groaning. His sister eased tentatively to his side with her eyes locked on our captors.

"Perhaps," Gen'tahn'Gen chuckled. It was a sinister sound that reverberated all around us. "The young one would feel more appreciative once he has been allowed to heal the one called Kelita." His expression changed to the softness of pity.

To me it looked like a mockery. I narrowed my eyes.

"Oh, she has been hurting for such a long time." Gen'tahn'Gen glanced at each of his guards, "Let us show our kindness and good will to her and her friends. Darvian, you may heal her. Your sister, Meisha should join you in your effort. I very much desire her to be completely and quickly rescued from her pain."

I glowered at our captor as he watched with rapt attention. I reached for Kelita's hand. The click my skin touched her, she gripped my hand so hard I bit my lip to keep myself from flinching and reprimanding her.

Darvian and Meisha picked themselves up and moved to Kelita. They talked quietly for a ray before both reached down and rested their hands on Kelita's swollen leg. She howled and whimpered from their light touch.

Gradually, the broken leg straightened and shrank down to normal size. Kelita bit down on her sleeve as she held back screams from the pain. I could tell she wanted to cry and thrash her upper body by the way her neck muscles knotted and shivered. Then, she did cry out. Her leg bent in the middle of her femur up toward her shoulder. Dots of blood oozed through her pants.

"We're hurting her," Meisha cried and withdrew her hands.

Darvian ignored Kelita's agony and grabbed her leg. His eyes betrayed the effort he exerted to stay calm.

"What do we do?" Meisha yelled after she'd returned to her brother's side and tried to help.

Gen'tahn'Gen spoke, "We will provide you the calm you need. You cannot work your healing unless your desire for your friend outweighs the concern you have for failure."

Airitha tore her eyes away from Kelita only long enough to shoot a flaming glance at our captor.

I held Kelita's hand tighter as blood in the shape of a corner of a dragon's mouth continued to darken her leg. "C'mon, Kelita, you're gonna beat me in the next Highland Games."

Whether she heard me or not didn't matter. I knew I should say something, anything, to help take her mind off the pain.

"I thought I already did," she forced out.

"We were on the same team," I replied as Kelita shrieked.

Darvian and his sister began working again with an unnerving calm. They were so calm that they could have been sitting in a mountain meadow full of flowers with buzzes slowly floating around the warm, fragrant air.

Her leg shifted again. This time it straightened and lay beside her good leg in perfect symmetry. Meisha wiped at the blood, but she could do no more than smear it around Kelita's pants.

Airitha stroked Kelita's sweaty cheek and whispered that they were done. Just like Ahdah, when Darvian had discovered his ability to heal by mending his broken leg, Kelita lay asleep. Her throbbing heart settled to the normal, slow pace which made her chest rise and fall like the breathing of other species.

"They did it," I smiled at Airitha who returned it with an extra glow.

"They—they helped us," Meisha's voice was faint, contrasting directly with her flashing eyes.

Darvian turned his back to us and ran his fists against the floor as he muttered angrily at our captor. The only thing I caught was, "Keep out of our minds." He also mentioned something about the Gah'Stotten, the soldiers from his world who had followed Shahn'Nahsh in invading Teluthia. I wished some of the black clad soldier would burst from the starship and destroy Gen'tahn'Gen and his guards. We could deal with the Gah'ten, but we couldn't handle Gen'tahn'Gen.

However, we had already dealt with the Gah'ten aboard the ship. They were all dead. Maybe if we had one of their MECs though, a weapon that shot deadly bolts of magnetic energy that could burn through nearly anything.

Gen'tahn'Gen peered at us for many long clicks. I lowered Kelita's hand to her stomach and assumed a defensive crouch.

"There's no need for that, Young Jax," the orange Ti'Kahn stated with a wave of his hand. "Put those dangerous thoughts to rest. Join the calm of plenty among friends. That was a good show your friends put on. I've never seen time turned back. It really is a valuable skill to have when healing someone, don't you think? Instead of waiting for the injury to heal, merely turn back the clock on the affected area and not even a scar remains. Most curious I may say, and most desirable."

I stared into his orange eyes that glowed with malevolent greed. They were the same type of eyes Tranto had unintentionally shown me a flashback of—hungry with a tinge of wild eagerness.

"All of you," Gen'tahn'Gen continued. "You're all so full of...life. Each of you with your abilities ripe for endless possibilities. Alas, I get ahead of myself in my excitement. You are all, no doubt, hungry. Will you join me in dining?"

I tried, once again unsuccessfully, to contact Tranto. In his absence, I turned to Airitha. She glanced at our captors before gazing into my eyes with a look of consternation. Her eyes narrowed the way eyes do when the person is so worried their brow bunches above the nose. Darvian and Meisha continued to stare in anger and apprehension at the orange Ti'Kahn.

I stared off distantly to the far right of Gen'tahn'Gen. Inside me, something gave way. My friends gathered around me would each give up whatever it took to keep us safe. Without consciously deciding it, I knew I would do the same.

Kammiel lay motionless. She was so small and looked so peaceful—almost as if her Ahdah had carried her to bed and laid her in the exact way she loved to sleep. Her delicate, light blue striped mul'li contrasted with the somber, dark floor and made her look even more delicate and fragile.

I reached down and touched Kelita's hand. She and I were inseparable. She was the friend I always wanted without knowing it. I think I liked her in the same way Ahdah and Omoah liked each other when they first met. Just thinking about her in that moment made extra blood flood the capillaries in my face.

Airitha pleaded softly, "We can't leave them, Jax."

I raised my gaze to her round face. She, a slender twig of a girl, beautiful in her own right, was perhaps the most stalwart of us all. She never backed down from what she believed to be true and necessary.

My chest felt immensely full, and my various injuries felt small and faded. I stood to my full height, which was only the average height for a boy twelve erans old and replied evenly, "We will not join you until our friends awake and are completely fine. Further, we will make the decision together."

Gen'tahn smiled. A breath of a laugh escaped his partially parted lips. "Very good, Young Jax. You show great devotion to those you deem worthy."

He declined his face slightly and flicked his wrist minutely.

Darvian jumped to his feet with a shout and rushed at him. The invisible barrier did not stop him.

"Darvian!" his sister shrieked as she shot out her arms to stop him. She was more than an arm's length too late, however. Her momentum carried her to the floor face first.

When she raised her gaze, the man accompanying Gen'tahn'Gen held Darvian by his wrists. Gen'tahn smirked at Meisha. His orange eyes glinted maniacally.

The man loosed his grip on Darvian. I stared in disbelief as he turned slowly and smiled at us. He held out his hand to his sister.

"Meisha, c'mon, let's go. They need us," he said as if he were still living with Airitha's family in their mansion and he wanted to show his sister the waterfall for the first time.

Meisha's face contorted as though she would cry, but no tears fell. With her gaze locked on her brother, she slowly pushed herself to her feet.

"No," Airitha shouted. "Don't go to them. Darvian, get back here. They're lying."

Meisha made no sign of hearing the younger girl's plea.

Darvian looked at Airitha and grinned, "It's alright. We'll come back when we're done. We can help them."

"Darvi," tears bubbled in Airitha's voice. Her lip quivered, and she knelt beside Kelita. "Don't go, Darvi."

I was stuck as if in thigh deep mud. Tranto would have known exactly what to do. Desperately, I flung grasping hands at Meisha. I clutched her arm and pulled. She merely shrugged and kept walking. I yanked on her arm the way I sometimes needed to in order to keep a dragon under control. She stopped and glared at me. I began to melt even before she torched me.

"Let go of me, little boy," her voice came low and wild. "Take your hands off my arm or I will see to it that you don't have any hands to pick your nose with." She twitched her head, and a distantness left her eyes for a click. For that click her expression shifted to remorse and horror, but then, the cloud descended on her again.

My hands dropped from her arm. Behind me, Airitha pleaded forlornly. I wanted to join her.

Gen'tahn laughed low and soft. A couple clicks later, he turned to leave with Darvian and Meisha in tow.

"Tranto, where are you? Why can't you hear me?" I screamed in my mind.

Numbly, I turned back to the three girls that were left of my friends. Kammiel and Kelita lay on the floor, while Airitha cried and watched Darvian and his sister disappear.

"They left us," her mouth could barely form the words. "They chose to leave."

Normally, I would have pointed out the way Meisha had reacted when her real self had peeked through the cloud, but I was changing inside more quickly than I could keep track of. Instead of trying to comfort her with words and reason, true though they would be, I knelt beside her and pulled her shaking body against me. My shoulder was soaked in layers of tears and snot before she finished.

Chapter 3

Airitha sniffed and peeled her cheek from the puddle she'd made on my shoulder. "Thank you," she whispered.

I returned her look, and we sat.

Kammiel flopped her arm and snorted. Airitha hurried to her side. "Kammiel," she called. "Kammiel."

"Omoah?" the disoriented, little girl responded as she came out of the final stages of sleep.

"Kammiel," Airitha called again, "it's me, Airitha."

Kammiel's brilliant, blue eyes fluttered open. She studied Airitha for a click, looking more and more confused.

"Why did that mean man make me sing him our languages?" she asked.

Airitha sighed a deep, soul-wrenching apology and scooped the little girl into her arms. "You're okay. You didn't do anything wrong," she said repeatedly as she held her.

"I don't like him in my mind," Kammiel stated.

"Neither do I," Airitha said.

I looked down at Kelita, hoping she would wake up soon, but also I was glad she was sleeping and allowing her body to adjust to being whole.

"Airitha?" I called gently. "If I can get to the ship, do you think we have a chance with some MECs."

She froze. Kammiel looked at her. I looked at her. Terror and horror threatened to tear her face into several pieces as they fought over control of her facial features. "Please, Jax, they'd probably turn you against us."

Part of me felt indignant that I was taking her suggestion, but the other part knew she was right. Yet another part of me, the largest one, was supremely happy that I took her suggestion. I glanced at the ship one last time but made no move to get up.

Airitha conveyed her thanks with her eyes.

"I'm thirsty," Kammiel said.

Airitha laughed grimly and replied, "We all are. We'll get water and food soon, I think."

She looked at me as an Omoah looks to her husband when she needs help with one of the children.

"If I can make it to the ship, I'll find something to drink and some food." I pushed myself up and looked down, "I won't bring any weapons. You're right. We shouldn't risk it."

Relief flooded Airitha's face. She'd lost so many friends in the last few periods that most people would crumble. To add to the hurt, each friend had chosen to leave just as if they had chosen to betray her. She somehow still functioned in the midst of such emotional pain. But, then again, I was joining her in the middle of that pain and choosing to make the things that she valued important to me.

A thought struck me as I took my first step, had she been right about the way I treated Rurin, my little brother who I often called a bother? I glanced at Airitha. She sat on her knees, cuddling the little girl who had also given more than she should have ever been asked to. She even volunteered much of her sacrifice, then, once these orange Ti'Kahn found us, she'd been robbed and left unconscious. I shook my head. Not even my Ahdah could have done any better defending my friends.

My attention turned to Darvian and Meisha next. Had they really chosen to leave or had they been forced against their inmost will? Meisha had shown evidence of the mind control we suspected, and Darvian had demanded that Gen'tahn get out of his head. Had they been set free only to fall into a much more dubious prison?

The black floor reflected the image of my confusion back to me. I grimaced at the haggardness and grime darkening my face. No barrier prevented me from reaching the starship and climbing the ramp.

A smell wafted down to me, the stench of death and burning. I plunged in with my nose pinched shut. My head tails could filter the oxygen from the air without me smelling it.

As I wandered the corridors with the metallic grating, I remembered how Tranto had cleared the way for us. He had slid beneath the grating and slipped appendages up through the gaps and smashed the Gah'Stotten soldiers with such force blood had sprayed the walls in some places. I hurried past those points, making my way toward the rear of the ship. I didn't want to go to the bridge and see the carnage there firsthand ever again.

At last, after almost half a period of wandering and opening doors, I found the kitchen area. Giant tubs of food stuffs and dishes lay neatly organized on shelves. Omoah would have been overjoyed at the precision and order. In a matter of rays, I was making my way back to the door with a large jug of water and a stack of cups. A makeshift bag filled with food also hung from my shoulder.

Airitha wrinkled her nose and looked away when I walked up. "It must smell really bad in there," she whispered.

I nodded, "I'm sorry I don't have any way to wash it off right now. Here's water and food. It's still good and will last a while longer yet."

"Thank you, Jax," Airitha overcame her disgust and gave me a quick hug.

Kammiel looked up at me, her eyes alight with gratitude, "You're smelly, but I like you anyway."

I squatted down to be eye level with her. "You're welcome. I think your attitude is good."

She looked at me questioningly. Airitha laughed, "He means he likes that you're not grumpy and demanding."

"Oh," Kammiel's face brightened. "That's because I'm not Heldinn. He gets really mad when he's hungry."

Airitha laughed, and I smiled.

"I think we can move anywhere we want," I commented.

Airitha glanced around the room, "I think," she said slowly, "we should stay right here."

"Let's move next to a pillar," I shrugged. "I want to be able to lean back against something."

Airitha responded, "Okay. What about Kelita?"

"I might need your help moving her."

I knelt next to Kelita's motionless form and called to her softly. She didn't stir. I tried shaking her awake with the same result. Airitha stepped briskly over once she had helped Kammiel settle with a cup of water and piece of crusty bread.

"Let's drag her. The floor is smooth enough," I said.

"Okay. I don't want to pull on her leg just in case," Airitha studied our friend and gently took her left arm.

I scooped up Kelita's right hand, "One, two, three." Kelita slid easily across the polished floor. Her head hung limply toward her back, but Airitha and I took care to be gentle as we laid her back down.

Making a pillow as well as I could out of my shattered armor, I supported her head. I lingered at her side, hoping she would wake up soon.

"Here, Jax, eat something," Airitha held out a greenish-yellow fruit.

I took it, peeled it and ate without tasting it as I silently willed Kelita to get up and start yelling at Darvian for the pain he had caused her. Then, she would notice she was standing on her leg without it crumpling beneath her, and she would smother Darvian in a hug of profuse thanks.

"What are they going to do with us? That guy, Gen'tahn'Gen, made it sound like they're going to make us do things for them," Airitha asked as she scooted across the floor and leaned against the pillar beside me. Kammiel lay against her chest sleeping deeply.

I turned my scratchy eyes to her, but no words came.

She bit back a response and nodded grimly.

Finally, I grunted, "I don't know."

Airitha leaned her head on my shoulder, "Jax?"

I looked at the top of her head and grunted.

"Do you think our parents know where we are?"

Anger built up behind a hastily constructed dam as I replied between partially clenched teeth, "I don't even know where we are."

Airitha gave a shiver and scooched closer to me. Kammiel's feet pressed against my legs. I lifted them gently and placed them in my lap. The intricate carvings on the pillar felt like wrinkles of stone in my back, but it was far more comfortable than sitting up with no back support.

"I'm scared," Airitha stated, "but I'm glad you're with us. You'll figure something out."

I craned my neck to look at her. She peered back into my forlorn gaze. "No," I breathed. "I can't do it alone. I need all of us here and working together." I dropped her gaze, "Things always go bad when I try to make things happen alone. Besides," I hesitated, finding it suddenly difficult to continue, "I think...I think I'm scared, too."

I felt Airitha study me as I played with the grime on my thigh plate. After several clicks, I glanced at her.

She said, "Let's solve this together, then. When Kelita wakes up, she'll help us."

I nodded solemnly.

Kammiel shuddered in her sleep and whimpered softly. Airitha rocked gently to help her reach peaceful sleep again.

In my mind, things crashed and leapt onto and off of every surface. Why had our friends been taken, for, it was clear to me, they had been selected and removed from our group?

The thought of Tranto leaving of his own free will tormented me most. I yearned for our connection. I had to have him. Only with him in our group did we stand a distant chance of figuring out how to escape our captors and their manipulative ability.

Airitha lay a hand on my forearm. I looked at her.

"We'll be alright. I wish they were here too," she said, barely holding back a fresh onslaught of tears.

"I miss Tranto," I found myself responding. "Why did he leave? Why didn't he stay to help us?"

"I don't know," Airitha shook her head as her face pinched with the effort of remaining calm but failing. "I know you're important to him. I don't know why any of this is happening." Her constraint broke, and small rivulets formed silently on her grimy cheeks.

"We just finished a battle," I scoffed at our circumstances. "We almost died, and now, we're prisoners and being abandoned by our friends."

"Oh, Jax," Airitha's final reserve of calm acceptance shattered.

She sniffed, but it was too late to keep the wetness from my shoulder. Kammiel woke and added some of her own tears to the mix.

"I'm sorry," Airitha said, peeling her face from my shoulder.

"Nah, it's what friends are for," I forced a smile.

Airitha gave a single laugh and sniffed again, "Friends shouldn't have to be there the way parents are for their kids."

I shuffled my feet. Kammiel adjusted her legs which still draped over mine. "I think," I replied tiredly, "our parents are a little too far away right now."

Airitha's chin and lips quivered, but she pulled herself together and said, "It's only for a short time until we get back home."

A dazed, distant expression played on Kammiel's face as she gazed at Airitha.

I changed the subject, "When Kelita wakes up, I think we should look around this room and try to figure out where we are."

Airitha nodded, "Okay."

"What about the bad men?" Kammiel asked, snuggling into Airitha.

Airitha pulled her tight and said, "We can deal with them if they show up again."

Chapter 4

I slept until the sound of running and fighting woke me. With a start, I reached for my sword, forgetting that it had been taken. The room we were in looked the same as before. The only difference was Kelita. She was no longer lying unconscious on the floor beside me. Instead, she ran from one pillar to the next, kicking each one viciously several times with her leg that had previously refused to heal.

Airitha and Kammiel turned in circles as they watched her. Groggily, I joined them and watched as Kelita sprinted without the slightest hitch of pain to the next pillar. Sliding to a stop, she raised her leg in a high kick that would have knocked anyone down with the sole of her foot planted firmly against their chest. The pillar didn't budge, but Kelita laughed gleefully.

"Is she practicing to help us get rid of the bad man?" Kammiel asked.

I didn't stay to hear Airitha's answer. I ran to Kelita's side and ran with her. When she reached the next pillar, she feinted from the pillar and struck at me. I was too slow to react and would have been knocked sideways if she had followed through with her kick.

"Good as new!" she said exuberantly. "I can spare against you and win any cycle now." She laughed and exercised and danced on her leg to show me.

I smiled like a victor as well. A sudden urge to hug her peeled my feet from the floor and wrapped my arms around her. She continued to laugh. Then, she planted a kiss on my cheek.

"That's because I like you," she said, growing suddenly shy.

I looked down at her as she tried to look away. "You can walk," I said as the heat of embarrassment steamed up my neck, passed my ears and seeped into my face. "You're leg's healed."

She leaned against me, snuggled against my neck and then pushed herself away. "I bet I'm still faster than you," she called as she turned and broke into a wild sprint.

My longer legs helped me considerably, but she was naturally far lighter on her feet and kept just out of my reach, utilizing sharp turns around pillars to keep a slight lead. We raced around the pillars, trying to keep from slipping on the polished stone. On the fourth pillar I cut the turn short and ran to the inside. Kelita rounded the pillar and plowed into me. That's what I wanted.

"Okay. You've proven you can beat me when you have a head start," I said as I grabbed her hand. "I'm glad your leg is healed."

The pinkness in my white markings grew more noticeable.

She grinned at me and giggled, "I like how red your face gets."

I looked away, wishing I had something to cool the heat in my face.

"C'mon, I haven't thanked Darvian yet," Kelita said lightly as she tugged on my hand. "Where is he?"

I didn't know what to say for several strides. Finally, I said simply, "He left. He and his sister left after they healed your leg."

"Why?"

"I don't know."

Airitha looked at us with a calm smile that seemed too stiff, "I think Gen'tahn'Gen and the others took them."

"Who?" Kelita asked before realization flooded her.

"You can run now," Kammiel danced the few steps to Kelita's other hand, snatched it and skipped beside her. "You're really fast. Maybe we can all outrun the bad man now."

"What's going on? Why would they take them?" Kelita asked me.

"There's something going on with our minds," I answered. "After they healed your leg, Darvian told them to get out of his mind. I've felt it too, though not very strongly, they can get into our minds kind of like what I told you Tranto and I can do with each other."

"So that's their ability?" Kelita demanded.

"We don't know," Airitha offered. "Scientists on Teluthia were working on a machine that can access memories and such. Maybe these people have the same sort of technology—only better."

Kelita pulled the left corner of her mouth back in an incredulous sneer, "Yeah."

"If it's their ability, that explains a lot. They knew who Tranto was." I quickly released Kelita's hand as she tugged it.

Crossing her arms she said, "Right, I remember that. They called him something strange and led him away. I didn't completely black out. I was just in a lot of pain when my leg broke again."

I looked at Airitha, "If it is technology, it would be a lot easier to think of a way to escape."

"Let's just take the starship," Kelita shifted her weight to her right leg and let her head lean toward the shiny bulk of the ship.

"We can't leave our friends," Airitha said aghast.

"Why not? If they chose to leave, why can't we?" Kelita bored her eyes into Airitha's for a long while.

Airitha blinked and replied without looking at any of us, "I don't think they knew they were making a choice.

They may not have even had a choice. You saw them, didn't you, Jax, how Meisha gave that weird look?"

I nodded slowly. Kelita jerked her gaze to look at me.

"Airitha's right," I said. "We're not leaving without them."

"But they chose to leave us," Kelita objected loudly.

"They can do bad things," Kammiel looked up at us with the softness I've seen only in young children's eyes. "They can make us do what they want even if we don't want to."

"Oh, Kammiel," Airitha knelt and hugged the young girl. "She's saying the truth. Kelita, I told you how they forced her to sing them our languages."

Kelita looked down at them with an unmoved expression.

"Let's figure out what this room is like," I said.

Airitha gave Kelita a long, hard look as she found Kammiel's hand and stepped toward me. Kelita snapped into action and placed herself deftly between Airitha and me. Airitha led Kammiel to my other side where the little girl reached up small fingers for my big hand.

"When we find Tranto, can you take me home?" she asked.

I walked stiffly for a few steps before replying, "We'll all go home as soon as we can."

"If they are using machines to make us do things," Kelita said thoughtfully, "can't Airitha make an anti-machine—something that will disable their device? We have an entire starship on our hands."

I caught the hint of arrogant supremacy in Kelita's voice and wished she wouldn't put our friends down so vehemently.

Airitha thought about it for a click before responding in a serious, contemplative manner. "We probably could figure something out," she said. "The key would be to build the device without them forcing us to stop."

"I need to pee," Kammiel looked up at Airitha, who, in turn, looked at me.

"The starship smells really bad," I said. "There should be a privy around here somewhere."

Glancing all around the room revealed nothing that looked like it led to a bathroom. I walked a little faster and angled us toward the nearest wall.

"There's a door over there," Airitha pointed to the right side of the wall. Kammiel dropped my hand as Airitha hurried her toward it.

"Airitha," I called sharply. "I don't think any of us should separate ourselves from the others."

I broke into a jog to catch up.

Kelita called from behind, "If she wants to leave us too, what can we do to stop her?"

I let Kelita's remark float into oblivion as the door opened ahead. An orange Ti'Kahn woman stepped out. The four of us stopped, and, out of the corner of my eye, I saw Kelita assume a defensive stance with arms ready to deflect blows.

"I ask you to us pardon," the orange, Ti'Kahn woman said. She wore the same orange fabric cloth draped over her body except she also had it looped around her neck before it spilled loosely over her right shoulder. The brown sash accentuated round hips. Her eyes flashed with the same fire, but with a kindness absent from Gen'tahn'Gen's eyes. She gave a stiff bow and held a hand out for Kammiel.

The little girl shrank back and clung to Airitha, who slowly bent and picked her up. Kammiel buried her cheek in Airitha's neck but kept her eyes carefully trained on the woman.

I drew up alongside Airitha. "Can we use the bathroom?" I wasted no time with my fear and did my best to sound calm.

The woman smoothed her cloth or dress or robe, whatever it was, and bowed slightly again, "Please forgive me. I am Hahn'Nik'Nik. The Great Gen'tahn'Gen wished me to remain in the hidden until need possessed you for things you have not."

"Can you take us to a bathroom, please. That's something we need and have not," Airitha asked in a voice that sounded as normal as though she were talking with my Omoah.

"Yes, of course, yes," Hahn'Nik'Nik answered with a suppressed giggle. Then, she executed a quick twist on her heel.

Airitha gave me a single, brief glance before following her through the door. I was only a step behind her.

"I'm not going in there," Kelita said with gruff menace in her tone. "Jax?" Her voice hoarsened, "Jax, I'm not going in there."

I bit my tongue between my molars, desperately attempting to not say anything. I turned midstride, raised my eyebrows at her and tipped my head toward Hahn'Nik'Nik. Kelita stuck her feet to the floor and glared. I turned my attention back to following our guide.

"Jax!" Kelita erupted behind us.

We were in a hall similar to the halls and back passages Airitha had shown me on her world before the cities had been blown apart and leveled by the Gah'Stotten's bombs. The intricately carved wood depicted scenes of what I assumed was everyday life for these orange Ti'Kahn. In nearly every carving, a tree overarched the scene. One scene showed a Ti'Kahn kneeling at the edge of a swampy pond. With the tilt of his head and the skill of the artisan, it looked like he conversed with strange looking creatures mostly submerged in the pond.

By the time we reached the end of the hall, Kammiel was walking beside Airitha and swinging the older girl's hand lightheartedly. Hahn'Nik'Nik opened a small, unadorned door, revealing a toilet system somewhat similar to those on Teluthia. The main difference was the presence of a bucket of water beside the toilet presumably to flush without running water. I felt proud of all I'd learned of Teluthia's technology in the relatively short amount of time I'd known Airitha and her people.

Kammiel let go of Airitha's hand and shook her head when Airitha asked if she wanted her to help her.

Hahn'Nik'Nik smiled and said, "Little ones mine are about the same age. Such children lovely."

"How many children do you have?" Airitha asked lightly.

Was the orange woman exerting some mind control over us? Why would Airitha drop her guard—not to mention Kammiel? If she were impressing her will onto us, I could feel no evidence. I'd have to be extra cautious of their ability or technology or whatever it was.

"Two I have," Hahn'Nik'Nik giggled. "My boy older is. They are up to mischief always."

Airitha grinned with that slightly absent look of not knowing. "My Omoah is pregnant right now with my only other sibling. I guess I can call Darvian a brother as well. He's lived with us for nearly an eran."

"And Darvian is the boy young, green?" Hahn'Nik'Nik clasped her hands in front of her and looked like she enjoyed the conversation.

Kelita tiptoed up behind me and rubbed her shoulder against my arm. The heat radiating off her nearly made me recoil against the lefthand wall.

"Tell her to stop," Kelita whispered wisps of smoke into my ear.

"Yes," Airitha looked down. "Where did they take him?"

Hahn'Nik'Nik looked grave, "He and his sister are attending the sick and injured we with us have at moment this."

Airitha forced a smile while I tried to interrupt. Meisha and Darvian were using their ability to help these people? Was that a bad thing? Did these people truly desire evil for us or were they simply exerting some sort of power over us because that's just what they do? The questions circulated with no rhythm. If only Tranto hadn't been taken, he would've been able to help me sort them out.

Kammiel came out of the bathroom and reached for Airitha's hand again. Then, a thought seemed to strike her. "Hahn'Nik'Nik, I heard you from the toilet. You talk funny. May I sing you our language so you may speak it correctly?"

Hahn'Nik'Nik looked at the little girl. Surprise and confusion etched lines between her eyes. She knelt and held her hands out in a shrug, "I didn't know that funny I speak."

Kammiel giggled and placed her hands on Hahn'Nik'Nik's temples. She sang softly after resting her forehead on the woman's.

"Oh," Hahn'Nik'Nik said, standing and looking down the hall behind us, "I did speak funny, putting all my modifiers behind my nouns. Thank you. Is this better?"

Kammiel giggled and reached for Hahn'Nik'Nik's hand, "You talk much better now."

The three laughed. Kelita and I exchanged frowns.

"They're crazy," Kelita whispered. "Keep an eye on them. They'll leave us next."

I marveled at the ease and grace of Kelita's steps as we continued down the hall. I had spent a considerable amount of time with her training for the Highland Games before she was injured, but she had hobbled around for so long that I had forgotten the strong, determined grace in her movements.

I think that was one of the things that drew me to her. She had always struck me as the prettiest girl at school, which also meant she was the prettiest girl I knew from my home world of Geoteous, and my eyes always followed her easily—until she looked in my direction. When she'd glance my way, I'd hurriedly find something else to pretend to have been studying for several rays.

"I don't feel any mind control," I offered.

Kelita replied with only a distrusting scowl.

Hahn'Nik'Nik talked easily with Kammiel as we rounded a corner and began passing doors on the right side of the hall. Airitha kept pace with them and laughed and giggled as the three of them conversed.

Chapter 5

When Hahn'Nik'Nik finally led us to a table laden with food, we all ate greedily. The supply of tart fruits and thick, sweetbread seemed never-ending. Kammiel spent much of the meal sitting on Hahn'Nik'Nik's lap, asking her to help her peel the different fruits. She amassed quite a pile of the dark husks of a small fruit Hahn'Nik'Nik called jeknetzo.

Kelita and I sat together in silence, staring at the three enthusiastically sharing stories and food.

"Please," Hahn'Nik'Nik laughed lightly, "call me Nik'Nik."

Airitha dipped her head and asked about Nik'Nik's kids.

"I must ask the Great Gen'tahn'Gen, but I think it would be alright for all of you to live with my family and me during your stay with us," Nik'Nik answered.

Airitha peeled back a husk on a jeknetzo. Juice from the yellow flesh flew toward Kammiel. She cut a look at Airitha before laughing and smearing it over her skin as she tried to wipe it off.

Hahn'Nik'Nik squeezed the little girl in a hug and said, "You'll have so much fun with Ahn'Ahn and Mik'Mik."

"Pardon my asking," Airitha's face was wadded in confusion, "but why do all the names here sound like you say them twice?"

Kelita rolled her eyes at me. I mouthed back, "I know." Fear built ladders in my mind and climbed to new heights. I had thought Airitha was going to help us figure out what was going on, but it was clear she could no longer be trusted.

Nik'Nik adjusted Kammiel on her lap and flicked her mul'li over her shoulders. "It's the nature of our language," she said. "Here, listen." She launched into a staccato rhythm of tongue clicks, grunts and pops that sounded like an insane nykor fleeing from a dragon.

Kammiel stared up at Nik'Nik for a click. Her eyes not really focused. Then, she responded with a series of pops, whistles and clicks.

Nik'Nik blinked and looked intently at Kammiel. Nik'Nik told Kammiel something else in her strange, click language.

Kammiel laughed and burrowed against her new friend.

"What did she say? What did you tell her?" Airitha demanded, obstinate about being left out.

Kammiel merely giggled and accepted the small, white berry Nik'Nik offered her. Airitha huffed and tore open another fruit.

"Why does everything have a thick skin here? Why can't it just be easy to eat like back home?" Kelita whispered.

"I don't know," I snapped.

"Jax," Nik'Nik addressed me in a conversational tone.

I slowly looked up from my work of peeling and met her fiery orange eyes. Biting back the urge to search desperately for Tranto in my mind, I forced myself to remain calm.

"Airitha tells me you live amongst animals that are huge and ferocious," Nik'Nik said. "I have seen Oogluk's acquired shape and can only imagine how dreadful those animals must be."

"You mean dragons?" Kelita whispered for my ears. "Oh, so terrible."

I was sure Nik'Nik heard her, but she made no response. I paused in replying. How much should I tell her? What would she do with the information? At last, I settled on what seemed like enough to satisfy her but not enough to be useful if we had to fight these new people.

"My Ahdah trains dragons, and I help him," I said. Fear for Tranto washed over me again. What were they doing to him?

"And they are used for beasts of burden once they are trained?" Nik'Nik asked innocently.

"We ride them. Get from place to place," I said with a shrug.

"Ah, but they cannot fly through space, the great emptiness that separates worlds?"

"No," as I replied, Kelita dug her heel into the top of my foot. "They need air to breathe. Tranto tells me there's no air in the blackness between the stars."

"Tranto? Is that what you call him?" Nik'Nik's face twisted.

"That's who he told me he is," I said, growing so nervous sweat beaded on my forehead.

Nik'Nik gave a single laugh and glanced to her right before finding me with her eyes of dancing fire, "That crazy creature. I mean I know they have a certain protocol, but to go and rename himself."

"What do you mean?" I leaned forward ignoring Kelita's hands clutching at my arm.

"Oogluk of course," Nik'Nik shook her head in disbelief. "I've heard stories about some of the old ones, but he," she tilted her head as she found her realizations extremely funny, "he tops the stories. How many erans has he been away? Oh, it must have been at least a millennium."

"Do you mean Tranto is over a thousand erans old?" Airitha asked. Her purple eyes were large and round.

Nik'Nik nodded, "He was one of the last, and our people have awaited his return for generation after generation." She looked suddenly sad and shifted her gaze to the tabletop, "I guess we should have known Tellitor'itor was not coming back after a normal lifespan passed."

"But Tranto can't teleport by himself?" I interjected darkly.

Kelita ground her teeth audibly beside me.

Airitha stared at me while Nik'Nik tilted her head and thought.

"Yes," Nik'Nik said slowly, "that is the same thing. It's an odd word you use, but I suppose it makes sense. Oogluk, or Tranto as he has you call him, left nearly eleven hundred erans ago with Tellitor'itor. They were only one team out of a vast number. I could not hope to remember how many without consulting the records."

"Is Tellitor'itor the same type of animal Tranto is?" Airitha asked hesitantly.

"Oh, no," Nik'Nik's eyes widened as she shook her head. "Oogluk is no animal. I would have thought you'd all have learned that after only a few cycles with him. He is as much a person as you or I.

"Back in that age we were curious about the possibility of life on other planets. Our astronomers searched the night skies tirelessly, hoping to dredge up inhabitable worlds to satiate our people's curiosity. The Neftim, Oogluk's people, pledged their support to us. Together our peoples united to explore the worlds despite the great dangers."

I tried to hide a knowing and scoffing laugh. Tranto and I had definitely learned about all that—or, had he known all along? I retaliated Kelita's glare with a look that asked what the big deal was.

Nik'Nik addressed me, "You must have had some experience I see. It is very dangerous, especially if the heart wavers even slightly. I am glad you have arrived safely to us."

"What did your teams do?" Kammiel asked. Wonder wrote itself into her wide, sparkling eyes as she looked up at Nik'Nik.

Nik'Nik settled her arms around the little girl and brought up a storytelling voice. "They found many worlds and reported to us about them. They found worlds where people with extraordinary abilities built incredible civilizations. Found, as well, were worlds where the people fought amongst themselves and killed for the slightest infractions. All of this was conveyed to our leaders at the time.

"However, contrary to what many of the exploring teams desired, the Great Ok'ton'Ok proclaimed that we, our people, were too dangerous to live amongst people who lack our ability, which seems unique to us. He determined that every team learn all they could from the peaceful, advanced worlds and bring that knowledge home. They were to leave the worlds untouched, and their presence was to be completely unknown to the inhabitants."

"How many worlds are there?" Airitha asked out loud but quiet enough she could have simply been talking to herself.

"What did you ask?" Nik'Nik shifted her orange eyes to her.

"I was wondering to myself," Airitha ducked her head. "But I do wonder; how many worlds there are?"

Nik'Nik looked somber for a few clicks before she replied, "We did not keep record. That or the records were destroyed by the Great Ok'ton'Ok. Stories have been passed down through the generations, but we know better than to believe every single one of them."

"How do you know what you're saying now is true then?" Kelita demanded.

Nik'Nik studied her for a click and then replied, "I don't. It is merely what I, and most people, accept to be true. All the technology, civilization structures, stories, writings and other things we gathered from other worlds was all destroyed in an attempt to keep the other worlds safe from our ability."

"Did your people go to Teluthia?" Airitha asked with piqued attention.

Nik'Nik blinked apologetically, "I am sorry, but I don't know. You see, each of the worlds we visited is remembered only by the names we gave them, and many of those names have not survived as I just explained." Nik'Nik gave an apologetic smile.

Airitha turned to me, "Do you think there's more creatures, Neftim, I think Nik'Nik called them, like Tranto on Teluthia, Hegnoranthe and Grael?"

I met Nik'Nik's gaze before responding. My resolve to keep my guard up deteriorated as I joined the conversation in full. "It's possible," I said, "but it sounds like Tranto was the only one that didn't return." I gestured with my eyes to Nik'Nik, "Am I right?"

The woman nodded and stroked Kammiel's head as she explained, "It has long been believed that the Great Ok'ton'Ok sent out word that all were to return. Oogluk and Tellitor'itor, that is Tranto as he has you call him, are said to have never responded and to have never returned. They were both thought to have been already dead before the summons reached them. Albeit, some thought them to be alive and merely ignoring the summons, which seems to be the case."

"How did you send the summons?" Airitha asked.

"Oh, the way we send everything," Nik'Nik replied. "We communicate with our minds. Distance is of little issue, but the location is. So, as long as we know where a person is—what world and approximate location on it— we can connect. For some it's very strong and immediate. For others it may be fuzzy and slow."

"How did you find us, then?" I asked as I strove to connect the dots on my own. Nik'Nik opened her mouth to reply, but I cut her off, "Wait, as Tranto and I started teleporting, your people sensed us somehow and were able to connect with Tranto...."

"But that would mean he knew about these people and didn't tell you or any of us," Kelita hissed from behind her scowl.

Nik'Nik laughed nervously, "Betrayal does not lie in Oogluk. He is altogether more altruistic than any of the Neftim I have ever met. Jax," she looked straight at me, "you are partly right. Once you and Oogluk began teleporting as you call it, we were able to apply a general location to him. However, you jumped in and out of our sight so much we couldn't fully connect. That's when the

Great Gen'tahn'Gen ordered this seeker to be built. We finally found you on your home world, and we were able to establish a weak, slow connection, but then you and Oogluk teleported to the other world. We were able to grab you and bring you to us because of the connection."

"Seeker?" Kelita whispered as she narrowed her gaze at Nik'Nik.

"Seeker? Is that like a starship?" Airitha asked one of my many questions before I could think of which one to ask.

"Yes," Nik'Nik bobbed her head. "You would call it a starship, but it has no propulsion system. It is hardly more than a tiny ball of rock large enough to hold an atmosphere and, therefore, remain in space while bringing us closer to our lost Oogluk to establish a stronger connection."

"Why do you keep calling him yours? Even if he did come from your world, he's a different species—his own person," I hadn't meant to sound so provoked, but it was too late to suck my words back into my larynx.

Nik'Nik bowed her head, "You must forgive us, please, Jax. My people have taken it upon themselves to help care for the Neftim after we had enslaved them. They are free now and have been for many of our generations. When I say 'our Oogluk,' I invoke only a term of endearment and not possession."

"So, Tranto was a slave?" Airitha looked horrorstruck. The section of fruit she held slipped from her fingers forgotten.

Nik'Nik bowed her head, "It is a grievance I and my people will never forget."

I looked at Kelita. The look we shared said we both believed Gen'tahn'Gen's attitude of possession much more readily than Nik'Nik's words which could easily have been a lie.

"I am happy to say that, despite our shortcomings, Oogluk's family has accompanied us on the seeker and have been reunited with him," Nik'Nik continued.

My jaw slackened while my staring eyes grew round.

"Oogluk has a family?" Airitha gasped.

Nik'Nik hummed confirmation, "His wife, they don't call them husbands and wives, but their term is too long to bother with. His wife, Tuca, and their offspring—"

"Wife?" Kelita mouthed to me.

"What?" Airitha apparently found it nearly as hard to believe as I did.

"Where are they? Why are we all being held captive? If they aren't slaves anymore, we can all go, right?" I leveled my gaze at Nik'Nik.

She shrank slightly, "None of you are captives. You may go see Oogluk and Tuca anytime you want."

"That's not what we could do out there," Kelita stood and pointed vaguely behind us.

"Begging your pardon, but you're not bound," Nik'Nik looked insistently at Kelita.

Airitha looked back and forth between Nik'Nik and Kelita. Kammiel crawled onto her lap, demanding her attention.

"Why couldn't we move out there? We were trapped by some barrier," I demanded. My legs were tense as if my body planned to stand beside Kelita.

Nik'Nik looked flummoxed for a click. Then, she calmly sat straighter and said, "The Great Gen'tahn'Gen does not take prisoners or captives or anything else resembling a slave."

"What?" Kelita scoffed loudly.

She looked ready to climb over the table and engage in aggressive, physical communications. She stabbed her arm back toward the huge room where the starship sat. I reached over and rested my hand on her back. I received a withering glare, but she held herself back from going over the edge.

"Why couldn't we move outside that small ring?" I had to force my jaw to open wider, so my words didn't come out as a growl. My friends and I shouldn't have been trapped at all if what the orange Ti'Kahn was saying was true. I urged myself to calm even more before adding, "It gave Darvian a headache."

Nik'Nik looked taken aback, but she recovered and said mystically, "The Great Gen'tahn'Gen obeys the laws of our people. If he does not, he does not remain in power."

"And where do outsiders fit into the laws of your people?" I asked.

Chapter 6

"Kammiel's tired. She can barely stay awake," Airitha said heavily. "If you go see them tonight, I won't go with you. I'm exhausted, too."

I took a long look at her. I was unsure whether to press her to come with us so more of us didn't get separated, but at the same time, I knew we were all worn out.

"C'mon, Jax," Kelita said, "maybe we can find them."

"Jax," Airitha called.

I turned, and she bit her lower lip. "We won't get lost," I assured her. She smiled thinly and nodded as if that answered her concern.

We left the house or dormitory or whatever it was. Kelita grabbed my hand as soon as we were walking side by side. Heat rose in my neck and cheeks, but I suppressed the urge to let go of her hand. Instead, I fumbled clumsily to get our hands to fit neatly together. The rush of energy muffled her words as she postulated theories about Tranto and his wife, Tuca.

"Maybe he forced himself to not think of her while we were connected," I offered as explanation when she asked why Tranto had never mentioned her.

Kelita wrinkled her nose, "That's an awful lot of careful planning and discipline to not think of someone, and something as important as that, the entire time someone can see every thought you have."

I held open a thick, arched wooden door. The relief carving on its panels portrayed a Neftim changing shape. "It's not like we can pry into every part of each other's minds. If there's something we don't want the other to see, we can block it off."

"But you still know something's there, right?" Kelita asked.

I shrugged, "I guess, but I don't really know."

We walked in silence for several steps. The hallway was supposed to have stairs at its end that led down to where the Neftim resided. Every four steps I called out to Tranto hoping that we would be able to connect. I tried using his Neftim name, Oogluk, as well, but I couldn't feel him.

"Jax?" Kelita stopped so fast I had to pivot and face her to keep from dragging her forward. "I have to ask you something."

"You've been asking me a lot of things," I said slyly.

"I'm not your little brother. This is a serious question."

"What? And everything you've asked so far hasn't been serious?" I did my best to look skeptical, but the burning in my cheeks made it hard to know whether I was creating the look I wanted.

"This is about us," Kelita said.

"Look, I like you," I blurted.

"We're only kids right now," Kelita acted like she hadn't heard me. "But we won't be kids forever. Only a few more erans and we'll be adults."

"Kelita, I think—"

"That's what I need to know, Jax," she looked at me innocently. "You don't really say or do anything to show me you like me, yet you talk about deep stuff with Airitha."

I would have rather teleported into the lava flows on Teluthia than stand there trying to look at her. "When have you ever wanted to?" I asked weakly.

"Jax," Kelita stuck her lower lip out and placed exasperation in her voice, "we're talking about deep stuff now."

"I don't think we should kiss," I stated.

"Jax!" Kelita wailed and let her face fall. She pulled her hand from mine and rubbed her forehead.

I stared at the floor. If I could have made my legs obey, I would've ran until I found the stairs, jumped down them and tried every door and every room until I found Tranto. Once I found him, I would—

"That's not what I'm asking about," Kelita said. Then, she smiled lopsided with a slight tilt to her head, "I wonder what it would be like."

"What what would be like?" I mumbled.

She smiled at me with confident innocence.

"You want me to kiss you?" I asked as the hallway tilted and darkness crept to the edge of my vision.

It looked like Kelita tipped herself forward and pushed herself onto her tiptoes. Then, she sank back down and brushed beside me as she called over her shoulder, "C'mon we can't be too far away."

It was a whole eight clicks before I was able to pick up my feet and follow. I replayed what had just happened in my mind until I couldn't even look at Kelita without feeling overwhelmed by the heat of embarrassment. Had she actually leaned forward to kiss me? Or, had my imagination played a trick on me?

Neither of us spoke until we found the stairs. The hallway didn't end the way I thought it would. Instead of ending into the stairwell, it continued on around the right side of the stairs and passed through an archway. Beyond the archway, natural-looking light flooded a room that looked like it was walled with glass.

Kelita stared at the sunlight for a few clicks before she turned to me. I immediately dropped my gaze to the floor and shuffled my feet across the floor.

"Do you think he's outside?" Kelita asked. "I thought we were on some sort of ship."

Airitha would have been able to answer Kelita's questioning observations much better, but I swallowed and attempted an answer that sounded like Airitha's people could have come up with. After all, I didn't possess a single doubt in my mind that Kelita would not like it if Airitha did answer.

"I think Nik'Nik said they were able to create this seeker, that's what she called it, so that it has an atmosphere of its own," I said.

Kelita responded, "You certainly paid attention to that orange lady's story."

"Are we going to find Tranto?" I glanced out the distant windows. The sunlight was turning a distinctive purple and red.

"You don't actually believe they made a planet and can fly it around space, do you?" Kelita crossed her arms and swung her hips so she could rest her weight on one leg.

I scratched my head. "I...I don't know," I admitted.

"It all sounds like a nice story wrapped up neat and pretty to make us think we aren't their prisoners. Well, come on," Kelita plunged down the stairs.

I followed with my head spinning. Kelita's way of causing me to question things felt right but so wrong at the same time.

I hardly noticed when the stair tread ended, and I stood in thick-bladed grass up to my ankles. We had indeed descended into the outdoors. A stiff breeze blew sweetly scented air over me, and tree leaves crashed together in natural music.

Kelita groped for me as she backed toward me. Her face angled up the same as mine.

Above us, an enormous slice of fruit hung suspended in nothingness. My heart beat once. The throb filled my ears. The fruit was Teluthia. Wrinkly red, vibrant green and scattered blue.

"Is that?" Kelita breathed.

"Yeah, that's Teluthia," I responded.

Breaking the spell cast by the planet, I grunted angrily and yelled Tranto's name.

"Jax, what's that?" Kelita raised her arm to point.

I didn't bother looking. "They *are* lying to us. We have to get Tranto and the others and get back to Teluthia as fast as we can. We'll take the starship."

"Look, please," she insisted.

"Airitha can fly it. Darvian probably can too," I growled without hearing her.

"No," Kelita's voice rose. "Look."

I peeled my eyes from the lush grass between the building and the forest. Kelita's arm moved slowly as if she were tracing the trajectory of a distant dragon. I stepped to her side and sighted down her arm. She pointed to a black speck moving across Teluthia's fruit-like appearance. It was incredibly far away and moving fast.

"It's a starship," Kelita whispered. "It has to be. They're coming to rescue us."

A sinking feeling drew my heart to my waist, "Teluthia doesn't have any starships left that can fly."

"Maybe it's one of those Gah'ten dropships," Kelita replied.

"We don't know when Gen'tahn'Gen is going to order us to be confined again or when this seeker is going to be piloted away from Teluthia. We have to find the others and leave now."

I glanced around wildly. Tranto had to be somewhere close by. I reached out with my mind and recoiled. Not one presence but too many to count lay open to me. Maybe not open so that I could communicate with them, but they were present in a way that I could feel them. The vast number of them nearly drove me to my knees as they threatened to overwhelm me.

"What's wrong?" Kelita steadied me.

"I can feel them," I said with wide eyes.

"Who?" Kelita pressed.

"All of them," I responded.

Chapter 7

Kelita commanded I tell her what was going on, but just as she finished speaking, thunder erupted all around as at least a dozen Neftim dropped from the sky with wings snapping taut.

Kelita staggered and froze. She gripped me as she stared nervously at the nearest semitransparent creature.

I felt each of them in my mind. They didn't invade, though. Instead, they seemed to be asking for permission to speak with me via thoughts the way Tranto and I did. I scanned them with open-mouthed wonder. They all took different shapes ranging from long and thin with ribbon-like wings to looking like a ball with the wings of a turit protruding from either side. Two even had more than two wings. None of them had shaped any sort of head for their bodies. They circled us with expressionless bodies that were sophisticated yet incomplete to my eyes.

At last, a Neftim with innumerable, shimmering wings moved closer to me. His presence grew stronger than the others. I stared at him.

"Thank you, Jax of Geoteous, for allowing this connection," the Neftim stated. His voice held a deep resonance and that same accent Tranto had only thicker. The Neftim lowered his body to rest on the ground. "I am grieved that it is only at the sacrifice of one of your number that we are able to communicate, yet I am glad we may speak.

"I am Ronthluque, and I speak for the Number. You have brought us one of our Number. For that we are most grateful."

A finger poked my side as a hand tightened on my arm. "What's going on?" Kelita asked.

"He says he speaks for the Neftim. He's glad to meet us," I hissed. "His name is Ronthluque."

"What's going on? Neftim? Oh, yeah. Why can't I hear him?"

"We," Ronthluque paused, "we would like to speak with all of your number. However, it is only you, Jax of Geoteous, that we are able to communicate with."

The Neftim circling us gave some impression of bowing with much rustling and shifting of wings.

Ronthluque motioned to each of them with his many wings and said, "All in our Number are pleased to meet you and Kelita, also of Geoteous."

I bowed. Kelita tried to yank me upright again.

The circle of creatures shifted again, and one by one, they took flight. The wash of their wings felt just like the familiar wind from dragon wings. The darkening sky was alive for several clicks with their sounds of flight.

Ronthluque took a step forward. His body formed lumps and distorted as he shifted his shape. His many wings joined into six, and his body elongated. "The one of our Number whom you call Tranto awaits you at our pools. Come, bring the woman beside you and let me take you to your friend. He, too, desires to see you."

"Jax," Kelita whispered between clenched teeth.

"He just asked us to fly with him. He'll take us to Tranto," I snapped.

The black speck Kelita had said might be a Gah'Stotten dropship had grown considerably against the beauty of Teluthia as Ronthluque and I spoke. The leaves rustled, and night animals began to sing.

"How far away are your pools?" I asked Ronthluque.

"They are not far," he said smoothly. "You would find them easy enough to walk to, but the journey would take a long time."

I nodded. Turning to Kelita, I asked, "Are you coming with me?"

"You wouldn't be able to leave me behind," she said and strengthened her grip on my arm.

I glanced at the resting, semitransparent creature. He was so much like Tranto I wanted to trust him fully, but he was not Tranto, so I fought myself. Ronthluque folded his wings and lowered his body to the ground.

"C'mon," I tugged Kelita behind me.

Tentatively, she stepped beside Ronthluque and followed suit as I sat, straddling his back. Kelita wrapped her arms tightly around me and glanced around, slapping me in the face with her mul'li.

Ronthluque wrapped himself around our ankles and calves. With a brief call of caution, he flung us into the air. He moved his three pairs of wings as if they were waves. The resulting flight was far smoother than a dragon's or anything Tranto had ever managed.

Darkening forests slid beneath us. The light remained relatively bright and reddish. Ronthluque said it was because we were so close to the planet that light reflected from it and bathed the seeker. After a few rays of flying, the cloying smell of decaying plant matter rose thickly to my nostrils.

Kelita wrinkled her nose and said, nasally, "It stinks."

I nodded and forced my eyes to pierce the darkness, "We're flying into a swamp. It might be the same one Tranto and I teleported to accidentally."

"These creatures must not be able to smell," she replied.

We flew on for nearly half a period. Bogs with foul smelling mosses and low, dying brush created vast holes in the forest canopy. Under the trees, I caught the glint of standing water. Countless night creatures chirped or croaked their songs for anyone who would listen.

I scanned the sky for the ship Kelita had pointed out to me, but I could not find it against Teluthia's light. Was it the Gah'Stotten trying to escape, or had Ahdah, Thaydrin and Vauriel gathered their soldiers and come after us? I thought it was farfetched, but it was still a possibility. We had not left Teluthia far behind as I had assumed when Gen'tahn'Gen first talked with us. Indeed, if the seeker was the cause of the ecliptic darkness, then it had hung in the sky over Teluthia for an entire cycle.

A thought suddenly struck me, "Ronthluque, why go through all the trouble for one Neftim if there are so many of you?"

The creature remained silent so long I wondered whether he'd heard me. A large, round tree rose from a smooth bog in front of us. I was about to ask about it when he finally answered.

"Friend of Oogluk, we are not the vast people we could be." Ronthluque groaned in his mind, "Our Number are not a vivacious group filled with the laughter and joy of young ones. War among us has gained our Number nothing save to drive wedges deeper about pointless disputes. Further, those of our Number required to serve the Great Gen'tahn'Gen," his thoughts possessed the feeling of spitting on the name, "dwindles us eran by eran." I was about to ask another question when the creature tagged on, "It is my suspicion, as well as that of some of the Number, that Gen'tahn'Gen desires conquest as in the cycles of old."

"You're slaves?" I asked. It did not surprise me that such a powerful people would be enslaved if they could be overcome. Nevertheless, hadn't Hahn'Nik'Nik just told us that the Neftim were no longer slaves? Had she lied to us? It seemed likely.

"That, Friend of Oogluk, is the spark that ignites our war," Ronthluque said wearily.

"Why do you kill each other over the argument of whether you're slaves?" I asked.

Ronthluque glided toward the round tree and replied, "Kill our own Number, we do not. However, our war separates us and divides those amongst our number who would otherwise bear little ones. Great pain you will find in our Number for many of us have been separated. Once, our families bound our Number together, but no longer. Now, our Number is perishing to the killer of unity.

"The Great Gen'tahn'Gen, may he die," Ronthluque's voice took on a dark, cracking edge, "has granted our Number this one favor of recovering one of our Number." He gave the impression of spitting, and anger boiled in the deeper recesses of his mind, "I see through his lies and deception to the heart of his despicable ploy. He would have all of our Number serve him. There are few who can see the way I see, but sight can be a curse of its own when it is joined with willful disbelief."

I strove to come up with something to say, but words escaped me. I wondered again at Hahn'Nik'Nik's story.

Kelita asked quietly, "Are we going to land by that tree?"

I nodded, "I think so."

"Jax?" she whispered in my ear.

"Yeah?"

She hugged me tighter, "If we don't make it off of here, this seeker thing, I'm sorry."

I thought for several clicks. "Sorry for what?" I asked when I couldn't figure her riddle out.

"For trying to make you see things my way."

"Oh," was all I could say.

"You don't want my apology?" Kelita asked, loosening her arms.

My head hurt and spun as I tried desperately to form a response that would satisfy her.

"It's okay," she said after several clicks of silence, "I'll try harder."

"No," I responded still hopelessly confused, "you don't have to try harder. I just want you to be safe, and I'll be by your side."

"Jax, that's the most romantic thing you've ever said—probably even thought," Kelita pressed her temple against mine.

I burned with embarrassment. Ronthluque chuckled into my mind. I tried to shrink, but Kelita interpreted it as me trying to snuggle her as she sat behind me.

She continued her train of thought, "I didn't know you were so amorous. I don't want to leave your side either."

I gulped at the lump in my throat and refrained from arguing against her assumption that I never thought romantic thoughts—whatever they were.

"Prepare yourselves," Ronthluque called.

I relayed his message to Kelita.

Less than a ray later, we landed lightly beneath the spreading boughs of the round tree. All around us, swamp grasses waved in the breeze. We stood on an island covered in small, dead leaves and ankle high bracken that tugged at my pants. Strands of silvery clouds hurried above us on their mysterious missions.

"They will come to us," Ronthluque declared. With that he set us down by the base of the tree and lowered himself to the ground in front of us.

"How long will it take them?" I asked.

Ronthluque answered, "It is a slightly longer flight for them, but they are nearly here."

I reached out with my mind to search for Tranto, but I could not feel him. Instead, I nearly stumbled at the immense number of Neftim present all around. They were crouched and waiting with bated apprehension, slowly stalking through the marsh grasses or flying in silent circles above us careful to not allow themselves to be seen except through my mind.

"Do you feel them?" I hissed in excitement to Kelita.

She frowned and glanced all around and at Teluthia's glowing shape. "No," she shook her head. "How many are there?"

"Too many to count," I replied. "I didn't think it was possible for this many Neftim to be here. They're all around on the ground and in the air."

Kelita shrank closer to me, and her hand twitched as if searching for a bow string or arrow. She found my hand instead. I wrapped my hand around hers. She looked at me, and I wanted to.... What? Hug her? I quickly looked down at the ground.

Ronthluque stated, "Your kind are strange to us, but she is clearly fond of you. I think she desires you. Do you intend to honor her choice?"

"What?" I asked dimly. I tried to wrap my mind around what he was saying.

"In our Number, it is the female Neftim who makes the choice of mate. The male chooses whether to honor her decision or leave into exile until he is able to join himself to another number. I understand it is not this way with your kind," Ronthluque continued in a factual tone. "We have, at times, observed the Tek'ekim, the people that are your kind here, but we do not study them nor do we share sensitive information with them. I think that is why they resent us so."

I understood—or I thought did. However, I was nowhere near able to discuss the topic with Ronthluque. My thoughts careened madly as I tried to catch them.

"We're too young to marry," I finally managed.

Ronthluque gave the impression of tapping his head with a finger. It was so much like Tranto that I thought for a click that he had reached us and had connected with me.

"Ah," Ronthluque said, "you are too young to forsake your parents, but not too young to love. This is a curious thing. I shall have to ponder this and see whether our Number are the same."

Kelita and I walked to the large, gnarled trunk. The bracken and dead leaves crunched beneath our feet. I turned my attention to the bits of sky poking through the canopy above. More and more stars continued to grow visible. Their tiny lights looked small and insignificant from where I stood.

"Jax?" Kelita broke the silence.

I glanced at her. She had a thoughtful look on her shadowy face. What was wrong?

"Do you think Tranto will be able to get us off of here?" she asked.

"I don't know. I still think we're prisoners." I shook my head and took my hand away from Kelita's. She reached for it, but I crossed my arms before she could catch it. "They say we're not prisoners, but Ronthluque says they, the Neftim, are held captive even though they have their freedom on the planet. None of this makes sense."

"Well, if we are prisoners, I can't think of anyone better to be trapped with," she smiled at me somewhat awkwardly.

I looked at the ground.

"Tell her the truth, can you not? Can you not tell her the truth?" the familiar voice I cherished said the same thing backward and forward.

"Tranto!" I reached out to him with my mind.

He gave me the sensation of laughing deeply.

Kelita shoved me lightly on my shoulder and studied my face. I knew I looked ridiculous staring up through the limbs of a tree with wonder and excitement radiating from me.

"Is he almost here? Did he bring his wife?" Kelita demanded.

"He says I should tell you something," I didn't take my eyes off the patches of sky.

She shoved my shoulder again, "What? Tell me what?"

Tranto conveyed a picture to me. Heat flared so hot in my cheeks it felt like they'd been slapped so hard they bled. What did I have to lose? Ronthluque and Tranto couldn't both be wrong, could they? Then again, they could. They didn't study our Ti'Kahn ways.

I caught Kelita's arm as she reached out to shove me again. It threw her off balance, and she stumbled against me. I wrapped my arms around her and bent my head down. My tunnel vision was so strong stars danced around her head. I kissed her.

Kelita's eyes grew wide, and she pushed herself away from me as quickly as she could. Her expression contorted from surprise to fear to uncertainty to joy and then to confusion.

I couldn't look at her. I had aimed for her cheek wanting to give it a little peck like the one she'd given me in the bunker on Teluthia. Somehow, whether my body

took over or Kelita moved slightly, or I just had really poor
aim, my lips had landed directly on hers.

Chapter 8

"Kelita," I tried to recover, "I'm sorry. I didn't mean to."

Kelita's voice came soft and a bit squeaky, "Didn't mean to kiss me at all or kiss me on the lips?"

"Sorry," was all I managed.

"Well, I'm not," she declared.

I pictured her with a defiant tilt to her head and a hand on her hip. When I peeled my gaze from the ground, that was exactly how she stood. Her eyes flashed with something she was trying to hide.

"You caught me off guard," she shrugged, "but I liked it."

My face flushed so much I didn't even attempt to say anything.

"Awkward, Friend Jax, is how all of us are when we are young," Tranto spoke softly into the distant part of my mind. "When we are young, all of us are awkward."

Was Tranto holding back a laugh or was he overflowing with joy from being with his wife?

"I didn't know you had a wife," I stated to Tranto to change the subject.

"A lot to discuss, we have. We have a lot to discuss. I, too, did not know. Perhaps, to say I did not remember would be more accurate. More accurate, perhaps, it would be to say I did not remember," he replied with a slight darkening to his mood.

"Was this your first kiss, too?" Kelita asked.

I stared through her without acknowledging her question.

"Oh," she dropped her eyes to the ground.

I shook my head and replayed what she'd asked. "No," I replied. "I haven't kissed anyone else. My first, too."

Kelita brightened, picked her way around a bramble and slid her hand into mine, all the while smiling at me. I stared at her and strove to think of something, anything, to say. With her free hand she tucked her mul'li behind her shoulders.

Two vast shapes dropped lightly to the ground in front of us. Tranto held his dragon shape and turned his fake eyes to appear as though he looked at me intently. The shape beside him must be Tuca, his wife. She looked a bit like Ronthluque except her four wings were much longer and thinner than his.

Ronthluque stepped forward into a bow beside us. Tranto acknowledged his greeting and thanked him for bringing Kelita and me. My face burned as they shared a joke about the kiss I'd given Kelita.

"What are they saying?" Kelita leaned and whispered in my ear.

"They're just welcoming and thanking each other," I said once I'd recovered enough.

"Is that his wife?"

"Friend Jax, may I welcome you to Tuca, my alambaralam." Tranto called. "To Tuca, my alambaralam, may I welcome you."

"Does that mean wife?" I asked hurriedly.

Tranto felt as though he were smiling as he replied, "To your kind that is the word you would use, yes. Yes, that is the word your kind would use."

"Greetings, young one from afar," Tuca spoke fluidly like a brook that knows its course through the rocks.

I felt the urge to bow, so I did and responded, "And greetings to you, oh loyal one."

Tranto's presence filled with laughter. My face swelled redder with even more embarrassment. Could I do nothing right?

"She would still have chosen to never leave my side even if she had known the erans she would be alone. Even if she had known the erans she would be alone, she would have chosen me," Tranto confided. "She has withstood the test of time and," words failed him as he struggled to say what would adequately describe himself. He completed the thought a few clicks later, "She has withstood the tests of time and the brokenness in which I have returned to her."

"Jax?" Kelita nudged me.

I blurted in a whisper to her, "This is Tuca, his alambaralam, wife. She has waited for him all these erans. He is very pleased and grateful."

"Isn't that a bit selfish of him?" Kelita hissed back.

Tranto addressed Kelita through me, "Perhaps best it would be for Tuca to speak of this matter. To speak of this matter perhaps it would be best for Tuca."

I ducked my head and whispered, "Tuca's telling me what she thinks," when Kelita elbowed me.

"For erans of loneliness, and for erans of grief could I be angry?" Tuca said gently. "Yes. In short, I would be justified for any action or thought or feeling that can be dreamed of for everything that Oogluk did." The two Neftim leaned close against each other.

"But," Tuca's presence brought so much sadness to my mind that I sniffed, "what I have learned since he was taken has validated my deepest and most secret machinations of consciousness. I remained true to him even when everything and everyone proclaimed him to be dead.

"'Why don't you move on with your life?' the Tek'ekim would have asked. The Number presented my predicament to me in numerous ways, yet I refused to realize their persuasions and lived on in loyal, mad denial.

Now, after all these long erans, I am at last reunited with the one I chose. He is still mine, and I am still his alone."

Kelita elbowed me again, "You're going to forget everything she's saying before you can tell me."

Tuca continued, "I know now the reasons that Oogluk left me and our children. It would be banal of me to say he had no choice. However, that is precisely the circumstances. The Tek'ekim administered him a drug which rearranged his mind causing him to utterly forget us. His memory of our family was robbed the same way a hungry wonkul may steal the eggs from a turit's nest. Nothing was left—not even the shell of those memories."

"What's—"

"She's saying they drugged Tranto and took him away from her. He didn't remember her at all," I snapped at Kelita as I kept listening.

"I have seen his mind. My dear Oogluk's damaged and battered interior." Tuca struggled to continue due to the raw emotions of deep care and empathy flooding every part of her mind, "He is not the Neftim I led a happy life with, yet he is no different. When they manipulated him with their drugs, parts of him were lost and other parts were jumbled into an incoherent mud. Damaged beyond repair some of him may be, but that does not change what we share and what I choose."

So, Tranto hadn't ignored me every time I asked about his past. He legitimately had no recollection.

"I have shared my memories of us with my Oogluk, and he has fully acknowledged them to be true and factual. It is no replacement for what was stolen as that was entirely from his own perspective, and so, was colored by his own self-reflection. I saw," Tuca pushed herself to say it, "I saw how much of him had died."

As she continued, I felt the sensation that I felt whenever I was around someone crying from desperation so deep that they can make no sound with their sobs, "He has assured me of your kindness and acceptance. You have been so very good to him. Helping him. Strengthening him. And, I don't know how, but bringing him back to me."

Tranto nuzzled his wife and spoke to both her and me, "Even in my state, I am more alive now than ever before. I am more alive now than ever before, even in my state. Because of you both, and our children, Tuca, the rest of my erans will be the ones I remember. The rest of my erans will be the ones I remember because of our children, Tuca, and you both."

I felt naked and ashamed as I asked the question that singed my mind, "Forgive me, but what about Tellitor'itor? How do you not remember him? What happened to him?"

To my surprise Tuca responded, "She is undoubtedly one of your ancestors in your old generations."

Tranto added, "I think she retained some of that drug and forced it on me before she died."

"Jax?" Kelita grumbled.

I had turned into a mess beside her, and my watery eyes must have made her anxious. I turned to her and looked at her with my eyes wide and my brow scrunched.

"What are they saying?" she tipped her head toward Tranto and Tuca.

I stared at her. My ancestry had Ti'Kahn from this place? Well, not from this place exactly, but wherever the seeker had come from.

"C'mon, Jax, what is it?" Kelita urged.

"They say Tellitor'itor is one of my ancestors."

"Telli-who?" it was Kelita's turn to look confused.

"Tellitor'itor," I replied. "She was the Ti'Kahn who took Tranto to Geoteous. They say she's one of my ancestors."

The news didn't strike Kelita as it had me. "That makes sense," she said. "That's probably why you can talk with them and I can't."

She was right. Why else would I be the only one to be able to connect with Tranto and the other Neftim.

Kelita gasped, "That's probably why your sister has yellow markings. And—and everyone else who has yellow markings is related to you."

"Related to me?"

"Somehow," Kelita shrugged.

"She speaks right. Right, she speaks," Tranto noted.

I sent my gaze out over the marsh grasses. They waved incessantly as though they had a dance that they never tired from. My gaze finally landed on Ronthluque. He had remained silent through the whole telling of

Tranto's history. When my gaze fell on him, he bowed and spoke.

"Jax of Geoteous," he said gravely, "you will always be remembered as a harbinger of good. Through you much healing has been worked in our Number."

I returned his bow and mumbled, "I don't know how I have done anything."

Tranto walked up behind me and wrapped me in an extension of his body, "Friend Jax, without you pulling me from my lake, where would I be? Where would I be without you pulling me from my lake?"

Tranto included Kelita in his embrace, and she was pressed against me. She studied me, but kept her lips pressed into a tight line as if she had to bite them together to keep from asking questions.

"Tranto or Oogluk?" I asked out loud.

"What?" Kelita said.

I waited for Tranto to respond.

At last, after much rumination, he replied, "Your kind tells stories in books. In books your kind tells stories. Books may be divided into chapters as parts of the characters' lives come to an end. As parts of the characters' lives to an end come, books may be divided into chapters. I think, Friend Jax, that a chapter has ended for me. For me, I think, a chapter has ended."

"So, you want me to call you Oogluk?" I asked. Deep inside the melancholy ache of loss welled up like when some toy that I had loved dearly as a child, but had outgrown, had been placed in a box and hidden away. The joys of the memories remained, yet I was unable to tangibly feel the comfort of the toy.

"Oogluk is who I am. Who I am is Oogluk," Oogluk said with a ferociously joyful tone.

I nodded solemnly.

"He wants us to call him Oogluk," I offered to Kelita.

We talked for several more rays, and then Ronthluque flew Kelita and me back to the Tek'ekim's building. With the surreal, reddish light glinting off numerous roofs and towers, it looked as if it were a palace when I beheld its silhouette in the dusky sky.

Oogluk and Tuca had remained behind after many long stories had been shared and theories disgorged. They claimed they would not be far away, but the click I was too far away to connect with him, I may as well have been a planet away.

Ronthluque landed by the door we had used earlier. "Jax friend of Oogluk," he said, "one of our Number will remain out here at all times, hidden of course. You will always find us when you have need."

I nodded tiredly and reached for Kelita's hand. She grabbed it and snuggled into my shoulder.

"You kept me up so late, I'm going to sleep in next cycle," she said with a yawn.

"You wouldn't have stayed behind if I could've tied you up."

"It's not nice to tie people up," she murmured.

I tilted my head and thought about kissing the top of her head, but I rested my cheek there instead.

Our feet scuffed the grass and then slapped the artificial floor of the building. We retraced our steps and found our rooms. My bed was piled with blankets, and I flopped on top of them and fell asleep.

Chapter 9

I awoke with a start. Something slammed onto my chest.

Airitha scolded Kammiel for waking me.

Nonplused, the little girl stated, "Airitha said we can find breakfast once we're all up."

"Not now, Rurin," I moaned.

"C'mon," Kelita dug me from the blankets, "this little groushan jumped on me too. It's what we get for talking so long with Tranto and his wife."

My bleary eyes caught Airitha's sudden, attentive jerk. She knew we had gone to see them. She had wanted to go with us but had stayed with Kammiel, who had been far too tired to go.

"Let's tell Airitha about it over breakfast," I mumbled. "I'm not enjoying being jumped on."

Airitha had few questions as we ate the breakfast of fresh fruits and juices laid out for us. Hahn'Nik'Nik was nowhere to be seen. Instead, we were waited on by a single servant who said nothing and refilled our glasses before they were half empty. When he wasn't hurrying to help with something, he stood in the corner with his eyes downcast and orange-entwined hands clasped in front.

Kelita made a sound of disgust and bumped me with her shoulder. I looked up from the fruit I had been sectioning.

Airitha walked over and sat down beside me. Kammiel leapt up and placed herself beside Airitha so that we were all on the same side of the table on the same bench.

"I'm worried," Airitha hissed around a bite.

I took a drink of red juice that looked like liquid candy and asked, "What about?"

Kelita sighed an exasperated groan beside me.

"We haven't seen Darvian or Meisha since they were taken…or left. Wouldn't they have come back by now if they could?" Airitha didn't try to hide her confusion at our friends' actions. Her brow darkened as she stated, "Darvian really didn't want to go. I don't know how they made him leave, but he definitely wanted to stay with us."

I glanced at each of our white, oval plates before responding, "That's not the only thing I'm worried about. The Neftim don't like these Tek'ekim. They don't seem to be in agreement about them, but Ronthluque clearly believes they're dangerous and not to be trusted."

"Jax," Kelita growled. When I glanced at her, she pointed with her eyes to the servant standing in the corner.

I spoke loudly, "If they're reading our minds already, then it doesn't hurt us to have an open conversation."

Kelita turned away with a pouting expression. Quietly, she said, "I guess you're right," and bit into a small, burgundy fruit.

"I like Nik'Nik," Kammiel piped up. "Mostly."

Airitha turned to the little girl and laughed with her. Then, she turned back to me, "I'm glad I'm not the only one who's concerned. If you figure out anything we can do to find out where they are, will you let me know?"

Why couldn't we just ask? Even prisoners were given answers of some kind, right?

I addressed the servant in the corner, "Where can we find our other friends?"

Kelita gave me a wide-eyed glare. I ignored her and hoped she wouldn't bring it up later.

The servant did not make eye contact and spoke in a slight drawl, "The one, Hahn'Nik'Nik, will escort you shortly."

Kelita faced me with her nose only inches from mine. She whispered so quietly only I would hear her, "How do we know we can trust him? What if they put some of that drug you said they gave Tranto in our food?"

I looked intently into her eyes. In my peripheral vision, Airitha looked at us with a question forming on her lips before quickly turning to the servant and asking him about something else.

"Kelita," I said, "they might have, but I don't know what else to do right now."

Kelita's eyes narrowed, and she flopped back onto her part of the bench. I thought I heard a muffled sigh escape her lips.

I refrained from rolling my eyes and made an effort to focus on my plate. If they had managed to drug us with their mind control or mind blanking drugs, what could we do about that? We had to eat. None of us showed signs of its effects either. We all sounded and acted normal—unless that was part of the effect it had on me. Would I notice if anything were out of place if I had been drugged?

A new voice reeled me back into the room and the present reality.

"The Great Gen'tahn'Gen will see to it," Hahn'Nik'Nik finished what she was saying.

Kammiel slowly got up and sat on the other bench beside the orange woman. Nik'Nik responded by pulling the little girl onto her lap and helping her peel an orange, three-lobed fruit.

The Tek'ekim woman sounded wistful as she murmured with a faint smile, "Once the seeker's back home, you'll be able to play with Mik'Mik. I've been away too long." She sighed long and slow as she raised her attention back to us.

"Nik'Nik," Airitha asked, "when will we see our friends again? Meisha and Darvian?"

Nik'Nik smiled brightly, "Those two are something else. The healing they bring is such a joy. They worked far longer than anyone anticipated yestercycle. I'm sure they will be in attendance with the Great Gen'tahn'Gen."

"She makes it sound like they hardly leave his side," Kelita whispered to me.

Nik'Nik shot a glance at Kelita and met my eyes. I gazed back with what I hoped expressed neutrality.

"We're worried about them," I offered. Worried seemed like a drastic understatement with the growing dread rising in me.

"I heard you were able to speak with Oogluk?" Nik'Nik shifted her legs beneath the table.

I nodded, suddenly conscious of not wanting to share anything about the meeting.

"I know some of them resent us," Nik'Nik said. "I wish it wasn't that way. Our two peoples could prosper so much more if we didn't have to barter and bargain so much. The Great Gen'tahn'Gen has promised to establish better relations with them, but they can be so stubborn we shall see what becomes of it."

We finished eating in relative silence.

"We must be on our way," Nik'Nik stated.

Kelita shot a dark glare at her back as she led the way down the hallway. "Just keep your Gen'tahn'Gen is so great to yourself," she muttered to no one.

I reached back and pulled her to my side so I could whisper in her ear. "What do you think she meant when she said this seeker is going to go home sometime?"

"I don't think it's very complicated," Kelita replied. "They said they made it big enough to hold an atmosphere. It came from somewhere, so it has to go back. Maybe it's a moon or something from there planet."

Neither of us had realized Airitha could hear us until she interjected, "That can't be or their planet would be destroyed—or at least normal functions would stop."

Kelita glared at her and tried to make me slow down and fall behind the rest. To her consternation, I jogged a few steps to Airitha's side.

"How do you mean?" I asked.

"Moons are responsible for tides and such in large bodies of water. Their gravity affects things. If it's a big enough moon, it might even help hold the planet in its orbit. I'll tell you more later. I don't think they'd like to hear us talking about mistakes we think they've made," Airitha said.

Just as we were about to walk through the ornate doors opening into the great room where we'd met Gen'tahn'Gen yestercycle, Kelita grabbed my arm. "We never got back to discussing the starship we saw," she said with a forceful realization tugging her eyes wide.

"I don't think we have time right now."

"But what if it's important?" she countered.

I looked at her and then gazed through the open door. "Look, I don't want to go talk to Gen'tahn'Gen any more than you do, but I don't know how we could get away with anything else at the moment."

Kelita frowned, "Let me know when you do know something."

I grimaced playfully, "I know I can outshoot you in archery."

"No, you can't," Kelita responded instantly with a prim toss of her head.

The familiar pillars, elaborately carved like trees, stretched their branches in greeting as our footsteps clattered on the dark floor. To my surprise, the starship lay exactly where it had the cycle before and looked untouched.

As we drew closer, pairs of guards materialized beneath the pillars. They stood perfectly still like hunting predators stalking their prey. Only their eyes moved as they followed our progress. They were dressed in the same orange clothes and pants. They held their weapons in their hands but also possessed rows of knives and other wicked-looking tools in their belts.

The air closed in around us the closer we drew to the crystal throne. Kammiel reached up for Airitha's hand and clung to the older girl.

Laughter echoed in the room as we rounded the final pillar.

There stood Gen'tahn'Gen in front of the throne. Darvian stood beside his sister to the left of the throne while an imposing array of guards stood behind them.

The nasty, whorled scar that had twisted Gen'tahn'Gen's face was gone. His face looked whole and even pleasant as he smiled at us with twinkling, orange eyes and unscarred lips.

Chapter 10

"Greetings, my young friends," Gen'tahn'Gen called as we came to a stop in front of him.

Nik'Nik bowed, bending at her waist. Kammiel shrank into Airitha's leg.

"Please stand," Gen'tahn tilted his head as though entertained. "This cycle is a great cycle for it is the first in which I stand whole before you to welcome you newcomers."

Airitha and I straightened from the shallow bows we had started. Kelita held her arms crossed rigidly with her weight resting on one foot.

"I trust you have found a breakfast suited to your tastes. We have taken great pains to procure the finest for our little sortie to bring back the one who was missing," Gen'tahn extended his right arm in a waving gesture. "Now that you have brought my Oogluk to me, we may return."

He bowed his head as if to end the conversation. With languid strides he stepped to the throne and sat slowly, leaning into the backrest. His orange eyes glittered with anticipation.

"Young Jax," his slow, popping voice articulated, "I thank you for your benevolent care of my Oogluk once again, but that is not entirely why I have called you to my presence this cycle."

I flinched when he addressed me and watched with apprehension as he leaned forward and clasped his hands together. Silver rings on his fingers glittered coldly.

I glanced at Darvian. He stood motionless, staring into the distance as though he hadn't even seen us. Meisha stood the same way but with a frown turning her mouth down.

"You see, my dear Jax, we, the Tek'ekim, have need of someone with your abilities. This seeker was not easy for us to construct, and we really must put it back where it came from."

Beside me, Kelita stiffened. She and I had the same ability to shape. If they needed me, they would most likely try to make her help as well.

Gen'tahn continued, "Once you have helped us return our seeker, we will escort you back to your world where you may continue to live and grow in peace." He drew out the 's' sound into a lengthy syllable.

He raised his hand and smiled, "Now, don't be troubled. The time it will take a person of your capabilities to help us will be quite a small scrap of time. Your friends have assured me that they will gratefully enjoy my hospitality until you have finished."

"No, we won't," Kelita spat. "Darvian, Meisha, let's go."

Kelita turned and marched to the nearest pillar. Darvian and Meisha remained rooted to the floor, but their heads swiveled toward Kelita.

Gen'tahn stood from the throne. A sneer cast sickly shadows on his face. For a click his face looked more hideous than when it had been misshapen by the scars.

Before he could speak, shouts, rattling weapons and earsplitting squelches erupted far behind us. An orange bolt burned into the ceiling above the left side of the semicircle of guards behind Gen'tahn'Gen.

The ruler's face contorted from a look of anger to confusion and back to a feral look of hatred. He snarled to his guards, who leapt into action, rushing toward the attack.

I dropped to the floor, pulling Airitha and Kammiel down with me. Kelita dove and landed on her stomach beside us.

"C'mon," she jerked her head toward the pillar.

We began crawling but were yanked to our feet and forced to run bent over toward the throne.

Another stray bolt sizzled to my left. It shattered the throne's crystals into a shower of black and white shards. I instinctively covered my face.

Kammiel whimpered, and Airitha hoisted her to her hip. She glanced over her shoulder as she did so and stopped so fast I plowed into her.

"Ahdah!" Airitha shouted as she struggled to keep her footing. "Over here!"

The Tek'ekim's weapons rattled like constant thunder in a storm, drowning out any words that may have been shouted in return. Thaydrin stood in his unmistakable, thin height dressed in white armor. The MEC in his hands flashed, spraying orange bolts at our captors.

Airitha screamed again, but then, we were forced through a door that slammed shut behind us.

"No," Airitha yelled and flung herself toward the door.

One of Gen'tahn'Gen's guards swatted her aside as though she were nothing more than buzz. She whimpered as she landed heavily on her side. Kammiel clung to her and cried and wailed like she was the one being beaten.

I rushed to help. Scooping Airitha gingerly off the floor, I tried to pry Kammiel from her, but the little girl would not let go. I pulled Airitha's free arm around my shoulder and helped her run-hop down the hallway.

"They're here, Jax. They're here to save us," Airitha cried.

I could think of nothing to say, and I couldn't do anything because the guards would simply beat me down.

Finally, I replied, "I know. I saw your Ahdah too."

We continued on. Any time we slowed, one of the guards gave us a shove from behind. We ran and ran and ran. Ahead Kelita disappeared around a corner. A few clicks later, we rounded the corner and spilled into a forest of thick trees curling gnarled branches toward the sky from mucky, green pools of stagnant water.

A path, paved in dark gray cobblestone, ran straight ahead. We were herded onto the walkway and pressed for greater speed.

"Let me take her," I called to Airitha.

Somehow, Airitha managed to convince Kammiel to climb onto my back where she bobbed like a piece of firewood thrown into a river.

The trees on either side of the causeway were well tended, and no branches tugged at our clothes or tore at our skin. The further we ran, the more Neftim I felt all around. Here and there the murky water swirled in eddies of algae from where they watched us. None of them connected with me, and I did not recognize Ronthluque, Oogluk or Tuca anywhere.

A huge explosion ripped through the air behind us. Airitha stopped and turned to look. Her pinched face said it all. She was afraid her Ahdah had been killed.

I slowed, and a hand pushed me from behind. Airitha caught me before I fell to my stomach.

Kammiel whimpered, and Airitha tried futilely to comfort her by holding her hand and talking softly to her.

A MEC bolt sizzled into the trees above us. Loud shouts rang in the swamp. I refused to look back. We had to keep moving so we wouldn't get caught unprotected in the middle of a battle.

Airitha turned and ran sideways. "Ahdah!" she shrieked.

She still held Kammiel's hand. Her feet scraped the cobblestone next to mine.

We had to find cover, but the Tek'ekim urged us forward.

Something bumped my foot. Airitha yelled. The cobblestones sent a punch straight for my face. Kammiel clutched me tighter as I stumbled.

I never hit the gray stones. I glimpsed a semitransparent tentacle as it retracted into a nearby pool.

I stood and watched as the guards that had been pushing us forward, away from Thaydrin and his troops, ran toward the burning palace behind. Their weapons buzzed, and their orange robes flapped. Fire shot skyward in another explosion. A white armored, Teluthian soldier knelt and fired his MEC. Thaydrin advanced in a high crouch with his own MEC spraying bolts into the charging Tek'ekim.

"Where's Airitha?" Kammiel cried.

A click later I saw her. Airitha crawled low to the ground to the right of the path. She had leapt into one of the pools and slogged her way through the mud toward her Ahdah.

"Airitha!" the little girl on my back shouted.

What about Gen'tahn'Gen? Wasn't he ahead of us? Wouldn't he come after us with more of his guards?

Kelita. I spun to look forward down the path.

"Kelita. No," I shouted as realization struck. "Stop. Just let them go."

Kelita barred the way of several of Gen'tahn's guards. She crouched in a fighting stance as she leveled a thick branch in front of her chest as if it were a sword. The guards twirled their buzzing weapons and lunged.

I stood torn between the two. If I followed Airitha, maybe her Ahdah would be able to save us. That would leave Kelita all alone. At the same time, if I ran to Kelita, wouldn't the guards overpower us and drag us away?

The first white armored Ti'Kahn I'd seen took a massive blow to his head from one of the Tek'ekim guards. His helmet flew off. Blood flowed in a river down his face, nevertheless, I instantly recognized him.

"Ahdah!" I shouted and raced toward him.

Before I'd gone two steps and before the Tek'ekim could raise his weapon again, a string of orange bolts burned through his chest. He crumpled to the path and slid into a pool. Ahdah dropped to his hands and knees before he was pulled back by two of Thaydrin's soldiers.

I stopped. I didn't want to run any farther. They were fighting in front of me, and I needed to get as far away as I could. What was I thinking? A stray MEC bolt would kill both me and Kammiel.

Muttering angrily to myself, I turned on my heel and raced, bent over, toward Kelita. She still faced off with the guards. Neither party made a move. The guards were clearly respectful of Kelita's ability with a sword—or branch. And they had good reason to. They couldn't overpower her with numbers because no more than two could attack side by side, and that, not very effectively for the danger of a stray blow landing on their comrade.

On impulse, I scanned ahead for Gen'tahn'Gen and my two friends from Grael. None of them were to be seen.

I was ten strides away from Kelita. Four guards stood against her, but she continued to hold her ground.

"What's going on back there?" she growled when I stopped several feet behind the guards.

"Ahdah and Thaydrin are leading an attack," I blurted. "They're here for us."

Something felt odd in my mind. Had I said something that wasn't true? Why did something feel out of place?

"At least I thought so, but they must not be here for us," I studied the ground as I fought to remember what I had seen. Ahdah had been there, and he had gotten hit in the head so hard his helmet flew off and blood streamed down his face. "I know my Ahdah's back there for sure."

MEC bolts continued to squelch, though less frequently. The heavy smacks and growling shouts of melee fighting took over.

"Did you see my Omoah?" Kelita asked.

She'd turned to me the slightest hair when she asked me. The two guards immediately in front of her lunged. Both rattling, buzzing weapons jabbed her in the ribs. She went completely limp instantly and crumpled to the cobblestones.

The guards didn't even look at me as they knelt and bound Kelita's wrists and ankles.

Kammiel sobbed the terror-filled cry of a young child all alone in a dangerous environment. I knelt and lowered her to the ground. Her wailing grew louder. Quickly, I scooped her up and placed her on my hip. Without hesitating, she wrapped her arms around my neck and grasped handfuls of my clothes. She burrowed her wet cheeks and runny nose into my neck like a soudis rooting in soft dirt.

I could think of nothing to say to her. Nothing was alright, yet, somehow, everything was fine. I rubbed her back and strove to think about what Airitha would do for her. My memory failed me, though. The only thing I could picture was her running toward the battle, and that was bad.

My vision blurred as though my eyes were crossed, and my mind felt muddy like the muck surrounding the pools of algae and murky water. What did I need to do? Oh, that's right. I needed to find Darvian and Meisha.

I helped one of Gen'tahn's guards lift Kelita's unconscious body and set off at a slow jog down the path with them. The din of battle melted slowly away behind us.

Chapter 11

Nearly a half mile later, the swampy pools gave way to a small lake. In the middle of the lake an island rose in mounds of dirt and stone. Trees reached out over the water before turning their large leaves skyward.

A building that looked like a castle stood stalwartly on top of the highest point of the island. It's brown, stone walls curved out and over the tops of the closest trees, and a tall tower sprouted from its center.

The cobbled path skipped over the lake in a wooden bridge with many sections. Each section ran flat while the rail arched far overhead at its zenith.

A girl screamed my name behind me. Kammiel peered over my shoulder as I kept jogging. A man shouted to me, but I didn't pay attention. Nothing was more important than reaching the island and the castle.

Our feet thundered on the bridge. The boards bowed and sprang haphazardly beneath me, causing me to stumble several times.

"Jax? Friend Jax?" another voice called to me.

Only one more section of bridge to go.

"Friend Jax, the wrong way you are running. You are running the wrong way," the voice said again.

A shape swooped down from my right. A huge, flying creature with two people riding on its back. I cowered, sliding to a stop behind the rail.

The creature bent its shape and slammed the lower portion of its body into the bridge. The bridge shook crazily as the section the creature hit disintegrated into slivers and chunks of planks floating on the water.

Kammiel waved and yelled, "Airitha, we're over here."

Just then, my body was blasted into the bridge rail. Kammiel's little body was forced so hard against mine that I was sure I would have a bruise shaped like her. My ears exploded, and pain sliced my head in two. I couldn't block enough of the sound even with my fingers plugging my ears.

Green light, so bright it hurt to look at, sliced out from the castle in a vertical line like a tree trunk hurled through the air. It flew faster than MEC bolts and barely missed the flying creature. More blasts followed in quick succession causing the surface of the lake to dance and the bridge to shudder.

The concussive forces from the blasts felt as though they echoed forever in my chest and head tails. My ears rang, and stars danced in multicolored pinpricks of color in my vision alongside black dots. My sense of balance teetered on the verge of collapse.

Kammiel stared unseeing into the distance. She jumped when I grabbed her shoulders and pulled her to stand.

The four guards hurried forward toward the broken bridge, and, one by one, dropped into the water. It came up to their chests. The one carrying Kelita did not even bother keeping her head out of the water, but that wasn't a problem. As Ti'Kahn, our head tails can filter oxygen from the water just the same as they pull oxygen from the air.

I pointed Kammiel toward the end of the bridge where the guards had plunged into the water. She clutched at me and wrapped her small arms tightly around my neck.

I drove forward. My balance was off. I staggered to the left and flopped into the water.

The winged creature returned and dove just overhead. I ducked beneath the surface of the murky water for a click.

I could hear nothing for certain other than the pounding of my heart and a piercing ringing in my ears. However, as I came out of the water, I vaguely thought I heard the shadow of my name. Glancing down at Kammiel, I realized she was too frightened to say anything. It hadn't been her calling to me.

Algae spun in eddies beside me as I surged forward. I wasted no more time on who had called my name or whether I had even heard it.

The Tek'ekim guards sprinted down the path in front of me. A part of me said I was forgotten, but then, I felt the reassurance that they simply trusted me to follow them. The path was so clear I couldn't get lost.

My heart throbbed faster as I urged my body to its fastest speed. It protested and demanded I rest, but I ignored it. With Kelita and Airitha unconscious and gone respectively, it was up to me to care for Kammiel. I would not let her down.

Vertical, green lines sliced through the air again. Now that we were on the island, the concussion was only a whisper of what it had been while on the bridge. Kammiel still flinched and went stiff as the air throbbed.

Snatching a glance over my shoulder, I watched the last few green lines dissipate behind the flying creature.

A flash of memory snapped in my mind. Tranto. Oogluk. Airitha and her Ahdah.

My footsteps slowed until I walked backward, peering up at the flying creature. Oogluk maneuvered as only a creature like him could. Thaydrin and Airitha clung to his back. It was a mad dance of death as the green lines erupted again. Oogluk tucked his wings and tail tight, spun and twisted like a ribbon in the hands of a skilled ribbon dancer.

I wanted to call out to them and tell them to get away, find safety.

What was I doing?

I needed shelter. I couldn't stand out in the open in the middle of a path and wait for a bolt to hit me. I tightened my hold on Kammiel and broke back into a run before I'd completely turned around.

Tree branches hid patches of the sky as we neared the castle. Oogluk danced back and forth with his riders clinging to him like turits clamping tight to an ee'nex's back to pick buzzes from its fur. Why was he the only Neftim out there? Where were the others?

Ahead, a dozen Tek'ekim charged like a river down the path toward me. Their faces were grim, and each held a buzzing staff in one hand and curved knife in the other.

Ahead, branches cracked and crashed to the ground. Oogluk dropped to the path, crouching with his fangs bared and wings bristling.

"Jax!" Airitha shouted my name.

Thaydrin twisted away and raised his MEC. Several squelches marked the bolts he fired.

"They have Kelita," I bellowed. My voice sounded distant and slow to me.

"We'll come back for her. We need to get out of here. Now!" Airitha yelled.

Oogluk lashed out, various parts of his body shooting out suddenly. I had seen him do that before against attacking wood dragons back home.

The memory of Ahdah taking a smashing blow to his face replayed in my mind. Where was he? Was he alright?

"Where's my Ahdah?" I demanded.

Airitha's voice was unsteady as she struggled against Oogluk's new dance, "He's alright. Get up here, and we can take you to him."

Oogluk reached out to grab me and carry me away. I pulled away. Kammiel screamed and flailed at my arms, trying to reestablish her grip on me, but I flung her into Oogluk's grasp and used her inertia to fling myself out of his reach.

"Friend Jax?" he questioned me.

"Take them and go," I commanded. "I'm going after Kelita."

Kammiel clung to Airitha's side. Thaydrin squelched off several more shots. The last of the orange staff-wielders fell with a hole in his chest and his robe bursting into flame.

"Jax?" Airitha was near tears.

"Go," I bellowed. "I'm going after Kelita."

With that I dodged off the path and into the mud.

"Jax!" Airitha's voice filled with raw terror. "Jax!"

Just go. Get out of here. Get somewhere safe. I'll meet you there as soon as I have Kelita.

"Friend Jax," Oogluk said before melting away, "I cannot return here again. Return here again, I cannot."

"Goodbye, Tranto," I said and pulled my feet from the sucking mud.

Chapter 12

I didn't look back as I slogged through black mud. I could see the entrance to the fortress through the scraggly branches of the moss-laden trees. I would not be going that way. I had no hope of making it past more guards alone.

A thought, distant and incomplete, formed in my mind. I should get out of the mud and give myself up. I shoved the thought aside. I was not going to believe those voices.

I ducked under a branch that clung to my clothes and knew I couldn't run. They would know paths that I couldn't even see. They would know where to step so their feet wouldn't be eaten by the mud. No, outrunning them was out of the question.

Fighting them? I didn't have any weapons. But I could shape, right? Yes, that was right. I needed to remember that.

After scanning the immediate swamp for any sign of bright orange Tek'ekim, I squished beneath a fallen tree covered with moss so that it made a sort of tent. A branch snapped off easily, and I called on my ability. Orange light enveloped my fingers. The wood responded.

I pressed my fingers together, feeling the wood fibers shift and realign themselves. First, I needed a melee weapon that could stop their rattling clubs or staffs. Kelita had shown me that even a simple, unshaped branch could accomplish that. Second, after I had a sword, I would shape a range weapon.

A bow and arrows seemed too extreme to make quickly, but perhaps several throwing spears would do the job. Unless I could find a MEC, I would be limited by the projectiles I could carry. Maybe the longer reach of a swordstaff would be better suited to fighting off the Tek'ekim.

My fingers went limp. Why was I trying to hide? The half-shaped sword slipped into the mud. Why didn't I understand I was still in danger and could be found and killed by the flying creatures?

I growled and pushed myself up. Mud coated my chest and weighed down my legs. I had to keep moving and stay away from the pools of water. A path through the maze formed in my mind. I saw myself hopping from one solid island to another.

With a struggle I reached under the moss to pull my sword from the mud. Clutching it in one hand, I followed the string of islands toward the castle.

I would arrive at the wall in the fast approaching night, scale it using my shaping ability and drop down inside. Then, I would find Kelita, and we'd sneak out together.

It was a good plan. All except for one thing: I couldn't shake the feeling that something was wrong. Something deep within me or something I planned to do just didn't fit.

The chill of night made me shiver as I crept beneath the looming shadow of the wall. Few stars shone through the veil of clouds, and Teluthia's bright presence created an ethereal, red glow from just beyond the horizon.

Turits clucked and called to one another as buzzes attempted to drown out their choruses. A few biting buzzes circled my head. I tried to shoo them away, but they were too persistent.

I emerged from the swamp about a hundred yards from the front gate, but something didn't seem right about scaling the wall there. The picture in my mind showed a place at the corner further down the wall. I shook my head. Why wouldn't the original spot work?

No Tek'ekim showed themselves behind the parapet. If they weren't patrolling, did they already know where I was or did they have a different means of detecting intruders? If it was the latter, was it deadly or would it capture me in a cage I couldn't escape from? Maybe it would simply send up an alarm and I would have just enough time to find Kelita.

I stared up at the top of the wall. It stood thirty feet above me. I had never perfected the art of shaping handholds as I climbed cliffs at home, but I could do it.

I shoved my sword into my belt and tried to remember what I had forgotten. As I searched my mind, I recoiled at a presence I hadn't known was there.

"It is I," the steady voice of Ronthluque hastened to say. "I've come to help you."

Vaguely, my mind surfaced memories of the Neftim. It felt like an age ago when I had last spoken with him.

With his ability to see my mind, Ronthluque said, "You have the tainted feel of the Tek'ekim. They have given you the drug they use on our Number."

"What do you mean?" I asked.

"You ask yourself what you have forgotten," Ronthluque explained, "yet, you also think that you never intended to shape anything more."

The image of a swordstaff materialized alongside a handful of thin spears.

"I don't have time to make those now. Besides they'd see the glow from my ability," I hissed.

A wave of pity washed through Ronthluque as he shoved aside the desire to say that it would be no different from me shaping handholds on the wall—the light would be seen either way.

"Where are you?" I asked. "Can you help me rescue Kelita?"

"I am on the edge of your perception," Ronthluque stated. "Once you go inside that wall, our connection will be lost. Oogluk warned us of the great fight that afflicts our

Number at these walls. His warning is well understood. Our Number have long felt the vile effects of the Tek'ekim near this fortress."

"So, you're saying that you can't teleport me in or Kelita out?" I asked in frustration.

Ronthluque gave the sensation of closing his eyes and hanging his head apologetically, "Alas, Friend Jax, I and my Number are unable to assist you further than to warn you and potentially pull you from the island once you and your Kelita are outside the wall. I and the Number with me will wait for you out here."

"How many of your Number do you have?"

Ronthluque closed off more of his already nearly walled off mind. "Friend of Oogluk, it would be unwise for me to say prior to you entering that pit," he said slowly.

I glanced up at the wall, trying to pick up any movement or any weapons I hadn't seen yet. Except for the skittering feet and mournful calls of night animals, the entire island and surrounding lake was silent.

"Friend of Oogluk," Ronthluque said, "Trust nothing in there. Do not trust even your own memory. What you take in with you, you may not return with. You must be quick and keep your mind guarded closely the entire way."

With that, Ronthluque's presence ebbed away, and I found myself standing beneath the dark wall wondering what had just happened. Ronthluque's words seeped from my mind like water from cupped hands. Only the residue of what he had said remained with me.

Muttering to myself, I reached up to form my first handhold. The wall was made of porous stone which reformed quickly under my influence. The orange light from my ability glowed brightly, but I ground my teeth and kept going. I had no other option.

What would happen if they caught me scaling their wall? I would have no way of defending myself. If I slipped and fell, I doubted the mud would cushion my fall adequately. These worries and others plagued my thoughts as perspiration washed away some of the mud on my face, leaving muddy streaks on my cheeks.

It took me ten rays to climb halfway up the wall. Once there, clinging to the wall like a buzz, I stopped and looked down. What was I doing? Why was I climbing the wall in the middle of the night?

The answers escaped me, but it must be important. I proceeded, shaping divots into the wall and pulling myself up.

Five feet from the top the memory of Kelita falling unconscious and being carried through the water to the fortress crashed into my mind. Fear gripped me. If I could forget that easily, how easy would it be for me wander around the fortress for the rest of my life and never know why I was in that strange place instead of at home? Would I even remember home?

I paused beneath the lip of the parapet, straining my ears to pick up any sound that could be a patrol. Only the night songs of the swamp greeted my eardrums.

Holding as tightly as I could to the faded memory of Kelita, I placed my hands on the parapet, pulled my body up and peered into the fortress.

Chapter 13

As I peered over the wall, an urge to drop down and run to the tower via a narrow causeway nearly overpowered my caution. However, after scanning the fortress for several rays and seeing no one, I slipped over the parapet and crouched, leaning my back against it. I was in.

No one was going to get me. Who had kept saying that? Someone I knew had kept saying, "They get you, and once you're gotten you don't come back."

I shook my head. No, I had never heard anyone say that. I was making things up—fabricating delusions.

Kelita. Right, I had to find Kelita.

I pressed my knuckles hard against my temples. I *had* to remember Kelita. She was the whole reason I had infiltrated the castle. Or was she? No, I had snuck over the wall because they needed my help. They were asking me to help them just like Ahdah asked me to help with things on the farm. We did have a farm. I could remember that, but what animals did we have on the farm? I couldn't picture them.

I shuddered. I had been told something important just before scaling the wall. What had it been?

Why was I huddled in the dark against the parapet?

I stood and looked over the parapet to the swampy ground below. No threat revealed itself.

Drying mud cracked and flaked off my chest and legs. Had I fallen from the wall? Was that why I had needed to climb it? Why hadn't I just gone to the gate?

My mind swam as I tried to sort it all out. In frustration I dropped my arms to my sides. My left arm caught on something. I drew it from my belt. A half-finished sword.

One word flashed through my mind—Kelita. What did that mean?

Shrugging, I strode toward the causeway leading closer to the central tower. I needed something from there. Or did I need to report what had happened to me?

My footsteps slapped lightly on the stone causeway. It had no railing or parapet. A few Tek'ekim walked briskly along their way underneath. Not a single one looked up at me.

I bumped into a door. It was so dark I hadn't seen it in the shadows. After a few clicks of groping for a handle,

I found it and opened the door with a slightly raspy squeak. Behind it, a circular staircase ran up and down.

Footsteps echoed in the stairwell. I stood just inside the door as the orange light of several torches illuminated an archway on the opposite side of the landing I stood on.

A pleased-looking Gen'tahn'Gen smiled at me as he and his torch-bearing guards stepped onto my landing. He held out his right hand to me and flicked his left wrist.

I grasped his hand, pleased that he greeted me so warmly. Then, I stared as a marvelously beautiful, young girl stepped forward from where she had trailed the procession. She had white markings just like me and was clothed in the simple garb of the Tek'ekim with the addition of a massive, white cloak wrapped about her shoulders and trailing on the ground behind.

I bowed to her as she stopped in front of me.

"Are you ready, Jax?" the girl asked.

I looked down at my clothes caked in mud. A rush of embarrassment flushed my cheeks.

"I'm sorry, Kelita," I said as I suddenly remembered the girl's name, "I think I need to wash up first."

Kelita turned from me and nodded to her right side. Two Tek'ekim pulled me gently to stand beside her.

Gen'tahn'Gen smiled broadly as he clasped his hands in front of him. Then, he raised them as if addressing a crowd he wished to silence.

"My family, I give you the repairers of our time." Gen'tahn gave a flourishing bow and said, "Come, my friends, we are ready to right the wrongs that have been done to our world."

Kelita hooked her hand in Gen'tahn's elbow and grasped my hand with her free hand.

The white cloak was placed on both of our shoulders as we passed beneath the archway.

Kelita whispered to me, "Isn't this great? We can help them repair their world."

"What happened to it?" I asked.

Gen'tahn'Gen answered, "My friend, Jax, we, the mighty Tek'ekim, took a portion of our world when we created this seeker in order to reclaim my Oogluk that had been stolen from me. I thank you and Kelita for agreeing to aid our reassembly. It was a dreadfully taxing project to make this seeker—one that cost many lives because we did not have your abilities available to us."

None of his explanation made sense to me, but I remembered Gen'tahn asking me to help his people with my shaping ability. I had readily agreed, and so had Kelita. I walked straighter as pride rose in my chest.

Kelita grinned at me. Her eyes shone with bright anticipation.

We were led deeper and deeper into the castle. On either side, rows of orange-clad guards stood at attention with their rattling weapons silenced. Torches glimmered from sconces whenever the narrow windows were absent.

After walking down a long, extraordinarily wide corridor, we entered what I thought to be the center of the castle. The cavernous room yawned open in a circular declivity. A chandelier held by thick chains hung high above a pool of dark water in the very center. Mosaiced geometric designs sent rays toward the walls where additional torches flickered in front of mirrors attached to the curved walls.

Countless, motionless Tek'ekim knelt around the pool. In the pool itself, dim shadows of Neftim floated. It was impossible to count how many there were, and I had no way of knowing how deep the pool was, so there could have been many more of the creatures buried under the water and layers of their brethren.

"Now, Jax," Gen'tahn came to a stop, "we are ready to depart this place, and I wanted you and Kelita to witness the greatness of our many millennia of work."

Gen'tahn raised his hand, signaling a tall Tek'ekim amid the kneelers. The man, in turn, gave a command in their native tongue. The water in the pool swirled as the Neftim reacted violently for a click, but almost before they'd started their agitation, they calmed and floated utterly still.

The tall man gave another command. Several previously hidden Tek'ekim came forward and removed several Neftim from the pool. I could barely feel a presence in them, even less than the vague shadows emanating from the others. They were unconscious, and that was right—the way it should be. They served us, and it was only a pitiful penance for what they had done so many erans ago.

Gen'tahn'Gen grinned, "So much work. So much work, but it accomplishes our needs. It's not so unlike your ancestor, Jax, who explored the far reaches of the universe."

I nodded. I was indeed thankful I had some of the Tek'ekim's blood in me. Without it I would be as blind and disconnected from the Neftim as Kelita.

I shot a wary glance at her. She was already looking at me with a wide-eyed, blank sort of stare as though she couldn't decide what to think.

"I guess our work is about to start," I said to her.

She nodded her head slowly as her eyes grew unfocused.

Kelita and I were ushered toward the pool. Gen'tahn and at least two dozen guards circled around us. A grinding sound like sand being crushed between two boulders filled the room. The floor we stood on sank slowly.

Once the floor stopped descending, Kelita and I were escorted down another tunnel. All along the walls of this lower tunnel large doors stood locked and sealed so tight I doubted air could even pass into the room behind. I counted eighteen doors on the right side, and each door was mirrored on the left.

At the end of the corridor, we turned left and walked until we came to another circular room far smaller and with a much lower ceiling than the one we had descended from. A raised dais formed an island in the center of the room.

"My young friends, please forgive me, but this is a necessary measure," Gen'tahn said.

Two guards bound orange cloth around Kelita's and my wrists and looped a chain through our bound arms locking us together.

Kelita scowled and raised her hands to look at the bonds.

Something deep in my mind stirred. A desire to fight against the bondage? But was that all?

A guard motioned for us to climb onto the dais. We did. Two Tek'ekim joined us—one on either side. Gen'tahn'Gen clapped once, and we were no longer in the circular room.

Chapter 14

Kelita and I stood in the midst of a barren, rocky expanse. Water cascaded over gray crags in the distance. The air felt sticky, dirty and hot.

Kelita wrinkled her nose and grunted in distaste.

"It's like someone set a swamp on fire," I said.

She nodded.

The two Tek'ekim who'd teleported with us beckoned us to follow them. Several more guards materialized where we had stood, followed by Gen'tahn'Gen a ray later. Their bodies formed from dark mist in less than a click.

"Please pardon our family for the precautions we were required to take. Unbind them," Gen'tahn said.

He turned slowly as he scanned our surroundings. I turned with him and saw the seeker for the first time in decent light.

It hovered over us easily as far out into space as a small moon, and that's what it looked like, mostly. Part of its surface was smooth like the face of a planet, but the rest was broken and jumbled like dirt clinging to a fence post that has been removed after many erans of use. Its lumpy, shattered appearance suddenly reminded me of the barren place we stood in.

Gen'tahn spoke, "Many months and many lives it cost us to build. That is why we have asked for your assistance. With your abilities, we will be able to reassemble our planet in far less time and with much less loss of life. I can see in your eyes that you have already perceived how our seeker fits into this grotto."

Kelita nodded gravely and turned to me, "It's clear we were intended to do this part from the very start."

"How will we bring it into position?" I asked Gen'tahn.

"Our family leaves that to the two of you. Whether you ask us to bring the seeker back piece by piece or in small manageable conglomerations, we will aid you." Gen'tahn's orange eyes blinked, "Only you may not attempt to replace it all at once. We have not the resources of Neftim for such a maneuver. Hence, why we have enlisted your services. We request only that you be careful to not disrupt our palace and grounds," Gen'tahn'Gen smiled. "Our family have Neftim and men at your disposal."

"Is there anybody who can help us from the original people who disassembled your planet?" Kelita asked softly as she brought her scanning eyes to rest on Gen'tahn.

The leader of the Tek'ekim made a nearly imperceptible laugh in his throat and stated flatly, "They all died. Our family grieves for them."

"Oh," Kelita looked at the ground. "I'm sorry to hear that."

I stood still and turned what Gen'tahn had said over and over in my mind. When had they died? Why had they died? If they had all died, how had the seeker been completed at all?

"Young Jax," Gen'tahn addressed me.

I snapped my gaze to lock onto his fiery orange eyes.

"You have many questions," Gen'tahn stated. "It is written in your face. I assure you, all will be alright, and answers you will have when the time is complete."

I nodded.

"Hahn'Nik'Nik will assist you in acquiring the implements you require," Gen'tahn added before turning and walking slowly away.

I traced his footprints in the dust coating the broken stone. After twenty feet, he and his escort vanished. In their place stood the woman I remembered well. I remembered her and—who else had it been that she had befriended immediately?

"Jax and Kelita," Hahn'Nik'Nik bowed hurriedly to each of us. Her face bore no expression, and she moved stiffly.

Kelita bowed beside me. I was slow to follow because I hadn't yet shaken aside the feeling that I had forgotten something.

"I want to personally thank you for agreeing to help us," Hahn'Nik'Nik smiled a little too rigidly and a little too thinly.

Kelita offered a brief statement of acknowledgment.

"You've been made well aware of our supplies to assist you. I will facilitate your desires to the necessary people and places," Hahn'Nik'Nik clasped her hands behind her and rocked on the balls of her feet.

"We should do it in small sections," Kelita said.

If we took the seeker apart piece by piece, it would be like putting a puzzle back together right after wearing yourself out cutting each individual piece. However, we would know how it went back together as long as we paid careful attention to how the whole unit was oriented and how each smaller piece fit into the whole. Smaller pieces would be easier and less dangerous yet more time-consuming. Then again, if someone got hurt, wouldn't that cost more time?

"Either way it's gonna be a lot of work. We've never done anything like this," I stated.

Kelita turned to Hahn'Nik'Nik and said, "We need to go back to the seeker to divide it into pieces."

The orange Tek'ekim motioned several guards to come close. Then, we stood inside the castle on the seeker.

I tried to stand straight, but my sense of balance had disappeared. I rocked back and forth trying to orient myself with the cobbled floor of the courtyard we stood in. Finally, I planted my feet wide and stood even though my mind told me I was leaning severely to my left side. A droplet of water dripped uphill.

Beside me, Kelita muttered angrily as she struggled to take a step.

Hahn'Nik'Nik let go of the two guards she clung to, swayed for a click and then spoke. "It is the gravitational pull exerted by Ekper'reppek, our planet," she said struggling slightly with the words. The seeker has moved closer since we returned."

I picked up on an edge of doubt or fear that crept into her voice. Wracking my mind, I tried desperately to decipher why that was a bad thing. The closer we were to the planet the shorter the distance we'd have to teleport the pieces of the seeker into place.

"Why is that bad, and how does that work?" I asked. "We're in space."

Kelita frowned and said nothing.

"Planets produce a force that pulls things to them," Hahn'Nik'Nik explained. "Have you ever seen the effect your planet's moon has on your oceans?"

Kelita and I both shook our heads.

"The gravity from a planet's moon or moons pull the ocean in rhythms called tides. That's why the oceans advance and retreat on the beach."

"We live in the mountains," Kelita stated with a shrug.

I found I didn't particularly care about it either. When would I live by the oceans? Probably never.

"Can we teleport to a new location close to a corner so we can separate it from the rest?" Kelita asked Hahn'Nik'Nik.

"Of course, we can. I ask you to hurry as we are running out of time. Our Neftim are not rested enough for another move of the whole seeker. If we do not act swiftly, the seeker will fall to Ekper'reppek. The results could be disastrous. Hold to one another."

Another disorienting teleportation ended in a cloud of dust and swirling wind. I stumbled as I struggled with the sensation of being sucked toward a cliff, undoubtedly the edge of the seeker.

Dried, scaly mud crumpled and cracked under my feet. The air was bitter as though it had been trapped in a foul-smelling oven for an eran. The few trees still standing stood as sentinels, dry and leafless.

Kelita met my questioning gaze and nodded. As one, we knelt and placed our hands on the crumbling, chalky dirt.

"Once we have this corner cut off, bring it down to Ekper'reppek. I can see right where it fits from here," I said with a brief glance at Hahn'Nik'Nik.

I didn't need to describe the location I saw or make any other requests. In my mind I knew that they knew what had to be done and how I wanted it done.

Kelita's hands glowed bright orange. Mine lit a click later.

Kelita snapped her eyes to lock on mine, "What was that?"

I had felt something too. It'd been like standing on a stone and having another stone crash into it—only without any sound. Only the faint vibrations provided any tactile proof that something had happened.

"I don't—," I began to say.

A thunderous boom sliced my ears with pain. I glanced wildly around but saw nothing.

Hahn'Nik'Nik spoke hurriedly with two of the guards. Clicks later they hurried off at a leaning jog. The other guards pressed in tighter and watched us more closely.

The guard to my right twitched as Kelita and I started up our shaping abilities again. His hand suddenly landed on my shoulder.

Another boom split the air.

Kelita launched her body at the guard's arm. She hardly began her leap before two guards grabbed her waist and all but threw her flat on her back.

I struggled against the hands grabbing at me, but it was hopeless.

As I, too, was flung to my back, light glinted so bright it blinded me for a moment. Then, a huge shape rose above the lip of the seeker in front of Hahn'Nik'Nik. I knew the shape. I knew what it was. I knew that I knew what it was, yet I couldn't place it.

"Don't bother struggling, Jax," Kelita said. "I don't know why I got so angry when he grabbed you."

I didn't respond. The huge shape roared like a rockslide and lowered itself to the ground.

An orange clad guard shouted in their clicking and popping language. Without turning to look, Hahn'Nik'Nik held up her hand in a gesture for the guards to wait.

The starship settled, and a ramp began its slow descent. A single figure emerged from the enormous door. He walked slowly toward us with both arms raised high above his head. A piece of white fabric fluttered in the gentle breeze between his hands.

Hahn'Nik'Nik held up her hand in a calming fashion. "Stop, wait," she said to the approaching figure.

The guard holding me let go and grabbed his weapon as all the others had already done. They crouched and spread in a semicircle.

When the man carrying the sign of peace stood a hundred feet away, Hahn'Nik'Nik raised her voice, "That's far enough. What business do you have?"

The man wore armor that had once been white but was streaked with mud and what looked like blood dried to brownish maroon. He wore no helmet or gloves. Even at that distance his incredible height was easily perceivable.

"I bring a warning and a request," he called. "May we speak?"

"We are speaking now," Hahn'Nik'Nik replied.

"Do we know him?" Kelita whispered. "His markings are red."

"Time is of the essence," the man called. "This satellite and the planet down there are well on their paths to destruction."

A glance at Hahn'Nik'Nik showed her mouth pressed into a hard line.

"And," the tall man continued, "I request that Jax and Kelita, both of Geoteous, be returned the care of their parents who are with me. Further, I request that Darvian and Meisha be returned to our care."

Kelita knit her brows together as we exchanged a look.

"We are curbing the present danger thanks to Jax and Kelita's voluntary aid," Hahn'Nik'Nik replied curtly.

The man stood silent for a click before speaking again, "We've just detonated two charges on the bottom side of this rock in hopes that it will adjust its orbit a little further out. From what information we have gathered, the planet itself is slowly falling toward its sun." He paused as if waiting for a response. When he received none, he continued, "I don't know whether we can save your planet or your people."

He lowered his arms, letting the white flag hang loose from one hand. "We are not your enemies unless you make us your enemies. We wish only to have our children returned to us and, if you and your people allow, to help you save your world."

Hahn'Nik'Nik swallowed visibly and twitched slightly as though she were keeping an intense show of emotion just barely at bay. When she finally spoke, her voice rang with the same just barely strong enough restraint.

"The Great Gen'tahn'Gen leads us well," she said. "It is he who has returned to our family what has been missing for generations, and it is he who devised the means by which we have attained it. It is he, too," she swallowed and pointed her chin, "who has provided repair for our world. The Great Gen'tahn'Gen does not wish you harm but know that he will spare no retribution for thieves, accomplished or would-be."

The man declined his head, "The Great Gen'tahn'Gen has spoken. I wish one last thing before I go."

"Then, speak," Hahn'Nik'Nik snapped. A thin, wet trail told of a tear's slow descent down her cheekbone.

"Jax, Kelita," the man called to us, "have you truly volunteered to help these people?"

I opened my mouth to respond, but Kelita answered for both of us, "Yes, sir. The Great Gen'tahn'Gen requested our help due to our abilities, and we are happy to serve him."

The man remained rooted.

"Please, get them back to work," Hahn'Nik'Nik said softly to one of the guards.

Kelita and I knelt and once again pushed our shaping abilities into the rock. I kept the man in the corner of my peripheral vision. He kept standing there as if he had more to say or something to do that he couldn't remember. At last, a group of the Tek'ekim guards sauntered toward him, and he slowly turned and retreated to the starship.

Chapter 15

Kelita and I fit the first piece from the seeker into the void on the planet. Hahn'Nik'Nik marveled at the nuanced picture I was able to form and convey to Kelita for its placement via teleporting.

"How many Neftim is it taking to teleport this?" Kelita asked after we had lowered the second piece into the grotto.

"We have ten working with us right now. We can dedicate more, if need be, but they supply enough energy to accomplish this rejoining," Hahn'Nik'Nik replied.

"That wasn't very hard to slice off the little bits to make it fit snuggly without rocking and cracking," Kelita commented. "Let's try the rest all at once."

I looked at her as I weighed the effort. She didn't know what it was like to teleport the pieces because the only thing demanding her energy was cutting the pieces. I felt the fatigue creeping into my shoulders just thinking about holding the focus for another piece. The Neftim and the Tek'ekim helped some, but I had to hold the image, tell my helpers where to maneuver the chunk of rock and also communicate to Kelita if she missed shaving off any of the awkward lumps that didn't fit just right.

I was still looking at her when we landed back on the seeker. The air was shifting and swirling madly, which blew leaves and bits of mossy debris into our faces.

"Is it getting warmer on here?" I asked quietly.

"Let's hurry up and get it moved back down. I don't like what that white armored man said," Kelita knelt and pushed her shaping ability into the remainder of the seeker.

Silently, I agreed with her, but a deep concern ran through the back of my mind. Had Neftim died to teleport the seeker back to its home planet? I had thought they were unconscious, but was it possible that the Tek'ekim, were killing them?

"Hahn'Nik'Nik," I called, "we need as many Neftim as possible helping with this one. We're going to move the rest of it with this move."

She nodded her head and looked far away for a click. Her face pinched, and she said, "We have six additional Neftim."

I nodded, hoping that would be enough and lowered myself next to Kelita. The rock beneath the swamps felt mostly solid, but tremors and whispers of some immense force tugged and pulled at it threateningly.

"They've got six more Neftim helping us," I whispered to Kelita. "We'll have to hold it together while we teleport. Do you feel all that tension?"

Kelita nodded, keeping her eyes closed, "Right. I've never felt anything like it before."

Five clicks later I gave Hahn'Nik'Nik the signal. The next click we were falling toward the planet's surface.

"We're too far away," I hollered.

"They've died," Hahn'Nik'Nik mouthed. She looked stricken and wide-eyed.

"What's going on?" Kelita shouted. "We're supposed to be a lot closer."

"Can they catch us?" I asked, whipping my gaze between Kelita and the orange woman.

"They're all dead," she replied slowly. "I was told they were fully rested and able to assist us."

"You mean *all* the Neftim you have available are dead?" I asked as I franticly reached out with my mind for any Neftim to connect with. I felt nothing save a suffocating shroud emanating from the surrounding Tek'ekim guards.

"You were supposed to keep us from dying," Hahn'Nik'Nik whispered as her face teared up. "You were supposed to keep our Tek'ekim workers alive."

"What about the Neftim? Can they catch us?" I shot at her.

"You killed them," Hahn'Nik'Nik's voice rose sharply. "The Great Gen'tahn'Gen said you would keep us alive."

"Are there any other Neftim who can help us?" I stood and glared at the orange woman.

Hahn'Nik'Nik smeared a tear with a fist and shook her head as if trying to clear her mind. Her expression went stony, "There's more Neftim planet side. They may be able to help."

Clouds whipped by in puffy mounds of white. Heat waves washed over us.

A mechanical whine split the air to my left. I turned and there was the starship flying straight toward us. Its immense bulk floated only twenty feet above the trees.

I felt something in my mind. I knew it instantly, yet I didn't know it.

"Jax?" the creature called.

I fought against the shroud separating us as it grew thicker. The creature growled. To my right one of the orange guards stumbled and sagged slowly to the ground. Two more followed clicks later. Then, every one of them dropped to the ground.

Kelita caught my gaze. I was too bewildered to speak, but she had no trouble voicing her thoughts.

"I'm going to strangle that Great Gen'tahn'Gen," she barked. "We're free now."

She looked down at her clothing and shivered in disgust.

She stepped toward Hahn'Nik'Nik, "We never agreed to help you or your precious Gen'tahn'Gen. You enslaved us. I hope you die with this hunk of rock. You and your planet of liars."

Hahn'Nik'Nik stumbled backward and fell. She didn't attempt to get away as Kelita continued her verbal rampage.

"Friend Jax," Oogluk said with a slight weariness, "free you are at last. At last, you are free."

"I'm not sure what happened," I replied. "I mean, I remember what I did and stuff, but I don't remember why."

"Manipulating your mind, they were. They were manipulating your mind."

My befuddled brain finally registered urgency. "Kelita," I shouted, "we have to go. This whole rock is going to crash into the planet down there."

Kelita ended her threats to the Tek'ekim abruptly and looked at me blankly.

"Tranto's on the starship. He and Thaydrin can save us," I offered in explanation.

"And my Omoah?" Kelita asked.

Oogluk confirmed.

"Yes, she's here too."

Kelita hurled the handful of mud she held at Hahn'Nik'Nik, splattering her right arm and face.

The starship landed, and the ramp descended.

"What are we waiting for?" Kelita smiled at me as she grabbed my hand. The mud residue was gritty between our palms.

Just then a small girl dashed down the ramp.

"Kammiel," I called.

My cry was mimicked by another voice. Airitha ran down the ramp. A look of terror plastered on her face, "Kammiel, get back here. Kammiel!"

"Go," I pulled Kelita forward and let go of her hand. "I'll get her."

I willed my legs to move faster as I angled at an intercept course to catch the young girl. She was faster than I calculated and shot past me. I turned, slipped in the mud and bounded after her. She ran straight for Hahn'Nik'Nik, who still lay in the mud.

"No, we have to save her. Nik'Nik!" Kammiel screamed as I lifted her.

We slid to a stop five feet in front of the orange woman. The revulsion I felt toward her boiled inside me. I found myself happy at seeing the mud Kelita had thrown on her. I wanted to kick more mud on her until she had no orange left to see.

"Let me go," Kammiel squirmed like my little brother. "We have to save Nik'Nik."

Hahn'Nik'Nik looked first at me and then at Kammiel. Her orange eyes clouded with remorse and fear.

"We have to save Nik'Nik," Kammiel turned violent in her attempt to get free of my arms and kicked me in the knee.

I grunted but didn't let go.

"No!" Kammiel wailed.

I shoved the urge to kick mud on my captor away and jogged toward the starship.

"Let me go," Kammiel shrieked. "Let me save Nik'Nik."

"She's not worth saving," I heard myself say. My steps slowed to a walk.

Kammiel kicked my knee again. She hit the sensitive place on the inside of the joint. I stumbled and barely caught myself. However, Kammiel threw her weight forward and away from me. She threw me off balance, and I toppled headfirst into the mud.

I groped blindly for Kammiel as she wriggled out from underneath me. By the time I had the mud scraped from my eyes, she had made it back to Hahn'Nik'Nik and was pulling at her hand. The orange woman slowly got to her feet and let Kammiel lead her toward me.

"We have to go, now," Airitha slogged up to me. She reached for my hand and for Kammiel's free hand.

Together the four of us jogged through the mud, up the ramp and into the starship.

No sooner had both of my feet landed on the floor inside the door than a vicious yell reverberated off the hard, smooth walls. A streak of white and purple rushed toward us.

"Get her out of here," Kelita yelled in such a growl it was barely coherent.

Many long hours of training with Kelita alongside her Omoah allowed me to see the kick aimed for Hahn'Nik'Nik's head well before Kelita brought her foot back. It was a strike she had often attempted despite her injured leg. Thaydrin and a Teluthian soldier lunged forward. Kelita's powerful kick caught Thaydrin on the side of his thigh just below his hip. His leg buckled, and he fell.

"She's controlling you," Kelita roared as her golden eyes burned like white hot coals into the little girl frozen at Hahn'Nik'Nik's side. "Get her out of here."

Kammiel's voice wavered, "She's not making me save her. She was nice to us."

"She's using you—all of you," Kelita glowered at each of us.

"Take her to her Omoah," Thaydrin said in a strained voice.

The soldier restraining Kelita nodded and turned her around. They started walking away with the soldier holding Kelita's upper arms, but after a few steps she shook his grip off and pouted with her arms crossed.

Hahn'Nik'Nik bowed and knelt on the floor, "I'm sorry. I'm so sorry."

Kammiel hugged her and rested her cheek on Hahn'Nik'Nik's shoulder. The orange woman sniffed and sobbed quietly.

Thaydrin bent down with a grimace, "You are not responsible for what your people have done. You are not all of your people, are you?"

"I'm so sorry," Hahn'Nik'Nik kept sobbing.

Thaydrin stood and remained silent. Airitha glanced between her Ahdah and me and then looked at Hahn'Nik'Nik.

I regarded Airitha with a blank, emotionless stare that I hoped hid my anger and disgust. I hung my head after several long clicks and said, "I don't know whether she controlled us or not, but I can't find it in me to help her."

I felt Airitha's eyes on me and raised my head enough to return her gaze.

She swallowed and gave the slightest nod, "What—and what does Tranto, I mean Oogluk, think?"

I pondered her question for a long time and wondered why she had asked it.

"I did not feel her exerting her will over you. Over you, I did not feel her will exerted," Oogluk offered apprehensively. "Dangerous is she, along with all of her people. Along with all of her people, she is dangerous."

"Does it mean we shouldn't help her?" I pressed.

Oogluk made no reply.

"He says she's dangerous just like the rest of her people, but he didn't notice her controlling me," I said lifelessly. "I don't want to help her, but," I forced myself to continue, "but I guess we should."

Kammiel wiped gingerly at some of the tears trickling down Hahn'Nik'Nik's cheeks.

Airitha and I watched her for a few clicks before she turned to me and said, "I'm not sure what's best, but I think Kammiel is showing us what's right."

Oogluk grunted in my mind and made no further comment.

I dropped Airitha's gaze and watched her feet as she stepped toward the orange woman and bent to give her a hug. It was a light, tentative hug, but it brought a fresh onslaught of tears to Hahn'Nik'Nik's eyes. I thought briefly of her children and wondered whether they would survive the impact of the seeker on the planet.

I looked up at Thaydrin, trying to gauge his response. However, he stood expressionless, giving no hint to his thoughts. Then, with a decisive gesture, he motioned one of the guards to his side, whispered some command and rolled his shoulders.

We waited for less than a ray before a Teluthian soldier hurried up and saluted Thaydrin with her arm across her chest. She held her helmet under her arm and stood at attention. Thaydrin spoke into her ear low tones. The soldier nodded once and saluted again.

Thaydrin stepped beside me. The Teluthian soldier greeted Hahn'Nik'Nik, who rose slowly and let herself be led further into the starship.

Airitha stared after the retreating forms as she planted herself by her Ahdah.

"It is as it should be," Oogluk broke the silence. "As it should be, it is."

I nodded, feeling slightly dazed.

"That is done," Thaydrin said softly. "Now, we must but find Darvian and Meisha."

Darvian and Meisha. I had all but completely forgotten them. Were they still on the seeker, or had they been transferred to the planet?

"One Neftim remains alive whom they thought to be dead," Tranto's voice was hard and laced with heaviness. "Whom they thought to be dead, one Neftim remains alive. Assures me, he does, that none remain on this rock."

"Can we save him?" I hurriedly demanded of Oogluk.

He responded with grief darkening his presence in my mind, "He tells me he is glad to have been one of the Number and that honored he was to have felt our presences. To have felt our presences and to have been one of the Number, glad he is. He is gone." Oogluk paused and repeated slowly, "Gone, he is."

I ran to the window beside the ramp and peered out. A ball of fire left a trail of smoke behind it.

Airitha bumped into me as she joined me at the window. She gasped and turned to look at her Ahdah.

A click later I looked at him for answers too.

"We were just in time," Thaydrin said evenly as he rubbed his forehead. "I should not burden you with this, but you have already guessed it. This does not bode well for their planet. They severed part of their planet's crust from the rest. This part we see below us is burning in the remaining atmosphere. Their planet's orbit is growing closer to its sun and will burn the same way."

Airitha and I exchanged glances.

"Can we do anything for them?" she asked her Ahdah.

Thaydrin directed his gaze out the window, "We may have only a few cycles to find Darvian and his sister."

Thaydrin placed a hand on each of our shoulders as we watched the burning ball until it had fallen from view.

Chapter 16

"I don't understand how someone, much less an entire planet, could be so stupid," Kelita fumed when she thought I was listening.

I studied my Ahdah's sleeping body. Thaydrin's doctors had done what they could for him, yet his nose was still severely crooked. His left cheek also caved in slightly. They said they had reconstructed his face as well as they could with the tools they had available, but the blow he'd taken had shattered the bone in too many places.

Why had he joined in the attack? He had sent me to train with Kelita's Omoah because he was no good with combat tools. He had told Almatem exactly that the cycle Kelita had chosen Kerelyn.

Where were Darvian and his sister? They didn't need any special tools to heal Ahdah. Why had they disappeared?

"Where are they?" I mumbled out loud.

"Huh?" Kelita asked. "You haven't listened to anything I've said, have you?"

I ran a hand over my face and walked aimlessly to the bench in Ahdah's room and sat hunched forward.

"Darvian could heal his face and make it look like nothing ever happened."

"I say forget them," Kelita placed her right hand on her hip.

In my mind's eye, I could see her glower.

"They've chosen to help those orange people. That Hahn'Nik'Nik," she spat the name like it was bitter-tasting water, "should be thrown back to her world."

"She didn't control us," I said slowly without looking up.

"I don't care. She's one of them," Kelita placed her left hand on her other hip. "They were going to kill us."

I leaned heavily against the wall that served as a backrest for the bench. Letting my weary eyes droop to slits, I studied Kelita. She glowered and chewed her bottom lip as she began pacing. Bags hung beneath her eyes, and her shoulders rounded forward as though she wanted to be invisible.

I felt her weariness and wanted nothing more than to sleep and wake up with everything fixed—Ahdah healed and everyone back in their homes. Unbidden, tears pooled in the corners of my eyes. Everything was turning out bad—just bad. Why couldn't we just go back to when some things were still good? Why couldn't we go back to when Teluthia was still whole? Back to when my family was celebrating my sister's marriage. When Oogluk was still Tranto?

Kelita sniffed. A shiny droplet fell to the floor.

My body fought me as I forced it to stand and walk across the metal floor. Kelita pressed into me as I wrapped my arms around her. She stood motionless, staring into space for a ray. Then, her mouth peeled apart, and she sobbed on my shoulder.

"I hate them. I hate them," she mumbled. "I hate the Gah'Stotten, and I hate the Tek'ekim. I hate them. Why did they do all that?"

Numbness settled in my mind. Words escaped my grasp.

Kelita peeled her face from my shoulder. Her golden eyes were shot with red and deep anguish. She studied me, her eyes flitting over every part of my lifeless face.

"Why do they destroy everything good?" she breathed.

I stared—maybe at her, maybe into space.

"Jax," she bit her lip so hard she left imprints in it.

Her body felt like the only thing living that I could feel. My arms dropped to my sides. Kelita pushed herself a few inches away.

"Aren't you going to answer me?" Kelita asked.

"I," I heard myself say, "I don't know why they do stuff."

"Well, they shouldn't. They should just live peacefully with everybody else," Kelita said.

"I think that's what everyone wishes," I responded quietly.

"Your Ahdah almost got killed by them," Kelita pulled away and started pacing again.

I couldn't find a comfortable way to stand as I watched and listened without really seeing or hearing.

"Why can't we just let them burn? That's what they did to their world. We shouldn't have to help them," Kelita fumed.

I slumped against the wall to the left of Ahdah's motionless form. Slowly, and without thinking consciously about it, my back slid down the wall until I sat huddled on the floor. I rested my head against the wall and stared forward unseeing.

Ahdah was hurt again, and Darvian and Meisha were nowhere nearby. Did Kelita truly mean what she said about leaving them with the Tek'ekim and letting them burn with their captors? Was she really that heartless? Did I agree with her?

The numbness in my mind deepened. It created shadows that hid memories and masked friendships. I slid down the slope alone. The ice was like the scales on a flip— it let me slide down, but I could not reverse direction without being caught. I wanted to feel angry just as I also wanted to feel numb.

I glanced up suddenly as Kelita's footsteps left Ahdah's room. I felt nothing at her leaving without saying goodbye.

Oogluk connected with me and pressed a question into my mind, but it didn't register.

Alone. I was alone, but not alone enough.

I sat so long in that position with my knees drawn up to my chest that my butt screamed at me to move and relieve the pressure of the hard floor. I dimly acknowledged it, yet I welcomed the pain. At least, I felt *something*.

Someone walked in front of me and sat slowly beside me.

After several rays of silence where I neither said anything nor looked at the newcomer, Airitha stated softly, "I heard you were in here."

I blinked and gave a single nod.

She lay her head on my shoulder, "I wish we could help your Ahdah. He fought so hard for you."

I blinked again.

Airitha grasped my left hand where it lay on the floor. "I'm glad you're okay, too. That was really brave of you to go into that fortress and rescue Kelita. It's the same thing your Ahdah would have done."

I blinked several times.

"I think he's just like you. You both help others and make the hard choices that show you care about those you love."

She rubbed my hand as I hefted my unfocused gaze from the floor and pushed it toward Ahdah's bed. I sniffed.

"I just want it all to stop," I murmured. "It's too hard."

Airitha squeezed my hand.

"Do you hate them?" I turned to face her suddenly.

She looked at me with her round, purple eyes and answered slowly, "I hate what they've done."

"Why does your Ahdah think we should help them?"

"Oh, Jax," Airitha wrapped me in hug and spoke into my shoulder, "this all must be extremely hard for you."

"It's easier to hate them and just walk away," I grunted.

Airitha gave a single cough of a laugh, "Yeah. That would be a lot easier."

I hung my head. A wave of vertigo hit me as I spoke out loud what I had just realized, "Ahdah would want to help them even though they did this to him."

Airitha said nothing but pulled me into a hug.

After a few rays, she said, "I don't think things get easier the older we get. I think the consequences get more and more costly."

"How are we gonna get Darvian and his sister back?" I asked.

Airitha released me from her hug and leaned back against the wall. She studied her lap for a few clicks before replying, "I think Ahdah is working out a plan."

Silence ensued externally, but, internally, my thoughts were anything but quiet as they ran wild, crashing into each other.

"Jax," Airitha looked at me, "I'm scared. This drop ship is huge, but it can't hold an entire world."

Awkwardly, I flopped an arm around her shoulders and pulled her close.

"Jax," Kelita's voice erupted, "how can you hug her when you won't even talk to me?"

I jerked my gaze to the open door. She stood with her eyes hard and flashing. Her arms lay crossed over her chest, and she leaned her weight on her recently healed leg.

Airitha slowly extricated herself from my arm and stood.

"Jax was just helping me," Airitha said softly.

"Shut up," Kelita's voice carried dragon sparks in it. Her face wadded up with pain and anger. She spun and ran out of the room.

Airitha looked down at the floor and then glanced at me. Feeling helpless and lost, I remained frozen to the floor.

"Friend Jax," I felt Oogluk's presence in my mind.

"Well, I got myself into a mess, didn't I?" I interrupted him.

"I think you do not see what is right in front of you. What is right in front of you, I think you do not see."

"Airitha's standing right in front of me. You know that. You can see what I see through our connection," I retorted.

"Please forgive me," Oogluk said softly. "Kelita is not alone in her hopes that you will choose her."

"Tranto, I can't think about all that right now," I rubbed my forehead. "I just wish Kelita and Airitha would get along without so many silent battles."

"Are you talking with Oogluk?" Airitha sat cross-legged on the floor in front of me.

I nodded, not wanting to tell her what we talked about.

"How long do you think Kelita will be mad at me?" Airitha asked in an undertone.

Resting my head against the wall and closing my eyes, I said, "I dunno."

Airitha met my gaze and looked down, "I know you like her, but she can be so spiteful. She's been jealous of you and I being friends ever since she saw me on your world the first time."

"Airitha," I began.

"No, Jax, let me finish," she interrupted. "You're not like other boys, Jax. There's something different about you. I don't know, but you seem more *real*—like there's all these different parts of you that you're okay with letting others see instead of hiding them."

My eyebrows scrunched involuntarily as I tried to understand what she was saying.

Airitha glanced up and smiled at me, "I like that about you. You don't always have to be the best whatever in the room, but you're always you."

Oogluk telling me that he didn't know how to be anyone but himself surfaced in my memory. What if Airitha was telling me the things she liked about me were the little things that Oogluk gave me to say now and then?

As if in response, Oogluk said, "Have care, Friend Jax. Care, have. Me, it is not that she is speaking of. She is not speaking of me."

"But I don't understand," I replied.

"I think few people truly do," Oogluk struggled to keep himself from repeating it backward.

Airitha scooched closer to me. Our knees bumped, and she leaned forward, resting her elbows on her knees. Our eyes met.

"Jax," she said, "I know we're young, but," she took a brief glance away, "but—," she broke off. She shook her head and started over, "I haven't told you this because I didn't want to be a burden or drive a wedge between you and Kelita, but I think, if I don't say anything, I'll be more frustrated with myself than if I continued to keep my silence."

The edges of my vision swam in dark dots.

"I've really liked getting to know you," Airitha blushed and gave a self-conscious smile. "Even when we couldn't understand one another's languages, you always seemed to understand what I said. I've been wondering what it was like for my Omoah when she met my Ahdah."

She stopped when I thought she needed to explain what she was saying. With scrunched brows, I looked at her. She, in turn, studied my face before looking down.

I grunted and asked hesitantly, "Do you...does that mean?   Are you thinking of my sister's marriage ceremony?"

Airitha gave a sloppy smile with her face angled down.

Oogluk mused to himself, and I caught only snatches of his thoughts through our connection.

My white markings turned pink as I said, "I think I know why you've been scared of Kelita."

Airitha offered a grimacing smile and ducked her head. I looked over at Ahdah as he lay with his face smashed. The attack and that blow replayed through my mind over and over. His helmet flying off, the blood and then him being carried away as the others pressed forward.

One of Airitha's slender hands rested on my shoulder. I felt her sit beside me as she snuggled into me. My thoughts raced as if a spoon were stirring them in a huge bowl. I didn't want Kelita to be mad at me. Airitha had just told me—something. Ahdah was severely injured and needed Darvian's ability. The Tek'ekim's planet was falling toward its sun, and we were somehow going to help while simultaneously rescuing Darvian and Meisha. Oh, and Oogluk's family, his wife, Tuca, and their offspring should be saved, too. What about Ronthluque and the other Neftim?

"Jax," Airitha breathed.

"Huh?" I didn't take my eyes off Ahdah.

"I'm sorry. I wish we had been able to escape before they came after us. He wouldn't have gotten hurt then," Airitha said.

I balled my fists in my lap and drew my knees up to my chest. "It's not your fault," I murmured. "We couldn't get away."

It was then that I realized hate welled up inside me. I would have to find Kelita and tell her that I did hate them. If they hadn't held us prisoner, Ahdah wouldn't have come to rescue us, and he wouldn't have gotten hurt.

Oogluk began speaking but stopped when Airitha mirrored his words, "I can find it easy to hate them, too, but I think if I did, then I'd be just part of the problem."

"What problem?" I demanded. "It's because of them Ahdah's hurt."

Airitha jerked back and hurriedly replied, "I didn't mean it like that. I meant only that if I were to hate them, I wouldn't really be me anymore. I'd be abrasive and dangerous."

"Abrasive and dangerous?" I repeated in a rhetorical question.

Airitha snuggled into me again. Her body was tense, and her jaw worked slowly as she rested her cheek against my shoulder.

I turned my gaze to look down on the top of her head.

"I shouldn't say anything," came her quipped response.

"Let it be, Friend Jax. Let it be," Oogluk coached.

"Are you telling me you understand what she's hinting at?" I demanded of the creature.

Oogluk was thoughtful as he responded, "Think about how she is drawing comfort from you. About you she did not make this comment. This comment she did not make about you."

"Thanks," I said without meaning it.

Oogluk responded by giving the sensation of laughing, and then, he withdrew from our connection.

Airitha gasped and stood, "I forgot I promised Kammiel I would take her and Nik'Nik to dinner with Ahdah so they won't have to eat with the soldiers."

I struggled to my feet. They'd fallen asleep and stung terribly.

"Come with me, Jax. You need to eat too."

I glanced at Ahdah.

"They'll have someone check on him and let you know when he wakes up," she said calmly.

"Okay," I said and hesitantly followed her.

Chapter 17

"We'll be going down on the sunny side," Thaydrin's aide barked. His words were no joke, however. He'd informed us of the temperature changes and other phenomena happening on the falling world. "That means," the aide continued, "that your armor will struggle to keep you cool. You'll be slogging through boiling swamps and baking mud. Any vegetation remaining unburned could spontaneously combust at any time at these temperatures."

He droned on, covering details of the mission and the stringent time allotments for each portion. Essentially, a medium sized strike force was to rappel from the dropship through the Gah'Stotten's launch bay doors and make their way quickly through the hot zone, which had been vacated by the Tek'ekim. The force would use the intense heat to provide cover as they approached the palace where we assumed Darvian and his sister were held.

Oogluk and I would join them once the temperature dropped sufficiently for Oogluk to safely handle it. He and I had wanted to teleport the entire team directly into the palace, but that had been cut down as too risky. I admitted I understood the danger of suddenly entering an intense mind attack. It was far better to lay out an invasion plan and enter the danger slowly and maintain the ability to retreat if necessary.

Kelita hadn't spoken to me since she'd run from Ahdah's room. We'd seen each other twice, but the first time, she'd stared at me blankly. The second time, she scowled and walked away.

Airitha hugged me, "Be careful."

My eyes were large as I replied, "I know what we're walking into. I won't let them take me again."

She tightened her hug momentarily, "I know."

"I won't be leaving for another two periods," I said, trying to sound lighthearted.

"But you'll be working with Oogluk to establish connections with other Neftim," she looked up at me with her round, purple eyes. "We won't be able to talk."

"Commander Jax, sir?" a burly man with the blue markings of Hegnoranthe saluted me. He stood almost twice my height, but his eyes showed nothing but respect and admiration.

"At ease, sir," I responded in my newly acquired and uncomfortable vernacular. Thaydrin had made me Field Commander of the strike team.

"With respect, sir, one of your people is requesting to join the team," the burly man said.

I glanced behind him and saw Kelita, standing stiffly in white armor with a pack strapped to her back.

"Kelita?" I could think of nothing more to ask.

"May I join this team, Commander?" Kelita said. Her voice sounded slightly hollow.

I took a click to think.

Kelita seemed to think I would refuse. She hurriedly explained, "I've attended each briefing and know the entire operation. Like you, I've experienced what we'll be walking into."

I felt the weight of my position weigh heavy on my shoulders. The burly soldier had been right in addressing me with Kelita's request. Under Thaydrin's actions, I was responsible for making this decision.

I wanted to ask her whether her Omoah consented, yet I didn't want to upset her further and overturn the shaky balance of our relationship.

"It's a dangerous mission," I said, hoping she would withdraw her request but knowing my statement would only solidify her decision.

"Yes, sir," Kelita saluted with her fist thumping her chest in Teluthian fashion.

Oogluk brooded darkly in the distant part of my mind. I knew the reasons for his hesitation and wished for more time to talk with him.

"Kelita, I think," I began. "I don't want you getting hurt," I redirected my tact.

Kelita raised her chin slightly, "I want to come."

"Anger and hate," Oogluk surmised, "are either a powerful asset or a blinding fire, but they are always a dismal companion."

I laughed once in my mind. "Let's hope they are a powerful asset," I responded to Oogluk. I felt as though I'd betrayed my friend by talking about her like that.

"Okay," I said to Kelita, "You'll be with Mahrwal here."

The burly soldier saluted me and proclaimed, "I'll bring her through alive, sir."

Kelita gave me a look that hovered somewhere between smugness and reckless ambition as she donned her helmet and hefted a MEC.

Mahrwal whisked his own helmet on and motioned his section of the strike force to the rappelling lines. His would be the second team to descend. Two more would follow.

The first team hung from their lines as the floor opened below them. Heat wafted into the dropship. I instantly dripped sweat.

A click later the lines whined as the twenty-one soldiers fell to the ground. The lines were drawn back, and the second team hooked onto them.

Kelita looked small but powerful as she grasped the cable with her left hand and leaned back into an almost seated position, which raised her feet a couple inches off the floor. The floor opened. The line whined. Team two was on the ground.

Airitha grabbed me for support as the dropship shifted quickly to the side. The last two teams would be dropped a half mile away.

"You'll come back with Darvi and Meisha. I know you will," Airitha wrapped her thin arms around me, trapping my arms.

I looked at her with sudden shock paralyzing me. We were doing this. We had started, and there would be no turning back.

I nodded, "We'll bring them back."

Airitha nodded and pressed her lips together as if to keep herself from adding more.

Oogluk shifted behind me, and Airitha let me go and ran to her Ahdah, who stood grim-faced by the door.

The floor opened twice more, and the final two teams descended the lines.

"Well," I said to Oogluk, "here we go."

Oogluk ignored my doubt and fears as we set to work reaching out as far as we could to search for Neftim. We were both fully convinced they would readily and

eagerly help us with the second goal of our mission—
capturing Gen'tahn'Gen.

The dropship skimmed the steaming surface of the
planet as we searched. It was fruitless. The few Neftim we
found were so near death and so scared that they did not
respond to us. We could sense them scurrying for any
cover they could find from the scorching sun.

"Perhaps," Oogluk grunted, "there will be some in
better health closer to the palace. Closer to the palace..."
he trailed off.

"I'm sorry, Oogluk," I said. "I wish more of your
kind were able to join us, but it's a good thing we didn't
count on them."

The creature responded heavily, "My heart is
saddened indeed. However, it does me some good to know
there are many yet alive. That there are many yet alive, it
does me good to know."

"We're approaching the cool zone," Thaydrin said
as he lay a hand gently on my shoulder.

"Yes, sir," I said nervously.

"Jax," Thaydrin said, "your Ahdah would be proud
of you. I know because I am proud of you."

I gulped but could find no words, so I nodded.

"We'll take good care of him when he wakes up,"
Thaydrin assured me.

"Thank you, sir," I replied.

He glanced at the black device on his wrist. "It's
time," he stated. "I know we can count on you."

I nodded and bit my lip.

The two extra MECs each of us on the team carried clipped to our packs gleamed with black luster as I strapped the pack to my armor.

A thin, purple arm with red markings reached out and handed me my third MEC I would carry in my hands. I hadn't seen Airitha reenter the drop room. She didn't say anything, and neither did I. We looked at each other, and I knew what she wanted to say.

"Ready, Friend Jax?" Oogluk called.

"Let's go," I said, pulling my helmet on and reaching for the creature's leg.

A click later, the dropship disappeared as it thundered on its way.

To say the armor struggled to keep the heat out was a gross misrepresentation of the truth. The heat beat down on me so harshly that my body sweated just standing in the small clearing amid wilting trees and cracking mud. A warning flashed red in the corner of my display inside my helmet.

"How can anyone still be alive?" I asked in awe of the intense temperature. "This isn't even as hot as what the teams had to deal with."

Oogluk, grim and stoic, made no reply. I felt the pain and discomfort he did not hide from me. His body was not designed for such conditions. I imagined feeling the water evaporating from his body like steam from stew on a winter cycle.

We wound our way under the trees and around what had once been green pools of standing water. However, we soon found that even though the dried pools stank, they were firm enough to hold our weight. In the wettest, I sank only up to my ankles.

We quickly traversed what would have been an impossible maze, had there been water, and soon reached a small hill that would have been an island where we could survey the soaring expanse of the city. The palace, easy to pick out due to its towering, ornate roofs, stood in the center on the only bare stone I'd seen on this strange world.

"The Great Gen'tahn'Gen likes his subjects to know his humility," Oogluk commented.

I had never heard him use sarcasm before, so I was just deciphering his meaning as he finished repeating the statement. I couldn't help but grin.

"That," Oogluk became distant for a click as he thought of Tuca, "is the result of learning again what I had been forced to forget." His tone darkened and grew more solemn, "What I was forced to forget.... Friend Jax, is it normal to be ashamed of what one has forgotten even when he has had no say in the forgetting? When one has had no say in the forgetting, is it normal to be ashamed of what has been forgotten?

"When Ronthluque told me he knew me and that my Tuca still waited for me, I was at such a loss I could do no more than follow him blindly. How lovely, sweet alambaralam Tuca was able to wait a millennia...? How do I not feel so despicable that I think it would be a favor to crawl back into my lake until I die?"

I crouched behind the crumbling bark and moss conglomeration that coated the dry trees and let my vision lose focus. Oogluk's question seemed like one I should have the answer to, but he had always been the one to guide me and answer my questions.

"I have not lost everything, Friend Jax. Though, I may not remember the why or the how of what I know, it does not change that I know it deep down and know it to be true. The why or the how of what I know, I may not remember, but what I know to be true, it does not change deep down."

"That's something else, Oogluk," I evaded his question a few clicks longer. "Since being back with your Number, you have been speaking more normally—not repeating yourself backward all the time."

"Yes," Oogluk acknowledged with the sensation of a shrug. "Such a minor thing it is, though. It is a minor thing. I am glad to be healing."

I knew I still had to answer his other question. The other teams would be in position in less than five rays, so I needed to wrap up that conversation just in case.

Just in case what?

"It is on my mind, too," Oogluk affirmed me. "Into a war we are walking. It is unknown whether we shall walk out."

"I think," I peered through the brown, crusty leaves, "that when we forget about someone we care about, no matter the reason, we feel bad because we knew we should have remembered."

"That sounds like a wise answer," Oogluk stated. "A wise answer that sounds like. I shall take time to ponder it once this is over."

"It's going to be over one way or another soon," I shifted my eyes to see the time piece hovering at the edge of my display in my helmet's visor. "It's time."

Chapter 18

The plan was that Oogluk and I would draw attention away from the main forces, and, as we did so, we would place ourselves in position to connect with any Neftim Gen'tahn'Gen might try to use to teleport away and escape. We would avoid an all-out assault, if possible, but we also had the numbers to overpower the Tek'ekim if it came to a firefight.

Oogluk gave a final negation of Neftim in our vicinity. He shifted his shape to an eight-winged creature, and we shot into the air. He said that we would be less suspicious flying in a shape that was more natural to the Neftim.

"Keep an eye open for those green line weapons," Oogluk reiterated a warning Thaydrin had given our entire force.

The dismal, dry swamps hurried by below us. They were utterly silent and still until we skimmed above Mahrwal's team. They looked like a pack of scurrying buzzes with mottled white, brown and slimy green carapaces. Kelita was one of them. Down there somewhere, hurrying over the uneven ground.

I glanced ahead at the imposing towers of buildings. If the Tek'ekim looked down instead of up at Oogluk and me, the strike teams would be seen too early. They had to reach at least the outskirts of the city before being spotted.

"They'll make it as long as we hold their attention," I said mostly to encourage myself.

Oogluk flew unhurried in a meandering path that looked uncalculated and as though he were lost or crazed with the heat. The first of the tall buildings reached up for us. Its roof of weathered wooden shakes looked like rectangular dragon scales. The scales joined wooden walls with many windows staring blankly into space.

As we passed over the building, the city behind became visible. I twisted around to look at the streets. The only thing was, there were no streets.

"I see it, Friend Jax. I see," Oogluk banked to the right. "Suppose, do you, that they are coverings they erected to ward off the heat?"

"I don't know," I muttered angrily.

If we didn't have a line of sight on the streets from the air, it would be infinitely more difficult to storm the palace. It would be a long, most likely, bloody fight. Further, if the inhabitants had covered the streets with sheets of wood, then most of them had probably remained to wait out the heat. Perhaps, refugees may have even packed any extra space there might have been.

"We don't have a choice," I clenched my teeth and gripped tighter with my knees.

Oogluk made no reply, but his stony determination washed into me like a mountain river that has flooded its banks.

"Marhwal," I whispered into my helmet, "the streets are canopied. I won't be able to guide you."

The soldier's voice crackled back, "Affirmative, Commander."

"Tell Anntoninn we'll be relying on him and his men for melee most likely. Everything is packed pretty close together."

"Yes, sir," Marhwal's voice died in my ear as he began relaying the orders to Anntoninn. This was his kind of warfare. We would see what the spear-wielding Hegnoranthians could really do. Each team had five of them accompanying them.

"Stay safe, Kelita," I peered toward the patch of forest where she and her team would be. I just caught a glimpse of dirty white through the dying canopy.

"Hold on!" Oogluk bellowed into my mind.

No sooner had he begun his warning than he shot skyward. My stomach lurched, and I slipped sideways against the creature's grasp.

A barrage of barbed arrows whistled past before arcing and falling back to the ground.

Stinging pain shot through my friend. A dark shaft fletched with bright feathers protruded from his belly. Oogluk was hit. Fear built in him and in me. He and I both knew regular arrows were nothing more than a tiny splinter to a Neftim, but the Tek'ekim would not use regular arrows. The arrows they fired at Neftim were either poisoned or laced with hallucinogens. Tuca had been the bearer of such information. Although she hadn't told me personally, Oogluk replayed the conversation from his memory into mine.

The silvery creature plucked the arrow from his body and let it fall to the wooden roofs below.

"If I turn crazy," Oogluk's voice rattled with the harsh rasp of fear and wrath barely held at bay, "you must make me teleport away from here. Away from here you must make me teleport."

"I can't do that to you again," I said appalled.

"Do not argue with me," Oogluk roared.

I cowered lower on his back. He arched his back and sent us into a dive.

"What are you doing?" I asked fearfully. "They'll shoot again."

Oogluk responded grimly, "Better they shoot at us or at our strike teams? At Kelita?"

I paused. Words fled from my tongue.

The black dots of arrows flocked toward us.

"She chose to volunteer for this mission," I breathed. Hatred stabbed me at that moment the way I could see the arrows doing in another click. I could have stopped her. I could have refused her request.

Pain flared in my neck. No, not my neck. A black shaft erupted from the top of Oogluk's silvery neck. The wicked-looking barbs were rusted—or covered in a reddish powder.

"Tranto!" his old name slipped out. "You've been hit again."

A silvery appendage ripped the arrow from his neck, broke it and flung it away.

A patch of fog grew in his mind like the smoke from a spark falling on dry leaves. At first, I thought it was the mindless fury fed by the fear coursing through every part of his mind. However, as the fog grew, it took shape in strange ways.

First, a cloud of purple in front of us suddenly turned into a mountain, only the peak pointed toward the ground, so, to me, who could see both reality and the false image, it was upside-down. To Oogluk it must have looked like reality. He rolled and pulled up hard in what would have been a steep climb had the mountain's orientation been real. What he actually did was send us into a vicious, upside-down dive.

"Oogluk. No," I shouted.

I felt his mind working slowly. Much too slowly. If he understood what I had said, by the time he registered it and acted on it, we would accomplish violent remodeling to one of the tall structures rushing up to meet us.

Then, the hallucination morphed from the mountain to a mirror image of the city. Even I could tell no difference between the two. I no longer knew whether we were rushing up to meet the empty sky or still falling toward the real city.

Oogluk fluttered between the two images in his mind. The instinctual part of him told him to fight against gravity pulling him downward, but the rest of him screamed in agonizing slowness that he couldn't trust his instincts; he had to rely on his sight.

An arrow whistled by my head. I hammered my fist against Oogluk's neck, but he paid no heed to me. Another arrow slammed into my shoulder. The momentum spun me to the left. The arrow shattered and glanced off without penetrating my armor.

A third voice joined Oogluk's and my own in my head. Grabbing my head, I pushed with all my mental capabilities against the intruder.

"Tuca?" Oogluk fumbled clumsily with his wife's name.

I let my barrier snap. Tuca could help us.

"Jax, so nice of you to let me in," Gen'tahn'Gen laughed low and malignantly.

Desperately, I tried to replace my mental fortress.

Gen'tahn'Gen paused his laughter long enough to say, "Pitiful, little boy."

My mind screamed at me that we were going to crash into a building or the ground.

"It grieves me that it must end this way," Gen'tahn'Gen stated in a tone that suggested he added a shrug to his words.

With enormous effort, I ignored the intruder and held my arms away from my sides. I recoiled when another arrow glanced off the vambrace on my right arm. Grinding my teeth, I called on my shaping ability.

"I'm sorry, Oogluk," I said as the orange light leapt between my fingers.

I hardened the air around my body into a protective bubble and braced for impact.

Shattered splinters erupted all around us. I was thrown hard against the top of the hardened air bubble. Oogluk's body contorted strangely as he bounced off thick beams and crashed through three floors of a tall building.

Dust billowed above me as I lay struggling to calm my shaking body. The MEC I'd carried in my hands lay in pieces all around me. I moved my legs. They worked. Pulling my right arm from underneath me relieved some of the taut, tugging feeling from my left side. As my adrenaline continued to fall off, pain flared, blazing like the heat from the planet too close to its sun. My arm was broken is what my mind told me.

I shifted my gaze around the room. Debris lay strewn everywhere, including on top of us. Oogluk lay unmoving beneath several beams and a section of the roof. Several more, large pieces of wood stabbed the air above my hardened shield.

"Oogluk?" I reached for the silvery creature with my mind.

His mind met mine, but it was so dim he felt nearly unconscious. The vision dancing through his mind was that of a turit spinning aimlessly in blank blackness with a rock growing beneath it.

"C'mon, Oogluk," I called to him, "you can beat it. We need you."

Had the strike teams seen what had happened? Of course not, they were rushing through the covered streets by the time Oogluk and I had been shot down. Were they facing fierce resistance?

Once my thoughts reached Kelita, I closed my eyes and fought the pain in my arm. I couldn't let her fight the Tek'ekim alone. She wasn't alone, I knew, but since I wasn't fighting beside her, I felt like I had abandoned her.

Carving a small hole in my bubble allowed me the access I needed to safely remove the debris laying haphazardly on top of it.

A few rays later, I dissolved the air bubble and clutched my arm to my chest. Boards shifted and groans of stressed wood sounded like the groans of a wounded man as I picked my way to Oogluk.

"C'mon, Oogluk, they need us."

Nothing but stillness met me.

"Well," Gen'tahn'Gen's voice cackled in wry anger, "you've brought a little, thieving horde with you, haven't you, little boy?"

"Get out of my mind," I roared with as much power as I could muster in my mind's voice.

Gen'tahn'Gen laughed, but his presence faded.

No sooner had Gen'tahn'Gen left than an onslaught of no less than twenty Tek'ekim reached for my mind. They grabbed, tore and did one effective thing. I pressed outward with all my resistance, pushing their probing fingers away from my mind. It kept them at bay, and I did not succumb to their control—until—until they placed the images. Or had they placed them? They were showing me my life, weren't they? Digging up my past experiences and plastering it in front of my eyes.

My parents' dragon farm came to mind first, only it was burning, and towering cliffs above our house crumbled. As I looked up, I saw myself clinging to the face of the rock just above where the cliff gave way. A look of blank astonishment held my face utterly passive. I remembered trying to shape the cliff. I had lost control, and a large chunk of stone had slipped from the mountain and crashed down on our farm. It had crashed down on the chimney, setting the wooden parts of the house ablaze.

Next, Kelita rode Kerelyn in front of me. She looped her dragon around a spire of rock while doing a handstand. Then, she fell. I dove after her on Raglod, but the big dragon was too slow. Kelita's body folded and crumpled on a boulder before it slid motionless into a stream.

I slipped and fell on the rubble of the wooden building. Only it wasn't rubble. The cool water of the river in Tennallium washed over my hands as I caught myself and reached for Tranto. Airitha's twisted look of pain at my abandonment lingered. It was like the hook in a flip's mouth once it's been set. I melted into the water and thought of screaming. The only sound I heard was the gentle gurgle of water flowing over stone.

The memory slowly faded to the stream by my sister's marriage ceremony garden. Shame washed over me the same way the stream washed the chilled drinks away.

A dragon tugged on a lead line. The line snapped. I fell to the ground, cutting my hand on the stones.

I ran past Gwarven's lifeless bulk. Her once beautiful, dark scales did not shimmer, and her inquisitive eyes were closed permanently. Ahdah told me he was sorry.

Why had I left the Tek'ekim with my promise left unkept? Had Kelita been the one to rescue me? But she was dead—along with everyone else. What more did I have to lose?

Oogluk thrashed in front of me in the final throws of clinging to life. His mind was dark, and what was left scurried out of reach and hid like a cornered nykor.

Nothing was left in my life that I cared about. I had abandoned Airitha—the last person I could have called a friend that might still be alive. No, she was dead, too. Her world of Teluthia had been decimated. The entire surface made just as dead and poisonous as the red mountains.

Why hadn't I just died there from the poison?

What could I gain if I kept going?

Slowly, I stood. My footing was uncertain as though I was standing in a small boat. Everything around me swayed in blurred lines the way a forest does in a storm.

Darkness yawned in front of me. I couldn't make my legs stop. I stepped, and the floor didn't catch me. I fell, numb and silent.

My lips parted in a whimpering scream, but it wasn't me. I hadn't just fallen down a flight of stairs and landed on my broken arm. I didn't have a broken arm. My body was whole just like my mind. I had to get rid of the ridiculous visions of lies pretending to be reality.

I swatted my cheek with my left hand to wake myself up. Pain flared all through my left side, but I couldn't tell whether it originated with my arm or with my face.

Leaves crunched under my feet, and I was climbing in the mountains by my home. Well, where my home had been before I had sent the cliff face sliding down the mountain when I tried to shape a secret tunnel my little brother didn't know about.

Rurin. Grief clubbed me in the middle of my back. He and I had been running for our lives from an angry, wild dragon. He almost tripped me, so I shoved him back. He fell, and before I could turn completely around, the dragon showered him in sparks. The blackened corpse of my brother swam in front of me. How old had he been? Had he been only three? Why hadn't I known shoving him would make him fall? I was old enough; I knew he hadn't tried to trip me on purpose.

My chin dropped onto my chest. Tears streamed from my eyes. I didn't care. No one was there to see.

My hand found a doorknob I didn't see and twisted. The door opened with a creaky groan and fell from its hinges. I smirked, wishing I could just fall and be done like the door.

Something tugged me on, though. I trudged through the dim desert. The heat made me sweat as the tall mounds of sand rose on either side of me. Turits screeched at each other. They were so close and so loud I cowered and crouched. Covering my ears made no difference. Their cries pierced everything, including my few remaining nerves.

Why hadn't I ever seen the truth about myself?

I screamed and sprinted toward the nearest sand dune. I would climb it and the next and the next until I either died and rid the world of myself or ran so far away that no one would ever find me.

Stars danced around me. Gravity pulled me down. My back thudded against the ground. Pain flared up my arm, setting my entire left side on fire. My neck ached, and my heart throbbed irregularly.

"He's ready now," a voice said.

"Tell the Great Leader we've broken him," said another; this one nasally.

The turits fought each other in another squawking match. My head split at the harsh sound.

My body was jostled. Patches of fuzzy blackness dotted my vision.

My left arm flopped with each stride of my bearers. Whether I whimpered or remained silent, I don't know. I don't know how much time passed or how far I was carried.

When I was finally set down, a rough pillar held me in a seated position. I paid no attention to the floor or any other part of my surroundings.

A voice clicked and smacked something that sounded like language. I knew I should know the voice and the words, but I couldn't force myself to search through my memories. I didn't want to know what else I had done and who else I had either witnessed be killed or remember how I had killed them myself.

The voice switched to a more flowing language, "Now, boy, heal his arm so we can take his armor off. Oh, the pitiful, little brat is nearly dead of heat. Quickly, boy."

I moaned as my arm was lifted and molten metal poured into the bones.

I woke with many hands pulling my clothes from my limp body.

"Quickly, boy," the heavily accented voice flickered with shrouded anger. "Make sure he doesn't die...yet."

A cool hand pressed against my forehead, and another grabbed my shoulder. Sweet coolness leeched throughout my boiling blood. My head lolled from side to side in utter exhaustion.

The cool hands pried at my eyes. Light stabbed painfully into my pupils.

"He needs water," cried a frantic, young voice.

Where had I heard that voice before?

A thick cup was pushed between my lips. Warm water sloshed into my mouth and dribbled down my chin.

"No, you gotta drink it," the young voice chided.

It should have been easy for me, but my tingling lips refused to seal on the cup. Only a few pitiful drops reached the back of my throat, where it felt like they evaporated on contact.

The dark smudges in my vision grew larger, and I felt myself slipping into unconsciousness.

"C'mon, Jax, I'm trying to help you," the young voice pleaded.

I felt my arms flailing to push away the voice's owner and the cup he pressed to my lips again.

Just before I blacked out, footsteps hurried toward me, clacking on the floor. Someone bowed low and pushed words quickly from his mouth.

"Oh, Great Leader," he said, "we can't hold them. They're at the gate."

I didn't even have time to wonder who was at the gate or what a gate was before I slumped into darkness.

Chapter 19

I woke with someone pounding on my head. I pushed them back, but my hands met only stifling hot air.

The pounding persisted. Each blow felt like the ringing blow of an ax against a hard tree or a huge hammer driving a long, metal stake.

After a few rays, the heavy blows to my head reached a crescendo and then subsided. Probing fingers felt around my neck and forehead.

A murky-sounding voice yelled, "He's over here. He's passed out, but he's alright."

Another voice responded in echoing reverberations as if it emanated from deep within a cave, "Get the green boy and girl to him immediately. Move."

The young voice rose and fell as it talked with another person. The other person responded with a higher pitch voice.

Three sets of hands moved me and prodded me. Something stabbed my arm, and my body shivered.

"Jax, can you hear me?" yet another voice called softly to me.

The young voice said, "His armor stopped working. It looks like it sustained a lot of damage. Although, that doesn't explain why they took it off him."

"Jax? Jax, can you hear me?"

I moaned.

"Oh, Jax, you can." The owner of the voice gave me a quick hug before she asked, "Gen'tahn'Gen? Where is he?"

The young voice answered for me, "He ran like a coward."

"Darvian?" I mumbled.

"Yeah," he replied.

"We came to," I tried to wet my lips. They were so dry they felt like paper. "We came to—to rescue...you and y— sister."

"We're all gonna be alright," Darvian answered.

"Relax and rest," Meisha encouraged.

"What about Gen'tahn'Gen?" I recognized Kelita's voice.

"Kelita?" I asked. "I thought you were dead. You fell from your dragon."

The other memories crashed into me in full force. I closed my eyes and felt my head shake as I tried, futilely, to resist them. They were true. They couldn't be. I needed them not to be, yet they were what I remembered.

"No, I'm right here, Jax," Kelita answered in halting confusion.

A voice I couldn't place barked several things in rapid succession. White shapes moved all around me. I was lifted from floor and carried across the shoulders of a man with white armor splotched with green, brown and sooty black.

"We need to catch Gen'tahn'Gen," Kelita yelled.

No one listened to her, and the soldier carrying me didn't show even the slightest catch in his pace.

"Hey," Darvian asked loudly, "what about Tranto? Can't he just teleport us all to wherever you're taking us?"

I closed my eyes and attempted to force myself to forget.

"He can't help us anymore," I managed to whisper.

Darvian shuddered and stared at me for several clicks before muttering, "They got 'im, then?"

"I'm going after Gen'tahn'Gen," Kelita called as she came to a stop. In her grimy armor, she looked no different from any of the other soldiers except she was much shorter.

But she had died. I had seen it happen. Oogluk had been poisoned and hallucinated as a result until he died. I had been hit with a few arrows as well. That meant I was hallucinating, right? Maybe I hadn't been hit with as much poison, and that's how I was still mostly cognizant. I was so desperate to be saved that I imagined the soldiers rescuing me.

Soldiers split around Kelita like a mudslide flowing around a tree trunk before it uproots it. But then, an order was given. Kelita flailed and screamed at the soldiers plucking her weapons away, and then she was lifted into a carry just like me. She screamed torrents of angry words and slammed her fist against the soldier's back.

We paused at a door. More orders were given, and everyone inspected their neighbor's armor. I was placed gently on the floor. Two soldiers fit armor to my body. It was too big, and I wondered who had died to provide it.

Darvian and Meisha had armor supplied for them, as well.

Once we were all ready and standing plastered against either side of the wide entryway, two soldiers threw the door open and leapt to the side. Orange flame danced madly and licked its way in through the door.

"Move," a commanding voice crackled in my ear.

I was immediately hoisted to a new set of armored shoulders.

Cool air produced by the armor curled around me, but it could not compete with the heat billowing from the hungry flames.

Kelita made plentiful protests, which hurt my ears. However, she was carried through the door right behind me.

Flames reached for me from all sides. The sky was a solid mass of writhing, orange flame. The crackling voices of so much fire was like deafening peals of thunder.

"Make for the outer wall," a husky voice instructed. "Once we're clear, they can pick us up. They'll know where we are."

"Yes, sir," said a chorus of other husky voices.

In a daze, I watched the burning buildings slip behind us as the soldiers' pace picked up from a plodding jog to a purposeful run.

"Watch out," a warning sounded in my helmet.

My carrier leapt to the right as I heard the crashing whisper of a charred building falling to the ground. Glowing, orange embers and white ash enveloped us. I could see nothing.

Without warning, we stopped.

"We should have continued through the city," a voice whined.

"He's right. We should've known these fires would spread like this," another voice said.

"We can't go back," the commanding voice responded.

The heat was unbearable. My armor couldn't pump enough cool air over my body. I felt like I was roasting on a spit over an open fire.

The soldier carrying me turned to look behind, which gave me a glance at what had stopped us. Several charred husks of buildings lay across the street. Flames leapt over twenty feet into the air above them. It was a mirror image of what I had been looking at behind us.

The soldier turned back around. I scanned the buildings beside us. They were engulfed in flame and looked ready to collapse any click.

"Set me down," I said weakly.

"Sir?" the soldier's reply came.

"Set me down. I can stand," I worked as much strength into my voice as I could manage.

The soldier obeyed, and I stood shakily. I reached for the soldier's arm for support.

"All of you Teluthians," as I said it, sudden realization that I was dreaming or hallucinating struck me. "All of you Teluthians," I said again, "gather in front. We need as much cool air as can be managed."

"Sir," a female voice objected, "very few of us can influence the air with our ability."

I searched for Kelita in the billowing smoke and glowing embers. Once I found she was part of my dream, I said, "Kelita, make a tunnel out of the air. Don't worry about making it wide; but make it tall enough to run through and as long as you can manage."

I couldn't see her face behind her helmet. I imagined something like fear shining in her eyes as the dark line of her helmet's visor stared at me.

Then, she struggled to free herself from the soldier holding her. "Let me go. You heard him," she growled.

Kelita waved her hands in slow circles. Nothing except the orange glow engulfing her hands like flame was visible. Several soldiers reached out to see whether they could feel anything. Startled comments followed as they bumped their hands into the hardened air.

"This is what you'll be cooling," I struggled to say.

Before anyone could confirm they understood, a section of the building to our left slipped from the upper floors and crashed to the ground. A large beam, mostly untouched by the flames, landed on one end. Splinters shot off like arrows. The largest struck the tall leader of the Hegnoranthe spear-wielders. He mostly evaded it, but the sharp tip slid underneath the pleated armor on his stomach. He stumbled with a groan and was caught by his men.

Darvian and Meisha raced to his side. The splinter was tipped with red when they removed it. Anntoninn groaned again as the two healed the wound.

I tugged on the soldier supporting me. We had to get the tunnel finished sooner. Kelita began working again as I struggled to her side.

"What's your plan after this?" she asked in an undertone.

"We just need to keep moving and get outside the city. We can get picked up then," I replied.

"What about Gen'tahn'Gen? Why aren't we going after him?"

"We don't have time to discuss that right now," I answered. Frustration, hotter and more unpredictable than the fire surrounding us, boiled just beneath my skin.

"He's going to have his people waiting for us. We're not going to be able to get past him," Kelita said sullenly.

"If he's there, then we'll capture him."

Kelita stopped her work, "Just kill him like Shahn'Nahsh."

"You killed Shahn'Nahsh," I said without thinking.

"He needed to be killed," Kelita responded with high-pitch smugness.

My energy drained from me far more quickly than I thought it would. That was okay, though, because once I made it back to reality, everything would be fine.

"Get the tunnel cold, and move it across those burning buildings," my voice came as a hoarse whisper.

The soldiers moved immediately. Flames curled around the tunnel in wild waves of orange. I watched intently as the end of the tunnel cleared of flame and opened on the other side of the burning debris.

"Anntoninn, you and your people first," the husky, commanding voice called.

"Yes, sir," Anntoninn replied, leading the way with his surviving spearmen.

"Commander Jax, you're next," the voice said.

I was carried through the tunnel. It was like walking through a raging forest fire that had its heat removed. The soldier had to crouch to keep from scraping my body on the ceiling.

The remainder of our team filed through and issued out on the clear side. They made a few quick, nervous celebrations before spreading out down the street to set up a perimeter.

With great care taken to scan our surroundings, we advanced toward the outer wall. Fewer fires dotted the city between us and the wall, but the danger only increased as the likelihood of ambush rose with each step we took.

What was Oogluk doing? Had he made it out of the building we'd crashed into before it burned? Would he simply pop up randomly someplace like characters in dreams often do?

As if on cue, Oogluk's presence touched the distant part of my mind. "Friend Jax, I have found you. You I have found," he said with palpable relief. "Transpired what has? What has transpired."

The effort of forming words to reply was too much for me, so I showed him a replay of everything I remembered.

"That is too bad about Teluthia," he replied somberly. "I grieve with you, Friend Jax, for your family and friends. For your family and friends, I grieve with you. These worlds have been bitter."

A huge shape made the sunlight blink. The soldiers stopped and watched as Oogluk, once again in dragon form, landed in front of us. A blackened, charred patch in the left side of his neck looked like a dragon had bitten a chunk out of him.

The expression in his fake eyes showed more realistic than he had ever managed before. I knew that if I were to look in a mirror, the same hollow grief and depth of things seen that should have remained unseen would peer back at me.

"I'm glad you're okay," I said to Oogluk. "I don't want to lose you again."

A deep sense of peace coupled with an equally deep sadness and filled the distant part of my mind.

"He can teleport us to the drop ship," Kelita was saying.

"No," I moaned, "I don't have the energy."

"Well, why can't I help him?" Kelita retorted.

"He won't allow you to," I responded. After a click, I added, "Besides, I don't think you could. You're not related to the Tek'ekim the way I am."

Kelita didn't miss a beat, "Then, let's keep running and hope your relatives don't kill us."

Chapter 20

We passed through a gap where a gate had once been, but it lay in mangled shambles on either side of the street. The sunlight, though sinking below the horizon, was unbearably intense.

I glanced toward the giant orb, easily four times the size of both of Geoteous's suns together, on the edge of sight. A cloud that looked like smoke billowed from the horizon.

They said the planet was falling toward its sun. Apparently, that meant it would burn well before it reached the burning ball of heat and light. If I were to remain on the planet, the sun would appear to continue to grow each cycle if I managed to stay alive.

A hot breeze stirred around us and rose in velocity until it whistled through the gaps in between the plates and pleats of my armor. I struggled to sit upright on Oogluk's back. Although he showed little sign of weariness or exhaustion from the heat, he was largely unable to block the searing pain that flowed through our connection.

"A long submerging in a cool pool of water sounds too wonderful to think about right now. Right now, a cool pool sounds too wonderful," he murmured when I asked what could help him.

I didn't have to look up to know the drop ship hovered above us, but I flinched when the lines fell beside us. Soldiers clipped the hooks onto their belts and rose into the air toward the cool interior of the starship.

Oogluk started. Kelita climbed up beside me. I didn't have enough energy to say anything to her. I just watched as she reached for the nearest line and smashed it into the hook on my belt. The mechanism closed, and I was hoisted into the air.

Oogluk spread his wings once all of us were inside the belly of the starship. With only two massive flaps, he leapt to the floor beside me.

He shook himself and said, "The light of that sun is nearly as murderous as the memories you shared with me."

I fell against his leg and replied, "I wish I had a family to go back to, now that we're leaving. What about you? Is your family still alive?"

The silvery creature stared down at the greenery wilting to gray for a whole ray before responding, "Felt any of the Number, I have not. I have not felt any of the Number."

I sat and leaned against him. Tipping my head back to rest against his nearly transparent scales, I responded, "I guess we're in the same boat. I didn't know anything could hurt so much."

A flash of anger flared inside the creature. It mirrored itself in me, as well. The belly of the starship closed, the two halves of the door sliding together. The door on our anger closed simultaneously, giving way to the barrage of grief and loneliness that snuffed the lights out. Somehow, I decided, it was better to dream and know the truth than to wake and live in it.

When I finally looked up, a girl who looked like Airitha stood talking with Kelita. She met my gaze just as I looked away. I didn't want to talk with anyone. I hurt too much, and seeing people that reminded me of my friends felt like dry dirt being rubbed into a deep cut.

"They told me you didn't want to go to the medical bay," the girl with the round face like Airitha's sat beside me.

"I'm fine," I muttered without looking at her.

"Something more than your arm breaking happened out there, didn't it?" the girl pried gently. She lay her cheek lightly on my shoulder. "Where's the Jax I know?"

"I suppose," I glanced to the opposite wall of the drop bay.

"You don't have to tell me if you don't want to. I just want to be here for you the way my Omoah is always there for me," the girl said.

Anger reared inside me like a dragon preparing to lunge at a challenger. I felt like breaking something by crushing it in my hands.

The girl who looked like Airitha lifted her head and looked intently at me, and then she scooched tight against me and wrapped me in a hug.

I tried to resist, but a tear trickled from my right eye, and I found myself speaking. "They're gone. All of them. Everyone I cared about."

"What do you mean?" the girl asked innocently.

"My family—Rurin was burned by a dragon because—because I shoved him when it was chasing us." I bit my lip to stop myself, but I couldn't contain it, "Kelita fell off her dragon, and I couldn't save her. You look like a friend, but," I clenched my hands tighter, "Teluthia got destroyed. I thought it was all just a dream or a hallucination from the Tek'ekim's poisoned arrows, but it's not."

The girl's hand moved in a slow circle on the back of my shoulder, and she stared at the far wall.

"And Oogluk," I continued, "his family is dead. We couldn't save them." I fell silent and then added as realization struck me, "I either killed them myself or couldn't do the right thing to save all of them."

A few clicks later the girl said my name softly just above a whisper. She didn't stop there, "I don't really know what you've been through," she said just as softly, "but I have felt what they can do. They can make us think something different than what's really happening or has happened."

I yanked my gaze to focus on the girl. She briefly met my eyes before squeezing me in another hug and continuing.

"Kelita's—well, she's alive and was apologizing to me. Something happened to her, too. Teluthia was decimated when we were yanked away, but we beat the Gah'Stotten. You helped us. Do you remember that?" The girl paused as though waiting for an answer. When I offered none, she ducked her head and went on, "And Rurin, your little brother. He's alive and wanted to come with us, but you protected him by not letting him, remember?"

I stared at the floor between my feet. "What about Gwarven, my dragon?" I asked numbly.

The girl swallowed before replying, "No. I'm sorry. She did die in the bunker on Teluthia."

I bit my lip and replayed each of my memories. The pain settled deeper.

"Your Ahdah is here," the girl offered. "He's in the med bay."

I stared at her.

She blinked and asked, "Would you like me to take you to him?"

I continued staring.

"I'm sure Darvian and Meisha have taken care of him. He's probably awake and asking for you."

How could I face my Ahdah after everything I'd done? Had I been facing him all along and just forgotten it?

"Jax?" the girl asked.

I wanted to disappear. Even my connection with Oogluk felt too exposing.

The girl pretending to be Airitha rubbed my shoulder, "I can see you're working on something in your mind. I'd like to help you with it if you'll let me."

I shrugged and kept gazing at the floor.

We sat like that for several rays. Then, footsteps rang on the metal floor behind us.

"Two men," Oogluk commented hollowly. "One like your Ahdah and the other like Thaydrin."

They both squatted beside us—Thaydrin by his daughter and Ahdah beside me.

Ahdah clasped his hands as if wondering what to say and then he sank to a cross-legged seat. Out of the corner of my eye, I saw his mouth move a couple times with no words sounding.

"Jax, I wish I knew what to say. I don't know everything you're going through," Ahdah said.

I didn't look up at him, but I blinked back hot tears and had to sniff to keep my nose from running.

"You've been through more than most men can handle," Ahdah copied my unfocused gaze.

"I'm sorry," I ground out through clenched teeth. Turning toward Airitha, I sobbed, "I'm sorry about the farm and that I made Rurin get burned up. I'm sorry."

One of Ahdah's strong, calloused hands rested on my back. I felt dirty and caked with so much grime beneath Ahdah's gentle touch that I flinched and would have shrunk away if the girl hadn't been snuggled beside me.

"Son," Ahdah began.

"I'm sorry," I blurted in between sobs.

Another set of booted feet rang on the floor behind us. A knee joint popped as someone squatted next to Thaydrin and spoke to him in undertones. A few clicks later, the newcomer rose and left. Oogluk offered me his perspective, but I didn't want it.

Thaydrin cleared his throat quietly and spoke. "Pardon me for my insensitivity," he said quietly. "We cannot remain here in orbit around this dying planet. I don't believe there's anything more we can do for it, and I've just received a report that we aren't finding any more life forms on it."

I bowed my head and collapsed into Airitha's lap. I didn't care if she wasn't the real Airitha, the friend who had always been there for me almost like Oogluk. It felt good to have her want to be next to me.

"It's my fault," I mumbled. My cheek pressed against the top of Airitha's thigh, which muffled my words. "I couldn't repair their world fast enough. Everything's my fault. I'm sorry. I'm sorry."

Ahdah's hand made little circles as he continued to rub my back. "Jax," he said, "no one is blaming you for anything. Please forgive my insensitivity, too. Thaydrin is right, we need to head back to where we can all be of the most help."

Oogluk's presence stiffened and formed walls in my mind. He pressed firmly against the wave of pain and sadness to keep it away from me, but I still felt it.

"They're dead, aren't they?" I asked him.

Pain, so deep and rending that I curled further into a fetal position, impaled me. I had said it—put words to it. His family was dead. I hadn't saved them either. I had failed at everything I'd been entrusted to handle.

"You don't understand," I yelled. "None of you do."

Physical pain lanced the back of my head as I sat up. Airitha held her lip, which was already dripping bright red drops of blood. I stopped for less than a click and stared. Our eyes met. I instantly looked down and ran for the door.

"Jax," Ahdah called.

I heard him take a few steps after me.

"Leave me alone. None of you know what it's like. You don't know anything," I screamed as I yanked open the door and collapsed headfirst into the corridor wall. I wanted to get away. I needed to be alone, but my legs would carry me no further. I was spent.

Slamming my palm against the wall did nothing for me. Anger, sadness and rage beat down on me like the dying planet's sun. Why hadn't it just killed me? I punched my leg and ground my teeth. It moved. I got both moving again. In a clumsy manner, clinging desperately to the wall, I stumbled to the end of the corridor.

I didn't think it was possible to feel anything more, but when I saw the barracks area complete with small bunks, my anger at myself doubled. I'd gone the wrong way. Countless people would be filing through to sleep, eat or clean their armor.

"So be it," I mumbled and dropped myself onto a bunk and pulled the blanket from the bunk above.

The blanket felt scratchy against my face as I rolled it around my body and turned onto my side. Behind me, two sets of booted feet came to a slow stop followed by the lighter ring of smaller feet.

"Sterran?" Thaydrin said.

"I'll let him sleep," Ahdah replied with a sigh. "He's right. I don't know what he's been through. Do you know what's going on? Either of you?"

The girl who was pretending to be Airitha answered tentatively and with a lisp, "He seems to think he did a whole lot of terrible stuff and killed his family. I don't know why, but I think the Tek'ekim have some way of messing with our minds."

"They must have drugged him," Thaydrin said heavily. "Hopefully, he'll be fine when he wakes up."

"I hate putting him under more pressure," Ahdah said hesitantly, "but do we have any other means of getting back apart from my son and Tranto?"

"We still don't know where we are for certain. Without a precise location, it's too dangerous to use the *Thecket Drives*. We're running low on oxygen, as well," Thaydrin laid out the situation I'd put us in.

"Airitha," Ahdah asked, "do you think Kelita can tell us more about what's going on?"

"She might," the girl said, "but Hahn'Nik'Nik might be the better person to ask."

Their feet shifted and then stopped.

"Are you coming, Sterran?" Thaydrin asked.

"No," I could imagine Ahdah waving them on, "I'll wait here for when he wakes up."

Tears, angry and hopeless, melted holes in my eyes until, at last, I fell asleep.

Chapter 21

Ahdah hovered over me with a steaming mug in his hand. A bitter, burnt odor jolted me completely awake. My heart pounded fast and hard. I darted glances all around, preparing for danger.

"How do you feel, Jax," Ahdah's voice was soft and lined with concern.

I shrugged my shoulders. I didn't want to be okay. I didn't want to feel alright. If I were fine, I would have to perform. The only thing I wanted was to leave my body right where it lay and do absolutely nothing.

"I'm sorry I've pushed you so hard, son," Ahdah said.

Silence, thick like the darkness in a cave, stretched between us. I glanced up without moving my head. I could barely see Ahdah's face in the blurry edges of my vision.

"You hate me, just like I do," I mumbled.

My legs became trapped by the blanket as Ahdah sat. I didn't think. I reacted, thrashing wildly like a flip on land and punching toward Ahdah. None of my punches landed, and he quickly leapt up.

"I'm sorry, son," deep pain and remorse colored his voice.

"Just get out of here," I growled as my eyes burned. "Find someone else who can make Oogluk teleport."

"Jax, I—"

"Leave me alone," I snapped.

I turned so I could watch to make sure he left. He stood to the side as the girl that looked like Airitha brought in a steaming bowl and another girl who looked like Kelita balanced a cup of water and small bowl of fruit.

I looked down as soon as Airitha met my eyes with a smile. Her lip was still split and had swollen like a fist inside her cheek.

"You didn't mean it," she said. She knelt on the floor and offered me a spoonful of white soup.

I stared at Kelita. Her sunken eyes looked hollow and dull. Yet, something deep, deep inside them flashed.

"You gonna get better or lie here the rest of your life?" she queried.

"I don't want everybody to be dead," I mumbled.

"Look at me," Kelita held up her hands in a full body shrug. "I'm not dead. Not yet anyway."

I did look at her. No playfulness brightened her tone or lightened her stance. She looked stiff like a solid part of the starship.

"We're running out of air," I mumbled with a wry grin. "So, you can die right after me."

"No one's doing any voluntary dying," Airitha stated.

"Why didn't you have your lip fixed?" I asked the question I feared the most in that moment. Had she refused to have Darvian and his sister heal it so that it would remind me of what I'd done to her? If so, why was she so cruel?

Airitha touched her swollen lump of a lip gingerly, "Darvian and Meisha are still sleeping. I didn't want to wake them up for something so small."

"Why are you so grouchy?" Kelita shot the question at me.

"I'm not grouchy," I mumbled.

"Well, whatever you call it, take a drink," she forced the cup of water into my hand, "and see if it washes it away."

"I'm not grouchy," I said again and took a drink. I didn't stop drinking until the entire cup of water was gone. Then, I held it out for Kelita to refill.

"Jax," she said quietly, "you and I both know what those orange people can do. If that story Hahn'Nik'Nik told us was true, that leader who ordered no more exploration did a good thing. I'm glad they're all dead."

The Tek'ekim were dead, too. What did it matter? The Neftim, all except Oogluk, were gone, and so were everyone else who had been on their planet. I tried not to consider it, but something was off—wrong.

Kelita's eyes widened, and she gasped, "What if they aren't dead? What if they teleported somewhere else?"

Airitha shifted her gaze back and forth between Kelita and me. Ahdah stepped closer, keenly alert.

"If they say they're dead, then they're dead," I sank back onto the pillow and closed my eyes.

"Maybe not," Kelita responded. "If they could teleport, which they can, they'd find another world to take over. They're probably enslaving everyone on Geoteous! Jax, you have to get us back home right now."

My only response was to let my frown deepen.

"Jax?" I heard her set down the empty cup. Then, she shook me. "Jax, wake up. We need you to get us back home."

I swatted angrily at her arms, but she kept shaking me.

"It's your home. I don't have a home," I spat.

Kelita held my glare and sent ice that quelled my fire. I looked down.

She whispered something to Airitha and then, with a brief, pleading glance at Ahdah, left the room.

Ahdah knelt beside Airitha. She turned to him with a horrified, questioning expression etched on her round face. "What if she's right?" she asked him.

Ahdah looked at her and said, "I think she is right."

A chill descended. Airitha glanced at me.

Ahdah looked stricken, "The place they know the best, apart from their own planet, is our home, where we live. You say they have some way of getting into people's heads. If they've done that, then they've seen our homes and villages, everything we've got a memory of."

The spoon and bowl Airitha had brought clattered to the floor. It was all a show I knew. They were acting to try to get me to teleport them where they wanted to go. Well, they shouldn't have had Airitha and Kelita pretend to be friends.

"Not your world too," Airitha said. "Teluthia's already destroyed. If Geoteous is under attack too...."

"Jax," Ahdah turned to me.

I looked away and frowned.

"I don't want to pressure you and Tranto," Ahdah continued, "but we need to get home."

"His name's Oogluk," I muttered. "His mind and memory were damaged when they made him forget his family."

Something clicked inside me. I glanced at Ahdah. He knelt motionless and looked at me with wide, suddenly understanding eyes.

I wanted to believe him. I wanted him to be right that the Tek'ekim had changed my memories. Everything inside me yearned for the reality of so much death and destruction to all be a lie.

"We should bring Oogluk here to talk with Jax," Airitha jumped up.

I threw the blanket off and sat up. "Leave him alone. He doesn't need more insensitive people putting on a show trying to make him do stuff," I yelled after her.

If she heard, she didn't slow down.

"Son," Ahdah said gently, "I know you've been through a lot, and you may not want to hear any of my ideas."

I glared at him.

He went on without changing his tone, "Based on what Kelita and Airitha have said, and now, what you've pointed out about Oogluk, I think you might be dealing with something similar to what they did to Oogluk."

"You don't know anything about it," I glared at the footboard. "You just want me to teleport us back to someplace so you can feel important. That's why you have Airitha and Kelita pretending to be friends."

An even deeper softness edged into Ahdah's eyes, "Jax, we aren't pretending. I don't know any more than what you and Kelita have told me about what happened to you both. When she came back with your team, she had this look in her eyes, and she would hardly let her Omoah hug her. Airitha, however, she let hold her while she cried on her shoulder."

"Kelita fell off her dragon while doing stunts," I said flatly.

Ahdah looked at me. When he spoke, his voice was unhurried and even, "I can't convince you to believe something you don't want to believe."

He reached toward me. I yanked my shoulder away before he could caress it. He made a fist and slowly lowered it to the bed.

"You can't prove anything you're saying," I mumbled.

"You're right. I cannot," Ahdah conceded.

"I don't want to be right, but I know what happened," I said.

We remained in cold silence for several rays.

"Friend Jax," Oogluk's presence felt like spring warmth thawing the ice of winter and like a fire threatening to burn me if I got too close.

"I see they found you," I said as I hastily erected mental walls.

"Yes, yes. Found me they have. They have found me," he shifted his shape and squeezed into the room. His nearly transparent, gray flesh blended like camouflage against the bare metal.

"Told me they have of their fears. Their fears, they have told me," he stated and sent a replay into my mind.

"So, what?" I asked.

"You try to hide your anguish alone, but it is mine, as well," Oogluk gave me a look that said he knew more than he was letting on.

"Are you going to try to force me to go back to that place too?" I snapped.

"Friend Jax," Oogluk responded calmly, "your memories are also mine, yet if a chance remains that Tuca may yet be alive, I am biased toward it. Biased toward it, I am."

"You're just like the others. You claim to know me, but if you did, you wouldn't demand something so cruel," I muttered.

Oogluk replied, "The fear you are feeding is poison only to you. Poison only to you is the fear you are feeding. Whether or not these friends are the same friends we remember, they are striving to help us."

"How can they help us?" I shot back. "All they want us to do is help them."

"Is there a reason to turn our backs? To turn our backs, is there a reason?" When I was silent for several clicks, Oogluk added, "They are people, too."

I fumbled for words, yet all I could come up with was a meager, "I don't want to."

"Weariness of the body can be solved by rest. Weariness of the mind can be solved by knowledge. But weariness of the heart—that is something else entirely." Oogluk remained motionless as he added, "The life one has is not interchangeable with the life of another. With the life of another the life one has is not interchangeable. Can one make a choice between lives?"

"Fine," I growled in my mind and aloud.

Airitha and Ahdah looked between Oogluk and me. Their looks were of curiosity and bated hope.

"I'll help you get to Geoteous," I said. "Once, we find nothing, I want to leave."

Oogluk made no comment I could discern. His mind lay completely hidden behind barricades, and I didn't try to get past them.

A picture of the training field at Kelita's house built itself in my mind, but I refused it and showed Oogluk the shore of the lake where he'd found me after I'd made it home from Prathniss. He conceded slowly as I insisted on a cliff overlooking the lake. At last, the location solidified in both of our minds. The familiar tugging and leaching of energy sang through my body.

Chapter 22

The shuddering vibrations of the starship's engines wound down and subsided. I stood with Oogluk and Ahdah near the ramp. I would have rather been anywhere else, but Oogluk had wanted me to stay close to him so we could escape quickly if the need arose.

Crisp, fresh air wafted in as the ramp descended. Both familiar suns shone brightly from the sharp angle of early morning and glinted off the lake in thousands of sparkling mirrors. Turits shrieked warnings to one another, the only break in the perfectly peaceful landscape.

I scowled and wondered how long I'd have to be there before Oogluk agreed to leave. We would find nothing amiss.

Kelita and Airitha stepped to Thaydrin's side where he stood stiffly next to several rows of armed and armored soldiers. He wore no armor yet looked more soldierly than his fighting men with his jaw set and his hands clasped behind his back.

The two girls whispered to each other. Kelita nodded and glanced at me briefly before she stood next to her Omoah. Airitha leaned against her Ahdah, resting her head on his side. He responded by draping his arm around her and pulling her tight. His lips moved, but I heard no words.

I realized it was Thaydrin's first time seeing Geoteous. A faint memory cast a shadow in my mind—me wanting him to see my home. How different this reality was. I loathed seeing my home world and didn't wish to share it with anyone anymore.

Oogluk interrupted my melancholy thoughts, "Friend Jax, whatever is out there, you and I will find it together. Find it together will you and I."

"I don't want to relive what happened," I replied.

"Friend Jax," Oogluk shifted his tone, "I do not want to argue with you. With you, I do not want to argue. I have been thinking. Thinking, I have been, about these people who appear to be the people that were missing. They claim to be our friends, as well. To be our friends they claim. My question is: what if we are mistaken to believe our memories? To believe our memories, what if we are mistaken?"

I withdrew further into myself.

"What I am suggesting," Oogluk explained after several clicks of silence, "is that, perhaps, we are the ones who are wrong."

"I know," I snapped. "Just because I have two trails of memory that lead to different things doesn't mean that I don't know the truth."

"Gaps we both have—"

"I know," I shouted into Oogluk's mind. "I can't piece everything together, but the things I did that caused people to die feels like what really happened."

Oogluk responded in undertones, "A war has waged in you your whole life."

"Don't tell me that nonsense again," I ground out.

As if he hadn't been interrupted, Oogluk finished his thought, "That war has caused you intense pain and feelings of rejection that brings the darker side of things foremost in your mind. I had nothing except fear when I hid myself away in that lake. Nothing I had, except fear. Now, shreds of light are what I strive to focus on. The light creates shadows by revealing my fear, but the light also provides a path."

"I thought your mind was damaged by the drugs they gave you?" I wanted to cut him off and cut him down.

"Pondered that too, have I," Oogluk replied. "I have considered that. I think now that the damage was done the same way the damage in your mind was accomplished. The same way the damage in your mind was accomplished, the damage in my mind was done, I think now."

"My mind's not damaged. I don't repeat everything backward."

The soldiers filed by and marched down the ramp. I remained rooted. Ahdah tried to pull me with his arm around my shoulders, but he let me go when I didn't budge.

"Our memories are vital for our lives much the same way our hearts are," Oogluk philosophized.

"You have internal organs?" I asked sarcastically.

Oogluk ignored my jab, "Just as my memory was wiped out—erased—by your ancestor, I believe your memory has been tampered with. Your memory has been tampered with I believe."

I scoffed and took a step forward. My eyes met Kelita's, and she moved toward me. She and I were the only Ti'Kahn still at the top of the ramp.

"Are you blaming that on me, now?" I asked.

Oogluk quickly negated my question and apologized, but I barely heard him. Kelita held her hands behind her back and studied the floor as she stopped in front of me.

"Jax," she met my gaze momentarily.

I waited silently as she shifted her weight from one leg to the other. She brought her hands forward.

"I found this when we rescued Darvian and Meisha," she held a broken sword in her hands. The hilt was wrapped in ragged, brown leather, and the blade gleamed orangish yellow from its two halves.

My mind was empty and numb as I reached for my sword.

"I'm sorry it's broken," Kelita said. "I thought about fixing it for you, but I was too scared I'd mess it up and the light would disappear."

The blade felt pitted and weak. Not at all how it had felt when Ahdah had given it to me. Had that been before or after I'd pushed my brother down?

"Thank you," I said flatly.

Oogluk mused to himself distantly but, otherwise, gave me space.

Kelita continued to shift her weight as though she were uncomfortable. Our gazes met for a click and then we both began talking at the same time.

"No, you first," Kelita said when we both stopped.

"Did I really kiss you on the lips?" I asked.

She looked down and tucked her mul'li behind her shoulders, "Sort of. I wasn't ready, and it seemed like you didn't mean to kiss my mouth."

"Oh," was all I said.

"Jax," something wavered in her voice. "I'm sorry. I don't know what I've been doing. I really don't know what I've been thinking. Everything is just cloudy, and I was so angry at Airitha. I shouldn't have treated her as badly as I did. I see what you two have together. I was wrong to try to keep you from her. I wanted to have you all to myself because I wanted to show her I was better, but she's been much more loving than I have. I've been a terrible friend. I'm sorry, Jax."

My mind jumbled all her words as I tried to decipher them.

"Aren't you going to say something?" Kelita asked tightly when I didn't respond right away.

I moved my mouth, but no sounds came out.

"If you don't want to be friends anymore, I get that," Kelita offered.

My mind spun wildly. I still couldn't pinpoint what she was saying.

"It's okay," Kelita sniffed. "I understand."

"Wait, Kelita," I called, but she was already at the bottom of the ramp, running to catch up with the others.

"Now, what?" I asked Oogluk.

"She has been honest with you and with herself," was all he said.

"You mean you understand what she meant?"

"Friend Jax, I think that with time, you will comprehend. You will comprehend with time." Oogluk shook himself and stepped toward the ramp, "Will you be accompanying me? Accompanying me will you be?"

I shrugged and walked beside him.

At the bottom of the ramp, I stopped and hastily shaped the two pieces of my sword back together.

"This way I might not accidentally cut myself with it," I explained to Oogluk.

The surrounding mountains felt like home yet looked foreign. We weren't far from Treniss, and I grew nervous that we would stumble across someone from the town. However, Oogluk and I caught up with the others where they stood above a waterfall shooting over a cliff. They stared and occasionally pointed far out over the foothills to the dark green plains.

I saw it after scanning for several clicks. A tall, thick spire of smoke billowed like a single storm cloud at the edge of sight.

"That is the direction of Prathniss, if I am not mistaken. If I am not mistaken, that is the direction of Prathniss," the silvery creature stated.

Ahdah turned at that click and saw me. I broke my gaze from him, and he trudged up the stony incline to me.

"You saw the smoke?" he asked.

I nodded.

"What do you make of it?"

I shrugged. Oogluk prodded me to tell the truth, but I remained silent.

Ahdah peered out over the foothills. He shaded his eyes for nearly a ray before turning back to me, "I'm sure it's from Prathniss." His voice darkened, "I think Kelita was more right than she knew."

I shrugged again even though Ahdah wasn't looking at me.

"How can we check it out safely?" Ahdah glanced first at the silvery creature behind me and then at me.

I shrugged and busied myself with studying the distant cloud. "If it is the Tek'ekim, then no one's safe close by," I mumbled.

"I think you're right," Ahdah crossed his arms. "I think their ability is to control minds—or, at least, influence people to do what they want. We don't have any way of fighting against that."

"One of our ancestors was Tek'ekim," I said.

Ahdah turned to me. A question arched his brows.

"That's how Oogluk came here. One of the Tek'ekim teleported here with him and then made him forget everything. That's why A'lii has yellow markings." Saying my sister's name felt funny, and I wondered whether I still had a sister.

Ahdah studied me. At last, he asked, "Is there any way to overpower their ability?"

Oogluk responded in my mind, "If we can convince the Number to turn against the Tek'ekim, we may be able to defeat them. They've been ruthless masters," he added. "Ruthless masters they have been. Some of the Number is there with them." His thoughts darkened, "At the least, they helped them get there. Dead, perhaps they are now."

"Oogluk says we should try to convince the Neftim to turn against the Tek'ekim. They've been holding them as slaves, so it might be possible," I relayed.

I thought of Ronthluque. If he had been real, and if what he had said was accurate, there were already a large number of Neftim trying to resist the Tek'ekim's power.

"Son," Ahdah shaded his eyes to look at me.

I tried to hold his steady gaze but failed.

"We're going to need you and Oogluk more than ever before," Ahdah said gently yet strongly. "I hate that it will come down to you two yet again, but we have no other recourse for the time being."

"Can't you use the starship?"

Ahdah nodded as though he hadn't thought of that. Then, he continued, "I don't wish to put you in harm's way anymore. I wish you could be done, but since it's not possible, what can I do to help you put the pieces right in your mind? I have seen the dichotomy tearing you apart. Reality seems incongruent with what you remember. I wish to help you if you'll let me."

I snapped my eyes to meet his. He looked solemn and determined.

"If we went home to see Omoah and Rurin, especially Rurin, would that be enough to help you know the truth and see through the lies?" he asked.

I felt my eyes widen as I shook my head.

"Sterran," Thaydrin's voice rang above the noise of the waterfall.

Ahdah held my gaze a click longer before turning and walking the few steps back to the cluster by the cliff. I heard Ahdah explaining the topography as he pointed in various directions.

Return home? Had Ahdah been serious about that? Wouldn't reality just get more confusing if I saw a boy that looked like my little brother? Ahdah had offered it with such confidence, it had to be true that he was alive, right?

Oogluk pushed his dragon-shaped muzzle against my arm. "I too wonder the same things. The same things I wonder. If I am to see Tuca, will it sort out my memories?"

I stared at the group of soldiers as Ahdah continued to speak to them. What could such a little group of people do against the Tek'ekim?

I didn't see Airitha step away from her Ahdah's side until she stood in front of me. "How can I help you?" she asked. When I didn't answer, she stepped to my side, hugged me and said, "I can see it's difficult for you being here. I wish I could understand why so I could help you with it."

I felt like a tall sapling bending beneath the weight of a strong wind, yet I was not a sapling and Airitha was not a destructive wind.

"I don't know what to do," I mumbled.

I wanted her to take the weight of my memories off me and discard everything that wasn't true. Instead, she leaned her head onto my shoulder and listened.

"Ahdah wants me to go home and see Rurin," my voice caught for a click as fear and adrenaline rose sharply inside me. "He thinks if I see him alive, I'll be able to sort everything out. Are you really Airitha? Is everything fine on your world?"

"Teluthia was attacked by the Gah'Stotten, and a lot of it is destroyed. That happened before we knew about the Tek'ekim." She pushed herself away so she could look me in the eye. "I am really, truly Airitha. I'm the girl who found you in the red mountains and brought you back to the roller where Ahdah, Thaydrin, was. We took you to our home and then to Hegnoranthe. You learned our language from their old leader, Elennethel. You and I met Darvian when you accidentally teleported away from Hegnoranthe."

I shuddered. I remembered that vividly. I had intended to abandon her—leave her right there in the river while I went home.

"You and Kelita won the archery competition at the Highland Games," Airitha continued. "She was still having trouble with her leg then. Darvian healed her leg, though, when—when," she swallowed and glanced down, "when we were taken to Gen'tahn'Gen's palace."

I felt my neck stiffen and my stare harden. I remembered all of that. I also remembered Kelita killing Shahn'Nahsh. Realization struck.

"If Kelita killed Shahn'Nahsh, that means she never died when she fell from her dragon," I said. "*If* she ever really did fall from her dragon."

Airitha smiled and nodded. She looked so happy she might burst into tears.

"If Kelita's alive and you really are Airitha, then do you think that my little brother might be alive too? Do you think I might not have made him get burned by that wild dragon?" I finished with my excitement waning and sinking darkly beneath a heavy, foul-smelling blanket.

Airitha nodded and replied, "Yes, I'm sure you never did that. I'm sure he's alive and wondering when his big brother and Ahdah are going to be home."

"How can you be so sure?" I asked.

Airitha glanced at Oogluk and then smiled at me again, "Because he tried to make you take him with us when we left your sister's wedding. He was so insistent that he had to come with us that he got really mad when you said he couldn't. You were annoyed to the point I thought you might shout at him and call him a bother instead of a brother again."

I had called Rurin that. I had also dumped all the drinks into the stream at A'lii's marriage ceremony.

"What's wrong, Jax?" Airitha laid her hand on my shoulder and ducked her head in an attempt to make eye contact with my downturned gaze.

"Nothing," I sighed. "I—I just.... Again? How many times did I call him that?"

"I think all siblings do from time to time," Airitha answered deep in thought. "Darvi can be a bit of a bother at times."

I thought again of how I had been mean to my little brother.

"It is okay, Friend Jax," Oogluk encouraged. "I think she will understand."

I gave a wry smile to the creature. "I just wish I hadn't called him a bother. If I didn't kill him, I'll never call him that again."

Airitha grew thoughtful, "Who knows? I might call my little brother a bother now and then. I certainly hope I can show him I love him the way you do with Rurin."

I jerked my eyes from the stony ground and met Airitha's rich purple eyes, "What do you mean? He must think I hate him."

"The way he always wants to be with you," she replied, "he likes being around you. If you didn't show him you love him most of the time, he wouldn't want to be like you."

"Come, Friend Jax, our friend, Airitha, has made me want to see the little fire again," Oogluk's attitude felt expectant and anxious.

"Hold on a click," I responded.

Then to Airitha, I asked, "Will you come with Oogluk and me?"

"What about your Ahdah?"

I glanced down at him. He was still deep in discussion with Thaydrin and the soldiers. "He's needed here. I think he just wanted me to see Rurin's alive so I would know what's real," I said. I still doubted I would find Rurin, but I worked hard to quell the fear and anger at myself and focus on the slim blade of light that Oogluk had descirbed.

"Okay," Airitha replied as she wrapped her arms around me.

Oogluk grabbed me, and the next click, we stood in front of the dragon barn. Loud snorts and a hissing growl emanated from within its dark depths.

Airitha shrank against me, while Oogluk sidled to the left toward the house.

"No! Naughty, Darthor. Leave him alone," the high pitch voice of my little brother shouted.

Growling ensued followed by the pitifully soft yap of a young grogul. I tore Airitha's arms from my body and raced into the barn.

Smoke filled the back stalls, and the smell of decaying blood nearly gagged me. In the dim light I could barely make out a small grogul pup, growling and yipping at the dragon in the last stall on the right. Rurin tugged on a leash tied to the grogul. He was so small he could not pull the grogul away from the dragon.

"Rurin, get back," I shouted. "Let go of the leash."

The dragon continued arching its neck right behind its head the way dragons always do before shooting sparks. Smoke poured from its nostrils.

"Rurin!" I bellowed.

He turned slowly and stared at me. The red glow of dragon sparks looked like red coals in the dragon's mouth. The grogul pup whimpered and tried to run, but it slipped on the stones lining the fire trenches.

I willed my legs to run faster and called on my shaping ability. A plate of hardened air formed on my right arm like a shield.

The sparks sailed through the air. The first few hit the grogul, which screamed in pain.

Rurin's wide eyes began closing. He turned his face away.

I pushed every fiber of muscle my legs possessed into a leap. I flew the last several feet and landed in front of my brother. Orange glittered and glowed all around as the dragon sparks glanced off my shield.

Rurin screamed, and two bodies collided into mine.

Searing pain ran along my arm. I wanted to drop the shield, but I couldn't. The skin on my arm began to melt and blacken as it charred. On accident I had shaped the shield directly to my skin. My senses began collapsing as the agony increased.

A tearing sensation followed by the absence of heat sang in my brain. Dimly, I saw Airitha holding the shield and walking toward the dragon. She didn't seem to feel any pain or get burned.

"Jax, I sorry. I sorry," Rurin blubbered as the dragon ended its barrage of lethal sparks.

The grogul lay dead in a smoldering pile of blackened fur and flesh much like my arm. The entire outside of my forearm was a gaping, oozing wound edged by charred skin.

"Friend Jax?" Oogluk called through our connection.

I could make no reply, but I didn't need to because he could see through my senses.

Rurin kept crying and apologizing. I barely managed to bite back howls of pain. Airitha dropped the shield, scooped Rurin into her arms and yanked on my left arm.

"Jax, we need to go," she said.

Her words echoed strangely in my mind. She sounded like Oogluk.

Oogluk fed me an image to teleport to. I snatched at it but couldn't focus.

Rurin settled down to whimpering. Then, he struggled to get down as three shapes raced from the house.

Omoah shrieked, "Rurin, sweetie, what's wrong?" Then she noticed Airitha, and me, "Jax, oh, Jax, sweetie. You're alive! Thanks be."

A'lii and Rithol scooped Rurin up as Omoah set to examining my arm.

"He shielded Rurin from the dragon. He's got third degree burns," Airitha hurriedly explained. "We need to get him to Darvian and Meisha."

"Well, Little Brother, what have you been up to?" Rithol asked in a distant manner that sounded like he was simply trying to give me something besides pain to focus on.

A'lii tilted her head as Airitha continued telling my family what Darvian and his sister could do and where they were at.

"A'lii," Airitha said, "you should be able to connect with Oogluk and help him teleport us to Darvian and Meisha. Your markings are yellow because of your Tek'ekim ancestor. Jax doesn't have yellow in his markings, so you should be even better at it."

"Oogluk?" my sister asked. "And what Tek'ekim ancestor? Who are they?"

Airitha closed her eyes, "Sorry, a lot has happened. Oogluk is Tranto's real name. If you connect with him, we'll be able to get Jax help right away. I don't think he can focus well enough right now, and we don't want to end up on a random world or out in space."

Omoah stared at Airitha with her mouth pressed into a firm line, but she made no objection.

"What do you mean?" A'lii asked. "How do I connect with him?"

"Jax, used to have to touch him, but now they can connect at a distance."

A'lii glanced at Oogluk and then stared at Airitha as she stepped closer to the silvery creature. When she was close enough to reach out and touch him, Oogluk shied away.

"Go on, Oogluk, you can connect with her. She's willing," Airitha said.

Incredible confusion, terror and insecurity rang like warning bells in my mind. "Do it," I managed to say to Oogluk.

My sister reached out a shaking hand and held it up for Oogluk to touch.

"Everybody, hold on to each other," Airitha called. "Oogluk, help her get us to the starship."

The silvery creature shook visibly as he eased his shoulder closer and closer to my sister's hand. Rithol clutched Rurin to his side and wrapped his other arm around my sister's waist.

Airitha grabbed Omoah's arm and clutched A'lii's free hand. Omoah held tight to me and shrieked.

We stood inside the drop ship in a wide-open room. Light streamed in through an open door.

Airitha, not at all surprised or disoriented by the sudden change of environment, peeled away from my family and shouted for Darvian and Meisha.

My sister stumbled to the side. Rithol caught her just as she puked.

Omoah hugged Rurin to her when he ran over to her. Her eyes were filled with terror, and she sat stupefied for a click. But then, she whisked into action. She inspected Rurin for burns or other injuries and then placed him on the floor beside her. She set to work gingerly peeling back my remaining clothes on my upper arm.

The ragged patches of skin that remained around the charred crust of my burnt flesh were bubbled and tender and stung, but her fingers were cool and gentle.

"Airitha, sweetie," Omoah called. She got no answer and looked up, only then, realizing that Airitha had left.

A ray later she stepped through the door with Darvian and Meisha in tow. Darvian raced for me as Meisha angled toward my sister.

Omoah held my left hand and let me lean against her as Darvian lifted my injured arm.

"Put something in his mouth to bite," Darvian said without emotion.

Omoah rolled up part of her dress. I bit down on it.

Pain stabbed white hot through my entire body. Omoah clenched me tighter, keeping me from writhing like a flip on land.

The next thing I remember was Omoah petting my forehead softly and singing an old song in a barely audible whisper. Darvian looked down at me with a satisfied smile playing on his sweaty face. Meisha's face joined his for a click and then Airitha pushed them away.

"Thank you," I said.

She smiled at me and said, "Now, that you're saved, are you ready to save the world?"

"Not so fast," Rithol jumped in. "What exactly is going on? How did my wife do that?"

I filled him in on the Tek'ekim and Neftim as quickly as I could. I told him how Oogluk had teleported to our world with one of our ancestors and how their mind abilities worked—at least the limited knowledge I had.

"We think they came here after their world fell too close to the sun," I finished.

Omoah gasped and pulled Rurin closer.

"So, there's more of these Neftim creatures here as well, and they're not on the Tek'ekim's side?" Rithol questioned.

"Right," Airitha answered. "Oogluk's family is probably here too."

"Airitha," I said, "can you finish explaining things while Ahdah and I go see what's happening in Prathniss?"

She nodded, and Oogluk and I left for the cliff where we'd left the others.

Thaydrin beckoned me over. A question burned in his eyes.

"Airitha's with my family in the starship," I told him.

Relief flooded his face.

Ahdah asked, "How are you, son?"

I nodded and said nothing as I shifted my gaze to the smoke cloud. "We should go check it out," I said.

Ahdah nodded and wrapped an arm around my shoulders.

Thaydrin held up a hand, "I think it may be best to remain far on the outside of the town just as you did not want to teleport directly into the Tek'ekim's city on their world."

I gave him a smile that said I had already thought of that and said, "We'll stay far enough away."

"Very well," Thaydrin said. "We'll wait for your return here at the starship."

Oogluk pranced like an excited dragon. He hadn't said anything, but I had felt a change in him once we learned that my most terrible memories had been lies planted by the Tek'ekim. He felt certain that Tuca was waiting for him.

"Son," Ahdah said, "may I see your sword?"

I handed it to him. The dull part where I had hastily shaped the two pieces together stood out like a bandage.

"We'll go right after I strengthen this section," Ahdah told Oogluk.

Kelita wandered over as Ahdah worked. "You found your little brother?"

"Yeah," I said. "Kelita," I took a step toward her, but she backstepped. "What are you doing?"

A pained expression flitted across her face, but she made no other reply.

"I just wanted to hug you and say I'll be back soon," I said haltingly.

Kelita gave a single nod and replied, "Good. Be careful."

I watched her as she climbed the hill alongside Thaydrin's soldiers. Had I changed so much she didn't like me anymore? Or did she have her own struggle with memories planted by the Tek'ekim?

"She's made her mind up," Ahdah said as he draped an arm around my shoulders.

"Huh?" I asked.

Ahdah handed my sword to me. The dull patch was still there in the middle of the blade, but he had strengthened it.

"I think she's chosen to keep her distance. If I'm not mistaken, she thinks she would be nothing but a burden to you," Ahdah offered in explanation.

"That still doesn't make sense," I said.

"Ah, I do not have the words now to be able to explain better. Besides, I may be far from the mark," Ahdah responded.

Oogluk reached for me, "Let us go, Friend Jax. Go, let us."

I allowed his excitement to take my mind off how Kelita had just behaved and asked Ahdah, "Ready?"

He confirmed, and we left the cliff.

Chapter 23

Ahdah and I peered over the brow of a hill. Prathniss lay in front of us over a mile away. The entire town looked like a giant bonfire. Countless houses burned out of control, and, as we watched, flames spread from one rooftop to the next.

"I don't see any Tek'ekim," I said.

"Right," Ahdah murmured. "How do we know this is their doing and not just a mishap?"

Oogluk stood quivering as he surveyed the surrounding fields with his senses.

"Should we get a look at the other side? Maybe they took shelter in the forest," I said. "We can't see all of the tree line from here."

Ahdah nodded, and I relayed the message to Oogluk.

We teleported to just inside the tree line a mile north of Prathniss.

"Tuca!" Oogluk called.

I felt a flutter of familiarity in the distant part of my mind. She was close by.

"She says she and Ronthluque and several others are planning an attack on the Tek'ekim," Oogluk conveyed. "I must go to her. To her, I must go."

"No!" I hissed as he crouched to leap into the air.

"Look," Ahdah pointed.

I followed his pointing finger. The fields between Prathniss and the giant trees were filled with people previously blocked from sight by the smoke. Some, with swords or any other weapon they could find, charged toward a line of orange clad Tek'ekim. Others stood stone still, peering into the distance with empty eyes while some wandered aimlessly with the same oblivion.

As we watched, a large man in a tattered, dark blue cloak lifted a huge longsword and yelled with such strength we heard him clearly from where we hid. No less than twenty townsfolk, wielding pitchforks and prods, rallied behind him. They rushed the line of Tek'ekim and cut their way through, but Neftim I hadn't seen, rose in monstrous shapes and beat them back. Two townsfolk beside the cloaked swordsman were flung high into the air and didn't move after they hit the ground.

Riders on dragons swooped down from the trees, but they could not control their mounts. Many riders fell from their rolling dragons. Other dragons slammed into the ground.

"We have to help them," I urged Ahdah.

His voice was strained when he replied, "I know, son. We're going to return to Thaydrin and tell him they can't tarry a click. Then, we'll get the word to the Coalition. I think that's Jamoal down there, and I doubt he had time to get word out."

"We have to help *now*," I argued.

"If we go out there now, we will eliminate any chance of getting help," Ahdah pressed down on my shoulder. "I may not be a soldier, but please trust me on this."

I swallowed, "But they need help now."

"Come," Ahdah whispered. "Let's go."

"Friend Jax, I must stay with Tuca," Oogluk said, crouching again to leap into the air.

"You heard Ahdah," I stated.

Oogluk limped just out of my reach. "Friend Jax," he said with such conviction I paused and stood still, "please do not make me to leave Tuca. To leave her please do not make me."

"I don't think we have a choice," I said.

"A choice we always have," Oogluk growled. "We always have a choice even if we do not like the outcome of one of the choices."

Oogluk hung his fake dragon head and let his tail drape around the trunk of one of the giant trees. A breath of wind wafted smoke around us. The suns' light danced in the white swirls as my eyes and head tails stung.

"I am sorry, Friend Jax," Oogluk stated.

The smoke swirled in fresh eddies. Muffled pops of wings catching the air to slow the Neftim for landing sounded beside us.

Tuca and Ronthluque landed beside Oogluk. They had formed themselves into four-winged creatures with plates of armor resembling those of the Teluthian armor.

"Friends of Oogluk," Ronthluque spoke into my mind, "we thank you for coming to our aid."

Oogluk and Tuca nuzzled and caressed one another as Oogluk slowly reshaped his hard dragon scales, mirroring his wife's armor plating.

Ahdah bowed at my side. Ronthluque returned his gesture of respect.

"How long must we wait before descending to rip and tear and crush? I wish to free Gen'tahn'Gen's shoulders of the burden of his head," Ronthluque gave the sensation of spitting when he said the Tek'ekim leader's name.

"We have Thaydrin and his soldiers who can come as soon as we teleport them here," I offered. "Ahdah also wants to inform the Coalition so they can send soldiers, but it may take some time for them to arrive."

Ronthluque hummed to himself, "So long it may not take if our Number were to help speed them on their way.

I will ask how many are willing. Though, I must warn you, we have long been eager for such an opportunity as this."

"Won't your Number need Ti'Kahn to help you teleport?" I asked.

Ronthluque gave the impression of laughter, "Jax, friend of Oogluk, we do not require help from Ti'Kahn when we are whole."

A new realization of what had been done to Oogluk flashed into my mind. I felt deeply grateful I had not been damaged so thoroughly and permanently by the Tek'ekim. Still, a new layer of shame tried to form deep inside me— my ancestor had done that to my friend.

"Then, Ahdah and I should spread the word and tell the Coalition to prepare and then you and your Number will follow behind us and bring them here."

"Yes," Ronthluque said.

I conveyed Ronthluque's request to Ahdah. He readily agreed. Oogluk, however, refused to leave Tuca.

"Very well," Ronthluque declared. "Will you, friends of Oogluk, allow me to bear you and speed you on your errands?"

I nodded and took a lingering look at Oogluk.

"Thank you, Friend Jax," he said. He did not hide the immense river of raw emotions coursing through him.

Tuca thanked me as well, and then we teleported to the Gah'Stotten dropship.

Thaydrin nodded grimly when I told him what was happening at Prathniss and that a Neftim would come shortly to teleport them to the battle.

"I wonder, Jax and Sterran, whether it would make sense to use the ship's weaponry?" he asked.

I thought hard about it, but Ahdah replied first, "Perhaps, it will be best to leave it here. What could be done if the pilots were overcome by the enemy's ability?"

Thaydrin rubbed his chy'li and stared into space for a click before grunting and saying, "That is a thought. It would be certain devastation if that were to happen."

He asked a few more questions and then set to work readying his soldiers.

I looked for Kelita, but I didn't see her and didn't have time to search the entire ship.

Ronthluque waited for us outside the ship. "Now, where must we travel?" he asked as we stepped down the ramp.

Ahdah paused beside me and stared at the Neftim.

"Your Ahdah is uncertain of the way we communicate," Ronthluque stated.

I tried to swallow the jealousy that sprouted up inside me. However, an edge of anger colored my voice as I explained, "It's Ronthluque in your mind. He needs to know where to take us next."

Ahdah shook himself from the stupor and asked, "You feel him like this all the time?"

"Only when we're close enough to each other," I explained.

"And he can see my thoughts too?" Ahdah sounded worried. I was about to respond but Ahdah spoke again, "Oh, he says only the ones I let him see, and he assures me he won't pry deeper into my mind than I want him to. Is this the same connection you have with Tranto—I mean Oogluk?"

I nodded. The anger I felt continued to grow. I had been the only one Oogluk would connect with. But now, my family was experiencing what had been only mine. It made sense that Ronthluque would connect with Ahdah since I didn't know as many towns as he did, but I still felt that something had been taken from me.

"Jax, friend of Oogluk, please tell your Ahdah to walk while he talks," Ronthluque's resonant voice broke into my brooding silence. "We have need for haste."

"He wants you to keep walking so we can keep moving," I said.

Ahdah shook himself and gave me a silly grin, "He did mention that to me, too. I was simply astounded."

Of course, you were. You didn't have to think that you were fighting and arguing with yourself. Oogluk would have checked my anger, but Ronthluque didn't even address it. He didn't even talk to me as we teleported from one town to the next.

Everywhere we went, Jamoal had raised the awareness of a possible attack, so the Coalition members were, by and large, prepared. Countless volunteers, mostly young men, also rushed home to grab dragons, armor and weapons after hearing Ahdah and I tell the story of the Tek'ekim.

Ronthluque was, by far, much better at mustering the soldiers than Oogluk would have been. I couldn't imagine Oogluk standing stoically amidst fearful stares or threatening glares in the town squares. He would have wanted to set us down where he could hide on the outskirts and have us walk into the square.

"That's about all the places I know," Ahdah said as he rubbed the back of his neck.

"Then, it is enough," Ronthluque stated.

We stood in the abandoned square of a tiny village far on the western slopes of the mountains. All the villagers had fled when we materialized right in the middle of their market. One man had grabbed a spear and tried to run it through Ronthluque, but the creature had snatched the spear and flung it far up the mountain.

Something whistled to my right. I knew the sound well. Ronthluque shot out a tentacle-like appendage, and an arrow dropped to the ground.

"Let us return to the battle," the Neftim stated. "We will find no help here."

Ahdah said hurriedly, "I've been undecided whether or not to go to Leitham. The Coalition doesn't extend its jurisdiction there. It's a large seaport, so large, in fact, that they organize their own version of the Coalition. They may hear us and give us aid."

Ronthluque and Ahdah conversed for several more clicks and then I heard the whoosh-crash of large waves.

Several people turned and stared open-mouthed at us, while others ran screaming from Ronthluque's appearance.

"Well, they've no excuse for not acknowledging something strange is happening," Ahdah murmured.

"This is a beautiful place," Ronthluque streamed a series of pictures from his mind. He showed me the surrounding hills with their soaring cliffs of gray and white stone interspersed with rich green trees and bushes. Next, he pointed out the countless tide pools scattered among the jumbled rocks of the coast and the numerous rivers and streams cutting through the hills and feeding fresh water to many additional pools.

"Our Number is a people without a home now," Ronthluque stated. "This land appears rich with the things we find necessary."

"The sea is salty. Can Neftim survive in salt water?" is all I said.

Ronthluque pondered that for a few clicks before stating he didn't know.

"Besides, I didn't think you'd want your people to live so close to my people. Oogluk used to show me memories of my people hunting him and trying to kill him."

Ronthluque shook himself, which gained several wary glances from the Ti'Kahn already giving us a wide berth. "Whether we shall always need to hide, I know not," he said. "I would prefer to be able to live without fear of death or enslavement if discovered."

We walked on in silence until Ahdah stopped and said, "Here we are. We'll inquire about volunteers and then we'll be on our way."

He went inside the ornate, stone building and returned less than ten rays later with a stocky man dressed in a leather jerkin embossed with a ship under full sail. Apparently, with the importance Prathniss played in trade, he hadn't needed much convincing to send aid. Ahdah explained how another Neftim would arrive after we left and how the teleporting would be a bit unnerving.

The stocky man nodded his head and eyed Ronthluque. Then, he said he could have two hundred men ready within the period. He turned on his heel with the briefest of salutes and charged back inside the building.

Before we were ready to depart, a dozen boys, a little older than me, raced from the building and scattered in all directions.

"We may see some of the best disciplined soldiers from Leitham," Ahdah observed. "I'm glad we came but let us be getting back to the others."

Chapter 24

Night fell quickly in the giant trees. Jamoal and his remaining, makeshift soldiers huddled in a group, nursing the wounds they'd received. Thaydrin sat beside the burly man. Somewhere in the group, Ahdah escorted Darvian and Meisha from one injured Ti'Kahn to the next.

The Teluthian soldiers hadn't joined in the fighting yet. By the time they'd arrived, Jamoal had ordered his men into the forest, and the Tek'ekim hadn't pursued.

I found myself wandering after having tried to talk with Kelita. She was with her Omoah and barely looked up when I sat beside her. She leaned away from me and mumbled only a single word when I asked her how she was.

"Jax, Friend of Oogluk," Ronthluque's voice sounded in my mind, "you are troubled?"

I sighed and sat at the base of a tree. A huge root provided a corner that I leaned into. "It's nothing," I replied.

"You have wandered restless about something for nearly a period. If you do not wish to discuss what is on your mind, you need simply only to say so," Ronthluque stated.

"It's nothing, but you're already in my mind anyway," I said.

"Is it about Oogluk?" Ronthluque asked.

"I said it's nothing." I just wanted him to leave me alone, yet I couldn't bring myself to say it.

Ronthluque's presence grew more distant, "I apologize for my intrusion. Pass the night easily, Jax, Friend of Oogluk."

"Goodnight," I mumbled to the creature.

I stared into the night and let my thoughts wander as aimless as my footsteps had been. A turit called a solitary note from among the branches reaching for the stars above me.

I shook myself. The wishful thought of Airitha hugging me and sitting beside me faded slightly.

The crunch of leaves and twigs snapping yanked my entire attention to a patch of darkness that looked murky. I drew my sword, failing to consider its glow would make me an easy target in the night.

"Friend Jax, it is I," Oogluk's familiar presence filled my mind. "I it is."

"I didn't feel you come up," I said as I sheathed my sword.

"I doubt anyone could have had they been as absorbed as you," Oogluk defended my lack of attention.

"What do you want?" I shifted my gaze to another part of the empty darkness.

"I, too, feel restless," Oogluk said. His nearly transparent body glinted dully as he lay on the ground in front of the huge root. "Restless, I feel."

"What about Tuca?"

"I am worried for her," he replied, abnormally vague.

"What's going on with Kelita? Why doesn't she want to talk with me?" I asked.

Oogluk gave the impression of rubbing his chin the way an old sage would before responding, "Friend Jax, I am learning that not much of what I thought I knew—"

"Just tell me what you think," I demanded.

"I know little of such things I am discovering. Discovering, I am, that I know little of such things."

"But you can see what's been going on," I pushed the memories of Kelita's and my recent interactions toward him. I met a wall.

"Friend Jax, I am not able to at this time."

"What do you mean?" I stared at the barely perceivable dragon-shaped head.

The creature responded patronizingly, "Things are not as easy as I had thought they might be. When two have been apart for a millennia, and one has no memory of the past...."

"You always helped me understand what was going on before? Why not now?" I felt discarded like the seeds from a fruit thrown carelessly on the ground.

"Tuca and I are vastly different," Oogluk stated. "She desires only to take revenge like Ronthluque. Understand, I do. However, my desire is for our people, the Number, to live in peace in a place that they are neither hunted nor enslaved.

"Friend Jax, they are a Number without a home. A Number without a home they are. If we could have a home, that would be enough to satisfy me. Enough to satisfy me, a home would be."

"Ronthluque said the same thing when we were at Leitham. It was one of the few things he said to me. Most of the time he talked to Ahdah."

I rubbed my back against the rough bark and wished I could feel the warmth of not being alone.

Oogluk reached out to me. His touch was welcome but empty, lacking the vitality that usually coursed in our connection.

"Are you sure, Friend Jax?" the creature asked me.

I nodded.

We vanished from the forest.

"Jax," Airitha sounded excited even though she was visibly tired, "what are you doing here? Is everything okay?"

"Yeah," I replied. "I just wanted to see my family again."

"Oh," Airitha glanced at the ground. "Rurin's sleeping already, but your Omoah and sister are outside. I think your Omoah is worried."

"Yeah," I grinned, "Omoah always worries about stuff. A'lii is probably trying to comfort her."

Airitha nodded.

Oogluk shifted behind me. The guards stationed at the door glanced at him and then turned their attention back outside.

"Where did you say they are?" I asked.

Airitha pointed, "They're over there on top of the hill."

I thanked her and turned to the door. At the top of the ramp, I realized Oogluk was not following.

"C'mon, Oogluk," I said to him without turning around.

"This is not why you came, is it? Not why you came..." he asked as though he already knew the answer.

"It's fine," I took a step down the ramp.

The stars were an immense, glittering ceiling, and the temperature was cooler in the mountains. The night was so calm and quiet that I cringed at the abrasive ring of my boots on the steel ramp.

I glanced behind me to see why Oogluk wasn't following. I just caught a glimpse of Airitha's mul'li as she spun and ducked behind the wall.

I trudged up the ramp to Oogluk's side. "Why are you staying in here?"

The silvery creature contorted himself to turn around to face out the door. His fake dragon eyes didn't look at me as he replied, "I think I begin to understand why you wanted to come here. Why you wanted to come here, I think, begin to understand I do."

I rolled my eyes and walked noisily down the ramp. Oogluk remained inside, but I didn't care. It wasn't until my boots scuffed through the long, tough grass that I realized my heart was beating harder and faster than it should.

After several steps, I looked back at the starship. Airitha didn't try to hide. She stood silhouetted in the doorway. Oogluk gave her a nudge and walked slowly down the ramp. Airitha's gaze followed the creature's retreating form before she met my eyes. I couldn't make out her eyes, but I felt the draw of her steady gaze.

I looked down until I heard her light footsteps ring on the ramp.

"Oogluk seems to think we should talk about something," she said softly when she stood in front of me.

I scowled at the ground and then looked up and said, "I wish he wouldn't always assume he knows stuff."

"Is Ahdah alright?" Airitha asked.

"There hasn't been a battle since he and the soldiers arrived," I replied. "You should know what's going on since they send you guys messages."

"Can they really be defeated?" Airitha's brow was pinched. "I mean with their mind control abilities, how do we know they'll stick to any sort of agreement?"

"The Neftim want to kill them all. They're really angry and want revenge. Well, most of them," I answered.

"Are there still Neftim being controlled by them?" Airitha glanced at Oogluk, who answered her question with a pained expression.

"They're gonna be hard to beat," I confirmed.

The three of us began walking. I glanced behind us toward the hill where I could make out two seated silhouettes against the starry background. They didn't know I was there or Omoah would've showered me with questions and "sweeties."

"Did you hear me, Jax?" Airitha touched my arm.

"What? Hear what?" I asked. A small bush grabbed at my leg.

"Do you think it's a good idea to use dragons in battle? It sounds like they were easy to use against us or simply kill."

Many of the Coalition members as well as the volunteers had brought dragons with them. It was just normal. My people never went anywhere without dragons.

"It's good to have a distraction, right?" I thought out loud. "And, besides, some of them will be able to get close enough to incinerate the Tek'ekim."

Airitha stopped me with a tug on my arm. I fidgeted with the pommel of my sword and had trouble holding her gaze in the dark.

"We should've brought a light," I said. "We could trip and fall off a cliff out here."

Airitha gave a single laugh, "You know this area better than I do, and I haven't seen any cliffs except the one where we saw Prathniss from. And that's over there."

I dug my toe beneath a rock and dislodged it.

"Jax, what about the Tek'ekim?" Airitha asked. "Don't they have families? Are they just looking for a home?"

"They attacked Prathniss," I said forcefully. "They need to be beaten or Gen'tahn'Gen will take over the whole planet. We'd be nothing but slaves."

"Kammiel—," Airitha started before I cut her off.

"She's Rurin's age. What does she know?" I quipped.

Airitha swallowed audibly. For a click I felt her glare. Then, with forced calm she said, "I was trying to say that Kammiel said Hahn'Nik'Nik thinks the problems would stop if Gen'tahn'Gen were removed."

"What about all the people loyal to him? Won't they just continue to control people?" I scoffed.

"Kammiel told me that Nik'Nik thinks there isn't anyone following him willfully," Airitha responded.

"There are always people wanting to control others," Oogluk pointed out.

I had forgotten he was with us.

"Oogluk says there's always people who want to control others," I declared, "and I think I agree with him."

Airitha thought silently for a few clicks.

"Besides," I added, "why should we believe Hahn'Nik'Nik? She was part of the group that made Kelita and me try to reassemble their world."

Airitha gave a tiny cringe when I mentioned Kelita's name, but in the dark I couldn't be sure of what I thought I had seen.

"What did she tell you when we got back with Davian and his sister?" I asked.

"Who? Hahn'Nik'Nik or Kammiel?" Airitha's voice was pitched higher with confusion.

"Kelita," I responded.

"Oh," Airitha quieted her voice, "she told me she didn't want me to tell anyone."

"Including me?"

"I'm sorry, Jax," Airitha said, "but I promised her I wouldn't."

I sighed, "It doesn't matter. She's not talking with me anymore."

Airitha chewed on her lip. I started walking again, and she jogged to catch up.

"I should get back to our army," I said.

She reached for my hand, but I snatched it away. She responded by stopping abruptly. I stopped a step later and turned to look at her.

"How will you know when you've won?" she asked.

"I don't think we have a plan yet. That's why I need to get back," I replied.

Airitha took a click to piece her response together, "When you go back, will you—will you ask Ahdah to consider what Kammiel said? Please."

"Alright. What'd she say, again?"

"About Hahn'Nik'Nik and about Gen'tahn'Gen being the problem," Airitha said.

Oogluk stopped walking and waited several paces behind us. The light spilling from the open door of the starship looked wavy and distorted. I looked up. Half of the sky was blocked by the massive ship.

Airitha wrapped her delicate arms around me in a hug. "What are you thinking about?" she asked.

I made something up and hoped it sounded plausible, "How do we know what's real? I was convinced that some of the memories the Tek'ekim had fed me were real." I shuffled a stone around with my foot, "Some of them would be easier to deal with than what's going on right now."

"The easy thing would be for me to tell you that you'll just know in your heart," Airitha replied after a few clicks of thinking. "I think, though," she laid her head on my shoulder, "we need to choose what to believe and live it until or unless proven otherwise."

"So, we're constantly living in a lie?" I wanted to push her away from me and keep walking.

"I don't think it's a lie," Airitha responded. "I think it's like acknowledging we'll never know everything exactly, so we find out all we can and don't let the rest bother us."

"Sounds like putting blinders on a dragon," I objected.

"Friend Airitha is saying that we cannot flip back and forth between believing two different things," Oogluk spoke through our connection. "If we do, we cannot live."

Airitha broke her embrace and looked at me. Then, she glanced into the distance, "Kind of, I guess. But I think we can see it—or, at least, see how it could be."

"So, what do you believe is real?" I asked, genuinely growing intrigued by the topic.

"The Tek'ekim didn't mess with my mind the way they did yours," she tried to meet my eyes, but I looked away. "I think it's incredibly wrong what they did to you and Kelita, but I don't know what to do about it or do about them." She paused thoughtfully, "They're kind of like the Neftim the way—"

"They're not at all like the Neftim," I interrupted.

"I just mean they don't have a home," Airitha explained.

"Oh," I conceded.

Without discussing it, we walked back to the ramp in unison. Airitha kept her head down in thought that looked so deep I didn't disrupt her. The artificial lighting from inside the dropship spilled far out from the door and gave everything an eerie, muddled color.

Oogluk gave the sensation of sighing wearily as he curled his armor plated, dragon shape on the ground at the foot of the ramp. I stared at him and wondered, not with the longing of times past, what it would be like if I had never met him. What if I had never chosen to take Raglod on the errand to Prathniss? Or what if I had stayed in the foothills until the storm had passed?

I tilted my head to look at the sky. The stars shimmered as they always did, bright and distant. The urge to sit with Airitha and study them struck me. I could tell her all about the constellations my people named. She wouldn't recognize any unless she had paid close attention the other times she'd been on Geoteous.

"Jax?"

I glanced in Airitha's direction. She sat on the end of the ramp with her arms folded to help ward off the encroaching chill.

"Huh?" I grunted.

"My home was destroyed, too. Ahdah and I have talked about it. At least, Omoah and my little brother are alright," she paused as if searching for the right words. "I wish all the fighting would stop. Too much has been destroyed. The Tek'ekim destroyed their world in order to get Oogluk back."

Oogluk raised his head as though he were curious about what was being said about him.

Airitha's brow was visibly tight, even in the shadow, as she finished, "What can we do? I wish we could make everyone stop destroying."

I stood still. Some of what she said rang inside me as if her words had plucked the exact chords that I wanted to play on a kaetinar.

"Maybe it does come down to one person," I said. As I said it, I wanted to disappear and hide from the thoughts that said I was one such person that I was talking about. "Maybe all the destruction is caused by one person who doesn't care about hurting others."

I argued with myself that I did care about other people and that I would never destroy worlds. However, the weight of the memories the Tek'ekim had planted slammed into me.

"What's wrong?" Airitha stood and clutched my arm.

I shook my head to clear the memories, but they wouldn't leave. "Rurin is alive. I rescued him from the dragon a few periods ago," I whispered to myself.

Airitha hugged me and said mostly to herself, "Why are some things so hard to forget? It seems like lies stick around longer than the truth."

"If it's not real and I don't believe it," I whispered angrily, "why does it stick around at all?"

Airitha hugged me tighter and pressed her forehead into my neck. I returned her hug. Something grew inside me. It was small and dim at first, but then it shot up and blossomed. I realized, then, that a cold, shadowy angst melted and dripped away.

"Thank you," I whispered.

"Time, it is," Oogluk stated.

"Jax, I'm scared your world will be destroyed, too," Airitha said with a sniff.

My gaze hardened. Maybe I really was nothing more than a calloused, little boy who thought only of himself. This girl hugging me certainly cared more about others' wellbeing than I did.

"Jax?" Airitha asked as she looked up at me.

I nodded.

Chapter 25

"Their 'bil'ty is pow'rful," Jamoal told Thaydrin for the second time how the Tek'ekim's first attack had progressed. "They pop up an' people jus' start doin' strange stuff—stuff they nevar done afore. An' some o' dem walk 'ight outta Prathniss."

The first sun shone brilliantly in golden light, slicing through the thick, green canopy above us at a sharp angle. The second sun crested the horizon, sending out soft rays of orange and pink.

Oogluk nuzzled Tuca beside me. Both Neftim talked at length with me about various strategies the Number had concocted.

"What the man, Jamoal, is saying," Tuca explained her latest idea, "is accurate. Our Number was fortunate to not get caught in the conflict. We may have been effective for a short time, but just as the Tek'ekim drove your dragons mad, they would have focused all energies on turning us to their devices."

A new question burned in my mind, "Would they have tried to control you if Gen'tahn'Gen were killed?" I hadn't relayed Airitha's message about what Kammiel had said yet.

Tuca hummed and thought for several clicks before replying. "That is too difficult to say," she said. "Our Number is a valuable asset for either side. We—"

She broke off. Silence lasted until Oogluk finished her statement, "Wish to fight our own, we do not." He continued heavily, "Those of the Number fighting with the Tek'ekim could be turned once the control is broken. Once the control is broken, those of the Number could be turned to our allies."

"I should've told Thaydrin what Airitha said already," I muttered.

Tuca shook herself as though trying to fling water from her body after a swim. "You will have time after this long-winded fire concludes his tale."

I nodded as Jamoal recounted how the Tek'ekim swarmed into Prathniss. After they had driven everyone out, they placed the unconscious townsfolk, who had attempted to fight against them, on a hill just outside the city.

"Kill everyone, they did not," Oogluk commented. "That is most remarkable."

"Nothing they do is admirable," Tuca interjected.

"Were they made unconscious by their weird, rattling weapons?" I asked.

Tuca replied, "Their weapons strike the resonance of the victim's brain, and the victim falls unconscious. Though those weapons are rarely fatal, they certainly are powerful."

I considered what she said and compared it with the hallucinogenic arrows they'd used against Oogluk and me. Every single one of their weapons was carefully engineered against the Neftim, yet instead of instilling widespread damage and death, they caused incapacitation. A dark realization struck me: such weapons allowed the Tek'ekim to subjugate their enemies versus outright killing them.

"And what about that green line they fired from the island fortress?" I shuddered as I remembered scaling the wall and falling under their control.

Tuca's presence was overshadowed by fear as she answered, "The green death is the worst possible way to die." She knelt until her stomach rested on the bracken and carpet of dead leaves. "The green death is sonic, we believe. Only a few of our Number have ever been struck by it, and they were burst apart into droplets that continued to disintegrate."

Oogluk gave the impression of wide-eyed astonishment as he processed the information. No small appreciation for having escaped the weapon sang in his mind as well.

"Some of our Number say they can still feel their screams of agony as their tiny parts continue to die. Such a death is agonizing and excruciatingly slow for our

Number." Tuca grew distant and numb as though she'd erected a wall of mist between us.

"Who were they?" I asked as gently as I could.

Oogluk's presence flared white hot in my mind before Tuca helped him settle himself.

If Tuca had been Ti'Kahn, she would have cried huge, silent tears as she said, "Our Kanook was one. Our dear Kanook. He was struck with the—with the green death. But he," Tuca struggled against her overwhelming emotions that she only barely kept from washing me away with. "But he saved his brother and his sister—along with the rest of our Number that had been caught by those murdering savages."

Anger boiled thick and hot in both creatures. I sought to disconnect but couldn't. Their anger, coupled with their grief, overpowered me. I could do nothing against it. I doubled over onto the ground clutching at my temples and clawing at my ears.

"Rend them to pieces," Tuca growled. "Avenge our Kanook."

Oogluk felt as fiery as his wife, yet he refrained from speech. Instead, he knelt over me and reached out to comfort me.

"Friend Jax," he said urgently, "sorry, I am. I am sorry."

Several other Neftim close by waved their heads from side to side and reared up on their hind feet. Tuca's wails of agony and hatred reached a peak and slowly descended to low, hot fire, the kind perfect for cooking.

Jamoal stopped talking, and everyone glanced around at the Neftim.

"Jax, what are they saying?" Thaydrin stared at me with a grim set to his jaw. "They've not acted like this before."

"They say that one of Tuca and Oogluk's sons was killed by the Tek'ekim," Ahdah said before I could speak.

Ronthluque stepped forward from the semicircle of Neftim. He lowered his armored head as though he were studying Thaydrin.

Ahdah delivered the message, "Ronthluque of the Number, declares this is not our war. He does not wish any more death, save that of the Tek'ekim, namely the death of Gen'tahn'Gen. Ronthluque speaks for his Number and says that he does not ask for aid, but any help offered will not be shunned."

Thaydrin rested his right hand on a handheld MEC holstered on his thigh. He declined his head slightly and spoke to the Neftim, "Mighty Ronthluque, you and your Number do have a personal quarrel with the Tek'ekim. Their enslavement of your Number has been a hard reality to bear, so I understand your motivation. However, I ask you to refrain your Number from engaging the Tek'ekim on the battlefield in such a frenzied state."

Ronthluque gave no indication as to what he intended, but many of the other Neftim ducked their heads and melted closer together in rough ranks of quivering semitransparency.

"My people and the people of Jax of Geoteous wish to stand beside you and your Number," Thaydrin went on.

"We must determine what a victory means. As of yet, we have agreed only that the Tek'ekim are a people homeless and destitute. I do not desire them to be utterly wiped out in a needless war."

The Neftim reacted with more erratic head bobbing and swaying. Several Ti'Kahn, all from Prathniss, cried out their desires for the murderers to die or to drive them out no matter how many women and children perished. After all, they shouldn't have brought them with them into a war.

Thaydrin held his hands up for silence. Jamoal stepped to Thaydrin's side and laid a big hand on his shoulder. The big Coalition man's mouth moved, but I couldn't hear what he said.

"Now, Friend Jax," Oogluk said. "The time is now to share what Friend Airitha reported from Friend Kammiel."

Ronthluque gazed at me with his unsettling eyes that never blinked. I swallowed and stepped forward into the open space between the leaders and the army.

"I have something to say," I cringed as I heard just how small my voice sounded. Hundreds of pairs of eyes fastened on me, and I froze.

Ahdah held out his hand, beckoning me forward.

Once I stood in front of the three men, I told them, "I went to the dropship yestercycle when it was dark. Airitha and I talked for a short time, and she said that Kammiel said Hahn'Nik'Nik thinks Gen'tahn'Gen is the reason for all the problems. If he were removed, then everything would be fine."

Jamoal was the first to respond, "'at's one thing and three people I don't know."

"The dropship is a really big starship," I explained. "Airitha is Thaydrin's daughter. Kammiel is the singer from Hegnoranthe, and Hahn'Nik'Nik is—well, she was a Tek'ekim."

Jamoal stared at me and stroked his chy'li. Ahdah and Thaydrin looked at the big man as he finally spoke. "I've 'eard 'nough abouten this Gen'tahn fella, but what's a singer know abouten this war?"

I swallowed and steeled myself for many more explanations. "Kammiel is the only one on Hegnoranthe that can use her ability to make people learn languages. That's how I can speak with everybody."

"There's more 'at could be said I see," Jamoal held his hand up. "I reckon I'ma jus' gonna 'ave ta larn as we fight. The biggest question I 'ave, an' I think lots o' others 'ave it too, is what are we gonna do with 'em once we win? Where they gonna go?"

Murmurs of agreement rose in a cacophony all around. Tuca and Ronthluque and some other Neftim all presented themselves in my mind. They refrained from placing words in my mind, but each played some sort of image that showed the Tek'ekim annihilated and absent from Geoteous. I understood that the same absence was to take place on every world they might have teleported to.

I hung my head as I considered Airitha's question. How would we know if we'd won? What if the Tek'ekim messed with our minds collectively and we just left them alone? Would we even know? What would happen to Prathniss and the rest of Geoteous if we did nothing.

Thaydrin broke the silence, but he spoke to Jamoal instead of addressing the entire crowd of makeshift soldiers. "Jamoal, it's evident we must discuss what victory means to us. It won't do to simply drive the Tek'ekim out of the town." He paused, and I could nearly see him thinking of his wife with her belly round with their unborn son.

"There's more than just soldiers in there," Thaydrin said as he peered toward the still smoking remains of Prathniss. "Much will need to be rebuilt no matter what we decide, but a cornered beast fights more fiercely than the beast which can run."

Jamoal nodded, "Saw some o' their little ones." He spat, "Too young ta be experiencin' such." He sighed and leaned on his sword hilt, "Gots our own little ones ta think 'bouts too."

Ahdah clapped a hand on his shoulder. The look in his eye was the crystal-clear fire of determination as he said, "You're a good man. We'll find a way."

Jamoal looked at Ahdah for a click before clapping one of his big hands on his shoulder and the other on Thaydrin's. "It don't matter where ya come from. Da invaders ain't gonna get da bes' o' us."

"It is up to us to ensure the deceiver is destroyed," Ronthluque murmured in an undertone that I wasn't sure whether I was supposed to hear through our connection.

"It is the only way," Tuca confirmed.

I stood still, staring at the three men as they continued to converse and lay plans. Numerous individuals were called into the group until it swelled so large, in order for the speaker to be heard by them all, he had to nearly shout. I had nothing to add to their strategy. I was like the shell of a seed that is forgotten once the seed sprouts and begins to grow.

I backed away from the group in the center.

"Ow," someone grunted when I stepped on his foot. "I've had enough of a job healing these people. There's somethin' wrong with their minds after the Tek'ekim get 'em."

"Sorry, Darvian," I apologized to the boy. "You and your sister have been busy I hear."

"Yep," Darvian gave a single, giant nod with his too-big head.

"Ask him what he meant about something wrong with their minds," Oogluk pressed with sudden urgency.

"You said something's wrong with their minds when you have to heal them. What do you mean?" I asked.

Darvian blinked his tired, green eyes and launched into explanation, "They get into people's minds an' change stuff. It's like they tear the brain and insert a new memory or something and then the person goes crazy. That's what they did to a lot of those dragons that dumped their riders, and I'm guessing that's what they did to the dragons that flew into the ground. Mah sister found it and figured out how to separate the real stuff from the fake stuff. It's worse than the Gah'ten getting you."

I stared at him as he shuddered and worked to brush aside the memories of the Gah'Stotten.

"Does she think it's their ability? Like I can shape and you can heal or turn back time on injuries?" I asked.

Darvian nodded, "She says it's like they get into minds from far away, kind of like the way you and those creatures talk." He glanced at Oogluk and Tuca.

"How far?" fear gripped me. If they could reach us where we were, then, they already had control over us. "They can't reach us here, can they?"

"Mah sister an' I talked about it, an' I guess we wouldn't know, would we?" Darvian kicked a root running along the surface of the ground.

"No, we wouldn't," I mumbled.

"Where are the rest of these orange Tek'ekim anyway?" Darvian asked with a jerk and tilt of his head. "They lived on an entire world. There's got to be more of them than what's in that city."

Oogluk walked up beside me and sank to his belly. "They must have been allowed to die," the creature said, "just like the rest of the Number."

I relayed what Oogluk said to Darvian, who visibly shrank and glanced warily around the way he'd done while we ran from the Gah'Stotten.

"It sounds like something the Gah'Stotten would do, doesn't it?" I said.

Darvian nodded. His round eyes fell on me for a click. I think I finally began to understand the terror he had lived in back on his home world. The Tek'ekim had messed with my memories, confusing me and causing me to act contrary to what I intended. Their influence lasted a long while after I was out of their reach. Yet, we didn't know we *were* out of their reach.

Another thought struck me. They had been able to track Oogluk and me when we teleported. They had even dragged us off Teluthia and onto the seeker. However, we hadn't experienced any mind control until we were in their presence. Did this mean their ability to feel and locate from a distance was much less limited than the mind control aspect? Could they not manipulate minds until the quarry was close by?

Oogluk nudged my shoulder with his snout, "Far more dangerous this all becomes. This all becomes far more dangerous."

I cringed. Wasn't Oogluk a prime example of the effects of the Tek'ekim's power? I smirked wryly to myself. Would we all say things twice, once forward and once backward, if the Tek'ekim won?

"I'm glad you found something to smile about," Kelita's voice snapped me from my dark contemplations. "We can't all stand around and smile like everything is funny."

Darvian whirled around and shrank against Oogluk's side. Kelita strutted forward importantly. I thought I wanted to reach out and greet her with a hug, but something cold and hard kept me bound, motionless and silent.

"Omoah says breakfast is ready and wanted me to bring you two. Darvian, your sister is with Omoah and was asking where you are." Kelita didn't wait for a response but turned on her heel and marched deeper into the woods.

The black barrel of a MEC glinted on her back where it was slung with a makeshift strap made from wood fibers.

My stomach growled as I took a step and turned back to get Darvian to follow.

"For me to follow, I do not think she meant," Oogluk stated, remaining planted beside the giant tree.

Ronthluque's presence invaded my mind, "Jax, Friend of Oogluk, bring Oogluk to the dropship. Our Number desires to speak with you."

Chapter 26

"Safely do so, we cannot," Oogluk objected. He stood at the base of the hill beside the dropship.

The ramp had been lowered by the guards when we arrived and the few people remaining at the ship walked slowly down it to see what was going on. Rurin pointed and waved excitedly when he noticed Ronthluque and the other Neftim. Omoah and A'lii both had the same apprehensive scrunch to their brows.

Kammiel held Hahn'Nik'Nik's hand as they wandered into the sunlight. Ronthluque gave the sensation of growling as he crouched as if preparing to spring. Hahn'Nik'Nik flinched and slowed her pace, but Kammiel kept walking and swinging her hand back and forth. She allowed the little girl to pull her the rest of the way down the ramp.

"Is something happening, Jax, sweetie?" Omoah asked as they drew near.

I nodded and replied, "But I'm not sure what."

Oogluk bellowed at Ronthluque in a conversation I hadn't been following, "Left here it was for fear the Tek'ekim would gain control of it. Here it was left."

Tuca stepped between the two as Ronthluque began slowly circling Oogluk.

"Omoah," I said quietly, "we need to get everybody off the dropship." I hadn't seen Airitha walk down the ramp. "Get everybody off the ship, now!" I shouted as I plunged up the ramp.

A'lii shouted something behind me, but whether she shouted to me or at the guards I couldn't tell, and I didn't stop to ask. Airitha could be anywhere in the vast bowels of the dropship.

"Friend Jax, care have, and find her quickly," Oogluk managed to convey to me before our minds were too far apart to remain connected.

I ran down the exterior hall, the one that connected the huge barracks rooms as a sort of common way and shouted for Airitha the whole way. A handful of guards spilled from the last room on the end. They didn't have their helmets and looked sleepy. I slid to a stop and thrust my hands into the air as they brought their MECs to their shoulders and aimed.

"It's me. Jax," I yelled. "We have to get everybody off the ship now."

Silently, they lowered their weapons, gave a single nod and salute in unison and, with the same unison jogged off down an adjoining corridor.

"Wait," I yelled after them. "Have you seen Airitha?"

Their only answer was the harsh ringing of their feet on the metal floor.

I tore into the barracks the guards had just vacated and searched for the door that I thought led to the central corridor. Once in the central corridor, I scanned the bare walls for any signs of how to reach the cockpit. Forward toward the front or toward the back?

I chose the front, remembering how the massive *Thecket Drives* were embedded in the rear and how the whole dropship looked something like a buzz. Rays later, I was awarded with a staircase. My feet rang on the metal treads as I called on all my speed and endurance.

My foot snagged on something at the top of the stairs, and I landed on my stomach with my arms pinned behind my back.

"Get off me," I shouted. "We have to get everybody off the ship. Where's Airitha."

"Sorry, sir," a woman's voice sounded above me.

The pressure on my arms eased, and two guards helped me to my feet.

"The king's daughter is in the cockpit," the second guard stated. "She asked to come up here this morning. The pilot and copilot are there, as well."

The door whisked to the side, and I stepped into the cockpit. Red lights glowed like candles on every surface. Dull light forced its way through wide windows of dark glass. Four stiff-looking chairs curled toward the controls.

Airitha stood with her face pressed tight to the dark window. She didn't turn to look at me but said, "Jax, I thought I recognized your voice."

I crossed the narrow floor to stand beside her and see what she stared at.

"What's happening down there?" She turned to me as she asked, "Why are you telling everyone to get off the ship?"

She caught my eyes for a click before we both turned to look at the two semitransparent creatures facing off.

"No, Oogluk," I shouted with my mind. "You can't win."

"Jax, what's going on?" Airitha's voice was pinched.

Oogluk had no chance of defeating Ronthluque in a fight—not without me, anyway.

"Get off the ship," I yelled over my shoulder as I sprinted from the stuffy room.

"Why are they fighting?"

"Just get everybody off the ship," I replied.

A heavy thud resounded down the ship's corridors. Airitha gasped, and I felt her footfalls right behind me.

"Jax, can't you stop them?" Airitha wailed as another thud echoed around us. "Can't you connect with them and tell them to stop?"

"I'm too far away," I yelled without turning to look back.

"What?" Airitha responded.

"Too far," I turned my head just enough to send my voice to her.

Together, we slid around the final corner. Our feet ringing against the floor didn't drown out Omoah's shrieks and the warning shouts she yelled at my brother, ordering him to get back.

I urged my body to run faster and nearly slid out the door and down the ramp when I tried to navigate the turn. Airitha grabbed my arm and steadied me.

"Look out," she cried and yanked me to the side with her.

A massive, semitransparent gray tail smashed against the ramp like a whip against a stump.

"Oogluk," I called repeatedly as I searched for his mind to connect.

"A'lii," Omoah shrieked.

"Oogluk, let me in," I demanded.

"Friend Jax?" Oogluk sounded confused.

I felt another presence in his mind then. At that click, Ronthluque whirled his body in an arc that caught his distracted opponent squarely and sent him slamming into the ship above Airitha and me.

Airitha squeezed my arm so hard it hurt, but I still reached for Oogluk.

"We can't win against him," I told the creature.

Oogluk hung above us and reached up with several tentacle appendages. As he pulled himself higher on the side of the curved side of the drop ship, he replied, "Let him destroy the Number, I will not. I will not let him."

Ronthluque materialized beside Oogluk. They both bristled. Oogluk stabbed at the other Neftim with parts of his body made into spears, but Ronthluque vanished and crushed Oogluk's body flat against the hull with a solid boom as he reappeared.

Pain lanced into my mind.

My sister cried out.

Oogluk dropped from the starship as though dead, but he landed on freshly formed feet and brandished a long tail with a ball of spikes at its end.

Ronthluque's presence invaded my mind then. "Give up, you dishonorable gumbat," anger and disappointment dripped like venom from his voice.

Oogluk responded, "Then, am I no longer to be admitted as one of the Number?"

"You know your number, gumbat," Ronthluque spat.

With that he vanished and reappeared just above Oogluk in the shape of a huge and evil looking spike.

Oogluk blacked out for a click as Ronthluque tore through him running his spike-shaped body over ten feet into the ground.

My sister cried out again.

Before I could decide what I was doing, I shaped an enormous disc of air and flung it to Oogluk.

Ronthluque vanished and fell from the sky again, but Oogluk swung the disc. This time, Ronthluque screamed in agony. His body fell to the side, nearly severed into two halves. Oogluk raised the disc like a warrior preparing to bear down on his enemy with the edge of his shield.

My sister screamed both audibly and in my mind.

Ronthluque vanished as the shield I'd made for Oogluk shattered rocks and threw chunks in a fifty foot radius.

"Enough," my sister shouted. "Stop it."

Oogluk froze with the disc of air still buried in the ground. Ronthluque quivered twenty feet behind him.

Incredible tension, like that of a hundred bowstrings pulled to full draw, thrummed through my mind. Ronthluque growled, and Oogluk yelped.

Slowly, with her feet dragging as if they weighed a thousand pounds apiece, my sister stepped between the two combatants.

Ronthluque's body joined itself back together just as Oogluk's leg had done on Grael after I'd cut him.

"Do not protect that traitor," Ronthluque hissed.

My sister pressed her mind harder against him. His clawed feet dug deep into the rocky soil as he strove to overcome the pressure A'lii exerted on him.

"The foul stench of gumbat," Ronthluque began.

"You will leave each other alone and resolve this peacefully," my sister said clearly.

Oogluk managed to pull the shield from the ground and turned with great effort to face Ronthluque.

"Let me kill that gumbat before he kills my Number," Ronthluque bared a mouth full of fangs that put the most wickedly sabered dragon to shame.

"It is clear," Oogluk managed to rise to a standing position on thick, powerful looking legs, "that I am not one of your Number. That I am no longer—"

"Oh, don't babble on, gumbat," Ronthluque snarled.

"Your Number is no longer a worthy entity," Oogluk ground out.

A'lii pressed against him more firmly, but that let Ronthluque claw a step closer to Oogluk.

Another presence reached for my mind. Tuca. She expressed no words, but the raw emotions of being torn in two spoke clearly for her. Airitha took my right hand and glanced at Tuca, who knelt beside me on my left.

"The Damaged One seeks an audience," Ronthluque mocked.

Omoah stood on the opposite side of the huge creatures. She looked on in horror with her hand covering her mouth. She looked torn between running to rescue my sister and snatching Rurin and backing away.

"You'll never be one of us," Ronthluque pressed harder.

Oogluk bared fangs of his own and shakily gained another step.

Ronthluque flashed more transparent as though he were cut off from teleporting at the last click.

My sister's legs quivered minutely. She turned and looked at me.

Then, everything snapped at once.

A'lii slumped to the ground. Ronthluque and Oogluk both lunged. Tuca slammed into me, throwing me against Airitha.

Omoah screamed.

Unbearable pain split my mind into little pebbles.

When I was able to look around, Tuca lay on the ground behind Oogluk. Her features grew rounder like a candle melting. Ronthluque lay in two halves behind her. One half formed a puddle of semitransparent gray. The other writhed until it, too, lay still and slowly collapsed into a puddle.

Oogluk stood stone still with the disc of hardened air lilting in his weakened grasp. A huge hole gaped in his fake dragon chest.

Tuca wept as she continued to collapse. She reached for Oogluk, but her body could not retain its shape. Ronthluque had slammed through Oogluk, creating a hole in my friend despite being sliced in two. Then, the once majestic Ronthluque had managed to start disintegrating Tuca.

Airitha yelled. I could not take my eyes off the carnage of the Neftim. She yelled again.

Somewhere in the distance Omoah screamed my sister's name. I looked back at where the battle had been fought. Omoah held A'lii in her arms. Blood streamed from my sister's face.

In a daze, I turned back to Tuca. The air popped and crackled. More than a dozen Neftim materialized around us.

Oogluk quivered back and forth as every nerve in his body screamed a single syllable, yearning that everything that had just transpired had not happened.

Tuca reached for him. Again, her body failed her.

The Neftim closed in on Oogluk.

I wanted to shout at them and tell them he wasn't to blame, but I could do nothing.

Oogluk suddenly collapsed on top of Tuca's dying body. Immediately, the Neftim flung themselves back, and the presence of Oogluk and that of Tuca winked out in my mind. Their bodies formed a single puddle that flowed downhill. The other Neftim hurriedly dodged out of its way as it flowed toward the cliff.

Stricken, I watched as the grayish mass trickled over the lip like a waterfall in a small stream. They were gone.

Chapter 27

"Somebody, help me!" Omoah screamed. "Her blood's pouring out. She's dying. A'lii. A'lii!"

I tore my gaze away from the cliff. I longed to see Oogluk shoot up from below and fly freely in his dragon shape.

The Neftim moved toward Omoah. She held my sister close to her chest.

"I'm sorry, Jax," Airitha cried silently beside me.

I felt her hand on my shoulder and brushed it off.

No words filled my mouth, but I walked to Omoah and knelt in front of her. Gingerly, I took my sister's limp body in my arms. Omoah pressed a wad of her dress against A'lii's nose. Turning to the closest Neftim, I looked at her and thought of Darvian and Meisha.

I didn't feel her brush my consciousness at all as she enveloped us in her wings. The next click, giant trees towered above us. Dappled sunlight danced all around as if trying to cheer me up. I looked around for either of the two green marked Ti'Kahn and growled when I saw neither of them.

Just then, Ahdah ran up. He took a single look at A'lii and charged away shouting for Darvian and Meisha.

"We're under attack!" a distant voice cried.

Jamoal ran by to my left. "To arms. To arms," he bellowed.

Omoah wrapped an arm around me and redoubled her care for A'lii, tipping her on her side and turning her head so the river of blood would not run into my sister's lungs or stomach.

The air vibrated behind me. The rest of the Neftim had returned just in time.

Fire and sparks showered through the treetops. Dragons cried and screamed feral growls above us.

Bows sang and arrows flew, but I knew they were little good against dragon scales. MECs squelched, and Gwarven's motionless body flashed into my mind, quickly followed by the gaping wound Kerelyn had suffered. I shuddered. Omoah cried softly beside me.

Rurin turned this way and that like a lost child trying to decide which direction home was. Airitha nearly tackled him as she threw her arms around him and pulled him beside our little group. A click later, a branch crashed to the ground where he had stood.

Someone nudged my arm. I looked up into the unemotional face of the Neftim that had teleported us to the forest. Her gesture seemed to coax me to go with her.

"Where?" I asked.

No answer.

"It's death to try to stop rampaging dragons," I attempted to explain. "It's like trying to stop stampeding ee'nex by standing in front of them and holding up your hand."

She nudged me again. Why wouldn't she connect with me.

A warning was shouted close by. A huge trunk, engulfed in flame shook the ground. Sparks and smoke shot in all directions. The dead leaves of the forest floor kindled immediately, and fire raced in all directions.

I pushed A'lii into Omoah's arms and raced to stamp on the fire before it reached us. Aritha and Rurin followed suite beside me. The smoke stung my eyes and head tails, but we kept it at bay long enough for Omoah to drag A'lii to the blackened ground that would not burn again. They would be safe until Darvian and Meisha arrived. Where were they? Why were they taking so long?

A man followed by three smaller figures came running through the smoke. Ahdah brought Meisha and Darvian to A'lii's side.

Meisha knelt and quickly examined my sister. Then, she turned to her brother and said, "I'll have to handle her. Go help some of those who got burned."

Darvian nodded and noticed me for the first time. His eyes were enormous, and I wondered how he was managing to function. Neither of us said anything. He raced back the way he'd come.

The third smaller figure strode toward me and held out a MEC.

The dragons still thundered above, and the heat from countless fires grew quickly.

A cheer erupted as the lifeless body of large, gray dragon thudded to the ground. It still had a saddle cinched to its withers.

I accepted the MEC Kelita offered and inspected it. The power supply read forty percent. I hoped it would last.

Once I took the MEC, Kelita turned on her heel and hurried to the nearest clearing where countless soldiers crouched, firing into the sky.

Fire and sparks continued to rain down. The attacking dragons flew wildly but always looped back around to spread their deadly sparks again. Two more of them crashed to the ground covered in smoldering, black spots and charred flesh torn back from deep, oozing wounds.

The Neftim nudged me again. "What do you want?" I demanded. "Just connect with me so we can talk."

Instead of connecting she turned to look behind. The Neftim stood in a meandering line between two huge tree trunks. I was their commander. But didn't commanders have to be able to talk with their troops?

"Talk with us you can," a familiar voice said.

My MEC hung forgotten, the muzzle still pointed into the air. I searched for Oogluk until I spotted him standing beside Tuca. Both looked perfectly whole.

I wanted to run to him, but all I could do was ask, "How?"

Oogluk rumbled for a click before explaining, "We Neftim are able to help those who are dying. Help those who are dying we are able. As I have helped Tuca, so we can do."

"So, you can help anyone? And keep everyone from dying?" I asked, desperately wanting to believe it.

Tuca took over the explanation, "We are able to help only our kind as far as we know. We have never attempted it with a Tek'ekim—I mean with a Ti'Kahn. A few of our Number mentioned it to Oogluk when they saw I was dying from Ronthluque's attack."

I glanced at Oogluk and then at the other Neftim. They all stood solemnly, ignoring the fire and chaos above.

Tuca continued with noticeable emotional strain, "A great price is paid every time, however, and none can say what that price will be." Tuca tried to mask the conveyance of tearful emotion, "My Oogluk has saved me, but he has paid for it with what we know not yet."

Oogluk interjected, "Even if the price had been my ability to speak, I would have considered it a trifle. I would have considered it but a trifle even if the price had been my speech."

Tuca stepped forward tentatively, then she knelt in front of me.

Oogluk spoke for her, "Change what has been done we cannot. Nor can we change the choices that were made. Choices that were made cannot be changed now. When the Number discovered us both alive, they teleported us here so that we may be of service to the savior of the Number."

"It's all Ronthluque's fault," I scowled and bit my lip. I wanted to scream and destroy—kill something.

Oogluk made no response but picked me up and whisked us both up a tree. From the top branches, I fired the MEC Kelita had handed me until my ears rang and the power supply flashed red.

Many dragons lay silent and bleeding out on the ground when we left the treetop. Several other dragons thrashed around noisily in the final throws of death. They bellowed and gurgled sickeningly. Besides their moans and screams of agony, the cycle was silent.

After climbing down, I sat with my back against a giant trunk and watched. The ringing in my ears separated me from the shouts of those helping the wounded or struggling to beat back the fires.

Tuca stayed close by, but the other Neftim wandered around our perimeter.

"What are they doing?" I asked Oogluk.

"Keeping watch are they," he responded.

A few figures coagulated in the center of the clearing. From my viewpoint, they were partially hidden behind the bodies of two dragons lying with their once majestic wings crumpled and twisted on the ground. Their eyes were glazed, and blood, which attracted swarms of buzzes, pooled at their mouths.

Shouts erupted to my right. I heard Kelita's voice rise above the others, "It's because of her. We were fine until she came here. Now they can reach all the way to us."

Several husky voices chorused their agreement. Kelita's Omoah held a hand across her mouth as she stared at her daughter.

I followed her gaze to see Kelita standing on top of the carcass of a dull green dragon. She pointed downward. Between the soldiers crowding in, I glimpsed a flash of orange. Oogluk lifted me enough to see over the crowd. Hahn'Nik'Nik stood with her hands bound together and a surly-looking townsman on either side of her squeezing her arms just above the elbow.

Oogluk acknowledged a flash of conversation from one of the circling Neftim. They were right. We should not have brought her back with us.

From my vantage point, I searched for my sister and family. Rithol bent over A'lii where she still lay in Omoah's lap, and Ahdah stood with an intense scowl creasing his face, listening to Kelita and her supporters. Rurin scampered toward the commotion.

I groaned. Just then, Kammiel's blue markings stood out beside Hahn'Nik'Nik's orange markings. I stared in disbelief as Airitha tried to comfort the little girl, and my brother ran up to Hahn'Nik'Nik and stood staring at her. Her gaze was trained down, but I don't think she saw Rurin.

Hahn'Nik'Nik flinched suddenly. Then, I saw another ball of spit smack her forehead. Rurin stared for a click and then shrank against Airitha.

The crowd erupted in shouts. Airitha tried to pull Kammiel away from Nik'Nik's side, but the little girl had planted herself like a climbing vine. She squealed as Airitha pushed her. Rurin tried to help Airitha, but Kammiel dodged them both and looped her arm more tightly around Hahn'Nik'Nik's leg. The Tek'ekim woman's head shook as if she were crying.

"Get us in there," I demanded Oogluk.

We both pictured standing on the carcass next to Kelita. I brought my focus to bear on that spot like a pin pressing against skin before it pierces. Nothing happened.

A ripple of confusion emanated from Oogluk's presence.

Nothing happened a second time.

Tuca's presence joined us, "The price, my dear Oogluk. This was the price," she wept. "My dear Oogluk. My dear Oogluk."

We tried one final time with the same results.

Oogluk sank to the ground, stunned.

"No, you have to get me there," I didn't take my eyes off the scene unfolding. Rurin, Kammiel and Airitha could all be hurt by the crowd if they lost just a little more control. Kelita was waving her arms and shouting again. She would undoubtedly rile them enough to cause serious damage to their captives. I cringed and laid my hand on my sword.

"Friend Jax, I am sorry. Sorry, I am," Oogluk murmured.

I froze as the truth finally sank in. He had given up our ability to teleport to save Tuca, his alambaralam. We would never visit the stars again.

"Let me go," I struggled to pry myself away from him.

His grip slackened, and I slipped away. The crowd chanted something I couldn't quite make out. Glancing up, I noticed Kelita had been replaced with a sour-looking man missing half of a head tail. Alakish, the man who had tried to swindle me for an extra hour of corral time when I'd purchased the seeds for my sister's marriage ceremony. A few more people climbed up beside him. They shouted into the crowd, but their voices didn't reach me.

I pressed forward. The crowd surged around me. Everyone pressed in as close as they could as if they wanted to tear Hahn'Nik'Nik apart with their bare hands.

A rope wrapped around my waist. I looked back to see Oogluk's strangely shaped body lift me above the crowd and lower me down beside the orange woman.

He let me go saying, "No more can I do, or they will hunt my kind as well as the Tek'ekim."

I nodded mentally and thought about what to do now that I was where I wanted to be. It was then that I realized I hadn't formed any sort of plan.

Kammiel held desperately to Hahn'Nik'Nik's arm and glanced wide-eyed at the crowd turning quickly into a mob around her. She had several dirty smears where she had been hit by spit and mud. I bent down to pick her up and pull her away.

"No!" she squealed and pulled herself toward Hahn'Nik'Nik when I lifted her off the ground.

"We have to get out of here. It's not safe," I yelled.

The little girl stared at me and shook her head violently.

"C'mon," I pointed toward Airitha and my brother. Grabbing her waist with my other hand, I attempted to break her hold, but her grip was like the cinch on a dragon saddle.

Somone stepped forward and slapped Nik'Nik on the cheek. Immediately, I thought of Meisha and the discolored and scarred side of her face when we'd found her as one of Shahn'Nahsh's aides. My anger flared that one of my people had just done the same thing Shahn'Nahsh had done.

Hahn'Nik'Nik fell to her knees. She was so broken already that she made no attempt to appear strong. She sobbed with her head hung so low her mul'li scraped the blackened remains of the forest bracken.

Kammiel let go of the orange woman's arm and gave all her attention to wiping the tears from the woman's cheeks. I could grab her and pull her away, but I didn't.

As if on cue, I heard the chant the mob ranted. "Feed!" "Feed!" "Feed!" they cried.

They wanted to feed Hahn'Nik'Nik to their dragons. I had heard about only a few towns ever punishing anyone in such a manner, and that had been in the far distant past.

My little brother pushed Airitha's restraint off and rushed to stand in front of Kammiel. He faced the crowd, and, even though fear flashed in his round eyes, he held his balled fists in front of his face as if preparing to fight a bully at school.

I drew my sword and stepped into a wide fighting stance facing the mob.

Kelita rushed me and shoved my shoulder. "Stop," she mouthed.

I turned on her, "You can't tell me this is what you wanted?"

"It doesn't matter," Kelita crossed her arms. "She's part of the problem."

The mob continued to chant, but some at the front grew still and dropped their gaze from Alakish to stare at us.

Sudden movement snapped both of our attentions to Airitha. She rushed Kelita with a growl. The two girls landed side by side in the mud. Kelita on her back and Airitha on her stomach. Airitha scrambled onto Kelita, pinning her beneath her. Kelita thrashed for a click before going still.

The crowd laughed and pointed.

Then, so fast I couldn't hope to stop her, Kelita drove her knee into Airitha's ribs. Airitha screamed and contorted. She fell to the side and doubled over with her face brushing the ground.

Kelita scrambled up. "Just stay away from me," she shouted.

Airitha moaned.

"Stop this madness," Ahdah's voice barely cut above the din. A glance showed him fighting the restraint of several townsfolk. He would never make it in time to help.

A woman stepped toward Airitha. "I say get rid of 'em all," she cried, turning in a circle to address the crowd. "No aliens on our world!" She bared her teeth and kicked Airitha in the side in the same place Kelita had kneed her.

"What's goin' on 'ere?" Jamoal's voice thundered over the reanimated din.

Another mob member ran forward and kicked Airitha's side.

Kammiel screamed behind me. A man held her above his head.

The mob rushed forward. I cried for Oogluk and the Neftim.

The next click, the dropship gleamed bright and glossy in front of me. The Neftim had removed us from immediate danger for the time being.

I glanced around. Hahn'Nik'Nik and Rurin huddled together by a rock. Airitha knelt doubled over, shielding her head with her arms. Kelita lay on her back pinned beneath the giant foot of a Neftim. Kammiel ran to Airitha, and Darvian and Meisha glanced around bewildered.

Without further thought, I rushed to Airitha. After she realized no more blows were falling, she held her side and tried to keep her sobs from shaking her body. I touched her shoulder lightly. She flinched and moaned.

Darvian and Meisha skidded to a stop beside me. Without speaking, they set to work. Airitha gasped and moaned, but never passed out.

When the two had finished healing her, she looked at me with slightly glassy eyes. Their rich purple pooled with emotion. Without warning, she grabbed me and sobbed loudly on my shoulder.

Kammiel pat her on the back and whispered to her that everything would be fine.

"Not without great effort will everything be fine," Oogluk spoke for his people. "We cannot stay here. Stay here, we cannot."

Rurin wandered over and tried to squeeze onto my lap. Airitha shifted more to my side to make room for him, and I lowered an arm to wrap him in the hug too.

"What are we gonna do now?" Darvian asked.

Meisha stood next to Hahn'Nik'Nik, rubbing the older woman's shoulders, "I think we have to get Hahn'Nik'Nik to safety."

My head swam.

Kelita shouted to be let loose. No one paid attention to her.

"What about the Neftim the Tek'ekim have right now?" I asked.

Oogluk attempted to respond, but Tuca silenced him, "Lost. They are lost to our Number." She broke down, and Oogluk comforted her.

Hahn'Nik'Nik sniffed and forced her shaky voice to form words, "I'm sorry. I'm so sorry. You're all so brave like my Ahn'Ahn and Mik'Mik are." She broke and wept for nearly a ray. "This is ridiculous," she broke again. "Why are we even fighting?"

We all waited silently for her to continue.

"Maybe you should hand me over to the Tek'ekim," Nik'Nik sniffed. "Maybe they're fighting so hard so they can reclaim me and punish me."

"But they'd kill you," Airitha said.

Nik'Nik nodded and sniffed. Wiping at fresh tears and old grime, she replied, "The Great Gen'tahn'Gen would not even try to save his daughter from the punishment of treachery."

"He's your Ahdah?" Airitha asked as we all leaned forward to make sure we'd heard correctly.

Nik'Nik sniffed and nodded, "Yes."

Meisha strove more vigorously to comfort the orange woman.

Airitha stood and walked toward the cliff. I wanted to follow her, but Rurin snuggled deeper into my chest and asked, "Who's Great Gen'tahn'Gen?"

Hahn'Nik'Nik scoffed loudly as she smiled wryly, "He is the man who destroyed our home world. Now, I think he wants to take over yours for himself. I would not be surprised if he contrived the seeker for just such a purpose. Therefore, making it necessary to begin exploring and conquering other worlds again as in the old stories."

Rurin wadded his face up and said, "I don't want him to have it. He must be mean if he's the one who kicked Airitha."

Hahn'Nik'Nik nodded and said, "I don't think he's ever thought of anyone but himself."

"But you wanted him to be killed?" I jerked my head to the side to see Kelita close by and bound with the silvery appendage of a Neftim. She was silent for the moment, but her eyes flashed with fire and ice.

Hahn'Nik'Nik swallowed and nodded as she looked at the ground, "I wish I didn't have to say that. If I thought peace could be reached any other way, I wouldn't have."

Kammiel walked slowly to Hahn'Nik'Nik and planted herself in her lap. The older woman stroked the girl's mul'li and cuddled her close, pressing her cheek to the top of her head, finding insurmountable comfort in the acceptance the little girl showed her.

We all stood in silence, contemplating the enormous ramifications of the events that had just transpired.

"We have to go back for Ahdah and our people," Airitha said wide-eyed as she returned to our group.

Chapter 28

"Stay close enough to maintain our connection," I instructed Oogluk and Tuca, "but if you're going to be seen, stay hidden and let our connection drop."

"But, Friend Jax?" Oogluk tried to object.

I gave him a hard look, "It will only make my job harder if you're seen."

"Go with the swiftness of our Number," Tuca breathed into my mind. "I'll hold this wild creature in check."

Oogluk argued with her, and the two bantered openly as I crept through the woods. The giant trunks were both good at concealing me and terrible at allowing me to see ahead.

The main thought coursing through my mind was finding Ahdah. I was worried about him after having seen some of the townsfolk forcefully restraining him when he tried to help my friends and me.

Part of my mind asked the same questions over and over about Kelita. I tried to shove the questions from my thoughts, but they resurfaced constantly, and I wondered why she had done what she'd done to incite the mob. Further, she'd been completely unrepentant when my friends started getting hurt.

Leaves crunched under my boots. That was the only sound I made as I neared the camp. The smells of charred flesh and drying blood made the air rancid. My skin felt as though it were covered in muck.

The two Neftim were silent, but I felt them searching every facet of my senses as they sought to help me.

I rounded a final, giant trunk I had kept between the camp and me as I approached. The space was empty. Everyone was gone. Not even my Omoah and sister were anywhere to be seen. The cooking fires had been scattered and stamped out. Only trampled mud and broken weapons remained as evidence that an army had camped there. The dragon carcasses remained where they had fallen in battle. Some of them were already bloating.

"The smell must have driven them to a new site," Tuca's presence wrinkled her nose.

"Well, where should we look?" I peered through the tree trunks as far as I could.

Oogluk hummed to himself before asking, "Use dragons, would they have?"

I scanned the vacated camp again and replayed the attack in my mind. "I doubt they have enough dragons," I said. "I think all the dragons left in Prathniss were used to attack us. They didn't have many tethered outside the camp either."

"He's right," Tuca agreed. "I think they would not have allowed the Teluthians to ride with them if they'd had sufficient numbers anyway."

Scanning the trampled ground, I walked further into the deserted camp. "They had to have left some good tracks," I said.

The two Neftim agreed, and I saw their shadowy forms glide through the trees on either side of me.

"Over here," Oogluk called softly.

I replied as I followed a trampled path with my eyes, "I think I got something, too."

I showed the two Neftim what I saw, and then Oogluk showed a churned up path he'd found.

"Make sense, it does," Oogluk declared, "that they split up."

"Yeah," I agreed. "Which one do you think is Thaydrin's soldiers?"

"Perhaps, we must follow each until we see some telltale sign. Until we see some sign, follow each, we must," Oogluk laid out the plan both Tuca and I agreed with.

"I don't want us to split up, though," I said.

The two Neftim fell into place behind me. We walked warily, scanning the trampled earth, the giant trunks and even the branches above us. The path led close to the edge of the forest, but remained far enough inside the forest's shadows that someone outside the forest would not be able to see us.

"It makes sense that they would come this way," Oogluk said. "The Teluthian people do not know your world, Friend Jax, and would fear losing their way in the depths of the forest. In the depths of the forest, they would fear losing their way. This way makes sense."

We walked on with the fields surrounding Prathniss always to our left. The further we walked, the less damage we saw. Turits called warnings to one another as we passed, and klonlin chittered at us from where they hid in the branches.

We followed the trampled path for a period before it ducked out of the woods.

"What do you make of it? Make of it, what do you?" Oogluk asked.

I studied the turn the path made. It crossed an open section of wild grass and dove into an orchard of well-kept connel berry trees.

"I really don't know," I murmured. "I don't see anyone. We're quite a bit further south, but I still don't think it's far enough to be safe to go out in the open."

"What if we were to fly a short way, staying close to the ground?" Tuca asked.

"No," Oogluk immediately countered. "It is not safe."

His fear alone would have been enough to keep us from such an action.

"It would be safer to climb a tree," I offered. "Maybe we'll still be able to see where this trail goes."

Oogluk whisked himself and me up a tree and deposited me further up when it grew so thin that it swayed with his weight. A small branch cracked. For a click, I thought I was falling from Raglod's back.

Once I recovered, I scanned the orchard below. The trampled path marched straight into the rows of trees, but then, it disappeared.

"I don't see anything," I said to the two Neftim.

"Doubled back on their trail, do you think they did, perhaps?" Oogluk asked.

Before I could reply, Tuca added, "Did they go out there to get food? They must have been hungry."

I peered more intently, trying to see through the trees to the grass below them. I shook my head, "I still don't see anything."

A large turit, pecked by three smaller and faster turits, soared by.

"I know I just said it isn't safe, but do you think we can fly for just a click? We'd be able to see more," I asked through our mind connection.

Tuca hesitated as if considering, but Oogluk gave a resounding no.

"Like this, I do not," he added. "Something is amiss."

Tuca pondered what we'd seen so far and offered, "Nothing we have seen points to either party definitively. Do we know that they did split up? Could they have regrouped, entered a battle and then retreated?"

Oogluk hummed and gave the sensation of stroking his chin like an old, wizened man might do, "Perhaps, any possibility we come up with is plausible. Plausible perhaps...."

Oogluk and I climbed out of the tree. I rested against a large root protruding from the soil. Hunger gnawed at my stomach. If I'd been thinking more practically, I would have grabbed something to eat from the dropship. An idea hit me.

"I'm hungry, so I could sneak out into the orchard, get some fruit and sneak back. While I'm out there, I would be able to see better where the path leads."

Oogluk shook himself and shifted his position, so it looked like he was scanning the waving trees attentively. He stood that way for a long time. All the while, I strained my ears to hear anything out of the ordinary. All was peaceful and compliant with a warm, summer's cycle, though.

At last, Oogluk answered, "Do not go out of range of our connection."

Trepidation coursed through my limbs and held me in the bracken at the edge of the giant forest for several long rays. The sunlight felt like it ate at the dark parts of my armor. Sweat trickled down the back of my neck.

At last, I stepped out of the bracken into to the trampled grass. I ducked, thinking I'd heard a bowstring twang. No arrow went whistling overhead, so I pushed myself toward the first row of trees a little over twenty feet away.

"This is too dangerous," Oogluk stated.

"I need to be able to listen with all of my attention," I hissed.

Remotely, Tuca mentioned to Oogluk that it would have been no different if we had found the townsfolk in the woods. I would have had to walk up to them alone just as I was doing.

Ducking under the branches of the first row of trees, I crouched and peered up and down the row, straining my eyes to look deeper into the orchard. Nothing looked out of the ordinary except innumerable, trampled paths. It looked like the townsfolk had split apart in all directions—probably to pick fruit for themselves.

The branches above me may have been laden with connel berries shortly before, but they were bare, apart from some small clusters of green, unripe berries.

"I'm going to have to go deeper in," I said.

Anxiously, I peered up and down the row again. Nothing and no one. Staying crouched, I ducked under the next row of trees. They, too, had been picked clean.

Finally, six rows in, I found berries that had been missed.

"No further," Oogluk declared. "Our connection is still strong, but we will not be able to help you quickly enough if you venture further. If you venture further, we will not be able to help you quickly enough."

I obeyed the creature and plucked every berry I could reach from the branches. They weren't fully ripe and tasted a bit sour. However, I wasn't going to argue with the fact that I was eating.

After I picked the first tree clean, I moved down the row until I found another tree clinging to missed fruit.

Both suns were right overhead, burning with brilliant light and heat. For a click, the terrifying thought that my world might be falling toward its suns made me pause and look around.

I had been keeping a good vigilance while picking the fruit, but were those eyes staring at me? Behind the low branches of a tree in the seventh row, two points glittered. They were the right size and distance apart for eyes. I ducked, and my heart throbbed harder.

The eyes blinked and looked away. The owner of the eyes grunted and mumbled.

"Certain you are those eyes were not orange?" Oogluk queried.

The person's mumbling grew slightly louder. It was the voice of an old woman with the accent of Prathniss.

Something big slid through the grass. The only noise it made was a slight hiss as it moved from the forest and into the orchard.

"Don't fear," Tuca said hastily. "I'm hiding as well as I can in the grass and coming out to be near you should you need to flee quickly."

I swallowed. The sound of her body scraping the grass unnerved me. I laid my left hand on my sword hilt and swallowed again. Tuning my senses to be even more highly alert, I stepped slowly around the tree I had been eating from and scanned the long grass between the rows.

Nothing moved. Behind me, Tuca paused.

I stepped into the grass. Fear and the desire to hide washed over me so strongly I dove back and lay on my stomach. Sweat trickled down my brow and hung, threatening to drip, just above my eyes.

"I can feel them," Tuca said. Her voice in my mind was filled with emotion. "They are not very far away."

I propped myself up and peered in all directions. "Who?" I asked.

"Gumbat," Tuca breathed.

"You mean the Neftim who Gen'tahn'Gen is using?" I asked.

Tuca did not respond verbally. Instead, I received a series of flaring emotions all centered around anger and betrayal. Her inner self burned and smoked like a wildfire.

"Go we should," Oogluk's fear carried through his urgent voice.

"The wretched ones must be freed whether by The Liar's death or their—"

"We cannot do that on—," Oogluk interrupted Tuca and then was interrupted by her.

"I will not pass up an opportunity to kill The Liar," Tuca fumed.

I felt some sort of resolution settle into place inside her. She scanned our surroundings, keeping up a hypervigilance. I froze. She found something—someone—else.

Tuca rushed forward to grab me. Even though she could see my thoughts and what action I intended to take, I dodged her and asked, "What is it?"

Tuca sharpened her focus, "It is Ti'Kahn."

Oogluk slid through the grass toward us. I could hear him even over the breeze rustling the leaves and the thumping drum of my heart.

I had seen eyes a few rays before. Where had they gone, and were they connected to the Ti'Kahn Tuca sensed? I plunged deeper into the orchard in the direction I had seen the eyes disappear so quickly I didn't realize I had even thought about it. Maybe I hadn't.

Tuca lunged for me, but her attempt stopped short. Oogluk howled in consternation, fear and anger.

Tuca's reprimand died as the words started crossing to my mind.

An old, weather-wrinkled woman cowered with both hands shielding her face. Her left hand held a cane, and a yellow shawl slipped from her right shoulder.

I stood perfectly still, eyes wide and mind racing.

"Run!" Oogluk's voice bellowed. "Run now."

A big shaped shifted the branches and grass behind me. Tuca stood ready to strike—semitransparent body roiling and poised.

"Don't," the woman begged. "Please don't. I mean no harm. I mean no harm." Her voice cracked, and she coughed, doubling over and leaning on her cane.

That voice. Where had I heard it before?

The woman recovered from her coughing fit. The grass at my waist shifted as Tuca slowly closed her gentle grip around me. The old woman's wrinkled cheeks smoothed out as she stared above me.

"Blessed earth," the old woman gasped and coughed as she stepped backward. She tripped, pulling her shawl from her shoulders. She would have sprawled flat on her back if Tuca hadn't reached out and caught her.

The old woman's hand tangled in her mul'li for a click as she struggled to roll to the side and stand.

"Let go of me," she coughed. "I thank you fer catching me, but I don't know what you are. Let me go."

Tuca seemed mildly entertained, but she accommodated the old woman.

"Now," the woman said, gathering her shawl into her arms as she sat in the grass, "that's no way to treat your elders. Scaring me near to death. What are you two doing?"

"Ann'Nadohn," I said quietly.

Ann'Nadohn stopped pulling at her shawl and flashed a look at me. "Your obnoxious creatures wrecked my seed shop."

I held the old woman's gaze as I replied, "Not Tuca. The gumbat must've wrecked it."

"The who?" Ann'Nadohn asked. "Oh, I don't suppose it matters much." She held up a crooked, bony finger and pointed it at me as she continued, "Now, those marauders—those people with the orange markings. Who knows where they came from. They just popped up in town and—and they drove everybody out. They didn't care about nobody. Some folks just walked out as if they were blind."

"Time for this we do not have," Oogluk said.

I stepped forward and offered my hand to the old shopkeeper.

"Oh, bless you, sweetie. At least you haven't forgot how to help an old lady."

Ann'Nadohn stretched her gnarled hand out and grabbed ahold.

"The ground is so much harder to get up from than my old rocking chair. That's not the only thing I miss already," she sighed. "Oh, well."

"Are there many more of your townsfolk hiding out here?" I asked the question Tuca voiced into my mind.

Ann'Nadohn narrowed her eyes and glanced at Tuca. "I couldn't keep up with the others," she stated flatly.

"I'm not on the Tek'ekim's side," I said, trying to sound as earnest as possible.

"What a strange way to mumble, sweetie," Ann'Nadohn said. "Is that what you call those folks that drove us out? Strangest thing it was. They showed up in the middle of town with woman and children, and most of us just got up and left. Then, those terrible creatures came and started crushing everything. They dumped my seeds and trampled my iscus. Such a shame. It was doing so well this eran."

Tuca received many more nervous glances as I tried to think of what to say. Oogluk was silent, which left me without the coach I needed.

"Our army split up," I finally said. "I think part came this way. Did you see them?"

Ann'Nadohn regarded me for several, long clicks. At last, she stamped her cane and, with a sad air, told me, "Yes, sweetie, some came through this way. They tried to get me to go with 'em. Said they were going to take back our town." She shifted so she faced Prathniss. "I wish I was certain they could take our town back, but," her voice took on a slight quaver, "after seeing what I did, I wish they would just focus on building our lives back. Let those orange folks stay. There's plenty of room for us all."

She glanced again at Tuca and jabbed with her cane, "This one seems to be trained well, but those others would have to go."

Tuca bristled behind me. She wasn't angry because Ann'Nadohn wanted to ban the creatures from the town. Instead, anger flowed freely through her emotions like a powerful undercurrent because she wanted the traitors, the gumbat, punished. She held no qualms about killing them.

"But they're your kind?" I urged her.

"They are not our kind," Tuca replied. "They forsook our Number and became gumbat. They are no longer part of us by their own choice."

"You spend an awful lot of time thinking, sweetie," Ann'Nadohn declared.

I nodded.

The old woman tapped her cane, "The townsfolk came through two periods ago. They gathered everyone else that was a'staying here with me. And, I say, they were in a huff. Like someone swatted a nest of stinging buzzes inside their heads. Even the old folks went with 'em. All except me."

Ann'Nadohn turned her gaze to the ground and turned slowly.

"Ask her whether she knows of the other group," Oogluk pressed.

"Ann'Nadohn?" I said.

The old woman stopped and wearily turned to look at me, "Yes, sweetie, what is it?" Her voice was soft and tired.

"Did you see the other group of soldiers? Most of them have white armor and MECs."

Ann'Nadohn shook her head solemnly, "No, sweetie." She forced a smile to her thin lips, "Just let me be, sweetie. I'll make a new life for myself and find some who'll help me."

Pity welled up inside me, and I said, "Don't move closer to Prathniss. Tuca says—"

"Oh, blessed earth no!" Ann'Nadohn spun so fast her shawl slipped from her shoulders and hung from her elbows. "I'm getting as far away as I can from those *creatures.*"

I had a retort on the edge of my tongue, but giant trees stood in front of me instead of the old woman. My anger flashed at Tuca, yet she made no effort to defend herself.

Oogluk rustled the underbrush at the edge of the forest and spilled into our sanctuary. "Back to the camp we must go," he said hurriedly. "We must go back to the camp."

Without waiting for me to confer with them, the two creatures grabbed ahold of each other. Tuca still grasped me, and we teleported to the old camp and landed facing the other trampled path.

I pushed my anger aside and prepared to be placed back on the ground to lead the way. However, Tuca, holding tightly to both Oogluk and me, plunged us down the path with a short teleporting jump. I barely had time to decipher our new surroundings before she teleported us again. We flew down the path, teleporting to the next farthest point we could see. I didn't have to supply any energy for the jumps, but it was still a nauseating experience.

Oogluk restrained his comments, but his apprehension grew, as did mine. We were recklessly teleporting into territory where we could be shot easily by guards wielding MECs. If a soldier saw us make two or three hops, he would have no problem seeing our pattern and, for all intents and purposes, ambushing us with a barrage of deadly bolts.

"Tuca." I tried to get the creature's attention. "Tuca!" I tried again.

Oogluk said, "She will not listen to you any more than she will listen to me. Than she will listen to me, she will not listen more to you."

"We have to stop this," I responded. "We'll be shot for sure, and I'm not as bolt-proof as the two of you."

Oogluk paused and then responded, "She wants to deliver you as quickly as possible. As quickly as possible, she wants to deliver you. Then, disappear, we desire. We desire to disappear. Back to the Number we intend to return."

I thought of my friends who were still with the Neftim. I did long to be with them. If only the war with the Tek'ekim had already been won.

The forest suddenly thinned and gave way to an enormous pile of scree. Tuca paused long enough for me to look up and up and up. The spire rose above us, dwarfing us like a dungle next to a house. A few dragons floated lazily on the updrafts of warm air. A flock of turits sang to one another as they circled the spire like a pylon.

On the ground, a row of white boulders moved— but they moved up the hill of loose stone.

"Oogluk!" I shouted into the two minds connected to mine.

"I cannot help," Oogluk growled and poised to spring an attack.

The white clad soldiers raised their MECs to their shoulders as Tuca saw what I showed her. She scrambled for focus on a point far above the jumbled scree.

"Call your creatures off," one of the soldiers snapped.

At that click, Tuca teleported us to the sheer side of the spire. Oogluk leapt. He would have plowed into the soldiers had we been standing where we had the click before. As it was, he leapt over vast nothingness and fell several feet before catching himself with his wings. An emotion, I guessed was embarrassment, washed through our connected minds, and he nonchalantly flew back and grabbed onto the spire a few feet to Tuca's right.

I scanned the ground three hundred feet below. The soldiers turned this way and that until one looked up and pointed. I braced myself.

"Only if they start shooting," Tuca murmured.

Oogluk studied the ground all around the spire. "Suppose we found them, and they do not want us either?" he asked worriedly.

If they were going to try to drive us off too...well, I didn't know what we'd do. Maybe we'd pick up Airitha, Darvian and the others and move to Grael. Would they even allow us to stay? Was there another world? Was it inhabited by another race of Ti'Kahn who didn't want outsiders? I sighed.

"Not so bad would it be if we Neftim had not been duped into their service," Oogluk commented.

"No," I returned absently. "But it's not your fault. I was tricked by them, as well."

"Yes, Friend Jax, but you have resisted every chance you had your mind to yourself," the creature countered.

I paused, wishing I had the time it used to take for him to say the same thing backward to think of a fresh argument.

"Being with Tuca has granted me much healing," Oogluk said.

"I don't know, Oogluk," I said. "They're probably controlled the whole time. You didn't experience it, but Ronthluque—"

"Speak not his name," Oogluk and Tuca snapped in unison.

"He knew how many of your kind died needlessly," I finished in a murmur.

"They're beckoning us to go down," Tuca observed.

I looked down at the soldiers. They waved, curling their hands back toward themselves, in a gesture to come to them.

Oogluk voiced his opposition to their wishes, "What if it is a trap?"

When Tuca didn't say anything, I said, "Lower me down. Maybe I can talk to them and see what's going on."

"Very well," Tuca said as she stretched her body into a thin rope, which allowed me to rappel down the spire.

I kept a close eye on the soldiers, but they never raised or even moved their MECs from where they hung in front of their chests.

When I was ten feet from the ground, the shortest soldier stepped forward, removed her helmet and helped me land softly on the jumbled scree. I kept ahold of Tuca and peered up at the soldiers, waiting for them to speak first.

"You're that boy, Jax, right?" the female soldier asked.

I nodded.

"Sir," the four soldiers saluted me with a hand thumping their chests. "It's an honor, sir."

"What about Thaydrin and his men?" I asked hesitantly.

The soldier standing directly in front of me stepped closer and pulled off his helmet. Holding a steadying hand on his MEC he motioned for the others to back off. They took up positions that allowed them to scan outward from the spire in all directions. Then, the soldier reached into a small compartment on the left upper arm of his armor.

He knelt and set a small, black device on top of his helmet and thumbed it on. The air between us lit up in a display like a diorama. Every little hill and tree showed up in the projection. Closest to me, the spire towered over the map.

The man pointed toward the base of the spire. By matching up the image with the real thing, I could see the place he pointed to was on the opposite side of the spire. "You'll find Thaydrin, Jamoal and Sterran here," he explained. "They relocated us further away after that attack this morning. You'll want to be careful walking in there with those creatures," he glanced warily up to where Oogluk clung to the rock face. "We aren't good at telling

317

them apart—which ones are on our side and the ones that would kill us."

"I think the other group went to attack the Tek'ekim in Prathniss," I said.

"Right, sir," the soldier said. He dropped his voice to a rueful murmur, "We don't expect any of them to return. I just hope we don't have to face any of them on the battlefield."

I swallowed and sought the Neftims' advice.

"Find Thaydrin," Oogluk said simply.

"We cannot stay and fight," Tuca observed, "but you made a promise to Airitha."

"She wants us to bring her Ahdah back and the others, so," the words caught. I had to force them out rapidly to finish, "So they can leave."

"We're happy to have you back with us, sir. Thaydrin will be happy as well," the soldier said and saluted before stowing the map projector.

Chapter 29

"I can't abandon my men," Thaydrin said firmly as he turned and clasped his hands behind him. "I will not ask my men to leave without setting the wrongs right that we have been a part of."

Jamoal cocked his head and stared at the Teluthian leader for a few clicks. Ahdah watched him and waited silently.

"The way I see it," Jamoal finally said, "these Tek'ekim were afta Jax 'ere an' his...his creatures."

Thaydrin turned to look at the worn and battered Coalition man. Their eyes met in a grim gaze before Thaydrin spoke, "A new era begins whether we have chosen it or not. As such, our actions at the onset determine the attitude of this new era. I will not follow the path that allows petty technicalities to drive a wedge between us."

Jamoal saluted in the Teluthian fashion, "I thank ya greatly, sir. With words like that, it'll be a era o' honor for certain."

Thaydrin placed a thin hand on Jamoal's bulky shoulder.

Ahdah strode forward, holding a longsword from slapping his leg. He glanced at me with grim appraisal. I looked down, feeling ashamed of how I had begged him not to fight.

Oogluk and Tuca stood warily at the base of the spire. Only a small mound of scree had built up at that part of the spire, and the trees reached branches out that nearly touched the stone. Their conversation was a constant, dull buzz in the distant part of my mind.

Ahdah addressed Thaydrin and Jamoal, "We have discussed the plan, and we see the necessity of separating the Tek'ekim from the Neftim they have fighting on their side."

Jamoal shot a glance at Oogluk and Tuca, but, otherwise, he remained placid.

Thaydrin nodded, "That will not be easy to do. What about the garrison you mentioned, Sterran?"

Ahdah shook his head, "They will not send more than fifty troops. Word already reached them, and they seem uncertain which path to choose: whether it would be more prudent to keep their soldiers back to provide defense if it comes to it versus a frontal assault."

I thought immediately of how most of the townsfolk had turned against my friends and tried to make an example of them.

"Jax," Thaydrin involved me in the conversation, "what would you propose?"

I stared openmouthed for a click. Then, I answered, "I think most of the Neftim don't know they're being controlled. If they knew, they wouldn't fight for the Tek'ekim."

Oogluk nodded in my mind.

"I met one of the people who fled from Prathniss when they first showed up," I said, fingering my sword hilt and trying to organize my jumbled thoughts. "She said they have women and children with them."

All three men nodded and closed their eyes in understanding.

Jamoal spoke quietly, "It's not like a 'ntenti'nal raiding party. 'at makes it more diff'cult."

Ahdah cleared his throat, "That makes open war something to be avoided."

Jamoal nodded and continued to study the ground.

"The questions we must ask ourselves," Thaydrin paused.

Vauriel rushed up to me and asked in a completely unmeasured voice, "Jax, have you seen Kelita? I can't find her anywhere."

I took a step back from the frantic woman. She looked the exact opposite of her usual calm and collected self. "She's with the others back at the starship."

"Oh, that girl," Kelita's Omoah closed her eyes and sagged with relief. Ahdah reached around her shoulders and helped her to a large rock. She flashed him a thankful smile and sat, resting her weight on her elbows on top of her knees.

Once Vauriel looked settled enough to participate, Thaydrin smiled and began again, "Thank you for joining us. We see the need to separate the Tek'ekim from the Neftim, and we also recognize that open war should be avoided at all costs.

"They have women and children with them," Thaydrin continued. "We suspected it and had many reports from the refugees and soldiers, but Jax has confirmed it.

"Thus, the questions we must ask ourselves are: How do we separate the enemy from those Neftim who would be friendly? How do we convince them of their plight? And, lastly, how do we overcome our enemy in a way that does not create a genocide? We do not know whether they are attempting to colonize other worlds at this time. Those out there," he motioned vaguely in the direction of Prathniss, "are very likely the only people surviving the destruction of their world."

"Jax?" Ahdah turned to me.

Why did he expect me to answer their questions? They were far too heavy for me to decide alone. Besides, I wished to avoid it all and have Tuca return Oogluk and me to my friends.

As if reading my thoughts, Ahdah stepped to my side and put an arm around my shoulders. He gave me his full attention, "I do not mean to bring you needless pain, so answer if you can and wish to. What was it like being with the Tek'ekim? Were you aware of what was going on and how they were using you?"

Jamoal and Thaydrin both looked at us curiously while Vauriel propped her chin on her hand as she crossed her legs. I glanced at her, hoping to see words forming on her lips, but she stared at nothing with her mouth in a straight line.

"I think I've already said I couldn't tell," I finally said.

Ahdah closed his eyes and then addressed the others, "This is one of my greatest concerns. We can outfight them in a battle waged with physical weapons." He studied each of the others for effect. "But how do we wage a war none of us are equipped to fight?"

His question caught me off guard. I didn't think he would give up so easily. But then, he *had* been bludgeoned by the Tek'ekim, and Kelita and I had been forced into their service. I reached out to Oogluk for an explanation.

The Neftim hummed to himself, and countless streams of thoughts whipped through his mind like hundreds of people muttering all at once. Nothing formed an intelligible response, however.

Tuca, who of course overheard, scoffed, "Leave the gumbat."

"What about A'lii?" I asked Oogluk.

"She is powerful in her mind. In her mind, powerful," he affirmed.

"Do you think she could convince the Neft—the gumbat," I quickly changed the term to keep from further angering Tuca, "to abandon the Tek'ekim?"

"Perhaps. Perhaps," Oogluk murmured as he gave the impression of stroking his chin.

I cleared my throat, settled my hands at my sides and said, "What about A'lii, my sister? She has a strong mind."

All of the leaders frowned. Jamoal crossed his arms and tilted his head slightly, "Ya woul'n't be tryin' ta jus' git revenge on yer sista, would ya?"

I wanted to growl and shout that I was a man and no longer played such petty games, but I settled on a silent glare.

The big man laughed and rested his forearms on his sword hilt, "Forgive me, young frien'."

"What do you mean?" Ahdah asked. "I don't think I've heard yet what happened to her."

"She stopped Ronthluque from killing Oogluk with her mind," I explained.

"Tell me the whole story," Ahdah commanded. A look of uncertainty clouded his face.

I didn't look at any of them as I told the story, "Ronthluque wanted to use the dropship against the Tek'ekim. I tried to tell him the reasons why it was a bad idea, but he wouldn't listen. Oogluk objected as well, and

Ronthluque circled him, preparing to attack. He would have attacked Oogluk then and there except A'lii leapt in between them and held them back from one another with her mind. Oogluk says she's really strong."

"But how did she end up injured?" Ahdah asked gently.

I glanced at Ahdah and then looked down as I remembered how A'lii had pleaded with me to help. "I think she got too tired," I said. "She could teleport with Oogluk, too, but he can't teleport anymore."

Ahdah studied me, and the others looked deep in thought.

Jamoal broke the silence, "I'm not sure I undastand all 'is talk o' teleporting and 'ese creatures."

"Nor do I," Thaydrin stated.

"How is all this going to help us against the invaders?" Vauriel asked the question it seemed everyone was silently asking themselves.

"We have to separate the Tek'ekim from the Neftim, if at all possible," Ahdah offered. "They're too strong fighting together."

Thaydrin nodded and glanced at each of us. "With them separated, we stand a much better chance at a bloodless victory. As Sterran has so adroitly pointed out, this war needs to be fought differently if we are to have hope of establishing the outcome we desire."

A long, thoughtful silence ensued.

Oogluk commented, "Complicated is this dilemma." Then, he grew confused, "I do not think I have heard the outcome they desire. Heard the desired outcome, I think I have not."

"It sounds like they want as little killing as possible," I offered.

The creature hummed to himself and ran numerous thoughts through his mind. I turned my attention back to Thaydrin and the others.

"Why these rotten wars?" Kelita's Omoah bit a fingernail. "First, your world; now, ours."

Thaydrin responded to her rhetorical question, "We don't have the answer to that at this time. However, you touch on the importance of ending this conflict as quickly as possible."

"We can't jus' wipe 'em out," Jamoal said, thoughtfully stroking his chy'li.

"No," Ahdah said. "We can't kill them all. That's another reason we can't use the starship."

"Can't they go somewhere else?" Vauriel looked teary-eyed. She bit another nail and then folded her hands firmly in her lap.

"And who would she suggest find the new world for them?" Oogluk asked.

"She doesn't know how hard that would be. Another world most likely means another race with another ability," Tuca chided.

"We can't do that," I blurted aloud.

The adults looked at me. Questions burned in their eyes.

"I know we'd have to find another world first of all," Ahdah prompted me to explain.

"Every world we know of so far had someone living on it already," I said quietly. "We'd probably find people with a more dangerous ability."

"More dang'rous than controllin' ya?" Jamoal scoffed quietly enough I shouldn't have been able to hear him.

Ahdah nodded his head and grasped his chin. Thaydrin frowned thoughtfully.

"Once we found another world," I finished my argument, "could we force them to accept the Tek'ekim? Wouldn't that be doing the same thing the Tek'ekim are doing to us right now?"

Kelita's Omoah said, "I agree with Jax. Look what other worlds and their inhabitants have already done." She shot a glance at Thaydrin, "No offense intended, of course. You and your people seem nice enough."

Realization flooded into me at the same time Oogluk grasped the meaning of our discussion. "Kill them all. That cannot be done," he mused. "Send them to a new world of their own is too dangerous—and would not be their own."

Thaydrin reiterated his deductions, "It is clear our task is not to wipe them out. Nor is it to relocate them to a distant, new world. The only option open to us is to discover how to allow them to live among us."

Jamoal raised his eyebrows, clearly considering the implications. He shifted his weight to one leg and rested his hands on the pommel of his sword. "It's peace. 'ats our on'y option."

Ahdah stared toward Prathniss, "How do you work out peace with someone who doesn't need to listen?"

"No," Vauriel shook her head. Her voice caught, "Not after what they did to my daughter and your son, Sterran."

Thaydrin clasped his hands behind his back, "I am not opposed to hearing other ideas." He lowered his piercing gaze, "But I think that all see the only viable option left to us."

I wanted to shout that we'd figure something else out. However, I remained silent outwardly while waging war against the idea in my mind with the help of the Neftim.

"What of the gumbat?" Tuca shot. "If the Tek'ekim are allowed to live, your people will have gumbat of their own."

"Trusted they cannot possibly be," Oogluk spluttered for words. "They are—sinister. Intend to use your people as they use the Neftim. That is their only intent. Their only intent that is. The answer death is not, but restrained such a danger must be."

"Would the Neftim teleport a bunch of smaller things together like moons and such to make a new planet for them?" I asked.

Tuca objected, "Too many would die."

"How to keep it from burning?" Oogluk added.

I could hear what Kelita would say in my mind. "They destroyed their own world. They aren't our problem. Let them deal with it themselves."

I shook my head, "No, they're here now, and we need to do what's best for everyone involved."

Ahdah looked at me with a curious expression. I couldn't tell whether he was appraising me as he considered what the Tek'ekim had done or whether he was inviting me to add to the discussion.

"Tell them of the gumbat," Tuca encouraged.

"I don't think they can be trusted," I said aloud. "Oogluk and Tuca both believe they would control some of our people, and I agree with them."

Kelita's Omoah snapped her distant, stony stare at me. Her eyes took a click to focus. "Don't let them have Kelita again," she breathed.

"The impossible, they will attempt, I think," Oogluk said. "Come, Friend Jax, there is no part for us to play here. A part for us to play here, there is not."

Tuca agreed with him, "Our Number will not allow ourselves to be within the reach of their control."

I felt obligated to relay their messages, "Oogluk and Tuca both say that they and the other Neftim do not offer their help for a plan that puts them close enough for the Tek'ekim to control them."

Thaydrin glanced at each person standing next to him. "We understand," he said slowly. "Please let them know that we welcome and we invite any help they are willing to give freely. It is completely their own choice."

I nodded as Jamoal objected, "'ese creatures is pow'rful allies on da battlefield."

Ahdah clapped a hand on the big man's shoulder, "We hope there won't be a battlefield."

"I been understandin' 'at," Jamoal acknowledged. "'owever, we got ta be thinkin' what if it don't wark?"

Ahdah opened his mouth to reply, but Thaydrin, staring at Jamoal, spoke first, "I think you're right. It would be foolish to place everything in a single, long shot that could fail."

Jamoal nodded and said slowly, "I don't get no joy from bein' pragmatic-like."

Thaydrin set up the map projector again, "Sterran, will you show us a defensible position between Prathniss and our current location?" He turned to the Coalition man, "Jamoal, will you run through every possible entry point for a small, diplomatic party that may need to flee quickly? Also, run through all the points that would be weakest for an attack—only if it comes to that."

I turned to walk back to Oogluk and Tuca.

"Jax?" Ahdah asked.

I faced him. A question was written on his face.

"My place is with my friends and the Neftim," I said quietly.

Ahdah ducked his head and walked toward me. He hugged me briefly but firmly, "I respect that. Keep them safe." He clasped his hand on the back of my neck, and we exchanged an understanding look.

“Yes, sir,” I said.

Ahdah nodded and flicked his eyes to the ground before taking one last look deep into my own golden eyes.

Chapter 30

"But they are sincere with their motives," I argued with Oogluk.

"Argue with you about that, I do not," the semitransparent creature replied mildly.

The dropship gleamed below us in the afternoon sunlight. My head tails floated out behind me in the wind from our momentum. Oogluk flapped his dragon-shaped wings and gave a very authentic dragon-like shake of his head as we flew over the cliff's edge and peered down at the Neftim exploring the stream at its bottom.

"What are the Neftim planning on doing?" I changed the subject. "They won't be allowed to stay here unless people change their minds."

"A star must continue to shine even when it has no planet to shine its light on," Oogluk replied.

"Does that mean you'll leave with them?"

A long silence passed. I turned my gaze to the distant clouds. Their puffy whiteness glowed surreal, like it couldn't actually exist.

"I do not hold much hope for the success of your people. Much hope for your people, I do not hold," Oogluk intoned softly.

A flock of turits whispered by below us.

"What else can they do? You heard the discussion."

"I believe your people would say that the grogul does not walk into the trap it sees but the nykor sees the trap and keeps going," Oogluk's thought formed in my mind.

I smiled despite the gloom bouncing around inside me like a buzz inside a jar, "Did you make that up? We don't have any sayings like that."

Oogluk gave the sensation of laughing, "Yes, Friend Jax." He grew serious, "Is it not true, though, that a foolish animal continues into the trap even after it is known? Even after it is known, continue into the trap, does not a foolish animal?"

I nodded. He was right.

"Maybe there's too many of them for the Tek'ekim to control all at once. That's why so many were able to keep fighting like Jamoal," I said hopefully.

"Perhaps," Oogluk said.

We flew for several more rays. It was peaceful, and the gentle motion helped me think. It wasn't like being able to sit weightless in space and stare at the stars, but it was good to get away from the others for a bit.

Oogluk glided over the cliff and angled for a treeless jumble of rock beside the dropship. My family and our friends sat at the base of the rocks eating what Omoah, Rithol and Rurin had foraged. They could barely choke down the food in the dropship, which was considerably worse than the food Airitha had given me when we'd first met.

My sister looked to be in a deep conversation with Hahn'Nik'Nik while Rurin and Kammiel leapt from rock to rock, chasing one another. As Oogluk spread his wings for the final slowing of momentum in our landing, Rithol pushed himself up from the boulder he leaned against and strode toward the small cluster of Teluthian soldiers left behind to guard the ship.

"Oogluk," a worry suddenly leapt into my mind, "will the Neftim help the Teluthians get home?"

"I think they are not so hardened as to turn their backs on the ones who helped them," he replied with a sad thoughtfulness that made his words form slowly.

Rurin saw us and started clambering up the rocks. Kammiel called after him to wait, but he didn't even look back as he yelled for her to hurry up.

Airitha shaded her eyes to peer up at Oogluk and me. I kept scanning the little group until I found Kelita. She was huddled against a rock by herself. What was wrong and what had happened to make her change her mind about Airitha? They had finally gotten along when we escaped the imploding world the Tek'ekim had called home. And then, she had instigated a riot that had divided our people from the foreigners.

"Friend Jax," Oogluk said as if he were trying not to disrupt me, "friend Kelita is hurting inside."

"She doesn't seem to want me around," I stated.

"A great war inside, she has. She has a great war inside." Oogluk picked his first two steps down the pile of boulders and continued, "The war she has is not one you have had to face, I think."

I thought about all the times Oogluk, when he had been Tranto, had told me I had wars raging inside me. How many wars could a person have inside him in a lifetime?

Oogluk left my question unanswered. It was rhetorical after all.

Rurin made it to me and asked, "Can I ride with you next time?"

"Rurin," I grumbled, but he wasn't listening to me. Ever since he'd overheard that A'lii and Ahdah had been able to do, he had insisted that he could connect with Oogluk as well. Oogluk had assured me that he did not let him connect. The slight offering of that privacy did not go unappreciated by me and constantly challenged by my brother.

Rithol saw me making my way toward our little group and pulled himself away from the soldiers. He met me at the last boulder of my descent so that I stood slightly taller than him.

He looked up, shading his eyes, "Well, Little Brother, can we talk with you for a ray?" He motioned to Omoah and A'lii.

"What about?" I asked before hopping down.

"We think it'd be best to return home," Rithol said loud enough for the two women to hear.

A'lii looked at her husband and smiled.

"Back to the farm?" I asked.

Rithol nodded, and Omoah stopped beside me as my sister reached around Rithol's waist. He copied her, and they looked at each other as if they were about to kiss.

"The dragons need to be seen to," Omoah described the situation. "And the food they have here is not fit to eat. It's no wonder that poor girl, Airitha, is so thin."

Rithol picked up where Omoah left off, "Would those creatures," he waved a hand toward the cliff, "the Neftim, or whatever you call 'em, be willing to help us out?"

My sister laid her head on Rithol's chest. I wanted her to stay. Even though jealousy made me wish she had never been able to connect with the Neftim, the capabilities of her strong mind could be useful.

"I thought you wanted to stay and fight?" I tried to convince Rithol and A'lii to stay.

Rithol glanced at the soldiers. "My place is with my wife. Besides, I'm not needed with the soldiers." he turned to look down at A'lii who smiled up at him. "It sounds like there won't be any fighting based on what they were talking about last I knew."

Omoah nodded. She had nearly melted into a puddle of relief when I shared the army's decision.

Rurin yelled from right behind me. The next click, he slammed into my back. His arms wrapped around my neck, pinching my head tails. I staggered back, trying to regain my balance, but my instincts took over as adrenaline shot through my veins. I no longer heard my little brother's playful war cries. I changed tactics and used my unbalanced momentum to throw my attacker into the rocks behind me. My attacker's arms loosened. I doubled over, and he slid off my back, thudding to the dust in front of me.

"Get off him," someone cried as I planted my knee on my attacker's chest and drew my hand back to punch him.

A strong arm pulled me backward.

"Stop it," Rithol called into my ear. "He's not trying to hurt you. We're safe."

Without thinking, I bent my neck and prepared to drive it back into the face of the one restraining me. That's as far as I made, though, because at that click, two presences called out to me in my mind.

"Jax, stop. He's your brother," my sister's voice sounded like a thunderclap in my mind.

The arms restraining me slackened slightly, and the dark edges of my vision began to fade.

Rurin lay on the ground moaning. Omoah bent over him feeling his ribs.

"Darvian," Rithol called from behind me.

A quick movement drew my attention to the younger boy and his sister hurrying toward us.

"Friend Jax, alright—"

"No, I'm not alright," I cut Oogluk's query short. I stared at my little brother. I had hurt him. It was nearly just like the time I had pushed him down when we ran away from a wild dragon. He had been severely burned then. Hadn't he died?

"That is not truth," Oogluk growled into my mind. "Friend Jax, you saved your brother from a dragon in your Ahdah's barn. In your Ahdah's barn—"

"I'm fine," I ground out audibly.

Rithol's strong arms slowly released me. I hung my head as Darvian healed Rurin's ribs I had cracked. My little brother had only been trying to play with me.

Rithol bent down and helped Rurin to his feet when Darvian sat back and said he'd finished. "I think you need to play different games with your brother," Rithol chided.

Rurin looked at me with questions pooled in his wide eyes. I tried to look him in the eyes, but I couldn't hold his innocent gaze.

"I'm okay, Jax," Rurin exclaimed and raced at me. Rithol tried to catch him but missed. Rurin plowed into me and said, "I'm not hurt anymore. Darvi healed me. I'm not mad at you." Rurin squeezed my waist as tightly as his little arms could manage.

"I'm sorry, Rurin," I said weakly.

"It's okay," Rurin grinned at me. "I not jumping on you back again."

He tugged me back to our group. I kept my eyes down.

Omoah tsked and hugged me, "It's not your fault."

But it was my fault. I hadn't seen my little brother's game, and I would have killed him.

"You've been through a lot," Rithol said softly. "I don't know how anyone could go through all that and not be changed."

Kelita stood on the edge of our group, looking at me. A curious tilt to her head was incongruous with the blankness of her face.

Airitha, Hahn'Nik'Nik and Kammiel stood behind her. Kammiel lifted Nik'Nik's hand, playing with her orange marked fingers. Airitha looked on with a look of understanding.

Hahn'Nik'Nik suddenly rushed forward. "It's not his fault," she cried. "My people tormented him and made him think lies were true. I'm sorry. I'm so sorry."

I had never told her about the hallucinations or the lies the Tek'ekim had convinced me of. I gawked at her as she continued to apologize and work herself into hysterics. Airitha tried to calm her, but she refused to calm until my sister smoothed her hand over the orange markings on her forehead and then hugged her. Hahn'Nik'Nik sobbed twice and fell silent.

"She'll be alright," my sister said calmly. "She's really worried about her kids."

“We need to attack the Tek’ekim,” Kelita announced abruptly.

We all turned to look at her.

Chapter 31

"Goodness! No!" Omoah exclaimed in response to Kelita's proclamation. She reached for Rurin and hugged him to her where she still knelt on ground.

Kelita shot a brief look at me. Her eyes sparked and flashed.

"Jax, just told us we're going to try to talk with them," Darvian stared with confusion parting his mouth and bunching his brows together.

"We all know they won't get anywhere," Kelita retorted. "They can't be reasoned with."

I found myself objecting, "But we can't just walk in there and kill them all."

"Somebody's gotta do something," Kelita said as she lifted her hands in a shrug. "We're just sitting around."

I opened my mouth to attempt further reasoning with Kelita, but Oogluk cut me short. "She will refuse to see things differently. To see things differently, she will refuse," he said.

"I want to go bring Kerelyn back home," Kelita's gaze hardened when I made no response. "Nothing should have happened to her. She deserves to be home."

"Take her, I think Tuca will not," Oogluk observed.

I stared at my friend. My mind did crazy somersaults as it tried to figure out where the real Kelita had gone and who had planted the imposter. Maybe that time when she fell from her dragon had been real. Maybe the girl in front of me was nothing more than a look-alike that my mind tricked me into thinking was Kelita.

"What am I supposed to do?" I asked Oogluk.

Tuca responded for him, "None of our Number will take her."

"What if I went to get her dragon for her? Would you take me?"

Silence answered me.

"Kerelyn can't live on Teluthia," I prodded.

"What would she do with such a beast?" Tuca asked with a menacing growl creeping into her voice.

The absolute truth was that I didn't know. The old Kelita would have been able to be reasoned with, but the new Kelita, standing in front of me, gave every impression of making erratic decisions leading to wild and dangerous actions.

"When this is settled, we will help you retrieve her dragon," Oogluk said with finality when Tuca refused to answer further.

Part of me was glad that Kelita was talking with me again, but the bigger part of me was scared and apprehensive about telling her what the Neftim had said.

"Kelita," I swallowed, "they won't bring Kerelyn back until this is all settled."

Kelita slammed her hands onto her hips and glared, "She's my dragon. She can't live on Teluthia forever. You're a bunch of stinking dragon dung."

"Kelita!" Omoah chided sharply.

Kelita's face went wide and blank and then wadded up just before she turned and ran toward the nearest pocket of scraggly trees.

I followed her with my gaze, wishing I knew what to say.

"I think it best to let her go. To let her go, I think it best," Oogluk stated.

Kelita rounded the first tree, stopped and flopped onto the ground with her back against the trunk.

Kammiel tugged on Hahn'Nik'Nik's hand, but the Tek'ekim woman shook her head and whispered something to the little girl. Kammiel looked hurt for a moment, but then she went to Airitha and tugged on her hand. Airitha gave me a pleading glance before letting Kammiel tow her toward Kelita. A'lii started to go along with them but seemed to think better of it and stopped.

Kammiel flopped to the ground next to Kelita who shifted to put her back to the young girl. Airitha reached out a hand toward Kelita. It was then that I realized Kelita's shoulders shook with sobs. Kelita didn't flinch or scoot away as Airitha rubbed her shoulder. Airitha's mouth moved, but I couldn't hear what she said.

Rithol addressed me, "Well, Little Brother, what do you think about getting us home? Will these creatures help us?"

I nodded slowly, "I'm sure they will."

Tuca confirmed they would.

"I want to stay here with the others," I told her.

"Very well, our Number will care for your family," Tuca replied. "I will allow your sister to connect with me to show me the way."

"A'lii," I called, "Tuca says she will help you get our family home."

My sister glanced between the semitransparent Neftim and me. She nodded and reached for Rithol's hand.

"Jax, sweetie," Omoah said, "won't you come home with us?"

I shook my head, "I'll stay here with Oogluk and the others."

"There's plenty of room for all of us at home," she pressed lightly.

Meisha motioned toward the Teluthian soldiers and said sweetly, "I think it best that we stay here. We'll probably be needed again, and we'll be able to hear news quicker here."

Omoah acknowledged her reasoning and clutched at Rurin.

My little brother squirmed and dodged away. "I want to stay too," he said.

Rithol caught him and flung him over his shoulder.

"Put me down," Rurin cried.

Rithol laughed, "Once we're on your farm, I'll drop you in the watering trough."

Rurin objected loudly, but his pleas were not heeded.

Two strangely shaped Neftim landed next to Tuca and Oogluk. My family started walking toward them.

"Wait, A'lii," I ran to my sister's side.

"Miss me already?" she smirked.

"How did you stop Oogluk and Ronthluque when they were fighting?"

"I thought you already knew," she said in genuine surprise.

"I've never tried to do that," I responded.

Had Oogluk been Ti'Kahn he would have clicked his tongue before he said, "Remember when you forced me to teleport?"

My sister explained, "I pushed on both of their wills—found what they wanted to do most and pushed against it. I'm not really sure what I did, but it worked until I got too tired."

"Do you think you could do it again if we needed you to?" I asked. I didn't have a plan, but it was best to be prepared, right?

A'lii narrowed her eyes, "What are you wanting me to do? I'm not going to get you out of trouble at school, so don't even ask."

We stopped in front of Hahn'Nik'Nik, and she eyed us curiously. "That's essentially what we do," she said quietly.

"What?" my sister turned to her.

Hahn'Nik'Nik looked down, "I said that's what my people do. We push on what people want to do and make them do the things we want them to do."

My sister wrinkled her nose, "I just wanted them to stop fighting."

Hahn'Nik'Nik nodded, "We aren't so noble, but you sound like you have our ability."

Airitha walked up then. "Why is she so selfish," she grumbled so quietly she probably thought no one could hear her.

I glanced at her then at Kelita, who had shifted her position to stand beside the tree instead of leaning against it. Kammiel skipped toward Rurin and Omoah.

"She can't be more disagreeable than my little brother," A'lii teased.

"Well, you and I both agree about Rurin, then," I quipped. No sooner had the words left my mouth than I felt awful for saying them. "I guess he's not that bad. I guess he's not a bother." I smiled wanly at Airitha.

She looked like she had something else on her mind entirely. We all waited silently. Finally, she spoke, "We need to stop Ahdah from trying to talk peace with the Tek'ekim."

"What?" I asked, uncertain I had just heard her correctly. Had Kelita convinced her to attack them?

"Ahdah and the others don't have a chance against them, do they?" Airitha frowned. "I mean, they'll just be controlled, won't they? I think we're the only ones who can defeat them. We have you," she looked at me, "and your sister. We also have one of them who says she will help us."

Hahn'Nik'Nik nodded slowly.

Airitha continued, "Can we get into Prathniss, capture Gen'tahn'Gen and then throw him out into space...along with Kelita?"

A'lii stifled a laugh, and I seriously considered her proposal.

"I don't think either of them would appreciate the other's company," A'lii said with only a hint of a giggle in her voice.

Airitha implored me with her deep, purple eyes, "Jax, will it be enough to get rid of Gen'tahn?"

I felt Oogluk's mind running through various scenarios and possible outcomes so quickly I didn't try to follow them. My own mind ran only one question over and over: Why is she asking me?

"How would we get close enough to him?" I finally asked.

"I don't know all that," Airitha scrunched her nose. "But couldn't a few of us get close enough with the Neftims' help? You and A'lii can shield us from their ability."

My head tilted subconsciously as I thought about it.

Oogluk objected to the plan, "Too close it brings us. It brings us too close to their control. Capture us like they did before, I think they will. I think they will capture us."

"But she has a point," I replied. "Can my sister and I shield us from their ability? Maybe Hahn'Nik'Nik can help us too."

"What are you and Oogluk discussing?" Airitha demanded.

I didn't answer her question. Instead, I addressed Hahn'Nik'Nik, "Try to control me with your ability, and I'll see if I can stop you."

Hahn'Nik'Nik looked at me aghast. She shook her head, "No, I won't do that."

A'lii caught on and said, "Just make him give you a hug or something like that. Or can you make him say he's sorry for ruining my marriage ceremony?"

Hahn'Nik'Nik ducked her head. I tensed as Oogluk stiffened and narrowed his focus.

"Okay," Hahn'Nik'Nik said softly. "Ready?"

I nodded. Hahn'Nik'Nik's presence was barely perceptible, but I felt it. I had a sudden urge to give my sister a hug and apologize to her. I pushed against it. The urge strengthened. I turned to my sister.

"Friend Jax!" Oogluk snapped.

Hahn'Nik'Nik's presence faltered momentarily. The next click, Oogluk joined his strength with mine, and, together, we pushed against her will.

The orange woman suddenly flattened on the rock she was sitting on as if a dragon had smashed its tail into her chest and knocked her backward. She gasped and gave a small whimper.

Her presence disappeared completely. I stared at Hahn'Nik'Nik as Airitha helped her sit back up. She rubbed her temples and shook like she was shivering with cold. My mouth hung open and my eyes felt like the huge eyes of a buzz.

"That was," Hahn'Nik'Nik struggled to speak. "That was not fun. As soon as—as your Neftim joined you, I was thrown out of your mind. I couldn't make you do anything."

"What were you trying to make him do?" A'lii asked.

"Apologize to you," Hahn'Nik'Nik smiled thinly. "It almost feels like a piece of me got torn out."

My sister raised her eyebrows, and I said, "I really am sorry. I didn't mean to be gone so long. I thought we'd be back before anyone noticed we were even missing."

She rolled her eyes and asked Hahn'Nik'Nik, "Do you think we could do what Airitha suggests?"

"There's a lot more than just one of my people who'll try to control you," she answered.

"You alright, Jax?" Meisha asked as she and her brother approached.

"Yeah," I didn't completely lie. The fear was not crippling, and I could tell which flashbacks were fake and which were real. That's what I told myself anyway.

"Can all the Neftim push back like you can?" I asked Oogluk.

"I do not know," he responded.

A'lii asked, "How many do you think we'd be up against?"

Hahn'Nik'Nik frowned and opened her mouth, but then she shut it and shook her head.

"They'll be trained to protect Gen'tahn'Gen," I said, remembering the guards he had clustered around him.

"What about you two?" Hahn'Nik'Nik studied Darvian and Meisha.

"We can heal people," Darvian said hesitantly.

Meisha thought for a click and added, "Maybe we can help strengthen someone's mind by healing them as they get tired."

"Should we try it?" A'lii asked.

"Oogluk says not to," I told the group.

My sister rolled her eyes, "But what if it helps us? Try it on me," she told Nik'Nik.

"I'm ready," Meisha stated as she reached up and anchored her hands on my sister's temples.

"Okay, I'll start easy."

My sister visibly strained against Hahn'Nik'Nik. She twitched and scowled, but a few clicks later she straightened, and the tight expression on her face softened.

Hahn'Nik'Nik ended her coercion.

A'lii grinned, "That definitely helped."

Meisha smiled shyly and blushed, which turned her green markings darker until they were almost dark gray.

I hadn't been aware of Rithol watching, but he stepped forward and took my sister's hand. "Well, how am I to know you won't make me walk barefoot through thorns if you're mad at me?"

A'lii caressed Rithol's cheek with her hand and shrugged as she said innocently, "You'd never know I was mad at you, and I would tell you that you were sleepwalking."

"I don't sleepwalk," he retorted.

"Well," A'lii used the same innocent tone, "you'll know what's going on if you start."

Rithol leaned down and kissed her on the mouth. As he pulled away he said, "I would appreciate not starting. It sounds tiresome."

My sister blushed and playfully pushed him away, "Go help my Omoah."

"But what about you?" Rithol paused. "Are you going to help capture that Gen'tahn'Gen guy?"

A'lii looked at me expectantly. Then, Rithol joined her querying gaze. The next click, all eyes were trained on me.

"It could work," I bought time. "I think we need to figure out what to do with him if we can capture him."

Everyone still looked at me expectantly, waiting for *me* to make the decision.

"Why don't we just kill him?" none of us had noticed Kelita join us. "If we get that close to him, we can kill him like Shahn'Nahsh." Kelita glared at Hahn'Nik'Nik, "*She* said he's the problem and needs to be killed."

Hahn'Nik'Nik had said as much, but it didn't seem like the right thing to do. If we killed him because of his ability, wouldn't we have to kill the rest of the Tek'ekim? A new thought struck me, if we killed Gen'tahn'Gen because of his ability, then my sister and I would also have to be killed. Did it make any difference how the ability was used? What if I controlled someone to save them from a terrible accident, would I be doing the same evil Gen'tahn'Gen was doing?

Oogluk's thoughts rumbled through my mind. He offered no direction when I asked him, however.

"C'mon," I prodded him, "what should we do? They want me to choose."

"This is too much for one person to decide. For one person to decide, this is too much," he argued.

"Then, help me. You and I make two together," I pressed.

"Friend Jax," Oogluk sounded tired, "This choice is for all people not just you and me. Not just for you and me is this choice."

"But they expect me to choose for them."

"Choose for you, I cannot, but death is not the answer," he said thoughtfully. "Death, the answer is not at this time."

I hung my head. I couldn't be the one to choose.

"Well?" Kelita demanded an answer.

Kammiel looked at her and said softly, "If controlling people's minds is wrong, killing them is wrong too."

Omoah, who had circled back to see what was keeping A'lii and Rithol, nodded her head once, "Well said, little darlin'. Oh, your poor Omoah must miss you dearly."

Kammiel bounced into Omoah's arms when she spread them to give the little girl a hug.

I continued to wrestle with myself. True, killing someone because of what they *could* do would not be the same as killing someone for what they *did* do. Where was the line between punishment and redirection? Was Gen'tahn'Gen merely acting in the best interest of his people? Would I do the same if I were in his place? Did that make anything he was doing alright? Did that make killing him alright?

"A'lii, Rithol?" Omoah said when she straightened from setting Kammiel down.

My sister hugged her and said, "I've changed my mind. I need to stay here for now."

Rithol and A'lii exchanged imploring looks.

"I know you want to help," A'lii hugged him, "but I don't think Jax will need anybody to fight."

"Little Brother?" Rithol turned to me.

I froze again. I didn't want to be the one to tell Rithol what to do. Yet he was asking me what I wanted him to do. "I think the fewer people we have with us the better."

"You're right," he said and snatched Rurin from the ground. My little brother laughed and yelled to be put down. Rithol complied and turned to A'lii, "How will I know you're safe? I don't want anything to happen to you."

A'lii hugged him tight, "They won't hurt me." She winced as she continued, "It's too dangerous for someone without the abilities Jax and I have."

Rithol's face darkened, and he pushed A'lii away as he held her elbows and looked intently into her eyes. "Everybody's got their sacrifices to make, right? But you won't be mine. Come back alive."

A tear trickled from A'lii's right eye. She grimaced as she held back the rest of them and nodded, "I love you, you sweet man." She leapt at Rithol forcing him to step back or draw her close. Their bodies became indistinguishable, and they kissed forcefully.

"I love you too," Rithol breathed before breaking the embrace, scooping up Rurin and placing Omoah's hand in the crook of his elbow.

Omoah suppressed her tears of worry as she turned her back on her daughter and son and marched down the hill with Rithol.

A slender hand took mine. Airitha whispered, "If I'm going with you, why couldn't he?"

I looked over the vast plain to where we'd seen the smoke rising above Prathniss. "You're not going with us," I replied without looking at her.

"Jax," her voice grew strained, "you can't be serious."

"You've all made it my decision, and that's what I choose," I answered sharply.

"But," Airitha fumbled with her argument. "But you and I have fought together before. Remember the screamers on Teluthia? How we threw firebombs at them and blew them up?"

I clenched my teeth, "I remember."

Three Neftim disappeared with the part of my family that was headed home.

"Why can't I come, then?"

I turned my hard-eyed gaze to her, "If everything goes well, there won't be any fighting. We can't have anyone who can't protect herself go with us."

"Jax is right," Hahn'Nik'Nik surprised us. "And he knows better than any of us just how dangerous it will be."

Airitha's eyes darted to the orange woman, and her lip protruded in the closest I'd ever seen her to pouting. "I know," she said wearily. "I'm just tired of being left out."

"We don't know what exactly we need to do, anyway," I offered as solace.

Airitha gave me a half smile and let Hahn'Nik'Nik lead her toward the dropship.

"What about us?" Darvian asked.

"I don't know," I replied.

"Come on, Jax," my sister said heavily, "let's work on a plan with the others and decide whether we're actually going to do this. The fewer details we have about it, the more impossible it sounds."

"Yeah," Darvian chimed in. "Let's get rid of 'em like we did the Gah'Stotten."

I relented and followed behind to speak with Oogluk briefly without interruption.

"The Neftim in your Number must be some of the stronger ones?" I asked through our connection.

"Believe they are the strongest, I do," he answered. "Any of them would most likely help willingly, but is it a part that I may play? That I may play, is it a part?"

Everyone wanted to help, and no one seemed willing to step out voluntarily.

Incoherent yells erupted from my friends in front of me. Then, I felt it, too. Intense mental pressure drove me to my knees. Oogluk reacted at the same time I did. Together, we pushed against the powerful attack. My

strength felt like a fraying rope being licked by a roaring
fire.

Chapter 32

Tuca dropped from the air and bristled her body into spikes and a large mouth filled with teeth shaped for slicing. She whipped to the left and right, ripping and tearing at marauding Neftim as they materialized and dove in every direction.

"Gumbat," Oogluk managed to convey.

I hardly registered his explanation because I was pushing so hard against the mental attack. Visions of giving up and lying on the ground buffeted me. Grinding my teeth, I rejected them.

Without realizing it, I retreated backward step by step. In front of me, the Neftim who were part of the Number joined Tuca, creating a wall of semitransparent death. Gumbat teleported behind the line, but they were quickly driven off. Countless times Tuca and her Number sliced down on empty air as a gumbat teleported away.

They fought wildly, much the same way Oogluk and Ronthluque had fought.

We continued to lose ground, and I soon found myself curving back in a loop until I was backing beneath the dropship. The ramp sloped up on my left. Oogluk danced up it and leapt off in his constant, vigilant circling of me. I glanced beneath the ramp. Two Teluthian soldiers knelt on the ground with their hands on the backs of their heads.

"Get up!" I shouted at them, but they didn't flinch or even twitch in response.

I gave a massive shove against the weight in my mind. It slackened. I didn't know whether I could help the soldiers, but I had to try. Reaching out with my mind placed me in a vulnerable position. Oogluk filled in some of the gaps I created in my defenses. The nearest soldier lowered his hands to his lap and turned to look at me as I pressed against his mental captor.

My head throbbed as if Rurin had crushed my head tails by dropping boulders on them. "Grab your weapons and fight back," I forced out.

The slit in the man's helmet remained blank, and he sat motionless for a click. Then, he slapped his neighbor, and, together, they picked up their MECs and raced around the ramp.

The mental strain threatened to crush me with blackness. I wanted to rest—just lie down and sleep.

"Friend Jax," Oogluk picked me up.

My body flopped from side to side as he lumbered on the ground. "Let me sleep," I mumbled.

"No, Friend Jax, fight back. Fight back," Oogluk's urgent cries felt like a light breeze.

Then, my senses soared to high alert. Oogluk felt like he was trying to lift an entire mountain with the force he exerted.

"I'm back," I gasped.

An explosion knocked us backward. Oogluk stumbled and collapsed on the ramp. Another explosion sent flashes of orange and yellow skyward. Pebbles and chunks of rock rained down on us. The ground vibrated. Two more explosions followed in quick succession.

I blinked. The pressure on my mind was gone.

"Oogluk, we have to fight back," I yelled.

"Those shots are ours," he replied, setting me on my feet. "Ours are those shots. From this dropship they came. They came from this dropship."

Glancing up, I saw a tubular protrusion swing to the right. Red light bolted from it a click later. Through the smoke and debris, I saw a body with orange markings and an orange robe fly to the left.

Two soldiers in white armor raced toward me. Their MECs pointed straight at my chest. I drew my sword at the same time I reached out with my mind. They fired before I found the mental pressure driving them to attack.

My glowing sword sliced the ramp as I dove forward and to the left. The ramp's pitch slid me to the leftmost soldier's side. I didn't want to kill him. I swung. My sword cut cleanly through his MEC. He reacted instantly, drawing back his right hand into a fist. I rolled, and an explosion sent hot shrapnel into my body. A few pieces burned scratches into the back of my head. I spun, raising my sword to kill if need be. I didn't have to swing, though. The soldier crumpled to his knees with blood spurting from where his left hand should have been.

The second soldier suddenly slammed into the ramp as if he'd fallen from a great height. Feebly, he tried to move. His legs and arms scrabbled for purchase on the blood-slicked ramp.

Oogluk shoved the soldier's MEC into my chest. I took it and added small, orange bolts to the red rain pouring from the dropship.

Smoke billowed like a storm cloud. I could hardly see. I didn't try to shoot the Neftim traitors, fearing that I would hit Tuca and the Number instead of the enemy. Besides, the small MECs were not much good against the creatures.

Oogluk cried out. His body roiled in strange lumps and slipped off the edge of the ramp.

"Tranto!" I called, forgetting his real name.

His presence slipped from my mind, and I slipped to the edge and peered down through the smoke. Ten feet below Oogluk fought two gumbat. The attackers' bodies held no definite shape and shifted in wild contortions like a small waterfall tossed about by storm winds.

I pointed my MEC to fire, but Oogluk pounced on the two at that same click.

A yell faintly tugged at me from behind. I spun and saw an orange clad man with a rattling club slip on the ramp. I fired. He twitched and didn't get up.

The huge, red bolts continued to blast the battlefield. The Tek'ekim were trying to get inside the dropship and kill whoever was operating the weapon. They could simply teleport inside if they had enough gumbat to do so.

Forcing my attention away from the dueling creatures below, I called on my shaping ability. The air hardened into two long, curved swords. They were nearly ten feet long and weighed so much I could barely move them. Next, I strained my mind to connect with Oogluk.

Once I made a weak connection with him, I showed him the weapons I had made him. Two tentacle-like appendages snatched the swords from beside me.

I scanned the ground in front of the ramp. Nothing except Tuca and the Number, forming a tight perimeter. The fighting slowed.

I glanced beneath the ramp. Two shiny puddles ran slowly downhill. Oogluk stood still as he watched. He had wanted to set the gumbat free and see them rejoin the Number, yet in the confusion of battle we had not been able to reach out to the creatures. Oogluk had performed the only option in such a situation. He and I silently cut our grief short and turned back to the battle.

The red bolts stopped. A click later the mental weight slammed into me afresh. I fell to my stomach. My head felt too heavy to lift. A voice I recognized instantly and hated vehemently sounded in my mind.

"Well, well, well, Jax of Geoteous, I have found you and your slimy, little hideout," Gen'tahn'Gen prattled. "You've put up a good fight." He laughed sardonically, "But for every one of my people you killed, I'll kill ten of yours."

Oogluk roared incoherently.

My thoughts raged inside me, but topping them was worry for my sister and Airitha. I was confident they had been the ones to help with the huge MEC. They must have teleported past me. I didn't want to think of what had happened to make them stop firing.

"Oh, you pitiful boy," Gen'tahn'Gen stated.

I could see his gloating glare as images of my sister and four Teluthian soldiers flashed into my mind. Blood and gore dripped from every surface of the small gunnery chamber. Gen'tahn was connected to the gumbat. He could see through them.

"He lies," Oogluk's fury would have had spittle flying from his mouth had he been Ti'Kahn.

Gen'tahn laughed, "Oh, my friend, I don't lie. I merely show you the truth," he dragged out the 'th' in truth.

Tuca's line folded in on itself as the Number gave up ground to the mental attack. A cluster of orange Tek'ekim strode forward through the smoke curling around their arms and legs.

"You shouldn't have given away your position, boy, if you didn't want us to find you," Gen'tahn's voice felt slippery in my mind. "Remember we can sense every time you teleport."

A dark object the size of a ghinto fruit hurtled down from above. Gen'tahn'Gen glanced at it. Twenty feet above the ground a wildly shape-shifting gumbat caught the object. Before it could teleport or fly away, the object exploded in an orange fireball inside its body. Charred, semitransparent pieces of its body flew in all directions.

Gen'tahn flicked a piece of the gumbat off his shoulder and continued walking toward me. He opened his mouth, but I couldn't hear what he said.

At that click, the huge MEC above me fired. A string of red bolts obliterated the ground in front of the ramp. The mental pressure on me lifted, and three sets of hands grabbed me and dragged me up the ramp into the dropship.

Airitha's worried expression filled my vision. Her mouth moved, but I could hear nothing over the ringing in my ears. She yanked herself away, and Darvian peered at me. His hands cupped my ears. A click later, my hearing returned to normal.

"Are you alright?" Airitha pushed Darvian out of the way as she knelt beside me again. "That was Gen'tahn'Gen, wasn't it?"

Oogluk's bulk blocked part of the light filtering through the smoke.

"Yeah, it was," I said weakly.

"Where's Meisha?" Airitha yelled. "He needs help with his mind."

I felt Darvian's hands on my head. My muddled thoughts began to clear.

"Did you shoot him?" I asked.

Footsteps rang on the metal floor. Meisha spoke hurriedly with her brother.

"Jax? Is he hurt?" my sister's voice rang in near panic as she knelt beside Airitha and reached out to feel my neck.

"I'm fine," I croaked. "Did you shoot Gen'tahn'Gen?"

"Oh, thank goodness," A'lii closed her eyes in relief. Then, she shook her head, "I don't know. I don't think we were quick enough. Two of those creatures got into the ship. We had to fight them off."

I shuddered. It must have been bits and pieces from them that Gen'tahn had shown me and convinced me was my sister and friends. "How?" I asked.

"It seems your friend here," she wrapped an arm around Airitha, "is quite lethal to those things. She touched them and, poof, they turned into clouds of ash."

Airitha attempted to veil a smile as she blushed. At least, I think she blushed. It was hard to tell with her markings already red.

"What about Tuca and the Number?" I sat up stiffly. Darvian and Meisha continued to work on my body, and I winced every time they found a new injury and turned back time on that part of my body to when it was whole.

"They are recovering," Oogluk answered.

"I think they're alright," Hahn'Nik'Nik said, looking out the doorway.

"Why did they attack?" Meisha asked.

No one had an answer for her. Eventually, I shrugged and told her, "Gen'tahn'Gen said he knew where we were because they can sense us teleporting. Maybe he thought we were gearing up for another attack on him and he wanted to strike while he thought we were weak."

Airitha stiffened, and a look of horror clouded her face, "Jax, your family. They could've sensed where they went."

A'lii didn't even wait for me. She raced past Oogluk as I scrambled from the floor.

"Wait," I called to her back, but she didn't slow.

Tuca whirled around, scooped my sister up and the two of them vanished.

Oogluk soared over me as I leapt from the ramp. "Friend Jax, wait. Gen'tahn may attack again. Attack again, Gen'tahn might."

"I need to help my family," I feinted to the right. The Neftim grabbed me and lifted me from the ground.

"Darvian or Meisha must go with Hahn'Nik'Nik," Oogluk insisted. "You are needed here in case more attacks come. In case more attacks come—"

"What's so important about staying here? The dropship doesn't matter. We can all go," I retorted. I didn't bother struggling. I had seen how fruitless it was to try to fight a Neftim without weapons.

"Would all of us suddenly teleporting to your home lead them to attack there?" Oogluk didn't repeat himself.

My mind numbed. Of course, it would. They had attacked us at the dropship because all of the Neftim had retreated from the conflict in the army at one time.

"You're right," I finally conceded. "Have Meisha and Nik'Nik go."

"You must tell them," Oolguk said. "Tell them you must."

I did. Clicks later, the two women vanished with one of the Number. I hoped they would not be too late.

"Alright," I asked Oogluk, "now what do we do?"

"Will your Ahdah connect with one of the Number?" Oogluk asked unexpectedly.

"Um, yeah, he would," I responded.

"Then, we must send them word of this attack. Word of this attack we must send them."

"But you don't want any of us Ti'Kahn to go, do you?" I already knew the answer to my question.

Oogluk confirmed that the Neftim would go alone.

Airitha placed a hand gently on my shoulder, "Is everything alright?"

I trained my eyes on her and then met her gaze. "We need to know Gen'tahn'Gen's next move. He obviously doesn't want peace."

"You're worried about your family, aren't you?" she didn't say it in a mocking tone.

"Watch out!" Darvian shouted.

An orange bolt squelched from the jumbled mound of rocks. It hit a Neftim as it materialized several yards away. My sister stumbled and threw herself to the ground as more bolts slammed into the creature.

Oogluk shifted his shape to something with longer legs than a dragon and heaved himself up the rocks. The bolts stopped when he was halfway up.

A small Teluthian soldier stood and pressed her hand to the side of her helmet. I knew she was using the functions in the helmet to see better.

Just then, the air shifted with a soft ripping sound. Meisha and Hahn'Nik'Nik raced from the Neftim toward me.

"They weren't there," my sister glanced around anxiously. "Did they come back here?"

My own anxiety roared, overpowering my senses.

"You didn't find them at their farm?" Airitha asked.

A'lii shook her head, sending her chalky yellow patterned mul'li dancing. "They weren't there," she said again. "I didn't see any signs of a struggle, but it's not like Omoah to not at least leave a note."

Hahn'Nik'Nik reached for my sister. She forced her to stop her frantic searching by pulling her into a hug. "They probably went to the spire. Rithol will take care of them," she said as she comforted my sister, who had tears trickling down her cheeks.

A'lii nodded and sniffed. "Okay," she replied weakly.

I glanced at the small soldier on top of the rocks. She was the right size to be Kelita. I suddenly realized I had completely forgotten her in the fight.

Another Neftim materialized. I reached for my sword, but it wasn't a wildly shifting gumbat. The Neftim that had gone to the spire stood still and scanned us slowly with its fake eyes.

Oogluk relayed the information to me, "Your family is safe with your Ahdah Talmir says. They were shocked by the news of the attack. Shocked with the news of the attack—"

He didn't get to finish repeating himself. Squelches and shouts broke out inside the dropship. Then, it was over as abruptly as it had started.

"Attacking he is," Oogluk shouted into my mind. He launched into the air and glided to the ground beside me.

"It's Gen'tahn," I yelled.

Airitha clutched at my arm. I didn't bother trying to argue with her. Oogluk plucked us both from the ground just as a huge, red bolt exploded behind us.

All around, Neftim disappeared. Darvian ran hand in hand with Kammiel until a Neftim swooped down and disappeared with them.

My sword glowed in my hand. Airitha grabbed my wrist.

"What?" I asked.

"We can take that MEC out," she said. Then, without waiting for me to ask how, she instructed me to make a bomb.

Sheathing my sword, I formed it while Oogluk leapt onto the hull of the dropship.

"Good," Airitha said, snatching the orb from my hands. In a flash it was glowing orange and red, and then it was so hot I had to duck to the side.

Oogluk grimaced at the pain from his burning flesh. He ran along the ship until we reached the gunport. Airitha lifted the glowing orb above her head and threw it. It flew straight toward the MEC and would have exploded in the small hollow between the barrel and the hull had a gumbat not suddenly materialized.

The traitorous Neftim looked like a crazed grogul with a huge hump in its back that looked like a wild creature was inside kicking furiously to get out. The bomb struck it and melted into soft flesh. Smoke and charred flesh floated into the air. Oogluk jumped, turned a flip in the air and flapped his wings hard to carry us away. The bomb exploded with a pop like a giant bone breaking. Pieces of the enemy creature splattered us. The MEC continued firing at my friends.

"Friend Jax, make me a long bomb like a spear, and form a device that will allow me to hold it," Oogluk showed me what he imagined.

Then, I wanted to draw my sword and slice the creature I rode to pieces. My hands moved toward my sword. Why couldn't I grab it?

"Friend Jax," a voice bellowed in my mind. "Fight it. Fight."

I stared blankly. A girl my age stared blankly back at me. Then, her fist slammed into my face. Her other fist crashed into my head tail.

The voice in my head grew fainter as it tried to get me to fight.

Another blow sent pain searing through my head as blood poured from my nose. Still, my hands would not move.

My stomach lurched and my head throbbed with pain as I fell.

"Fight it, Friend Jax. Push him from your mind. That is it," I recognized Oogluk's voice.

The girl paused with her hand halfway to my face.

"Airitha?" I asked aloud.

She wadded her face in confusion and withdrew her hand. Her knuckles were split and bleeding.

"Airitha, it's me, Jax," I smeared at the blood running into my mouth and nearly howled in pain as I brushed my nose. Something inside me said it was broken.

The girl shook her head and stared at me. Then, a look of horror washed over her, and she lifted her fists and stared at them.

"Yes. Yes, you hit me, but we gotta work together," blood flew from my lips like spit.

"I have flown us far enough away he is not able to control you," Oogluk said. "Hurry. Make the weapon and give it to me. The weapon, make."

I struggled to focus on the task with every slight change in course or bump of shifted air causing new flashes of pain in my face. Gradually, the giant arrow took shape. Then, I added a separate, curved stick to throw it like an atlatl.

Airitha fumbled with the weapon and burned Oogluk several times.

"Now, guard yourself and Friend Airitha. Yourself and Friend Airitha, guard," the semitransparent Neftim instructed.

We looped around in a long arc and shot skyward. The cliff fell away below us, and the shiny skin of the dropship glistened in sunlight. Smoke and dust billowed from the ground. The MEC squelched wildly left to right as the Neftim fought the gumbat.

Oogluk shifted his wings and nosed down into a steep dive. I nearly blacked out from the pain. Oogluk drew both Airitha and me into his body. The weapon glowed bright orange, almost white, in his grasp. I could feel his pain from the intense heat even though he tried to block me from it.

A hundred feet above the MEC, Oogluk hurled the weapon. Immediately, he snapped his wings open and clawed for altitude. I did black out then.

When I came to and looked behind us, nothing but a gaping, black hole smoldered in the dropship where the MEC had been.

I felt the Tek'ekim contending with Oogluk. The dark oppression and abnormal tiredness and desire to give up fighting clutched at me. Oogluk fought it off, but he was growing weary.

Groggily, I pushed back with my mind. Oogluk sighed with relief.

Airitha came to from the G-lock a few clicks later. She looked around, bewildered. Then, she saw the battlefield.

Neftim still fought the feral-looking gumbat, and my friends held the Tek'ekim at bay with heavy MEC fire.

"We have to go back," I urged Oogluk. "They can't hold them back for long."

Oogluk turned and dove toward the battle. "Another weapon," he said as if gritting his teeth.

Exhaustion reached for me as I completed the projectile. Airitha heated it until it glowed. She moved slowly and somewhat jerkily as she handed it off to the creature.

Oogluk launched the projectile. It flew straight for the center of the Tek'ekim just as we did.

"Oogluk, pull up. Stop diving," I screamed.

Airitha stared at the ground.

"Oogluk," I beat my hands against his body.

Painfully slowly, he changed our course. We would not slam into the ground, but the weapon would explode right in our faces if we didn't turn.

The mental pressure grew nearly unbearable. I tried to yell to Oogluk to turn, but I was too tired.

I shoved against the mental attack. We started turning to the left toward the dropship.

"Not this way," I wanted to scream, but no sound left my lips.

"Too late it is," Oogluk whispered in exhaustion.

The weapon exploded. Heat, flame and dirt crashed into the underside of Oogluk's body. The force threw us against the dropship's hull. Airitha screamed, and pain overloaded my senses.

Oogluk's body slipped from the ship and landed on the ground. I was too weak to move, but Airitha grabbed my hands and pulled. She collapsed as a figure materialized above us.

"A very good fight, but a pitiful attempt to kill me," Gen'tahn'Gen laughed long and low.

My arm quivered as I lifted it to shield my face.

The four-legged, wingless gumbat Gen'tahn rode stepped closer. Its head twitched as if it wanted to look to the left, but an invisible stick beat it back to looking straight forward.

"Bind them," Gen'tahn smiled. The bright orange markings on his face were like additional teeth amplifying the sadistic look of his smile.

I could do nothing to resist as thin chains were wrapped around my wrists. My head fell limply to the side where I glimpsed Airitha being bound as well. Then,

Gen'tahn's gumbat lifted us by the chains and draped us over its neck as though we were corpses being flown to town.

Gen'tahn pulled on my chains and whispered, "What price will you and your little princess bring?"

Chapter 33

"Good. Good. Keep worrying," our captor gloated as we found ourselves surrounded by burned out husks of once colorful houses and various wooden buildings on one side and the ransacked shopping square on the other. Gen'tahn'Gen walked slowly out of sight.

Numerous banners and canopies lay strewn about the dusty ground. Stettin's Grill lay in a jumbled heap of splintered wood, turned-out bags and smashed cupboards. I shuffled in a slow circle, taking it all in.

"This is Prathniss," I whispered to Airitha. "What's left of it."

I found it odd that I still had my memories, and they hadn't been tampered with. Taking stock of everything in my mind, I realized that nothing was amiss—except for the feeling that I should be able to do something about the chain still wrapped around my wrists.

"It must have been a busy place," Airitha replied. "Is that Stettin's Grill, the place you told me about?"

"Yeah," I pointed. "And over there was Ann'Nadohn's shop. The gumbat smashed it."

Airitha grabbed the chain binding her hands and carried it around the pole it was anchored to. I had to do the same to keep my own chain from growing shorter and shorter as I pointed out different things to Airitha.

"Do you think they'll come for us?" Airitha asked quietly.

"They'll come," I replied quickly.

"Ahdah's going to be furious. He probably already is," Airitha tried to smile.

"Yeah, mine too. I hope my Omoah doesn't know."

That brought a small giggle from Airitha, "She'd call you sweetie so much you might call her a bother instead of your little brother."

I looked down at the dust.

"I'm sorry, Jax," Airitha said. "I was simply trying to make a joke."

"I just want to be free and have Gen'tahn'Gen pay for what he's done," I mumbled.

Airitha stepped as close as our chains allowed. We still had five feet between us even when we held our arms stretched to the side. She hadn't cried a single time since being captured, yet the softness in her eyes hinted that tears could start at any time.

"I'd like revenge, too," she murmured just loud enough for me to hear. "Ever since we found Darvi running from those Gah'Stotten monsters, we've been trying to escape one thing or another."

It's amazing how many different colors of granules you can spot in sandy dirt when you study it. I counted six before Airitha sniffed and continued talking—not really to me, but still to be heard.

"I think I understand a bit how Kelita feels," she said. "If I could overpower them and make it so they could never hurt anyone again, I don't think anyone could stop me."

I grunted. Her mention of Kelita had little effect on me. I was in the middle of wondering whether it would be worth being mad at Kelita when Airitha asked, "What about you, Jax?"

"Me...what?" I glanced at her as new anxiety shredded another piece of my calmness.

"Do you blame the Gah'Stotten and Shahn'Nahsh?"

I realized the truth in that moment. I could really blame only myself. I had chosen to fly Raglod to buy the perpengold seeds. It was because of that choice that I had fallen into Tranto's world. That had been a choice I'd made in arrogance. Further, we had discovered Grael only because I had wanted to abandon Airitha on Hegnoranthe. Things certainly could have been so vastly different that I never even learned of the existence of other people on other planets had I chose differently.

Averting my gaze, I responded, "Yeah, I think so."

Angry tears frayed Airitha's voice, "Why do they do that? Why do people do stuff like that?"

I opened my mouth to answer even though I had no idea what to say, but Airitha didn't stop.

"And Gen'tahn'Gen—the Great Gen'tahn'Gen—why won't he live at peace with us? Why does he think he needs to take over your people's town by force?"

"Your Ahdah has never taught you to respect your elders," Gen'tahn's heavily accented voice sounded inside my head. Airitha cringed and hugged her arms around herself. "I would begin lessons now, but, fortunately for you, you'll fetch a better bargain unharmed."

Airitha sank to the ground, drawing her knees up and hugging her ankles. She glanced at me with her face twisted by fear and imminent tears. Then, she buried her face in her knees.

Anger boiled so hot in me I felt like I could melt the chains on my wrists. That was it! I had forgotten about Airitha's ability to heat things up.

"Airitha?" I called. She only sniffed. "Airitha, you can free us."

She lifted her head as if it were too heavy for her neck to hold and peered at me with unfocused, bloodshot eyes.

"Your ability," I said. "You can melt the chains." I held my hands up to show her as if she couldn't both see and feel the chains around her own wrists.

"No...I can't," she mumbled. "I'm not like you." Her face scrunched and she pushed herself farther away from me, "You. You're the reason I'm here. You're working with Gen'tahn to capture me. You could've freed us whenever you wanted, but you let Gen'tahn capture us. Now, you're pretending to be captured too. If you weren't, you would've used your shaping ability to set us free."

I shook my head, "No, I don't have an ability like you." I brightened, "You can do it. The heat won't even bother you. You've handled fire with bare hands lots of times."

Airitha pulled herself into a tighter ball and then lashed out with her verbal sword, "Gumbat. You don't care about anyone but your new friends."

I yanked on my chain, trying desperately to get closer to Airitha, "No, I care about all our friends. I care about you. I want to get us freed, but I need your help."

"Once you're free, you'll join the Tek'ekim and help them capture me again," Airitha sobbed.

"Airitha, no," I pleaded. "You can do it. It wouldn't take more than a click."

Airitha screamed and turned to face away from me. Her shoulders shook, and she clenched her ankles so tight the tendons bulged in her neck. I was about to say more but stopped myself when her head began to shake as if she were shivering.

I stood, looking at my friend's back for several rays. She was convinced I had turned against her, and she repeatedly denied possessing the ability that could save us. Something tingled at the back of my mind, but it remained out of reach.

My hands stung from my bonds cutting off the blood flow. I retreated closer to the pole that served as my anchor point. We had to escape before our families bent to the Great Gen'tahn's demands. If only we had a Neftim with us. They could teleport, right? No, it was shapeshifting they could do. I frowned. It would be incredibly more difficult to get away if I kept second guessing myself.

Suddenly, my chains rattled and slapped against my forearms. I opened my eyes to see a huge, semitransparent creature yanking the pole Airitha was chained to out of the ground. Turning around, I saw a second creature, this one with a rider, reaching out for me.

I scooted backward, but a calming voice sounded in my mind, "Friend Jax, you are safe. Safe you are."

The rider slid from the creature's back. She looked like a Tek'ekim with orange markings standing out brightly against her purple skin and fiery eyes taking everything in. She ran to Airitha, who was trying to escape the creature's grasp by beating on its oddly shaped hand. The orange woman's mouth moved, and Airitha froze, staring up at her.

The creature holding me stumbled and fell to the ground. It held me safely above the dust, but I hardly registered it as the flood of mental pressure nearly knocked me out. My sight went black on the edges, and dizziness made the decimated market square tilt.

A door creaked, and footsteps padded quietly toward us. I felt like I was in a nightmare where I was trying to run away from a monster, but every step felt too heavy to take and forward progress was next to nothing.

The newcomer spoke out loud in the Tek'ekim's clicking and popping language. I couldn't understand what he said.

The orange woman feebly pushed herself up from the dirt and, glaring at the newcomer, returned a string of pops and hisses.

The footsteps stopped, and Gen'tahn'Gen spoke thickly, "Let us not keep our distasteful words from our guests. I am glad you have chosen to return, daughter."

"There is no claim you have on me," the woman said, slightly slurring her words.

Gen'tahn's eyes flicked to the left and right. I didn't turn to look as several footsteps sounded on either side. "I do not lie, daughter," the leader of the Tek'ekim gloated. "I am glad you have decided to initiate a reunion. It has been so long since you infiltrated their ranks that some of us were uncertain whether you would return."

The woman fought to straighten her back and pressed her hands down her sides. It was as if she had brushed away uncertainty. She stood tall with a look of defiance pressing her face into hard, resolute lines.

"Come now," Gen'tahn held out his right hand palm down, "let our little disagreements remain the trivial things they are."

He stepped close enough for the woman to bow and kiss the back of his hand, but she remained straight and tall.

"We need not have this little display of defiance. Others would not be so gracious, but I am willing to accept you back into our community. You need only to denounce this insubordination and take your rightful place beside me. Ahdah and daughter, that sounds endearing, does it not?"

My thoughts were so muddled I couldn't form an opinion or decide what I wanted to see happen between the two. The footsteps stopped on either side of me. A quick glance revealed four Tek'ekim, holding long sticks sharpened and stained on one end.

"You are deranged, Ahdah," the woman growled. Then, she spat on his outstretched hand.

Gen'tahn slowly retracted his hand. A gleam played in his eye, and he smirked. "Please forgive me, daughter," he said pleasantly.

In a sudden flurry of movement, the Tek'ekim leader coiled and struck out with the hand the woman had spit on. She shrugged into a cringe and let a small whimper escape. I expected the backhand to snap her head sideways, but the blow never landed.

Gen'tahn's hand stopped an inch from the woman's cheek, and he laughed low and cruel, "When have I ever struck you, daughter?"

The woman opened her eyes and looked ready to spit again. But instead of spit flying from her mouth, she wet her lips and proclaimed, "I may be scared of you, but you will burn in the furnace you yourself have created."

Gen'tahn's expression darkened into such a deep scowl that his face looked scarred once again. He parted his lips but didn't have a chance to speak.

The market exploded with the tearing sound of many creatures teleporting. Fire crackled to life all around. As if on cue, my mind snapped into focus. I stared at Hahn'Nik'Nik. She moved with the speed of a diving dragon. She ripped her tunic aside, grabbed a handheld MEC and pointed it straight into Gen'tahn's face.

"Get down," Oogluk's voice burst into my mind.

I didn't have time to react before he grabbed me and pushed me to the ground. His weight nearly crushed me, but then, he dragged me into his body. Our connection thrummed with energy.

Shaping! Airitha had been right after all. I could cut through my bonds with my ability. The chains fell away, and I urged Oogluk to move to Airitha. However, she already ran to us—her bonds cut.

I glanced to either side. The bodies of four Tek'ekim guards lay in the dust. Several blackened holes smoldered in each of their chests.

Hahn'Nik'Nik stood calmly, pointing the MEC at her Ahdah. Gen'tahn, scowling in dark rage, stepped forward until the weapon pressed into his chest. Hahn'Nik'Nik had to look up as she held the MEC. She had been the one to suggest that killing him would allow us to gain the upper hand. She could pull the trigger.

Hahn'Nik'Nik's mouth and eyes widened as if in shock. Gen'tahn pulled his hand back and whipped it in a tight arc that snatched the MEC from the woman's hands. A sharp, red object fell to the ground. Hahn'Nik'Nik sank to her knees, her expression never changing. Gen'tahn'Gen raised his left leg and kicked Hahn'Nik'Nik's shoulder. She spun halfway around and landed on her stomach. As she'd spun, a huge patch of red revealed itself on her chest and red droplets turned brown as they landed in the dust.

"Nik'Nik," Airitha screamed. She raced toward the woman.

Gen'tahn raised the weapon, but he faltered partway up. A'lii stepped barely into view to my right. She stood in tranquil grace with her gaze locked on the leader of the Tek'ekim.

Without thinking, I bent, snatched one of the sharpened sticks and threw it as hard as I could at Gen'tahn. I hardly believed what I saw. Airitha dove, grabbed Gen'tahn's robe and fire engulfed the man. The spear sailed through the air where his chest had been a click before.

Arrows whistled all around. Some found their marks, but most screeched and thwacked as they glanced off armor. Screams of both fear and pain contended with the squelching roar of MEC fire as bolts flew in all directions.

"A shield," Oogluk shouted. "Create a shield around you and your sister. Around you and your sister."

A tall man in white armor discarded his helmet that had an arrow protruding from the visor slit. Thaydrin rushed toward his daughter. Wild light glinted in his eyes.

I spun until I found my sister. She ducked and then leapt with a twirl as an arrow tore through her sleeve. I caught a glimpse of Hahn'Nik'Nik surrounded by a puddle of red and forgot what I needed to do. Where were Darvian and Meisha?

"The shield. The shield," Oogluk hollered.

As if I had to think about each action in slow motion, I snapped back to my sister. An arrow shaft glanced off my back. I called on my ability. My fingers glowed orange. Another arrow lodged in the hardening air. I snapped off the tip, careful not to get scratched by it. A click later, Oogluk carried the half egg-shaped shield of hardened air as my sister advanced toward Gen'tahn'Gen.

Two figures darted out from behind a building. They wore white Teluthian armor except for their bare hands wrapped in green markings. The taller one reached Hahn'Nik'Nik's motionless body first, rolled her over and pressed her hands against the woman's wound. Hahn'Nik'Nik's eyes stared into nothing, but her mouth split in a silent scream at Meisha's administrations.

Thaydrin plucked Airitha from the ground and helped her limp to the shelter of a doorway.

A blackened, Ti'Kahn shape writhed in the dirt. A'lii continued to step determinedly toward it.

"Help me," my sister said.

Dark pockets of weariness shadowed the underside of her eyes. Her feet delved dusty furrows with each struggling step.

I reached out with my mind and found Gen'tahn. His pain washed over me. The burns were unbearable. I tried to push it off me, but it was too strong.

A white armored soldier fell face down in front of us. A'lii pushed my shoulder to move the shield around his body.

Gen'tahn stopped writhing. The pain of the burns nearly crippled me. I stumbled. Gen'tahn shoved himself to his feet. His orange eyes spit fire at my sister and me. He couldn't see the shield of hardened air. He pointed the MEC. A string of orange bolts sizzled and smoked against the shield. My sister ducked.

Thaydrin rushed from the doorway. Gen'tahn whirled to point the MEC at the new threat. Orange bolts lanced toward Thaydrin.

A white clad soldier slammed into Gen'tahn from behind. The two went down and rolled in the dust. The pain Gen'tahn unloaded onto me buckled my knees.

"Push back," Oogluk instructed franticly. "Push his pain back to him. Back to him."

The ground shuddered. Wildly shifting gumbat dropped from the sky, crashing into the Neftim. The air split and tore and smoke shifted crazily as countless gumbat and Neftim teleported as they fought.

My sister looped her arm around my shoulders. I leaned into her for support.

Reaching out, I found Gen'tahn's mind and pushed. Some of the pain eased from my body. I pushed again. Strength, I didn't know I had, yanked me to my feet. Together with Oogluk, I shoved Gen'tahn. His body spasmed, and then he seemed back in control. The soldier flew off. Gen'tahn bared red-stained teeth as he stood and poured three bolts into the soldier that had tackled him. The Tek'ekim leader stumbled. Beside me, A'lii pressed her right hand to her temple and stopped advancing. She faltered, and I barely caught her.

Gen'tahn weaved to the right as if suddenly free, snatched the smaller figure from beside Hahn'Nik'Nik, and, pointing the MEC against Darvian's head, backed away from the square.

Chapter 34

I could do nothing but watch openmouthed as Darvian was dragged away. Gen'tahn would force him to heal his burns just as he'd made the two healers turn back time on the scarred flesh of his face. That seemed like an eternity ago.

"Follow him we must. We must follow," Oogluk bellowed into my mind.

A gumbat materialized in front of us before I could reply. Clutching my sister with one arm, I reached for my sword. The gumbat's head looked disconnected by the way it jumped up and down and to the sides like it was a ball tied to the center of a multiway tug of war. Its head jerked upside down. It swung a massive paw at me. The shield held, but my sister and I were hurled above the battle.

My entire left side screamed with pain as we landed on top of a wooden, three-story building. My sister moaned and reached out an unsteady hand as if to regain her balance.

A silvery mass cracked through the flat roof beside us. Another gumbat—or it was the same one coming to finish its kill. Sliding from beneath my sister, I stood shakily, wincing with every movement. I drew my sword and focused on the creature, trying to anticipate its next strike.

It shot out a tentacle from its center of mass straight for me. I dodged, stumbled and swung my blade. I felt no resistance as the glowing blade sliced cleanly through the tentacle. It fell with a sickening flop.

The gumbat teleported to my right side. An entire thicket of semitransparent spears stabbed at me. They faltered suddenly and retreated.

"Help Meisha," Oogluk ordered.

Meisha stumbled toward me from the edge of the roof. I raced for her as Oogluk plowed into the gumbat. The two creatures fell in a tangled mass of roiling silvery gray.

Meisha's armor was covered with blood and blackened marks. More than one arrow shaft flopped from the white plates on her back, lodged in the armor but not punctured through to her skin. I grabbed her hand and pulled her toward A'lii and the remains of our shield.

The building shuddered and splinters rained down on us. Meisha and I stumbled.

Oogluk and the gumbat rose out of the shattered wood. Oogluk bore down on the gumbat with his enormous mouth stretched wide to bite his opponent in half.

The gumbat teleported behind him. He tried to block the spear as thick as a log, but the gumbat stabbed it right through him. Oogluk's pain flared in my mind. Before he could move, the gumbat shifted its shape to form a knife and sliced upward and then down through my friend and the building's roof. My friend's pain blossomed white hot. The gumbat disappeared with a tearing sound.

Meisha dropped my hand as I stared. I wanted to scream and run to Oogluk's side, but I couldn't force my body to respond. Oogluk flopped to the roof—part of him falling away from me and the other falling toward me.

"No, Oogluk," I cried. "Oogluk."

Then, I had a wild thought. "Tuca. Tuca," I screamed with my mind. Nothing. She didn't reply. Was she still alive?

I limped across the shattered boards, grimacing against the pain I felt everywhere.

"Friend Jax," Oogluk's weak voice sounded even more distant in my mind, "save your friends, and let me go."

"I won't leave you. Tuca's on her way," I felt a sob trying to escape. Suppressing it, I continued, "She'll save you."

"Leave me," Oogluk labored to say. "Forsake not those you can save. Those you can save, forsake not."

The tears rushed over the dam I attempted to hold them behind. "I won't leave you," I cried. "Tuca! Tuca!" I shouted.

Oogluk gave the sensation of shaking his head as his presence grew fainter and fainter, "She cannot hear, Friend Jax."

"Oogluk," I finally made it to his side and struggled to my knees. I reached out intending to stroke the piece of my friend closest to me. "Don't die."

The click my fingers touched Oogluk's flesh, several things happened all at once that I still do not posses adequate words for. I fell forward into a deep, dark pit with only silence all around. The battle melted so completely away I literally forgot about it. Next, a searing white flash of pain sliced through my head. Lastly, I lost the ability to tell where my friend's consciousness ended and mine started.

The next click, I felt naked—exposed. Nothing was hidden. Everything about me was visible. The unchecked freefall stopped, and vibrant colors danced in slowly shifting patterns and strings as though I were inside an enormous loom as a master craftsman wove an intricate blanket.

All pain left my body. I reached out a hand, but, even though I could feel it move, I could not see it.

An unbearable cold clutched me for a click and then warmth wrapped me in its arms. Oogluk's presence filled my mind. I touched it with my mind. We were two distinct beings again.

Someone shook me. I groaned and fought to open my eyes. Sounds of fighting crept slowly into my awareness.

"Friend Jax?" Oogluk's voice urged. "Friend Jax?"

He shook me again. I winced as pain flared up my left side.

"Ouch," I moaned. "What's going on?"

"Gen'tahn'Gen, we must capture him. Capture him, we must," Oogluk responded.

"What was all that?" I asked.

Trepidation flooded Oogluk's presence, and he remained silent.

I blinked against the light of the two suns. Smoke rose above me, and squelches, shouts and screams echoed from below.

My sister and Meisha knelt beside me. Darvian's sister had removed her helmet, and her face looked haggard and lined. She spoke softly as she ran her hands over my injuries. The pain worsened and then melted away to nothing.

"C'mon, Jax," my sister held out her hand to me, "we gotta find Gen'tahn'Gen."

I took her hand and let her pull me to my feet.

She turned to Meisha and asked, "Can you come with us?"

Meisha glanced down at the square. "There's too many," she replied shaking her head.

Oogluk picked up all three of us. He flapped his wings twice and glided to a calm corner of the square. He helped Meisha gain her footing on the ground before leaping back into the air.

"Who else can help us?" A'lii leaned toward my ear.

"We should pick up Hahn'Nik'Nik and Airitha," I yelled back. "We could use a few people who can shoot long range, too."

"What about Kelita? She's a good shot," my sister responded.

A pang stabbed me. "I don't know where she is," I answered.

Oogluk swooped down. Thaydrin, Aritha and Hahn'Nik'Nik were sheltering together, and Oogluk reached out to bring them all with us.

Thaydrin held up a hand.

"We need to catch Gen'tahn'Gen," I yelled to him.

Hahn'Nik'Nik cringed but darted to us quickly.

Airitha looked at her Ahdah, begging him to let her go with us, but he laid a hand on her shoulder and shook his head.

Just then, a group of Teluthian soldiers hurried to Thaydrin's side. Airitha slipped away while his attention was diverted.

"What about Jamoal?" I asked Oogluk as we tore into the air.

In response, an image, sent from another Neftim, of the burly man charging toward a line of orange robed Tek'ekim brandishing clubs and bows filled my mind.

"Too busy," I acknowledged.

"Are we going to get Darvian back?" Airitha asked.

"We've gotta catch Gen'tahn'Gen," A'lii replied quickly.

Oogluk swerved abruptly as a gumbat materialized in front of us. At first, it didn't seem to see us, but then it bore down on us intently.

"Jax," my sister shouted, "push against its mind. We should be able to drive the Tek'ekim out of it."

I joined her in her effort. The controlling presence in the creature felt slimy, and it mirrored the same wild shifting as the creature's shapeshifting body.

Oogluk rolled to the left, barely escaping its attack.

With enormous effort, I finally locked onto the foreign presence in the gumbat. I pushed. The presence scrambled like a nykor attempting to find purchase on an icy hill. Then, it slipped and disappeared. A'lii gasped and recoiled into Hahn'Nik'Nik.

"I could control her now," my sister shuddered.

I felt her presence retreat from the creature. Briefly, I saw the square through the creature's eyes. It was nearly the same as when Oogluk shared an image with me of what he saw.

The creature's body stopped its wild shifting, and she hung in the air as if confused. Oogluk reached out to her with his mind, and the Neftim banked and flew just behind his left wingtip.

"You can set them free," Oogluk stated emphatically. "Free you can set the Number."

I glanced at my sister. I felt as tired as she looked. "I don't think we could manage many more like that. If we did, we wouldn't be able to challenge Gen'tahn."

"Rightly said," Oogluk acknowledged and flew on. "Once the great gumbat is captured, the Number shall be freed."

"Yeah, that makes sense," I said.

"There he is," Airitha cried. She pointed to a small figure in white armor lying face down in a narrow street.

I almost said we were looking for Gen'tahn, but I wanted to make sure Darvian was okay nearly as much as, if not more than, I wanted to catch the leader of the Tek'ekim.

Oogluk dove sharply and snapped his wings open with a thunderclap to slow us enough to land gently beside Darvian.

Airitha raced to him and skidded to a stop on her knees. "Darvi?" she asked with her voice laced with panic. "Darvi?" she gingerly shifted his helmet.

Hahn'Nik'Nik reached them next. She helped Airitha roll the boy onto his back. A'lii and I approached slowly, scanning every nook and cranny of the surrounding buildings.

By the time I got to Darvian's side, his head was cradled in Airitha's lap, and Hahn'Nik'Nik pressed a cloth to the side of his head. His helmet sat on the ground. An ugly, black streak burned into the right side of it.

"Is he alright?" I asked.

Hahn'Nik'Nik didn't look up as she worked, "Glancing blow. He seems alright. He should be fine if he doesn't overexert himself."

She pulled back the cloth. It was covered in yellowish fluid and little, black flakes of blackened skin. Darvian's right temple was a solid mass of bubbled burns with a streak of black running through the center of it.

Airitha whispered to him, and he moaned in response. She looked up at me and said, "I don't think he can tell us where Gen'tahn went. I'm going to stay here with him."

I stared back at her. Her brow was knit with concern. "No," I finally said. "We need you with us."

"I'm not going to leave my brother," her voice was low and determined.

"If we catch Gen'tahn now, there won't be any more people hurt...or killed," I tried to make her see the importance of our mission.

Airitha clutched Darvian's head tighter. He moaned, and Hahn'Nik'Nik laid a hand on Airitha's forearm. She relaxed slightly.

"I can't do it, Jax," she said quietly. "It's just like in the starship when we escaped Grael. I can't kill them." She sniffed but still didn't look at me. "I know what they've done and what they'll do if we don't stop them, but I can't. I can't fight to the death. I don't know what's wrong with me. I should be standing up for what I know is right, but that's just too much. I don't want anyone else to get hurt. But—but I can't be the one to kill them."

She glanced at me. I had nothing to say.

Airitha continued, "I don't know how you do it. You can fight for the ones you love and protect them no matter what it means. I can't. I don't know...maybe I'm too scared. I could've killed Gen'tahn when I set his robe on fire. I could have burned him the way—the—the way I killed the gumbat." She broke down in tears that dripped onto Darvian's face.

None of us moved. The only sound was Airitha's soft crying.

"You probably all think I'm terrible and weak. I can't do what's right to save the people I love," Airitha wept louder.

Darvian moaned and raised a hand to Airitha's face. He caressed her cheek with his hand. Her whole body shook as she sobbed.

I could think of nothing to say, but my body moved almost of its own accord to Airitha's side. I reached my arms around her as she had done for me countless times. She cried for nearly another ray. Darvian could hold his hand to her cheek no longer.

Airitha sniffed, "I'll come back for you the click we have him. He won't get away."

Darvian's weak voice was little more than a whisper, "I know you will."

Airitha sniffed and smeared at her nose. Collectively, we made Darvian as comfortable as we could in a flowerbed, taking care not to trample the flowers so they would hide him somewhat.

I tugged on Airitha's hand. We had to keep searching.

She turned to me with a grim smile and sniffed.

"Where could he go?" A'lii asked.

Hahn'Nik'Nik replied as she glanced around, "He could be hiding anywhere."

Countless buildings and houses lined the narrow, dusty street. Some of the taller buildings joined together with no alleys or yards between them.

"We will find no tracks on the street," Oogluk observed the hard packed dirt. "Perhaps, in the buildings we should look. In the buildings we should look, perhaps."

"He still has a MEC," I responded. "And he can probably feel us coming."

My eyes widened with the sudden inspiration, "A'lii, Nik'Nik, we'll be able to feel him with our minds."

Hahn'Nik'Nik shuddered, "He will know where we are if we do that."

"Won't he know anyway?" my sister pointed out.

Hahn'Nik'Nik lifted the MEC she carried, "How do I use this?"

I explained as quickly as I could. She thanked me and explained how Thaydrin had given it to her without teaching her to use it. I almost asked her to give it to me so I could use it, but I decided it would be better for me to be prepared to harden the air into a shield as quickly as I could if Gen'tahn opened fire on us with his handheld MEC he had gleaned. I had my sword anyway.

Gen'tahn was probably in one of the buildings, but Oogluk couldn't weave his way through them very well. If we had him help us from roof to roof, our progress would be slow, and we'd have tons of stairs with blind corners to contend with.

"If he's going to use his mind to sense where we are," I said aloud to no one in particular, "it'll be best for us to know where he is. Even if we both know where the other is, it's less dangerous than searching around blind corners and climbing up and down stairs."

"What if he gathered a bunch of his bodyguards around him?" A'lii asked.

"They won't be easy to defeat," Hahn'Nik'Nik offered with a grimace.

An orange bolt sizzled past my sister's head striking Oogluk in the shoulder.

"No need to keep arguing," I managed to shout before mental fatigue descended on me. I pushed back, but it wasn't enough. I felt myself falling.

Chapter 35

My knees protested as they hit the hard packed dirt of the road. Oogluk scrambled to pour his strength into me as I dropped forward onto my hands.

Orange bolts slammed into the ground and buildings all around us. Hahn'Nik'Nik returned fire, but her aim was no better than Gen'tahn's.

My sister growled venomously beside me. I pushed myself to my feet. A small gap in the mental pressure opened. I pressed on it and was instantly repelled. The force had been so strong, I felt disoriented and stumbled backward. Oogluk caught me and formed a sort of wall that my sister and I could lean against.

I stole a glance at A'lii. Blood trickled from her nose, and her eyes were half-closed. Her chalky yellow markings stood out sharply in the bright, afternoon light.

"Keep pushing," she murmured.

An arrow thwacked into the street by my feet. I broke my concentration long enough to see Tek'ekim guards with clubs streaming from the ground level door of the building Gen'tahn'Gen stood on and several Tek'ekim archers on the roof of the building to Gen'tahn's right.

A'lii groaned and bent over. I redoubled my mental attack but was unsure where to attack. A'lii straightened.

"Gen'tahn," she breathed. "We take him down."

Hahn'Nik'Nik shifted her MEC back and forth between the archers and the guards running toward us, firing a few bolts each time. They all flew wide, though.

"I'm going to make a shield," I told my sister.

She nodded and ground her teeth as I shifted my attention away from Gen'tahn.

The guards were only ten paces away—barely enough time to form a shield from the air. I reached inside, summoning my shaping ability. My metaphoric hands grasped at nothing. It wasn't there. I glanced at my hands. No orange glow. Franticly, I called on it again. And again. Nothing.

"Jax, help," Airitha cried as she dropped and pressed both hands to the ground.

I watched, dumbstruck. The ground beneath the Tek'ekim's bare feet smoked, and they leapt back in pain and fear. My own feet felt cold—too cold for the heat of the cycle.

Oogluk's attention snapped to me, "You saved me in the way the Number can save each other. You have paid a dear price, Friend Jax. A dear price you have paid. I am sorry. I am sorry."

Grief from Oogluk flooded me for a click before he managed to shield me from it.

What could I do? Gen'tahn pressed vehemently down on us mentally, the guards on foot paced back and forth as they slowly retreated from the spreading heat and the archers continued to rain arrows down on us.

Oogluk answered my question by gripping the façade of the nearest building with countless tentacles. Then, with a shout in my mind, he ripped it from the building and thrust the wooden shield in front of us.

"Your sister, help," he snapped at me.

A'lii shivered with exhaustion. I rejoined her effort to overpower Gen'tahn.

Hahn'Nik'Nik ceased firing, and the only sound became the crack of arrows embedding in the wood. A few found their way through the windows.

Airitha's face wrinkled with exertion, "I can't keep heating the ground much longer."

"That's enough," Hahn'Nik'Nik said. "You can stop cooling the ground for us."

Airitha sighed, and Hahn'Nik'Nik moved to the side of a window and began firing again.

A crack opened in Gen'tahn's concentration. I forced my way into it. Fear burst into my mind. That was the first time I'd felt that emotion from the Tek'ekim leader. My sister felt it too and wedged her way in. She was growing fatigued, though. Her body was covered in sweat and the trickle of blood from her nose turned into a river.

Gen'tahn lashed out. I couldn't hold him back. My sister collapsed. And spasmed on the ground as though she were having a seizure.

But the effort had been too much for the Tek'ekim leader. I pressed against his offensive, and he broke. I saw through his eyes as he slumped forward, got hung up momentarily on the parapet and then tumbled down. He landed on two of his guards who crumpled beneath him, breaking his fall. Gen'tahn blinked, and I saw his perspective as two orange bolts ripped through two of his guards.

Gen'tahn'Gen's thoughts turned to denial and deeper anger. He shoved the dying guard aside before he fell on him and struggled to his feet. His left leg barely supported him and bent at an awkward angle. He embraced the pain and fed it to his anger. His feet smoked and sizzled as he ran toward us, but he only used that pain the same as he did the pain from his shattered leg. One thought ran through his mind. Kill.

The arrows stopped smacking the wall that Oogluk held. Hahn'Nik'Nik twisted away from the window just as Gen'tahn'Gen charged through the door.

"Stop," I spoke into Gen'tahn's mind. Immediately, he stopped. Everything went blank in his mind, and that same blankness settled across his face.

Hahn'Nik'Nik's MEC pointed at his face only two inches from its barrel. She stood stone still, but visibly fumed with erans of hatred flaring her nostrils wide and hardening her eyes.

Gen'tahn'Gen had tried to kill her. He had stabbed her in the square only rays before. With an Ahdah like Gen'tahn'Gen, she didn't need any further reasons than what she had grown up dealing with undoubtedly.

She would pull the trigger.

The orange woman screamed an earsplitting groan of emotional agony, and, with the strength of a man twice her size, she coiled and smashed the MEC into the side of Gen'tahn's head.

His vision went black, and he nearly disappeared from my perception just like what had happened to Oogluk when he was unconscious.

Chapter 36

"You and Darvi have got to be the two worst patients I've ever had," Omoah scolded.

"That's because Jax is used to giving orders now," Darvian teased me. "He can't stand lying in bed."

"And you can?" Omoah peered down her nose at Darvian who quickly looked away.

"Why are you fussing over us so much?" I asked as lightly as I could. "Meisha healed us. That means she turned back time on our scratches, so it's just like they never even happened."

Omoah placed her hands on her hips and glared at me for a click. "The state you two were in," she began. It was going to be a long explanation.

I threw back the covers and bolted from the room. Omoah's scolding ricocheted down the hallway behind me.

A second set of footsteps sounded behind me, and I pushed myself to run faster.

"Hey, slow down," Darvian called. "She's not following us."

I glanced back and slowed. Darvian's sister had completely erased the burn on the side of his head. He claimed he couldn't remember ever having been shot to Omoah, but I knew he was trying to trick her into letting him out of bed.

Once Hahn'Nik'Nik had knocked Gen'tahn'Gen unconscious, Oogluk bound him securely and carried him quickly, along with my sister, back to Thaydrin and the others attacking the Tek'ekim. They'd made a huge spectacle of his capture, and it was only a matter of about a period before all the Tek'ekim surrendered. They'd even released the gumbat whom, once free, despite being shunned and distrusted by the Number, looked and acted no different from the other Neftim.

"I don't want to miss Gen'tahn's trial," I said over my shoulder.

"The Great Gen'tahn'Gen," Darvian mocked as he'd learned from Hahn'Nik'Nik, "can go swim in a dragon trough. I just want ta see mah sister."

"She's probably going to be at—," a small body bounced off my leg, and I dove to catch her before she fell to the floor.

A set of hands with orange markings caught her first. Hahn'Nik'Nik looked at me and smiled. Then, I noticed two young, Tek'ekim children trying unsuccessfully to hide behind her legs.

Kammiel reached up and hugged me. "I can go home soon, right?" she asked.

Apart from Anntoninn and his surviving warriors, she was the only one from Hegnoranthe, and she had never really felt at home with the fighting men.

Hahn'Nik'Nik tugged the two children, a boy and a girl, out of hiding. "This is Ahn'Ahn and Mik'Mik," she told me. She told them my name, but neither one wanted to look at me. Mik'Mik, the girl, shyly grabbed Kammiel's hand, and the two of them started skipping down the hall. Ahn'Ahn ran after them yelling for them to wait.

Darvian peered after them while I asked a question that had yet to be answered, "Have you heard yet where your people will live?"

Hahn'Nik'Nik forced a smile and looked at her hands, "We don't know, yet. Your Ahdah offered my kids and me a place at your house...as long as your Omoah agrees." She swiped at a tear and forced herself to continue, "My husband," she bit her lip and tried to squeeze back tears. "He—"

When she couldn't finish, Darvian stepped around me and hugged her. She blinked down at him and sniffed at the tears flowing despite her efforts. "We'll have to start all over again without him," her voice ended in a gasp.

Hahn'Nik'Nik's cheeks pulled her lips back in such a look of forlorn anguish I wanted to back away and pretend I hadn't seen her.

Darvian pulled out the spherical stone with the groove. I hadn't seen him rub it for some time. Hahn'Nik'Nik fumbled with it as Darvian handed it to her.

It rolled in her hand, and her thumb found the groove just as Darvian's had all those months ago.

"Thank you," Hahn'Nik'Nik managed around her tears as she knelt and hugged Darvian.

"Mah sister and I have our place, but she and her kids have nowhere," Darvian said as we exited the school made hospital.

A cloud settled over me. I couldn't decide what it was, but it felt heavy, and uncertainty loomed in its hidden corners. Like so many others, I had lost something irreplaceable. I flexed my hands and ran my fingers over one another. They would never glow with the orange light of shaping again. Darvian had tried more than a dozen times to bring my ability back to me, but the sacrifice had been more than even Meisha could manage. They had both worn themselves ragged to help me.

"Friend Jax," Oogluk's semitransparent bulk created a thin shadow that blocked part of the sunlight the way smoke does, "where are you off to?"

"I'm headed to see what they're gonna do with Gen'tahn," I said with my mind. "He's looking for his sister," I indicated Darvian.

"That is a story that repeats itself over and over. Perhaps, we should chain the two of them together. The two of them together, perhaps, we should chain," Oogluk attempted to cheer me up.

I gave him a wry smile. "Where's Tuca and the Number?"

"They have no taste for the deliberations of your kind," Oogluk stated with careful annunciation. "Believe that they are deliberating on what is to become of our Number, I do. I believe they deliberate on what is to become of our Number."

"I'm glad you decided to start including yourself when you mention your Number," I replied. Heaviness bent my back. "I don't want to lose you, Oogluk."

Oogluk bent down and rested his fake dragon head on my shoulder. I stopped. A line of dungles scurried across the dust, oblivious to how easy it would be for me to squash them.

"What's he saying?" Darvian asked brightly.

"He says he's worried about how big you're growing," I covered up my feelings. "You must be a whole head taller than when I first saw you, and your head doesn't look too big for your body anymore."

Darvian's green markings darkened, and he studied the ground as he thought. Then, he said, "That's because of how your Omoah feeds me. Can she come with mah sister and me?"

As far as Darvian knew, his parents were dead, gotten by the Gah'Stotten. How many other kids on his world of Grael didn't have parents?

"I don't think so," I said hesitantly. "It'd be nice to have a break from being called 'sweetie,' though."

"Right," Darvian agreed. "Did Kelita ever come back?"

Oogluk fell in step behind us. "No," I answered. Kelita had checked on me once I had woken and told me she and her Omoah were going home. She asked me to bring Kerelyn, when I could, and she would pick her up at school.

School. It sounded so normal that it no longer fit in anywhere.

"Dah!" Darvian exclaimed and jogged forward.

Looking up, I saw Thaydrin sitting on a low bench on the edge of a once beautiful garden. The flower stems had been trampled and broken by someone searching for edible roots judging by the numerous plants that lay uprooted and wilting.

Thaydrin enthusiastically returned his adopted son's embrace. Only then did I notice Airitha snuggled into his side. I slowed my pace and felt my face turn pink as Airitha met my gaze. She was beautiful, I had to admit to myself.

Thaydrin stood and offered me his hand. I shook it and waited for him to speak first.

"I see you want to ask me why I am not at the council," he said with a slight grin. "Bah, I've already made my decision while I still have the emergency powers given to me."

A large group of kids Rurin's age ran by, laughing and shouting to one another. I followed Thaydrin's gaze and saw Rurin, Kammiel and Hahn'Nik'Nik's kids among them along with several other kids with the orange markings of the Tek'ekim.

"Jax," Thaydrin asked suddenly, "what is it that makes a person an enemy?"

Darvian smiled, though not entirely without fear playing in his green eyes, "When they always try to get you."

Thaydrin and Airitha laughed with him, but I found I could do nothing but look on from the outside.

Then, Airitha stood in front of me, close enough to take my hand. "We'll be heading back to Teluthia soon. I'll miss you."

***

A period after the council handed down its decision about Gen'tahn'Gen, I wandered aimlessly through the streets just outside the market square. Several families were busy rebuilding, while others carried large packages of food that had just been brought in on dragons or ee'nex carts. They all had something to do. I had nothing except to wait.

I paused midstride. Ahead, Jamoal clapped Ahdah on the shoulder and strode off briskly.

"Ah, son," Ahdah said with a weary smile, "you're one person I won't have to look for now. It's good to see these townsfolk rebuilding their lives already. We're a resilient people."

The only times he dodged around what he wanted to say were when he still felt too angry to talk about what

417

needed to be discussed. That was something I noticed about a lot of men. Maybe it was something I did myself.

"You don't like the decision the council reached, do you?" I asked.

He gave me a grim smile, "It's hard to get over the fact that your own people accused you of colluding with the enemy. But then, you know firsthand."

Something Oogluk had said formed in my mind, "I guess they have good reason to fear us. A'lii and I have some of their ability."

Ahdah placed his hand on the back of my neck and pulled my face close to his. He was still taller, but I was catching him. "We are not Gen'tahn'Gen." His grip hardened, "We are not guilty of his atrocities merely because some of the Tek'ekim's blood flows in our veins."

He released me, biting his lip.

"I think it was the right decision," I offered hopefully.

Ahdah looked back at me. "I'm sorry you had to hear that. It can be an ugly business being an adult." With a sigh he rubbed the back of his head and then placed his hand on his the low fence at his side. "What you and A'lii did to that man," he shook his head. "He became utterly harmless. There was no perceivable trace of his mind control ability at work."

I knew it was something to be proud of, yet inside I didn't feel much different from a mug buried in the dirt. I shrugged, "I guess he and I share something more in common than ancestors from thousands of erans ago."

"Very few things are worth whatever price is demanded," Ahdah said slowly. He gripped my shoulder, "I'm proud of you, son."

I couldn't be sure, but I thought a tear twinkled in the corner of his right eye. I wanted to be little again so he would scoop me up, hug me tight and whisper that he understood. I blinked repeatedly and nodded.

And then Ahdah hugged me tight and whispered in my ear as he wept, "I'm so proud of you, son. The sacrifice you made is priceless. You're the kind of man I wish all men would be."

"I'm not that fantastic," I said into his shoulder. I felt distant and dirty like I was covered in gritty, smelly and used dragon bedding sand.

Ahdah held me at arm's length, "Will you come straight home after you and Oogluk take the Teluthians back to their home?"

I pressed my mouth tight. Anger and grief overpowered me. I wanted to scream or wail or do something equally juvenile. My lips began to quiver, so I pressed myself back into Ahdah to hide it as I explained, "Oogluk can't teleport anymore. He's broken, too."

Ahdah's hand felt warm and strong as he stroked my back in calming circles before settling it on the back of my neck. The only thing he said was, "You both are far from broken."

"Why does it hurt so much?" I cried into his shoulder. "I don't care that I won't be able to shape ever again. I don't care that Oogluk and I can't teleport anymore. I'm glad everybody's alive." I coughed, and Ahdah remained silent. "It hurts though—so much. Did it hurt like this when grandahdah died?"

"It did, son. It did. We were never made to lose things."

Ahdah continued hugging me and rubbing my back until I could cry no longer. Then we trudged back side by side to the makeshift hospital.

***

Purple light from the first sun setting deepened the richness of Airitha's skin that evening as the Teluthians, a portion of the Tek'ekim and a few Neftim assembled by the Gah'Stotten dropship. She blinked as she looked into the suns at me.

"I wish you weren't leaving so soon," I said before she could say something similar.

She hugged me quickly and stepped back, "My little brother will be born soon." She smiled broadly, but a hollowness settled in her eyes.

"It feels like the first time we said goodbye," I mumbled.

"Yeah," she replied nervously, "but nothing's going to be the same on Teluthia."

I bit my lip.

Airitha reached for my arm. I pulled it out of her reach. "I'm sorry," she said barely loud enough to hear.

A fresh wave of shame washed through me. I had blundered my way through everything that had led to—well, everything.

"It's not like I knew what I was doing when we saved everybody, and Oogluk's stayed away with the rest of the Neftim most of the cycle," I said, hoping Airitha wouldn't bring up anything else. I didn't feel heroic at all. Instead, I felt small and dirty like a clod of dirt a pecked at by a turit.

"Forgotten you, Friend Jax, I have not," Oogluk suddenly spoke into my mind.

"I know you wanted to help us rebuild," Airitha peered up at me with pity softening her already compassionate eyes.

"You should go," I said, straightening my back.

"Not until you promise," Airitha returned.

I looked at the ground. What did I have to give to her—or to anyone?

"Look," she busied herself with straightening the collar on my tunic despite my halfhearted swat at her hands, "we've been through a lot. I'm not going to pretend it isn't going to change me. I think it already has.

"Jax," she took my hand and massaged my large fingers with her slender ones, "I've realized how good it feels to have someone like you fighting alongside me for what we know is right."

With her red markings, it was impossible to decide whether she was blushing.

"You're right," she released my hand, "I should go."

I caught her hand and stumbled around in my blank mind. Finally, I grasped what Oogluk was repeating. "We couldn't have done it without you." I pulled my gaze from her astonished expression and bent slightly to kiss her hand. As I touched my lips to her hand, something bumped me from behind so hard I had to hug Airitha to keep from falling.

"This is not my place. Blame that Oogluk of mine," Tuca laughed clear and bright into my mind.

Airitha didn't even glance at Tuca as she leapt over us and drove hard with her wings to clear the dropship. She stared at me with half-lidded eyes—leaning up toward me. My eyes closed as if they had a mind of their own. My lips tingled, and my mind buzzed as Airitha pressed her lips against mine.

She wrapped both arms around me and smiled up at me, "We aren't that young, are we?"

The answer I should have given was a resounding, "Yes, we are too young," but that's not what I said. What I did say was, "I'm going with you. I'll talk to my parents. They'll let me finish school on your world."

She wrinkled her nose, "School? I guess we are that young."

Of course, our kiss could not go unnoticed with all the people around. Rithol sidled up, holding A'lii's hand in the crook of his elbow, "What have we here, Little Brother? I believe the garden is still serviceable. I'm sure you'd stay in it longer if you were the one getting married." He raised his eyebrows innocently. My sister scolded him behind her hand.

I'm sure my markings turned as red as Airitha's as I extricated myself from her embrace.

"He's a little rough around the edges, pouts when he loses and fights our littlest brother for the connel berries, but," Rithol shrugged and held out his hands apologetically, "maybe you can train him. I don't think he's entirely hopeless."

"Duck," Oogluk ordered. I hadn't noticed him or Tuca return.

I ducked, and Airitha copied me a click later. Rithol began to laugh, but his laugh quickly turned to an alarmed sound like that of a frightened nykor as Oogluk plucked him from the ground.

A'lii faced me, shaking her head, "You better watch yourself, Jax."

I stood and helped Airitha up.

"And," my sister tipped her shoulder, "we worked well together." She turned and walked briskly, but primly, in the direction her husband had been taken.

"I like your family—all of them," Airitha said brightly.

Epilogue

Twelve erans later I stand above a lush valley, looking down on a small cluster of buildings nestled beside a lake which is fed by a spring and snowmelt. The air is chilly and dry. My tunic is work-stained, and my hands thickly calloused. Seeing the small, mountain village in the midst of the greenery melts layers of fatigue from my shoulders.

It's good to be home.

I say goodbye to the Neftim who has carried me. Somehow, I know this won't be the last time I travel so far from home, but I think to myself that maybe I'll go only one more time.

Little, brown turits call to one another as they flit from tree to tree. Their song is one I consider happy and carefree. I smile at their antics as I move down the side of the valley.

There's a white house with pillars overlooking the lake at the end of the street. A pregnant woman stands at the top step, beaming at me as she swipes tears from her eyes. A young child, four erans old, leaps down the steps and races for me with a shout.

"Ahdah's home, Omoah!" Kai'lia shouts.

She doesn't slow at all as I brace myself to catch her. We hug, and she launches into the stories she's been dying to tell me all week. I do my best to listen to every syllable, but I can't help stealing a glance at Airitha. She rubs her round belly as I climb the steps.

Kai'lia pushes herself higher in my arms and presses her forehead to mine so that our eyes are a mere inch apart. "You stopped listening, Ahdah," she admonishes.

I hug her tight until she squeals. "I miss your Omoah the same way you missed me," I tell her, nuzzling her nose.

Her purple eyes twinkle as she asks, "Can I listen to the stories you tell her?"

I laugh and reply, "You can listen until your bedtime."

I've reached the top step. An aircutter whispers by overhead. Airitha holds out her arms. Shifting Kai'lia to my hip, I lean over my wife's belly so I can hug and kiss her.

"You might be just in time," she tells me.

I raise my eyebrows and look down at her belly appraisingly.

"Omoah already came out, and Ambrohl's in the hangar annoying the mechanics," Airitha says.

"Your brother does have a way of inserting himself into situations," I chuckle.

"How are Darvian and Kammiel?" Airitha asks as we head inside. She's moving slowly and taking small steps.

"Why can't they come visit more often?" Kai'lia rocks back and forth, upsetting my balance.

I shift her to my back and tell her, "They got some very important work. Do you remember how gray and sad it was on their world?"

I can't see my daughter's reaction, but I can sense her wrinkled nose, "I didn't like it there. It was scary."

"You wouldn't recognize it now. Now, it's almost like Grandahdah and Grandomoah's world."

"Where you grew up?"

I nod, "Part of my work has been to help Darvian and Kammiel establish a sustainable agriculture."

"Sustain, what?" Kai'lia asks.

"Agriculture," I give her a bump in the ride. She clutches me tight and giggles, demanding that I run with her.

When I don't immediately comply with her wishes, she says, "Oogluk and Tuca took me swimming yestercycle."

I grin as I remember what swimming is like with Oogluk.

I glance to my side, but Airitha is a few steps behind.

"I'm coming," Airitha smiles. "Are those two getting along better?"

I briefly consider saying that they are, but I settle for the truth instead, "You know how they are. The way they bicker, everyone's surprised they ever married. Kammiel does have a sharp tongue, but she's got a sweet spot. Whenever Darvian's too affected by flashbacks and such, she's right there helping 'im through it."

"Sometimes I still wish she were that sweet little girl who was too shy to talk to us when she first met us on Hegnoranthe," Airitha surmises.

I loop my arm around Airitha's waist, and she stops abruptly.

A look flashes across her face, "It's beginning."

This concludes:

A Constellation in Ashes

If you enjoyed *A Constellation in Ashes*, please give it a rating and a review! This not only encourages me and helps me know you enjoyed *A Constellation in Ashes* but also helps it become more visible so that other readers like you can find it and live in Jax's universe for a short time too. Thank you for joining in the adventure.

Read Jax's complete story:

The Trouble with Dragons and Strangers

A Journey of Unknown Skies

The Cycle the Shadow Came

A Constellation in Ashes

Find the author and his other works at:

moleculesofstory.wordpress.com

moleculesofstory T. M. Bennett on Facebook

Timothy M. Bennett on Goodreads

Also by the author:

Short Stories:

A Unicorn Named Nothing

Remember

Novels and Novellas:

Star Sky Series:

(#1) The Trouble with Dragons and Strangers

(#2) A Journey of Unknown Skies

(#3) The Cycle the Shadow Came